UNACKNOWLEDGED

The Possible Biological Mother of Howard Hughes

Ora Smith

Lighten Press, LLC

www.lightenpress.com

Published by Lighten Press, LLC
www.lightenpress.com

Printed in the United States of America

ISBN
978-0-9980410-7-0

Cover design by
Jenny Quinlan @ Historical Fiction Book Covers

Cover photograph courtesy of
iStock-182742455 SuperflyImages

Photograph of Howard Hughes, Jr.
Alamy stock photo P0R8W5

Photographs of Emma Butterfras Hydrick, Buddy Hydrick, George Hydrick,
Ernest Hydrick, Mary, Eva and Henry "Hy" Butterfras
Given to Ora Smith by family members

BISAC Subject Headings
FIC014000   FICTION / Historical / General
FIC074000   FICTION / Southern
ET020   CULTURAL HERITAGE
FIC041000   FICTION / Biographical

Get free novellas, sign up for Ora's newsletter,
and get to know Ora at www.orasmith.com
amazon.com/author/orasmith
bookbub.com/authors/ora-smith
facebook.com/AuthorOraSmith
instagram.com/authororasmith
twitter.com/AuthorOraSmith

Dedicated to

Nick Smith

1990-2017

"We hear about people who go back to their roots. That is good, but don't get stuck in the root. There is the branch, the leaf, the flower—all reaching toward the immense sky. We are many things...In the ability to connect with one people lies the chance to feel compassion for all people...In knowing who you are and writing from it, you will help the world by giving it understanding."

Writing Down the Bones by Natalie Goldberg

CONTENTS

PREFACE

I can't help but feel sentimental when I see families reunite and forgive one another. Maybe you've watched those television shows where a mother meets an adult child she gave away at birth. They should be virtual strangers but, somehow, they're not. There appears to be an innate desire for most humans to know their family origins. Exactly how much did Howard Hughes Jr. know about his?

His possible biological mother and my great-grandmother Emma Butterfras Hydrick, lived an obscure life around the turn of the twentieth century. I didn't know her. She died forty-two years before I was born.

But I wanted to know her. Her images from the two photographs I own are hard to decode. She looks like she's thinking *I know something you don't* and about to burst out laughing. Her hair, wavy and pulled back, appears either black or dark brown. Her eyes are lighter brown, seductively intelligent in one photo, mysterious in the other. One of the photos is color-tinted, and she wears a gauzy blue dress with a watch hanging from a wide lapel in the fashion of her time. It's a modest dress as is the white, high-necked blouse and dark skirt she wears in the second photo. The clothing was a deception to who she really was. Or was it?

The photos never hung in my house. My father kept them in a leather folder with his family research charts and notes behind closed doors in a small, dark cubby. When I found them as a child, I stared at Emma for a long time, as I'd done with every old photograph we owned, prompting her to let me know who she was, what she cared about, and if she knew I belonged to her.

As an adult, I asked a lot of questions. Emma's son, my Grandad George, talked about all his relatives—except for Emma, his own mother. If my father or I probed, he became indignant, his face coloring and jaw clamped tight. When it came to his mother, it appeared there were hurt feelings and perhaps even shame.

Eventually, finding the truth about Emma explained much as to why my grandfather acted as he had. Enlightenment is the added benefit of understanding human reasoning. And truth can bring empathy and healing. I am not a psychologist, but the study of cause and effect on people's lives strikes my interest. What exactly was passed down from generation to generation?

I'm a genealogist and while doing family history research, I always work with incomplete evidence. Abusive families keep secrets. When those secrets are three generations deep, digging up the hidden details can seem almost impossible. My aunt Jeanette and great-uncle Ernest both told me Emma's tale was "hush, hush." A secret.

My first reaction was to keep her story hidden too. After all, the generations before me painted her as disgraceful. Why should I hang out my family's dirty laundry? When I first began to research her life, that was the question that went around and around in my mind. What I've concluded is this—if writing Emma's story would hurt people, I wouldn't do it. But those who cared to keep it hidden are now deceased. It's time to bring to pass healing.

This book is about family identity—Emma's and my own. What is the connection of family? And why do I search for my own roots? One reason is that I like to solve mysteries, which means visiting libraries, museums, archives, and any place that might hold clues to an ancestor's life.

Another reason is my enthusiasm for history. It's fascinating to imagine what my ancestors' lives would have been like in their own day. If I can find facts that tell me *exactly* what they were like or what experiences they had, then I don't need to imagine anything. This is what I strive for as a genealogist.

I have other reasons for doing family history research. I believe in an afterlife—a realm where people reside with their full memories of life on earth. Following that belief, I reason those who have died still carry their personalities, but perhaps are more enlightened as to what their lives—and existences as a whole—

are really about. People who had mental and physical disabilities on earth no longer have them in this realm. And as on earth, all those who have died continue learning and having experiences that deepen their journeys.

What goes hand-in-hand with those beliefs is my conviction we have relationships in the afterlife. Those whom we care for the most—our family and friends—are those we want to be with and share our "new" existence. And they will do the same with us. My goal is to understand my ancestors' lives because I believe I will see and associate with them one day.

I want to treat whomever I am writing about with respect. I do not want to misrepresent anyone. I don't know all the facts and probably never will, but that doesn't mean I'm not striving for the truth about their lives.

This book is written in a nonfiction and historical fiction blended format:
- If I'm assuming a situation, forming an opinion of someone's thought process, or using conjecture about someone's personality traits, that section of the story will be told in my ancestor's point of view in a narrative form and have a dated heading. I do this to give the reader a fuller sense of my ancestors' lives.
- The historical fiction scenes are based on fact and circumstantial evidence.
- All acknowledgements of source materials used for *both* the nonfiction segments about my search and historical fiction scenes are indicated in the Chapter Notes at the end of the book.

It's impossible to capture the whole person in a biographical account. In this effort, I've had to decide what facets of Emma to bring forward to best explain her motives as well as share her story through my own commentary and reactions. Keep in mind, Emma's story is a framework of what could have happened. In writing it, I often felt as though I was looking through a telescope, wishing I had a microscope.

I am who I am because of how I was raised and because of my experiences as a daughter, sister, wife, mother, friend, student, and many more roles than can be listed here. During research for this book, I discovered information concerning my family that was not expected nor desired. In analyzing that data, I've had to decide what the facts meant to me. I discovered layers of myself I was unaware of that changed me in many ways.

I chose to write about Emma and Howard Hughes Jr. due to the interest it might generate, but also because it was a mystery for me to solve. There are always two sides (or more!) to any story. I don't want to sensationalize any human being. I am only striving for the truth.

Descendants of Emma Butterfras Hydrick

Emma A. Butterfras
born: 28 July 1882, Houston, Texas

her child	her child	possible child
↓	↓	↓
George Neverson Hydrick	Ernest Albert Hydrick	Howard Hughes
born: 19 January 1900	born: 20 March 1902	born: September 1905

↓   ↓   ↓

children of George: (no progeny)   (no proven progeny)

George Neverson Hydrick, Jr.

"Buddy" Owen Hydrick

Mary Lucille Hydrick

Rick "Sonny" Plymton or PG Hydrick

Donald Hydrick   ↓

Jeanette Hydrick

↓

child of Sonny Hydrick
Ora Hydrick Smith (me)

INTRODUCTION

Buddy Hydrick

I knew my father's brother as Uncle Buddy. I recall meeting him once when I was a teenager, however my mother told me I met him many times as a young child while living in Southern California. Buddy was a gregarious man—friendly and talkative. Always with a smile, his brown eyes made contact with everyone he talked with. His sister, my aunt Jeanette, who was fourteen years younger than Buddy, said he was "kind at heart." When he realized his time on earth was coming to an end, he decided to tell her a family secret that he'd concealed for fifty-nine years. He attempted to tell her on the phone but couldn't bring himself to say it aloud and instead gave her clues. He told her their grandmother, Emma Butterfras Hydrick, had a child she gave away, and that child became someone famous. When Aunt

Jeanette questioned him as to who that might be, he said this child's initials were HH.

Uncle Buddy is dead now, and I can't guess at why he went as far as giving her the initials but wouldn't say the name outright.

He started the following letter to Jeanette the day of their phone conversation, finishing it four days later. It is a handwritten letter, still in Aunt Jeanette's possession. I have typed it in its entirety, leaving grammatical errors, punctuation, etc. as Uncle Buddy wrote it:

April 13, 1996
Chula Vista, Ca
Fini: April 17, 1996

Hi! Baby Sister,

I'll drop you a few tidbits if the hand cooperates.

You are in the right church with the H.H. but the wrong pew; if he had been Hugh Hefner he would have been our brother, not Dad's. Our uncle was Howard Hughes. Dad's half-brother.

Jeanette, I only know this to be true because of what was told me many years ago by an unimpeachable source and research many years later by me. As you may see I could never bring it fore while Dad lived. And, I thought none of you would have enough inquiring mind to care. I am glad it is you who does.

On a long ago, beautiful spring day in 1937 on a porch of a house on North Airline Dr, in Houston, Texas. Our Great Aunt Eva (the one legged lady), it was the same day that Uncle Bert cut his index finger off on the fan-belt pulley of the truck. He would have blet to death if it hadn't been for me telling Aunt Eva in time. He was the one who took the gas in France in World War I. He was a horse trader. And a hell of a nice guy!

Aunt Eva (when she had two legs) and her young Sister Emma of a Sat. nite used to go dancing at the finest ballroom in downtown Houston. Emma, as you should know was one of the three most beautiful young ladies in Houston of those days. One dance night she met a very hansom young dude she only introduced to Aunt Eva as Howard. Aunt Eva said she later in life spent much time with a man she called Sonny.

Back to Airline Dr and Aunt Eva. Just before Christmas 1905, Emma, who was living in Galveston, Tx showed up at her place with Dad, Uncle Ernest & heavy laden with child. She asked her sister if she'd keep the boys for a couple weeks. Eva kept the boys. Our Grand mother came back without being laden with child, Aunt Eva, who was the first & greatest live & let live person, said she only told her it was healthy boy and it was with a good Houston family and she did it because she could only take care of two. She asked his father to call him by the nickname of Sonny. She took Dad and Uncle Ernest to go back to Galveston and the years went by as years will do.

Aunt Eva said when ever our Grand mother was in Houston she would search each paper for any mention of the Hughes Tool and Die Co. (which was growing by leaps and you know what) or anything at all to do with the Hughes boy. That is all I can recall the Grand Ole Lady tell me on that lovely spring day on No. Airline Dr. in 1937.

In 1928 we lived in Houston when Plympton, P.G., or Rick was born. He was nicknamed Sonny by our Great Aunt Eva. And, as strange as coincidences can become Howard Hughes Jr's nickname, which he dearly hated, was Sonny.

And now soon, when I go, that part of our history will live on thru you, my darling sister. And I don't give a damn what sinister critics may be bewilder and baffled by the revelation. [Our brother] George was not there. He was on a cow ranch.

And so, I'll say Goodbye with some hope we'll meet again, don't know where, don't know when, but I know…some sunny day.

Tell Danny, Howdie and keep pumping and each of the others I think of them. And I love you very much. You are the Best.

[signed] Old 72 Bud

Sometime in the early 2000s, Aunt Jeanette sent me a copy of Uncle Buddy's letter, along with old family photos and items she believed would be of interest. When I first read the letter, I laughed outright and called my husband into the room. "You have to listen to this," I said, and then proceeded to read the letter to him. He shook his head and enjoyed a good chuckle too. After the laughter, I read it to myself a few more times to determine why Uncle Buddy would say such a thing. *Could it be true, and why would he keep it a secret?*

I called Aunt Jeanette and asked if she believed the letter.

"Yes, Buddy would never lie to me." Her firm tone gave me pause.

Did she really think this was possible? Even if she did, what did she expect me to do? "Why did you send it to *me*?"

"You are the family historian and I thought you'd find it interesting."

After we hung up, I called my father and teased, "Did you know Howard Hughes was your uncle?"

He chuckled. "I heard tell of it."

He knew? I was shocked! "Do you believe it?"

"I do, but it's a family secret. *I'm* not going to be the one to tell the world."

I tried to get more answers, but he claimed not to know anything else and changed the subject. I brought up the family secret a time or two through the years, and either he couldn't or wouldn't answer my questions. He later showed signs of Alzheimer's and didn't remember who I was, let alone any of our family secrets.

I thought of the letter occasionally, broaching the subject with a friend or two, to see what kind of reaction I would get, not knowing if I was a complete fool to consider its validity. They usually found humor in the idea and certainly didn't take it seriously.

One day, I told a fellow coworker, Chris, about Buddy's letter.

Chris didn't laugh. She leaned closer. "Where did your great-grandmother live?"

"Houston and Galveston," I said.

She nodded. "I've read a lot about Howard Hughes and know there are seeds of doubt surrounding his birth date. Can I see the letter?"

The next day, I brought a copy of the letter to work. I handed it to Chris with a tinge of embarrassment, but also curiosity and excitement to finally have someone outside the family read it and give their opinion.

In the time it took her to read it, her expression went from interest to wonderment. She grinned wide and handed it back. "This could very well be true, Ora. You know how to do family history research. I think you should look closer."

"I'll do that," I said, intrigued to have someone confirm the possibility.

Chris asked, "Do you have a photo of Emma?"

"Yes."

"Can you bring it in tomorrow?"

I did the following day. She pulled up images of Howard Hughes on her computer and we were stunned at the likeness between Emma and Howard. Their noses and eyes were almost identical—their foreheads, ears, and the shapes of their faces amazingly similar. Staring at those two faces with strikingly similar features was the moment it all seemed possible.

That evening, I started my research to see if I could connect Howard Hughes to Emma Butterfras Hydrick. Through the following months, I searched online, read a couple Hughes biographies, viewed microfilms of Texas vital records, and called some Houston hospitals. I didn't find anything to corroborate Uncle Buddy's letter, other than online rumors that Howard Hughes's mother, Allene Gano Hughes, was never pregnant, and that the Hughes' neighbors said the child just showed up one day, and Allene claimed him to be hers. Many months after Howard's birth, on October 7, 1906, Allene traveled to Keokuk, Iowa and had Howard Robard Hughes Jr. christened in St. John's Episcopal Church.

The research discoveries were interesting, but I needed birth facts I couldn't find, not rumors floating on the internet. I placed the Howard Hughes research aside and went on with researching my mother's side of the family, which yielded much more success in linking children to parents.

Seven years passed, and I often wondered about Emma. What had her life been like? How could she give away her baby? I decided that though I might not be able to prove Howard Hughes was her child, I could still find more about Emma's story. Through old family letters, I discovered that she most definitely gave away a child. But I couldn't be certain who that child was. If I couldn't prove it was Howard Hughes, maybe I could disprove it by finding the missing great-uncle.

Buddy and I weren't the only ones in our family with a desire for answers. My father, Rick—also known as Plymton, P.G., and Sonny—researched his family for a short time in the 1960s, and again in the 1980s. Following are two letters he received regarding questions he asked of his father, George, and uncle, Ernest.

Letter from Ernest to his nephew, Rick:

> [excerpt]
> Dear Nephew Sonny,
> Aug 25, 1980 Monday

It was a surprise to here [sic] from you and give me some Info. …I was checking into my back ground I found a lots of answers I don't understand the more I checked into the records the worst it got so I forgot it…

There was another son born to Emma Butterfras Hydrick I can't tell you anything about it cause I don't know if he died at a [sic] early age everything in those days was Hush Hush they didn't tell us anything and didn't want us to ask questions.

Uncle Ernest

Letter from George to his son, Rick:

[excerpt]
Dear Rick   9-14-80

Now Rick, In reference to my past. I have told you I cannot tell you a thing. As I grew up I never looked back. As of now I am still looking forward. What you have found in research is fine. You will find more.

In the early 1900s there was no official Birth registration in the state of Texas…

I lived with Uncle Paul for a few years. He practically raised me. I told you there was another brother thats all I know…

Now please ask me no more let my past be. I will answer no more questions. Received a letter from Ernest. He tried to find out about the family. He said he is tired and give up. He wants to live in the future. Not the past.

Sorry I can't help you...
Love, Dad

Obviously, George and Ernest knew of another son born to their mother and that the son was given away.

In his letter to Jeanette, Buddy said he knew Howard Hughes to be his uncle not only because of what Emma's sister, Eva, told him, but because of his own research. I was enticed by that statement. What did he find when he researched? Would I find it too?

Emma and Howard Photographs

Emma Butterfras Hydrick

Howard Robard Hughes Jr.

CHAPTER ONE

Ora

E mma has a story to tell. Sadly, no personal letters or a diary of hers can be found. Through exhaustive searches of archives, courthouses, museums, societies, universities, and libraries, I pieced together what I could of her life. I interviewed my elderly family members and those who descended from Emma's siblings. I visited the places she lived and her gravesite in Galveston, Texas. I researched the history of women in the early twentieth century, and the histories of Houston and Galveston. Even with all this, I cannot know Emma's heart. I can only wonder at how much she could control her circumstances.

When researching, it can seem as if the life of a human being is made up of a series of events. In reality, life is something to be lived, not fabricated. Emma's reactions and choices to the events in her life are what would have defined her. I cannot know the emotional strength she displayed under tension and strain. But I do know she gave away a child—an act unfathomable to most mothers—and I want to try to understand her decisions.

***

Emma ~ Summer 1891, Houston, Texas

The neighbor boy flailed his scrawny arms. "Can't get me, ugly Emma." He pushed filthy hair from his eyes. He jumped onto, then off her home's planked walkway, taunting her in what was supposed to be a fun game.

Emma stood her ground. She turned her face from him, his words cutting deep. Tall, she pulled-up to her full height and raised her chin, trying to look older than nine.

When she'd found this time for games instead of gathering the chicken's eggs, she snuck out of the house. She didn't care that it was the meanest kids who could play—the kids whose parents didn't know where they were. All except Lila, that was. Lila's parents loved her. They told her so every day.

Emma and the other six children divided up on either side of the walkway, ignoring the morning chaos of a busy market Saturday. Wagon wheels crunched along gravel in the road, heading up the street to Market Square.

Emma was "it." She counted, "One, two, three, go!"

Taunting her and shouting, the children scrambled across the walk.

Lila squealed, narrowly being missed by an ox-pulled wagon loaded with country produce.

"Mind your way," the driver yelled at her. His wagon rattled on, another one close behind.

Emma reached to tag a friend without stepping out of bounds—off the walk and into the dirt of her yard. She made contact with Lila's arm. "You're It!"

Lila stomped her foot then pouted.

The door banged against the house behind Emma. "*Ich habe headache!*"

Chest tightening at Papa's bellowed words, Emma spun to see him.

"Halt your hollerin', *der dummkopfs!*" he shouted.

Heat filled her face. Was he drunk again? Why did he drink so much? Almost every day now. She stared harder at him on the porch.

He stood tall without swaying. His paint-splattered overalls and hat with the flaps that covered most of his gray hair, told Emma he was ready for work. His white whiskers, still wet from a washing, glistened in the morning sun. His blue eyes stared with unclouded recognition.

Her chest loosened.

He was sober.

She nodded. "Yes, sir, we'll stop."

In a nightdress covered by an apron, Emma's mama stepped barefoot onto the porch and handed Papa his lunch in an old lard pail.

Emma frantically glanced to either side, but the children had already scattered. She barely glimpsed the back of the last two as they rounded the corner of Leeland Street. Still, how could Mama come out like this—not dressed for the day? Where anyone passing in wagons could see her.

If they could see the ornately framed photo hanging over the mantle instead, they'd know. Mama had once been beautiful. Before the War. Before her family lost everything. Before Papa got so mean.

People often told Emma she looked like Mama with her small nose, full lips, and brown eyes. But did they mean she looked like the beautiful Mama in the photograph . . . or this Mama on the porch with messy and limp hair hanging to her waist? Sometimes her hair stayed down like that all day unless Emma brushed and plaited it.

Mama's eyes fell on Emma. She furrowed her brow. "Come in the house and tend to Hy and Eva."

Emma's little sister, Eva, toddled to the open front door. Her pudgy fingers grasped the doorframe as though she would come outside.

Emma hurried up the steps and boosted Eva onto her hip.

Papa turned toward the open door. "*Vere das* devil is you, son?" He didn't holler the way he had earlier at Emma and her friends. The yelling sounded more like there was some kind of joke between Papa and her brother—a chiding they would laugh about later.

Paul rushed out, combing his fingers through his blond hair. He was tall for fourteen—taller than Papa even—and thin as a railroad tie. "I hate working on Saturdays."

"Now *das* you're a man, I'm sure you realize vee must take jobs vhen vee get." Papa spent more days at home than usual—often with a sick headache and smelling of whiskey.

Mama grasped at the apron covering her nightdress, twisting it in her fists. "Will you be back with the wagon before dark to start the move onto Hutchins Street?"

Emma's mouth fell open. "What do ya mean? Is we moving?"

Mama pursed her lips and squinched her eyes at Papa. Her shoulders slumped, then she went into the house.

"Papa?" Emma faced her father.

He patted Eva on the head and turned toward the open doorway, calling to Mama. "I don't *kennt.*" With that, he stomped down the steps and headed to the side-yard stable.

Emma glanced at Paul.

He shrugged. "It's the first I've heard of it. See what you can get out of Mama today, and I'll ask Papa while we ride to work." Paul placed a hand on her arm. "Don't worry—"

"Emma, get to work on those dishes!" From the sound of Mama's voice, Emma had best get moving.

"Yes, ma'am," she called as she watched Paul trot toward the side-yard, then she went inside their one-story home.

It took a second to see in the dim room. Mama kept the only window at the front of the house closed with heavy curtains, as if to keep out all the happiness. Sometimes when Mama napped, Emma pushed the cursed curtains aside and opened the window to catch a breeze, if there was one. But if she forgot to close them before Mama got up, Mama would shield her eyes with her arm and reprimand Emma, yanking the curtains closed again.

At least there wasn't much to clean. Two bedrooms, a bathroom, one open room with a kitchen along the wall, and a sitting area in front of the fireplace. She hated how they were all squeezed in, but it used to be much worse before Emma's three older sisters moved out. Even so, it was the only home she'd ever known.

Why were they moving?

Four-year-old Hy sat eating cold cornmeal mush. With his elbow on the table, he leaned his head onto his hand, brown hair still mussed.

Emma placed Eva on the chair with stacked, old Montgomery Ward catalogs on a crate, boosting her high enough to eat her own cold breakfast.

A few steps away, Mama sat in a high-back cushioned chair staring into the cold fireplace.

Emma inched closer to ask about the move. Were those . . . *tears* on Mama's cheeks? Emma bit her lip and backed away, then went to the sink to do the morning dishes.

Soon Mama passed behind her. "When you's done with those, go to Market Square and the grocer and see if anyone's willin' to give up an empty crate or two that we can pack our belongings in." Mama went into her room and came back with three pennies that she placed on the drain board. "If you can't get 'em for free, then perhaps for a penny."

Emma stared at her hands in the graying water where grease floated along the edge of the sink, smelling metallic. "Where is we moving to?"

Mama walked back toward her room. "The other side of downtown to a smaller house. Your pa fell behind on payments." She entered her bedroom and closed the door.

A chill flowed through Emma's body. What about her friends? She'd have to attend a different school where she wouldn't know anyone. How could she ever live without Lila and being able to spend time at her house where her parents' asked questions about how her day went or if she'd like some lemonade.

After she finished the dishes, she fed the goat and chickens, gathered eggs, changed Eva's nappy, and brushed Hy's hair. She looked to Mama's closed door, wishing for help, but knew she'd get none. She shrugged her shoulders and took the little one's outside to load them into the hand-wagon.

They joined the busy street travelers heading to Market Square, about a mile up Milam Street, past some of the tallest three and four-story wood buildings in the city. Merchants bustled in and out of stores, gunsmiths cleaned and stared down barrel stocks, and blacksmiths' hammers clanged an off-beat tune.

A sweet yeasty smell came from the bakery, and Emma's mouth watered for a jelly roll.

A couple blocks further than Market Square flowed Buffalo Bayou. Emma liked going there with Paul, but she'd never go alone. It was a loud place of sawmills, iron foundries, and brick kilns. They'd dredged the bayou deeper years before so fancy steamers and large ships could sail its waters, bringing products to build Houston. Emma loved to sit with Paul on the banks and watch the ships glide by.

The unusual mixes of spices from Mexican, German, and Negro food vendors filled the air as they reached Market Square. Emma breathed them in and smiled. If she got the crates for free, she could use the pennies for dinner.

Vendors called out to travelers, shoppers of both high-class and low. People of every color and language pushed through the crowds. Dogs sniffed for scraps and were shooed away from piles of tomatoes, peppers, melons, and sweetcorn. Sun-browned women in full skirts and loose blouses exchanged money for food.

Wherever Emma found empty crates stacked, she asked if she could have one. If someone said no, she held up a penny and said, "For a penny?" If the answer was still no, she moved on.

After about an hour, she had two crates, but probably better to find a couple more. Hy now walked alongside the wagon, making room for the crates stacked next to Eva. Blisters had formed on Emma's hands where she grasped the wooden wagon handle.

She approached a perspiring and sour-smelling man selling tins of tobacco. "Excuse me, sir."

He cocked an eye at her. His face reminded her of a baked apple—the folds on his cheeks too heavy for him to tug into a smile. "Whatcha want?" He stood with his legs far apart, as if he needed to balance himself from toppling sideways.

Something about him told her to run, but she never liked being scared, so she gulped down the urge. "Do you have a crate or two you can spare?"

"Ya lil' beggar. Dun come 'round here askin' fer no handouts." The man raised his hand, and Emma flinched and closed her eyes, ready for a blow that never came. "Now git goin'!"

She ground her teeth and grabbed the handle of the wagon to move on. She hated jackasses. Why couldn't grown-up men be nice?

Anger at Papa stabbed her chest. Men were supposed to take care of their families, not care so much about drinking that they lost their houses.

"Slow down, Emma!" Hy ran to catch up.

She stopped and took deep breaths. "Don't worry, Hy. I'd never leave you." At least *she* knew what it meant to be trustworthy.

CHAPTER TWO

Ora

To learn more about Emma, it may help to get to know her parents.

In 1851, with Darmstadt, Germany at Peter Paul Butterfass's back, and a ticket in his pocket for passage to America, he walked toward his future dreams. Sixteen, tall and handsome, blond-haired, blue-eyed Peter had come into this world in 1835 with the label of bastard—a dishonorable branding he would never escape as long as he stayed in Darmstadt.

Now that he'd finished his apprenticeship and had saved money, he hoped to find work as a glazier and painter. He would remake himself and join the thousands of artisans and household craftsmen sailing to America.

***

Peter ~ March 1851

In the countryside, Peter scaled a low wooden fence, his worldly goods shifting under the cloth bundle attached to his back. The items wouldn't be enough to get him where he was going. When he arrived at the port in France, he planned to buy supplies to make it through the thirty-five-day Atlantic voyage.

Early morning sunlight glistened on droplets of dew that moistened the hem of his pants as he climbed the hill. To his left, the forested Odenwald mountain range reminded him of his youth and playing among the towering trees. He looked away, determined to not let himself get sentimental about leaving. He had to leave. He needed a future of opportunity.

In the foreground, vineyards ascended the hills. He would scale the slope and then head west to the Rhine River, ferry across, and find passage to Le Havre.

He was told Louisiana would be hotter than the mild climate of Southern Hesse with its warm, humid summers.

Peter stopped to rest and gazed at the valley below. He sat. The city of Darmstadt lay in the Rhine Plain, surrounded by a lush country of rolling, grass-covered hills and distant mountain ranges. Castles built from local stone by royalty dotted the landscape. The large city center with its steepled palace and tall, ornate buildings was one of the wealthiest cities in Europe, making him more aware of his poverty.

He wasn't alone in hardships—many people had begun to protest their working and living conditions. But these small revolutions failed to bring democracy and Peter was one of thousands leaving Germany. Many of his neighbors had already left.

Darmstadt had a rich cultural heritage that Peter had nothing to do with, such as opera, dance, and theatre. The world's oldest operating chemical and pharmaceutical company, Merck, was founded almost two hundred years ago in Darmstadt. But Peter had worked hard to become an artisan and had no interest in long hours spent or low wages earned in that chemical factory.

Gazing at the distant city, he felt no pull to go back. He had no lands to inherit or relationships to care about, and he could no longer watch his mother spend what little money he had earned on liquor. He stood and turned away from Darmstadt for the last time, continuing his trek west.

***

Lucky for Peter, the harbor at Le Havre was the thoroughfare of emigration from Germany, so he easily found German-speaking shopkeepers who helped him with what he'd need for traveling in steerage—or what they were calling "between-deck." While sailing, he was told he'd be pressed between strangers and no meals would be provided, but America was freedom. America was worth it.

With it being the sailing season, several thousand-people waited on the docks to leave. Seabirds squawked, looking for crumbs and scraps of food.

Peter knew no one but stood near those speaking German. Because he already had his ticket, which he had to show proof of at the French border, he was not obliged to lodge for weeks near the docks as other foreigners did.

A scrawny crew member who looked as if he'd been baked in the sun, his face like leather and clothes as faded and thin as the old kitchen curtains Peter's mother never washed, loudly repeated, "Those sailing on the *S.S. Gallia* for New York City, board now."

Peter moved toward the ship with over a hundred others, all carrying baskets, bundles, and trunks. Holding with one hand a small new trunk of food pressed to his back, Peter descended a steep ladder through a hatch that led from the main deck into steerage—which he found overcrowded, damp, and dim. The sour smell of unwashed bodies sickened him. His jaw clenched with foreboding.

With the ship originally built to hold cargo, he was, in reality, in the cargo hold. After stowing his trunk against the wall, he lashed it in place with ropes and then ventured further into the hold. He edged through the crowd, the low ceiling inches above his head, listening for German-speaking men who appeared to be without family. The press of the crowd was worse than he'd thought it'd be.

Adding to the chaos, crew members called instructions in French. Peter had no idea what they barked or if he was supposed to do something that would be of importance to his journey.

He continued to move down small corridors of tiered bunks positioned to run from fore to aft, where partitions of cloth or crates were being erected to maintain some privacy for families.

Finally finding a group of young German men standing near an outer wall, Peter introduced himself and dropped his bundle of bedding on the straw mattress of a top bunk built for four, claiming a quarter of it as his own. For over a month, he would be sharing this bunk made of rough boards with three strangers.

Recently full of dreams for his future, he suddenly felt out of place. He swallowed back the familiar sense of alienation.

That evening, passengers lit lanterns and released both apprehensions and excitement for the forthcoming events by singing. One man played a violin as accompaniment. A few danced in the tight corridors. Peter clapped along and forced smiles, but his mouth was too dry to sing. Shifting uncomfortably on the edge of his bunk, he reminded himself no one knew him here, and it would be best to act pleasant among his countrymen. He could make of himself anything he wanted. The past was behind him.

The journey was long and difficult. For days, he suffered from seasickness and stayed above deck as much as possible, retching over the rails with scores of others. During storms, there was no choice but to go between deck. To keep water from rushing in, the hatches were closed, blocking out ventilation, and the stench became unbearable. Vomit and human waste-filled pails sometimes tipped over from the rolling, rough seas. Back and forth, back and forth the ship rolled. During particularly bad weather, when the boat moved up and down the sea's high peaks, Peter had to lash himself to the bunk.

In calm weather, he stood in line on the brig where he used one of a few cooking hearths. He mostly ate hardtack, crumbled into water, or if he was lucky, hot coffee. He wore the same clothes the entire trip and did not bathe, other than an occasional douse with a bucket of cold seawater brought up with the brig's pump and poured into cisterns.

Being a young man, Peter was expected to swab decks, empty waste basins, and anything else the crew determined needed doing. The work helped him pass the time and usually kept him out of the disease-rife steerage below.

Weeks later, at the southern tip of Manhattan, Peter gratefully disembarked on a pier in front of the sandstone walls of Castle Garden—a building that looked more like a fort of defense than a depot. He stood on solid ground, but without the back-and-forth cradling of the sea, his legs trembled, and his body maintained an illusion of motion.

He wished for a bath and a decent meal, but first had to stand in a long line awaiting an examination by a medical officer. His appearance was scrutinized, teeth checked, and eyes tested for blindness. It was determined he wasn't a cripple or a lunatic. He grunted at that piece of news. When he stepped into the large and crowded room of the rotunda, he waited in yet more lines to exchange his foreign money and acquire a German-speaking boarding house in the city. His trunk filled with all he owned, he had it sent to that address.

When he stepped outside to an expanse much like a graveled park, April's mild temperature encouraged his optimism that this place held a bright future. An American flag drooped from a pole, having no wind to flutter it open.

Knowing little English, he trailed behind the Germans he'd gotten to know aboard ship. Many were greeted by kinsmen with hugs and back-thumping, then taken away. He would need to fend for himself.

A man dressed in a suit caught his eye and walked directly toward him, not taking his focus away. Peter had been warned about unscrupulous money changers and peddlers preying on immigrants, so he turned and quickly walked another direction, zigzagging through the crowd. He shook-off his stalker.

The smells of savory meat and bread pulled him toward street vendors in front of a grassy park. Green never looked so lush as that park and food never smelled so irresistible. Flowers lined the walkways and the leaves on the trees were in full canopy. Horse-pulled hackneys stood in line along a dirt road at the edge of the park, waiting for traveling customers.

Drinking a beer, that he never knew could taste so good, Peter bought a sausage sandwich. He ate his dinner of thanksgiving while standing near benches filled with weary travelers. Even after waiting in long lines for hours, he was happy to stand. He wanted to savor this moment for the jump into freedom that it was.

The ship's voyage was in the past, a trial of hell he promised to never repeat. He was in America to stay. The unfamiliar feel of foreign ground, smells of unknown foods, vendors calling out to sell their wares, chaos of people speaking many different languages, and sounds of horse-drawn vehicles, came with both anticipation and fear.

He hired a hackney to take him into the city, spending precious money, but it was too far for him to walk, and he didn't yet know the city's layout. His next step was to find a job. A big city like New York would certainly need another window glazier.

Most comfortable alone, he moved into his future. A future of dreams he hoped were more than delusions.

***

Ora

I have no record of why Peter sailed to New York City and not New Orleans, since his final destination was Louisiana. He may have created friendships with the Germans he met on the ship and traveled south with them where he learned to speak and write English.

From 1840 to 1880, Germans were the largest group of immigrants coming to America. A wave of political refugees known as the Forty-Eighters fled to America because of the German Revolutions of 1848. Like Peter, many were from the peasantry who were affected by feudal dues and high food prices.

When Peter arrived in Louisiana, there was already a large German settlement outside New Orleans along the fertile lands on the banks of the Mississippi River. Over a hundred years before Peter came to Louisiana, John Law organized the first colony in French Louisiana with indentured German immigrants. As with Peter, those first five hundred immigrants embarked in France. Another nine thousand Germans, who had moved to Arkansas and found themselves unhappy there, traveled to New Orleans for passage back to Europe. John Law's The Mississippi Company convinced them to stay by giving them lands along the Mississippi River. They settled what came to be known as the German Coast, clearing the land and farming the soil, supplying New Orleans with rice, corn, eggs, and meat. Peter found his place there and worked installing windows and painting homes and furniture.

Then war came to America—a war between North and South over property, slaves, and pride, and probably a war that Peter wouldn't have cared much about, but he was in the South where people felt their way of life was being threatened.

Now in his twenties, he piloted a Louisiana Confederate gunboat, the name of which has been lost to the family. The gunboat was most likely the *S.S. Diana*, which was destroyed in April 1863, fifteen miles north of Pattersonville. Eighty soldiers aboard the *Diana* came under fire by the Union on Teche Bayou, near the town of Franklin. Only forty Confederates survived the deadly onslaught. An eyewitness, Major Thomas Ochiltree, described it as one of the bloodiest struggles he had ever seen, with blood running two inches deep on the deck. The survivors abandoned ship and fled through farmlands and into the town of Franklin. Most were caught by the Yankees, but not all. There is no complete record of those who sailed the *Diana* and escaped, but I suspect Peter to have been one of the lucky liberated ones. He then traveled south to Pattersonville and joined a Confederate regiment.

Before the war ended, Peter met and married the young and beautiful Mary Clark sometime around 1864. He was about twenty-eight and Mary sixteen. Her common name of Mary Clark has made it difficult to discover much of her past. The Butterfass family has one stylized photograph of a charming Mary, her dark brown hair styled ornately and tied at the top of her head with a bow. She wears what appear to be precious stones on her ears and a lace collar on a fashionable dress. Her right eye is a bit higher than her left, and her brown eyes are deep set, her lips full and unsmiling, and her nose perfectly small. The large photograph has been tinted with color and is enclosed in an opulent Victorian-style gold frame.

I envision Mary as a Southern Belle, imaginably losing family members and wealth because of the War. Perhaps marrying young was a blessing when so many marriageable men had been killed in the war.

Peter and Mary's first child, Barbara Matilda—Tillie—was born in Louisiana, four months after the war ended. As a veteran, Peter was entitled to governmental distribution of food, but it was not enough to alleviate his family's poor conditions. Destroyed crops threatened Louisiana with starvation. Struggles with reconstruction and the disruption of the cotton and sugar trades made the state's economy slow to get back on its feet. Planters were fleeing to Texas. The growing railroad network contributed to Houston's growth, and more than the planters were heading that way.

German colonization in Texas had been encouraged since the early 1800s resulting in one of the largest migrations from

Europe. With Houston's offerings, Peter hoped there would be ample work from new construction of businesses and homes. In 1868, he relocated his small family and was moderately successful.

Mary gave birth to nine children total—Emma being her seventh born.

Butterfass Photographs

Peter Paul Butterfass

Mary Clark Butterfass

Family of Peter and Mary Butterfras

Peter Paul Butterfass
born: 22 March 1835, Darmstadt, Hesse, Germany
married to
Mary Clark
born: April 1847, Louisiana

their children
↓
Barbara Matilda "Tillie" Butterfass, born: 3 September 1865 in
Louisiana
Charlotte Emilie Gertrude "Lottie" Butterfass, born: 24 October
1868 in Texas
Wilhelmina Catharina Butterfass, born: 1 August 1871 in Houston,
Texas, died young
Name Unknown - probably a child born and died in infancy
John Butterfass, born: about 1875 in Houston, Texas, died at age 2
Paul Peter Butterfras, born: 9 May 1877 in Houston, Texas
Emma A. Butterfras, born: 28 July 1882 in Houston, Texas
Henry A. "Hy" Butterfras, born: August 1886 in Houston, Texas
Eva Anna Butterfras, born: 5 October 1889 in Houston, Texas

CHAPTER THREE

Ora

For the first nine years of her life, Emma lived with her family in a small home on Milam Street south of Market Square. After they left the Milam Street house, they moved every year or two, which made it difficult for outgoing and friendly Emma to make and keep friends.

Emma grew up in some of the most densely packed sections of downtown Houston. In 1892, Houston had started to build its first electric power plant and had already created a telephone exchange. At the time, New York was the only other city building an electric power plant.

Houston offered free public schools and mule-drawn trolleys to take passengers up and down the dusty dirt roads. For years, immigrants had been streaming into Galveston Port fifty miles south, contributing to Houston's population rise to over seventeen thousand. The legendary Chisolm Trail cattle drives were obsolete because railroads had reached Houston and other Texas cities with refrigerated railcars keeping butchered meat safe for consumption. By 1890, the city had two-hundred and thirty-four trains arriving and departing each day. Houston had rail links with the fashionable town of New Orleans, bringing such trendy entertainment as vaudeville and early jazz. The Texas Rangers had subdued the Indians for the most part, and the era of cowboys and outlaws moved toward civility.

In the 1900 United States Federal Census, Mary is recorded as having given birth to nine children. I have found names for eight. That undocumented child, and the deaths of both Wilhelmina and baby John, placed a wide gap in ages between Peter and Mary's first five children and the last four. It was almost like having two families. Emma was the middle child of the second set, with Paul five years older, and Emma's siblings Hy and Eva born after. The second set changed the spelling of their last name from Butterfass to a more phonetic, Butterfras.

By the age of seven, Emma was the oldest female child in the home, and her passive mother depended on Emma as if she were the first born. Sensitive to her younger siblings' needs, she perceived she needed to assume the parents' roles. Eventually, strong-willed, but insecure Emma rebelled against her submissive mother and selfish father.

In a taped, oral interview given by my father on July 6, 1980, George Hydrick said, "They was a close-knit family. Emma and Eva—they stuck together."

***

Emma ~ July 28, 1894

"Hello, family!" Emma's older sister, Lottie, called cheerily as she stepped into the dark house with her two small daughters.

Emma's other sister, Tillie, arrived behind her, an even rarer occurrence. Emma didn't know they were coming but grinned wide. Seeing them made a bad day so much better.

The women hugged briefly, Lottie bending over her mid-section swollen with her third child. They chattered like they were happy to be together. Lottie kept her arm around Emma's shoulder an extra-long time too. Without Papa, the visit felt like a party. Maybe they'd secretly come for her twelfth birthday and were waiting to surprise her?

Tillie fanned herself. "It's miserably hot and humid in here. How nice it would be to catch a breeze in the yard."

They took the old, mismatched kitchen chairs outside under their neighbor's canopy shade tree that reached over and above Emma's narrow but deep backyard.

Eva didn't have a chair and leaned against Emma, which made sweat trickle down her ribs. Not wanting to push Eva away, but wishing she'd leave, Emma whispered, "Why don't you go play with Beulah?"

Lottie's daughter, Beulah, who was four like Eva, sat in the yard's overgrown ryegrass with a rag doll. Her baby sister, Mabel, toddled around the yard, picking up bits of plant growth and rubbish and sticking them into her mouth.

"I don't like dolls," Eva whispered back, but when Emma sighed, Eva frowned and moved away to sit on the ground and pick at the dirt with a stick.

Emma's mom and sisters talked while Hy played at the far end of the yard on the trunk of a fallen elm tree. It had collapsed the year before in a storm, knocked off part of the shed roof on the goat's pen, and still lay where it had fallen—gray and decaying, consumed by ryegrass and weeds. The chickens pecked around it looking for bugs.

Dark clouds blocked the sun, but even without the sun's rays, everyone sweated heavily. Emma couldn't pull in a deep breath. The moist weight of the air all but drowned her. The clothes she'd pinned on the line that morning hung motionless, still wet.

As uncomfortable as she felt, she loved being with her family. She didn't see her sisters much and wished they'd come more often, especially Lottie who'd been like a mother, listening to her worries and making her feel safe. Lottie married and moved away when Emma was seven and Tillie married when Emma was two. Emma didn't even remember Tillie living in the house. Now divorced, Tillie lived in Galveston.

Mama frowned. "Where's Freddy?"

Tillie's son was eight, the same as Hy, but no one had seen him in years. "With his father." She gave the same answer she always gave, then turned from Mama. "They're buildin' a new opera house in Galveston." She started a different conversation in a voice that sounded like a circus announcer. "Y'all should come on down for the celebrations when it opens."

Mama nodded as if she'd do just that and fanned her face with a bamboo and paper fan with the words "drink Coca-Cola" across the upper edge.

She'd never go. She rarely left the house and even stopped wearing her corset.

Mama wiped at moisture on her neck where fuzzy white hairs curled from the humidity. Her gray hair, pulled sloppily on top of her head, sagged to the left.

Wearing the most recent style dress with a zipper down the back, Tillie sat perched on her chair like a real lady. "Come early, and we'll all have a picnic at the park where they give concerts.

Then we can dance at Garten Verein, a garden club the Germans built."

Eva jumped up, throwing her stick aside. "Can we, Mama? Oh, please?"

"We shall ask your father," Mama said, not looking at anyone in particular.

Emma's heart sank. Papa would never spend the train fare for all of them to have a day's outing. But she wanted to go. Just like she wanted Tillie's life where she could do whatever she desired and sleep late into the morning and wear pretty clothes.

Emma dreamed often of these things. She needed money to make her dreams come true. She'd ask Tillie what she needed to do to become rich.

Eva ran to Tillie's side. "Can we go swimmin' in the ocean?"

"Why sure!" Tillie gave Eva a squeeze.

Eva's face lit with excitement. Not yet five, she didn't know most of the time you didn't get what you wanted.

Emma all at once felt so much older than Eva. Sadness settled in her belly. It wouldn't be long before Eva's hopes would be as smothered as Emma's.

Lottie shifted in her chair and wiped the perspiration from her face with a kerchief, then pulled at her clothes around her belly. "I fear we wouldn't be able to join your little party until after the birth of the baby."

"Your life must be terrible dull." Tillie feigned sadness.

The two sisters rarely got along, fighting about the simplest matters.

Lottie made a face as if she had been pinched. "I'm satisfied."

"What's your day consist of? Changin' nappies, wipin' faces, and keepin' your husband from strayin'?"

"Tillie!" Mama's outburst showed more emotion than usual.

Lottie raised her hand to quiet Mama. "I don't live in slavery, Tillie. It's the wife's responsibility to provide for her husband's needs, and I'm more than happy to do so."

Tillie smiled sweetly. "I'm lucky enough to earn my own livin' and don't need to depend on no man. Sometimes I think I'm happier than anyone on earth."

Fascinated by Tillie's words, Emma wanted to visit her in Galveston to see this happy and mysterious life.

Lottie frowned. "We have different roads to travel. I'm happy with mine, and if ya don't like it, so be it."

"Oh, sister, no need to be melodramatic." Tillie rolled her eyes. "Being independent and secure is very sweet, and all women secretly want it."

Lottie shrugged a shoulder, sweat glistening on her face.

Emma wasn't sure which sister to believe. She loved Lottie and wanted to take her side, but Tillie acted so much happier.

Feeling the barest whisper of a breeze, Emma looked to the sky. Please let it rain. The bunching dark clouds hung low. A flash of lightning briefly lit the clouds farthest away. It smelled like rain.

"Oh, I almost forgot." Tillie leaned forward and pulled a small red, white, and blue box from her bag. Across the front were red words, *Cracker Jack*. "This here's a new confection they're sellin' in Galveston." She ripped off the top of the carton. "Try some." She passed it to Mama first, but Eva jumped to where Mama sat, showing an open palm.

This was it. They were going to talk about Emma's birthday. She could hardly wait. "Is this my birthday treat?"

Mama's eyes grew wide, and her face pink.

"Why Emma!" Lottie said, "How old is you?"

"Twelve."

"My little Emma's growin' up." Lottie grinned at her with wonder.

A loud crack broke the sweetness of the moment.

At first Emma thought the sound was thunder, but Mama jumped away from her chair too fast. Before she reached the steps leading to the back door of the house, Papa swung it open so violently it banged against the inside wall with a sick thud, sending the brass knob into the wall. "Vy are ya all out here, and vehr's my supper?"

All the sisters stood. A drop of rain landed on Emma's nose. Another on her head. Jagged lightning lit the sky. Rain fell in big, heavy drops.

"Come children," called Lottie frantically to Mabel and Beulah. "It's time to go."

With eyes wide, they rushed to her and she gathered them under each arm and ran toward the back gate.

Lottie whispered to Emma as she swept by, "Happy birthday!" and pushed the open box of Cracker Jack into her hand.

"Peter . . ." Mama cowered. "The girls come by unexpectedly and—"

"I vork to keep food in *deine* belly and expect it in mine, v*erdammt*!" He pointed a finger at her. "I'm tired, voman."

Bent forward, Mama slowly climbed the stairs and squeezed past Papa.

Paul stood sullenly in the dark kitchen beyond, still in his painting coveralls.

"Vell, vaht are you vaiting for?" Papa stared hard at Emma.

"I don't miss this!" Tillie grabbed her chair to carry back inside out of the rain. "Ya ol' drunkard. Some things never change." Chin high, she moved toward him. "When is ya gonna stop bossin' these good women?"

Emma had never heard anyone speak to Papa that way. She cringed. What if he rushed down after Tillie and hit her?

But Tillie didn't seem worried. She kept moving forward. When she went up the steps, Papa would either have to move to let her by or . . . what? Emma didn't know.

Tillie stopped before mounting the steps and she and Papa stared hard at one another, his hands fisted.

Whatever was going to happen, Emma didn't want Eva to see. Quickly looking around, she found Eva far back in the yard, sitting on the fallen tree trunk with Hy at her side, staring with big eyes. Rain flattened their hair, and they had crossed their arms over their bellies. They were watching it all.

Something inside Emma's chest broke free. She turned back. "Don't hurt my sister!" The words rushed out of her mouth almost by themselves.

Papa quickly started down the stairs, not toward Tillie, but toward Emma.

She froze in place.

Tillie swung her chair wide and hit him at the knees.

He fell with a crack onto the chair and rolled to the ground, moaning. Thunder boomed and lightning flashed as Papa pushed himself up. Mud covered his paint splattered canvas overalls. The chair lay in pieces.

Fear kept Emma from moving.

Tillie's body trembled. "Ol' fool! Did ya have to go after a young, helpless girl?" Tillie's expression shifted, like she'd said something that hurt her personally. Was she crying? It was hard to tell with the rain streaming down her face.

Thunder boomed again.

Papa was still on his knees. A twig dangled from his white beard.

"It's me ya wanted," Tillie yelled, eyes beseeching for his confirmation.

Crying, Paul bounded down the steps to Papa's side and grasped his arm. "Get outta here," he told Emma and Tillie, helping Papa stand. "Go," he pleaded again.

Tillie rushed to Emma and grabbed her by the upper arm. The carton of Cracker Jack flew to the ground. Carmel popcorn and peanuts spread across the mud. Tillie pulled Emma out the side gate and along the road's edge.

They walked quickly through the down-pour without saying a word, looking back to see if anyone followed. No one did. Emma kept wiping the wet hair from her eyes. Her skirt clung to her legs. Tillie never let go of her arm. After about twenty minutes, they reached Grand Central on Crawford Street.

Tillie pulled Emma into the station. "Come with me to Galveston for a while."

Emma tingled from head to toe. Galveston! A place where she didn't have to do chores. A place without her father. The tingle faded. "Who will take care of Hy and Eva?"

Tillie clutched Emma's hands. "Why do you care about that? They have a mother, don't they?"

Yes, *her*. Emma swallowed hard.

"Has Papa touched you?" Tillie drew her mouth tight and looked away.

Emma narrowed her eyes. "What do you mean?" Sometimes Papa looked at her body like he would reach out at any moment and caress it, but he hadn't. Those stares made her skin feel like he *had* touched her. She shivered.

Tillie pulled her forward. "We have a train to catch. Just come for a visit and return when Papa has settled down some." Tillie raised a brow in question, her impatience straining her features.

Emma bit her lip, went against everything her gut screamed at her not to do, and followed Tillie to the train. Going with her would be the best way to learn how to earn money and get the things she wanted.

CHAPTER FOUR

Ora

I'm not sure if Emma lived with Tillie in Galveston or just visited for a short time. In her early teenage years, she went back and forth between Galveston and Houston, with her main residence in Houston at her parents' home.

When the Panic of 1893 set off an economic depression, a financial crisis developed in the United States that lasted until 1896. The Houston City Directories of the time show Peter employed, but his salary was doubtless reduced. This could have played into Peter's demons and his problems with alcohol. Perhaps it was also his wife's unhappiness at being forced to live below the means to which she was accustomed, or the overwhelming responsibilities that had been with him for years while securing the wellbeing of eight children on a painter's salary. He could have been prone to the excessive need for alcohol by genetic disposition, learned the habit from his mother, or been driven to drink as a response to the Civil War traumas that likely still haunted his memories and nighttime dreams.

As Emma grew into her teen years, her mother's depression and submissiveness and her father's alcohol problem impacted her decisions. She suffered in ways that would affect the rest of her life.

***

Emma ~ 1898

Emma rose from her chair after buttoning her beaver-felt shoes. She placed the button hook on the old bureau with its chipped varnish and viewed herself in the full-length mirror, a crack running its length and giving her a fractured, double view of herself. She preferred a more stylish shoe, but they were her best and would have to do.

Her home-sewn skirt flared wide like a bell with a short train on the back, hopefully full enough to keep the shoes covered, other than perhaps when she danced the two-step or a polka. She sighed and promised herself that new shoes would be the first thing she'd buy when she got a job in Galveston the coming summer. She had no plans to go back to the boring monotony of her Houston school. She also needed to be away from Papa's reach. Living with Tillie off and on had given her a worry-free life that opened her eyes to possibilities.

She viewed herself a few moments longer, practicing smiles and making her eyes seductive and her face look older than her fifteen years.

For the past year, she'd gone to Houston dancehalls on Paul's arm, pretending to be his girl. They would laugh about the deception with friends, who offered Emma alcohol and cigarettes to add to the thrill of the indecent behavior. But tonight, her brother had a date, so she planned to go to a new dancehall with a girlfriend where chaperones were unnecessary.

Emma placed her quail-feather hat on her head, secured it with a hat pin, pulled on form-fitting gloves, and went to the front room where Mama sat napping. Papa had left earlier in the evening for his new job as an auditorium watchman. He would be gone all night, come home drunk in the morning, and sleep it off until he had to be back at work the following evening.

"I'm fixin' on going out," she whispered to Hy, not wanting to wake Mama. "Be sure and tend Eva while I'm gone, ya hear?"

"I can take care of myself," Eva whispered, pushing out her lower lip. "But I'd rather go with you." Only nine, the girl was too headstrong for her own good.

Emma laughed softly while glancing at Mama, who was still asleep.

"Please take me," Eva whined.

"You remind me of myself."

"She's as feisty, all right," Hy said.

"Someday I'm going to be big enough to sneak out of the house," Eva puffed out her chest.

Emma chuckled and kissed the top of her head. She liked Eva's free spirit the same way she liked Tillie's.

At the dancehall, Emma rarely remained seated. She spent most of the evening with a wealthy, older gentleman who wore fine clothing and a waxed handlebar mustache. During a waltz, he held her tighter than was appropriate. She laughed and pulled away. He pulled her closer, but she didn't mind his attentions because he bought her drinks.

"You'll squeeze the breath outta me, sir," she teased.

"You are quite enchanting, you know. How would you like to spend more time together and get to know each other in a quieter setting?" His smile was forced and he smelled like cloves and whiskey.

She briefly imagined living in an opulent home with china plates and silver settings. The maid would help her dress and style her hair. She'd have new shoes. She all but sighed. "I'll be leaving town soon."

His brow crinkled. "Where are you going?"

"I hope to find work in Galveston." She stood a little taller and held her chin higher.

"Oh? I heard about those working women in Galveston." He chuckled.

Emma stepped back, peering into his face to try and understand his meaning. His grin made his handlebar mustache stretch longer, distracting her, but their interaction gave her a thrill and she decided to play along. "I don't take your meanin'. I like to feel in charge of my life is all. I plan on being on my own soon."

"If you want to head down that track, I'll run after you."

She laughed softly near his ear. "I'm hard to catch."

CHAPTER FIVE

Ora

One night, while I was visiting with a newly found Butterfras cousin, he told me about Galveston's history and how it was infamous for prostitution, gambling, and drugs. The conversation developed into a lengthy discussion of why Galveston became known for salacious activities, and how the illegal practices survived for so long. It finally occurred to me that he might be telling me, in a gentle way, why Emma worked in Galveston. I asked some leading questions, but he wouldn't confess to his motive. Finally, I bluntly asked, "Do you think Emma was a prostitute?"

"Yes," he answered without blinking an eye. "I think she was."

Seconds ticked on the clock. I stared at him. He stared at me. My reaction was first one of shock and then sadness because it probably meant Emma had suffered sexual trauma at a young age. And then the ah-ha moment of understanding came. Emma's son, George—my grandfather—always seemed ashamed and bitter at the memory of his mother. Could this be why?

I headed to Galveston the next morning with the purpose of finding clues to these new questions about Emma.

***

Emma ~ Spring 1899

One week in four, Emma resided in her parents' downtown Houston home on Main Street, the other three weeks she lived and worked in Galveston, a city with a vibrant nightlife and unlimited vision for its future.

Leaving her parents' home, she traveled on a trolley one-and-a-half miles to Grand Central Depot and then boarded the train that would take her to work. The daily Short Line to Galveston left late afternoon. Well acquainted with the train ride, Emma settled into a red velvet, cushioned seat and prepared to wait the ninety minutes it took to arrive at Galveston Island's Union Depot.

Based on the looks men gave her, Emma knew she was an attractive young woman. At sixteen, she had the looks of a twenty-year old—especially today, in her ribbon-trimmed straw hat, high collared long-sleeved white blouse, and a belted blue skirt. Her dark brown wavy hair was parted in the middle and pulled back into a bun at the nape of her neck, giving her a modest look.

Many men told Emma her eyes were her most interesting feature. "Soulful eyes," they called them. Brown, with the irises set a little higher than most people's, making the whites visible before meeting her lower eyelid, giving her the appearance of innocent seduction. Her narrow, feminine nose complemented her full lips and wide smile. Even when she wasn't smiling, her eyes seemed to find joy in her surroundings.

Looks could be deceiving. She knew that well enough because she trusted no one. Her mirth that day was for the freedom she enjoyed.

She sat alone with no escort, which kept others from sitting on the bench next to her, even though the train was full enough to have a few cordial gentlemen standing. She was used to the looks of disapproval from women dressed in finery on the arms of older gentlemen, as if they didn't know it was almost the twentieth century. Emma didn't need a man at her side.

Oh, she'd been educated, but not with what one might call a first-class education. During her limited public schooling, she hadn't learned French or etiquette, but who cared. She'd learned to read and write. Even picked up some German from Papa.

She glanced out the window. The train left Houston's tall buildings behind and traveled south past opulent houses, then smaller, modest homes, eventually through shanty town, and finally those that couldn't even be called a shanty. If she wasn't careful, she'd soon be living in that neighborhood.

Buildings gave way to marsh grasses and swamp lands, and the steward came by to punch her ticket.

The late spring weather warming the cabin made her ask, "Can ya open a window, please?"

"By all means." He opened the one nearest her and moved on to other customers.

The breeze mildly smelled like rotten eggs. The woman across from Emma raised a kerchief to her nose.

A few passengers were Galveston's working class, obvious by their dress. Their faces were familiar to Emma, but she never exchanged pleasantries other than a simple head bob. Most passengers were typically heading for an evening out, or perhaps a few days in cosmopolitan Galveston where they could enjoy beach bathing, promenades, picnics, concerts, and dances.

The train moved up an incline onto a bridge. The usual low rumble changed to a hollower sound. They slowly crossed above Galveston Bay, two miles wide. As the train swayed slightly along the flimsy wooden trestle, fear was evident on the faces of the fancy women. They tightly grasped onto their cushioned armrests or gentleman's arms and looked to and froe to judge the reactions of others, gauging the danger they might be in. Emma smirked with disdain.

The descent off the bridge brought them to more grasslands and past dirty train yards and large storage buildings fanning out from the wharves. All sizes of ships, including a passenger steam liner, filled the slips. Since the end of the Spanish-American War the year before, the wharf thrived as Galveston's lifeblood.

Workers were leaving the docks by the hundreds, some on bicycles, but most walking. Night was coming on and subtle changes in the air magnified the salty breeze coming in through the open window. The early evening air of the Gulf Coast felt moist on Emma's face.

Nearing her stop, the train passed both old and new European-style mansions with slated mansard roofs. Some of the more elegant homes had walled gardens with luxurious hedges of purple, white, and pink oleander and bougainvillea, blocking their occupants' view of the dirty wharf. Emma wouldn't mind living in even some of the oldest houses with outdated and neglected cast iron verandas and gates corroded from the salty atmosphere.

Entering the bustling eastern end of the island, the downtown area, the train pulled into the depot. Emma disembarked with the crowd. Smells of fried clams and baking pastries mingled with the train's smoke. Her pulse quickened at being in such a vibrant place, and she smiled.

She walked south with most of the travelers who headed toward The Strand where they could find refreshment, lodging, or shopping. Piano music drifted from an open saloon, and a trolley bell rang down the street.

Emma ambled past a shop window displaying fine lace gloves and parasols. She often shopped at the elegant stores. The merchants were glad to see her spend money on fancy underclothes, evening dresses, and beauty preparations and treatments. Shoppers with children strolled by, unmindful of who she was. Emma made a point of dressing more conservatively east of 25th Street, to not bring attention to herself.

She walked past opera houses, theaters, and luxurious hotels. Closer to the Gulf, there were beer gardens a-plenty, and hostelries for the less affluent. Gambling and saloons brought in men of all vocations and lifestyles.

Past The Strand, the crowd thinned, and Emma continued into a residential district where palm trees swayed. The gulf breeze cooled the city and brought in a misty fog, causing the night to come early. Now walking alone, she passed a man lighting gas streetlamps on one of the few streets that hadn't yet been electrified. The homes with electricity were easy to spot because their windows shined more brightly. These were probably the same houses that had a telephone.

Since the city was barely above high tide and prone to flooding, some buildings stood on stilts. The highest elevation was Broadway, a wide boulevard that ran east to west, bisecting the city. Emma wouldn't be going that far. Her destination was Postoffice Street, where rows of white two-story houses had lattice-work porches shielding front doors from the view of passersby and green-shuttered windows closed for the night. She crossed the intersection of Postoffice and 25th, then turned west into a back alley where most people didn't venture. The alley was dark, but she knew each washhouse, stable, and quarters for servants. She arrived at the two-story, batten-board house where she worked and entered the back door of the bordello.

CHAPTER SIX

Ora

Prostitution. Not the plot line I expected to write about. And if I were naming my characters, I'd certainly never have sisters with names so close in spelling such as Eva and Emma and Lottie and Tillie. And then of course, there's Peter, Paul, and Mary. But the truth is what I'm after, so the truth is what I'll write.

When I first drove into Galveston, it was a morning of clear blue skies and little traffic. I traveled the bridge across the causeway, entering by Broadway Avenue, turned left onto 23rd Street, and parked at the visitor's center. After speaking to the kind folks there, I was pleasantly surprised to learn I'd arrived on Mardi Gras weekend, which I thought was only celebrated in New Orleans. I left with a handful of brochures and a plan to stroll the Entertainment District and return by way of a walking tour of old historic homes.

I walked north on 25th Street, not knowing its infamous history. When I crossed the intersection of Postoffice, my thought was how odd that the two words "post" and "office" were joined to make one. The sidewalks were raised a foot or more above the streets—I assumed due to occasional ocean waters entering the city. Some buildings were in decay, but I especially enjoyed the architecture of the intact taller business structures, with their elaborate flourishes and cornices at the roof-lines, showing the wealth once dropped into Galveston's economy.

I played tourist, shopped, and ate a delicious lunch, then gathered with the noisy crowds to watch the Mardi Gras Pet Parade. Costumed animals in wagons and pet carriers colorfully decorated with flowing beads, feathers, and sequins traveled down The Strand. There wasn't a lot of bead throwing—that was reserved for Fat Tuesday.

After the parade, I left the business district and continued my walking tour in the nearby East End Historical District. Because Galveston's an island, its efficient homes were built narrow and close together to conserve space. The architecture reflected a variety of styles—including Victorian and Greek Revival. The houses ranged from small, simple white cottages to large, stone mansions with turrets. Many charming homes were painted in soft pastel colors of blues, greens, and pinks with stained glass windows, wide welcoming porches, and wrought iron fencing, similar to what you would see in New Orleans. I imagined what Emma would have seen and what life would have been like in her day.

When I visited the Rosenberg Library and Research Center a couple days later, I learned that when Emma worked in Galveston in 1899, prostitution had already been a thriving business for over seventy years. The section of bordellos along Postoffice Street was famously known as "The Line." It was located a few blocks south of Union Depot and west of 25th Street, within a working-class, single-family home neighborhood. Sprinkled among the bordellos were also small commercial businesses. The area attracted locals, tourists, and men who came to the city for gambling, drinking, and sex.

At the library, I discovered enough circumstantial evidence (explained presently and in Chapter Notes) to convince me Emma was indeed a prostitute. *Why?* I kept asking myself in heartbreak. I wanted to know her sufferings and sensitivities and most especially her dreams for life. *Who had hurt her? Who had loved her?*

In Emma's day, Galveston did a large export-import business at its bustling wharf, surpassing New Orleans to become the top cotton port in the nation, bringing in many sailors desiring a prostitute's services. The bordellos in Galveston were segregated by race and economic standing. The city had a toleration-silence policy regarding prostitution.

I suspect the day Emma's life changed forever was a day like most others. Pansies flowered in pots outside shop doors, blocks from the bordellos. Spring was the best time of year on the island for the residents because summer brought muggy heat, mosquitoes, and too many beach goers and vacationers.

There was no slow season for Postoffice Street, even though it appeared almost deserted by day other than the patrons of second-hand stores and pawn shops. In the evenings, the big spenders came for the casinos. Liquor flowed and prostitution thrived.

***

Emma ~ April 1899

"I'm the best entertainment in town," Emma called to a seaman from the open parlor window of the bordello.

He pulled his pockets wrong-side-out to show her he had no coin.

"Come by after payday." She grinned and waved goodbye, then settled onto the low windowsill.

As the sun descended and cast a golden glow on the sand-colored buildings, she worked the window soliciting customers. She competed with other prostitutes at their bordello windows, calling out to the same occasional passersby. She hoped her youth, tight blue gown, and upswept hair with a white feather pin—along with her charm and good looks—would lure men in. She wasn't as shapely as most of the girls and had smaller breasts, but she knew her clientele well and did her best to appear high-class. She raised her chin a little higher and called to another seaman lazily walking down the street. He ignored her. Perhaps he was drunk and satisfied?

Most days were good, bringing in more money than her father ever made in a week. But this night, she had a feeling of foreboding. Sitting at the open window, looking at an abandoned street, she had time to think about how mere blocks away, other men—the kind who kept away from The Line—had women who stayed home to care for their children, cook, clean, and prepare for their evening arrival. Emma imagined the women shopped or had their groceries delivered by the many stores that offered the service by wagon or a young man on a bicycle. The same women visited with their neighbors or walked their babies in prams along the wooden sidewalks, attended church and charity events, played bridge, and socialized while sipping tea.

When Emma saw people on a picnic or strolling the boardwalk or beaches, she sometimes wondered if she wanted what they had. If their lives would keep her gratified. Would she *want* to move among decent folk and flock to plays, private dinners, and restaurants? Her seedier activities denied her that. And even if she did want association with such people, how could she? Her childhood hopes of marrying a gentle and dependable man unlike Papa were gone.

She leaned against the window frame and sighed, thinking about how her biggest concerns now were how she looked and smelled and who she attracted for business. Not only her looks, but the overall décor of her bordello and the quality of amenities were reflected in the price she'd receive. The customer paid for her by time spent—anywhere from fifteen minutes to all night. Usually, Emma received sixty percent and the retired prostitute who managed the bordello forty percent. Prostitution paid better than most jobs open to women like hand sewing, shop girl, teacher, secretary, or nurse—things she had no interest in. She knew herself well enough to know she needed a thrill and a job where she wasn't expected to do anything that lasted more than an evening.

She shook her head. These were thoughts she'd had before, and nowhere in her dreams could she reach a conclusion of what she truly wanted other than money. A lot of money.

"I don't hear you workin' that window, Emma," Bones called from within.

Emma glanced over her shoulder to her madam. Bones wore a shimmery burgundy evening gown, her skin sagging on her thin frame, making Emma think she must have been fat at one time. Her nickname was actually Skinny Bones. Most called her Bones. She was fair to Emma and cared for all her girls, as long as they worked hard and were honest about how many customers they serviced.

"Can't interest a man if he ain't there," Emma called back.

Bones cackled. "Maybe we need a breeze to carry yer parfume to the docks."

Bones was sometimes called "the landlady" by customers who didn't know her. She seldom took customers herself, being well-occupied with superintending her establishment. Often, she had high-paying guests with whom she'd visit and share drinks. She always pushed the sale of liquor and music and made sure that drinking guests didn't cause trouble for her girls. Threats of violence and harassment occasionally took place, and muscular Jax, the piano player, took care of the thugs.

Emma had never been in any trouble, which made her one of Bones's favorites. The shrewd woman was known to pay bribes to law enforcement authorities to allow the bordello to operate. Normally, prostitution was openly tolerated in Galveston by city officials, but residents often complained, and the police had recently made a show of cracking down. Bones occasionally had to pay attorney fees when girls were arrested, and she didn't hesitate to pay fines to release her girls from jail.

As night came fully on, Emma finally lured in a customer. The gas-lighted doorway of the bordello was hidden behind lattice, concealing his identity from the gaze of others on the street as he stepped inside. Bridget, the maid, ushered him into the subtly lit drawing room, ornate and welcoming.

Emma stepped toward him, gracefully brushing her hand over the airy softness of peacock feathers sprouting out of a Rookwood pottery vase. The room added to the atmosphere of seduction, its wallpaper in a sinuous plant-like design with stylized long-stemmed poppies and lilies in muted colors of sage, mustard, lavender, brown, and gold. Emma believed the dream-like flowing lines and curves lent themselves well to statues and wall prints of delicate nude girls draped in sheer fabrics.

"It smells like I've entered a French salon, the perfume is so thick in here," the customer said in a smooth voice.

"Have ya been to France then?" A man who has traveled to France was of great interest to Emma. Perhaps he was more than a seaman and had money. She moved in closer.

"Many times," he said as he slid an arm around her waist. A thin man with a high forehead, he stood a little over Emma's height. "Although the women are lovely there, they are not as beautiful as you." He smiled and his clear blue eyes showed interest.

Emma guessed him to be close to forty.

She laughed and placed a hand on his chest, applying just the right amount of pressure, at the same time swallowing disgust as a memory of Papa came unbidden, as it often did when her customers had blue eyes. "Do ya wanna dance? For a nickel, you can get a song from our pianist."

Emma motioned to Jax seated in the corner in front of his instrument, watching the room closely, waiting for a request.

The man who had been to France walked over and placed a nickel in Jax's jar. "How 'bout 'When You Were Sweet Sixteen'?"

"Sure thing, boss," Jax said.

The song was slow and the customer a good dancer.

Emma loved to dance and would prefer to spend more time doing that before they went upstairs, but Bones had her rules, and Emma knew she needed to try and cajole the customer into spending money on liquor or even opiates before luring him to her room.

When the song ended, Jax received a request for "Happy Days in Dixie," and the mood in the room picked up with the lively ragtime music.

Emma asked over the din, "Can I get you a drink?"

The customer nodded, and she showed him to a corner chair covered in chintz next to a low-lit lamp with a cut-glass shade depicting languid wisteria. By the time she brought him the drink, the room had filled with more men, a few with girls on their arms. Some danced. Others lit cigarettes and watched.

Music and light poured into the street whenever the door opened for a patron. Some were tourists, others boisterous seaman, and sometimes a young boy or two from the nearby medical college. The room filled as the evening progressed. Emma served more drinks. Bones brought in extra girls dressed in low-cut, silk evening gowns. They greeted their guests and asked if they cared to dance, or they worked the room to let the men look them over until they made their choice.

Youth was a desirable quality, so being sixteen gave Emma the advantage. Many of the customers were foreign sailors who couldn't speak English, but they easily made their desires known. As long as they were generous with coins for music, drinking, or entertainment upstairs, they could stay as long as they pleased. Otherwise, Bones asked them to leave.

Emma liked this brothel, but she planned to work her way up. There were a few bordellos sprinkled within upper-class residential areas and near the beachfront outside of The Line. A popular brothel was a large two-story house on Broadway, set back behind mature trees and a tall fence. It often had fine carriages parked in front night and day. Emma's goal was to work there someday.

After teasing and small talk, she sensed a subtle change in her john's mood. "Would ya like to go upstairs?"

"Lead the way." He grinned, showing yellow teeth and a generous amount of gums.

At the bottom of the stairs, Bridget handed Emma a pitcher of water and a towel.

The customer said, "Fifteen minutes." He gave Bridget money.

Ascending the stairwell, Emma let her hand trail along the wall of stenciled designs that followed the stairs to the upper landing.

The rooms used for entertainment were also the girls' personal bedrooms. Emma showed him into her room and shut the door. The house didn't have running water and so, for cleansing, she filled a basin with water from the pitcher. At the end of the night, her towels would be collected and counted. The number must match the number of customers that had been recorded in a ledger by Bridget or Skinny Bones.

"All well in there, Emma?" Bones asked on the other side of the door.

"As it should be," Emma replied, not surprised Bones was letting the customer know she was close by.

Since the house's entrances were on the lower floor, having the bedrooms on the second floor made it easier for Bones to keep track of the girls. For their safety, there were no locks on the bedroom doors, and glass transoms over the doors were left open so Bones could determine what was going on inside. The transom controls were located on the outside of the room.

Before Emma came to Galveston, there was a time when prostitutes were required to take out a license for $2.50 every three months and have quarterly doctor visits. Emma was glad

Bones continued the doctor's exam practice. She cared for her girls and paid the doctor bills for cases such as recurring venereal disease and childbirth. Bones allowed her girls to give birth at her establishment if the girl was a high wage-earning worker and stayed off drugs and alcohol. If Emma and the girls weren't cared for, it reflected on what Bones earned and sometimes how the girls acted. Emma had seen many girls with mental health problems, and one committed suicide in the last place she'd worked. If Bones had these issues, she tried to keep them from the public and press.

Fifteen minutes later, Bones knocked on the door. "Time to git a move on," she called.

When the customer left, Emma dressed and went back to the drawing room to entertain another customer. If she was lucky, she'd service six men that night.

***

Ora

The birth control methods used in 1899 were primarily douching, pessaries, or condoms made of a strong elastic rubber. These methods were not fail-safe.

On this night in April, Emma had a customer, possibly a stranger, whose last name was Osborne. I know this because he impregnated Emma and left behind his DNA to travel down three generations to myself.

CHAPTER SEVEN

Ora

I am the product of a whore and her john. That knowledge hurt at first. A secret perhaps best left unsaid, as my grandfather felt. This revelation flew in the face of all that family meant to me. *Family*—my identity.

Instead of a connection, I had a disconnect. "Do I really know who I am?" I asked myself. What are my ancestral connections to the Osbornes, and what were their traditions, practices, beliefs, stories, and culture? Was I just a DNA inheritor?

What exactly identifies who I am?

I thought ancestry was everyone's foundation. How many times have I heard that we can't know who we are until we know who we came from? Were my people—these Osbornes—artisans, inventors, engineers, blacksmiths, scientists, or what?

What are the fundamentals that make families relevant, effective, resilient, happy?

I once read an article in the *New York Times* by Bruce Feiler where he wrote that when he researched how to make families work more effectively, he discovered that the "most important thing you can do for your family may be the simplest of all: develop a strong family narrative." It has been proven that children who know details about their ancestors tend to do better when they face challenges. They have a stronger sense of control over their lives, higher self-esteem, more resilience to help moderate the effects of stress, and better overall health and happiness.

Knowing my ancestors helped me as a child. I knew I belonged to something bigger than myself. The family narrative was about how those before me endured the Irish Potato Famine, fought in wars, helped settle the American continent, and even participated in state leadership. But now as an adult, I was learning a new narrative.

Emma made choices that affected generations. Besides those aunts, uncles, and cousins who came before and after me, I have seven siblings, five children, five grandchildren, twenty-three nephews and nieces, sixty-four great nephews and nieces, and five great-great nephews and nieces—all a product of Emma and her "customer."

I suddenly needed to know what Emma's trials were and how she survived.

I did the math. Three months before she turned seventeen, she was pregnant. On January 19, 1900, she gave birth to my grandfather George. He would later take on the last name of Hydrick. There is no birth record for George, but he claimed to have been born in Houston, not Galveston. When he was six months old, the 1900 United States Federal Census was conducted, and he was not enumerated in Houston.

Emma was enumerated in her father's home, but George was either not reported to the census taker, or he was living someplace else, perhaps in a bordello. I had to swallow that likely scenario. I was gaining empathy and understanding for my grandfather.

George was also not recorded in Galveston. It is my guess he was with Emma that day in Houston, and she didn't report him because then she would have had to answer questions about her marital status and whether or not the father lived in the household.

As expected, Emma's occupation was not recorded in the census either. Almost all the young women living along Postoffice Street in the 1900 Census reported themselves as laundresses or seamstresses, historically common euphemisms for prostitutes in the nineteenth century.

When I initially conducted my research, because of George not being recorded in the census, I was concerned that perhaps he wasn't Emma's child and came to her through her marriage to Jack Hydrick, a year and a half after George was born. I had autosomal DNA testing performed and found that George did carry the Butterfras genes and was Emma's biological child. And as I have already mentioned, yDNA was also conducted, with the results being a paternal match to the Osborne family.

A bordello consisted of its own kind of family. If there were older children, they often watched the younger ones while their mothers worked or slept. The madam sometimes charged a fee for the inconvenience of having an extra person in her household but often enjoyed associations with the innocent children. I like to imagine Emma had friends in the bordello who helped her with baby George, and that he was given the loving attention every baby deserves.

***

Emma ~ Winter 1900

The baby's cries disturbed Emma's sleep. With great difficulty, she awakened enough to lift her head from the pillow. It throbbed from too much whiskey the night before—or was it only hours before? She collapsed back onto the pillow.

The crying gained momentum to bawling.

One of the girls banged on the wall. "Shut that kid up!"

Emma groaned and pushed herself out of bed, crossed the room, and pulled back the green damask curtain hiding the cradle.

George's pinched-up face grew redder as he howled.

She picked him up, his over-full nappy sagging with urine, and took him back to bed, pushing her breast into his open, wailing mouth.

Like a customer, he latched on. His cries muffled, his little chest spasmed until he relaxed and rhythmically sucked.

Hours later, Emma awoke to a cold room and a shaft of sunlight streaming through a crack in the heavy velvet curtains.

George laid quietly awake, staring at the shaft of light. Her head still ached, she was thirsty, and her bed linens were soaked with his urine. She should have changed him earlier.

He fussed while she cleaned him with cold basin water and dressed him in the last clean nappy and a white baby gown.

Slipping into a light blue satin robe, much too thin for winter, she took George down to the kitchen where she found Fereby adding thin slivers of wood into the already warm cook stove. The room smelled of coffee. Emma dropped into a seat. She wasn't any good for conversation until she'd had her coffee, and Fereby knew it.

The old, portly servant woman poured coffee into a fine china cup and set it on the table in front of Emma then took George from her arms. "How's de big man today? Ain't ya a cute one!" she cooed, rubbing her dark finger along his pale cheek. "Momma needs to put some fat on dose bones. I knows just the thing." She placed George in a large metal laundry tub half-full of clean towels on the floor.

He gurgled and kept his hands close to his mouth.

She left by the back door, and a gush of crisp air flowed in. She soon returned with a jar of cold milk she'd retrieved from the cellar. Opening it, she poured some into a tall glass, usually used for liquor. "Here, Miss Emma. You drink dis for lil' Georgy."

Lily and Val came into the kitchen, conversing about an Italian sailor who'd come in last night and used both their services, tipping generously.

Fereby set coffee in front of them, then retrieved a heavy black skillet crusted along the outer edge from years of use, and placed it on the stove. She scooped a spoonful of lard out of a tin and plopped it into the skillet. "You girls want some griddle cakes and fried pork strips?"

Emma's head had started to clear, and she agreed to the meal, as did the others. The cozy, warm kitchen with its homey smells was her favorite place. The winter had been long. In February, they'd had a freak ice storm that closed the city down for days.

A knock sounded at the backdoor. Assuming it to be food delivery, the girls let Fereby answer.

The refined voice of a lady said, "I'm Mrs. E. W. Nichols, the matron of Bethesda Door of Hope. May I step in and speak with the girls of this establishment?"

Fereby stammered some and then said, "The landlady ain't gonna like dat."

"I don't think she'll mind. I won't take but a moment."

Fereby glanced over her shoulder.

Emma shrugged. What did she care?

Fereby stepped aside, and a tall woman moved into the room like the angel of mercy she probably assumed she was. All business, she was dressed in a stiff gray wool coat over a darker gray dress, her back as straight as a ship's mast.

Emma didn't bother to pull her robe closed, and Val threw her leg up on a chair, as if to say, "I live by my own rules."

"You poor, soiled doves," Mrs. E. W. Nichols said with a false note. "Let me gather you to a cleaner nest. Won't you come to my rescue home on 27th Street and find peace with God and respect from your fellow men?"

Emma laughed out loud.

Mrs. E. W. Nichols acted as if she hadn't heard. "I could give you a decent home, and no one would be the wiser of your fallen state."

Emma tried to speak, but the formidable lady continued, "We will take precautions against temptations and place you in employment such as clerical positions, teaching, or nursing."

"How much would I get paid for that kind of work?" Lily squinted.

"The average annual wage is $235."

All the girls tittered. Lily got up and left the room with coffee cup in hand.

"How do you put a price on respect?" Mrs. E. W. Nichols called after her in a high voice.

"Is there someone there who would tend my baby while I go to work?" Emma asked, pointing at George in the laundry tub.

Mrs. E. W. Nichols displayed a quick moment of shock, then quickly covered her temporary loss of composure by running her hands down the front of her long coat. She glanced at George again. "I didn't realize there would be an infant involved. We could arrange to adopt it out to a good, church-going family, and it would be none the wiser."

"If I wanted to give my baby away, I would have done it already. Obviously, I have chosen to keep *it*." Anger filled her chest, and she wondered why she hadn't left with Lily. This pious and judgmental woman didn't deserve her time.

Mrs. E. W. Nichols turned to Val. "Do you have a child?"

Val shook her head.

"If you live in our home, work a full-time job, go to church, and marry and have children, then you'd become respectable. That is our goal for all the women of the night."

Emma guffawed. "There's at least a thousand of us in this city." No one could be counted on to take care of Emma but herself. She'd learned that lesson as a child.

Mrs. E. W. Nichols pursed her lips and said nothing.

"I don't guess I could," Val stated. "It's too late for me, and all your fixin' ain't gonna change my past."

Having believed Mrs. E. W. Nichols done with her, Emma jumped in surprise when suddenly the hawk turned her talons back to her. "You may know a lot about men, but how much do you know about babies?"

The question startled Emma and hit where she was most vulnerable. She knew little of babies, only those things she learned at home when caring for Hy and Eva. Mama taught her nothing of caring for a newborn. It had been Fereby who showed her what George needed. The schedule of when he slept and when she worked had been the hardest to undertake. Now six weeks old, he was awake for longer stretches of time. Her worries of George needing more attention than she gave gnawed at her insides. Maybe she should relinquish him to a home where folks could give him a better life and education. But something inside her wouldn't let go of him. "I can learn. I think you should leave now."

Fereby turned from what she was cooking on the stove, obviously having listened to the whole conversation, and stepped toward the door to show Mrs. E. W. Nichols out.

"We're at 1311 27th Street if either of you change your minds. Spread the word to the rest of the girls." Mrs. E. W. Nichols placed her calling card printed with fancy, swirling letters on the table. "And remember, we are all God's children and need to be saved, including that baby."

Saved from what? Emma wondered.

CHAPTER EIGHT

Ora

At some point in Emma's childhood, she'd lost her sense of belonging. From that, I imagine her desires grew to wanting to be independently secure. I do not know who inducted her into the profession of prostitution. There is no evidence Emma was thrown into the occupation against her will. It may have started with visits to the dancehalls in downtown Houston, or the influence of an older sister or someone else, or it may have been much more complex.

Why would a woman turn to prostitution? The most typical reasons were money, sexual curiosity, abuse as a child, homelessness, or avoiding some kind of uncomfortable situation in their daily life such as sorrow, poverty, emotional pain, or bitterness. Of all these, it has been found that childhood abuse is the leading cause for young people to turn to prostitution. Some estimate that 85% of prostitutes were sexually abused before they entered the profession. Few of them would admit to it in the day that Emma lived. When questioned, they typically gave the answer that they were "not welcomed at home."

While Emma was in the profession, she did not break her ties with her family in Houston, but instead it appears she stayed with them on her week off—probably the week of her menstruation. Since she felt responsibility for her siblings, I would suspect checking on Hy and Eva drew her home.

Was there a sense of hopelessness for Emma or did her rebellious spirit push her toward selling her body for money? Did she know that prostitution would change her world and set her apart from decent society of the late Victorian Era? Did she care?

I only have circumstantial evidence of Emma being abused at home, but I do know that patterns of abuse can develop in families and carry down generations. It happened in my own family.

When we think of family, we think of people looking out for each other's welfare. The reality for Emma was her parents expected their children to take care of themselves. Peter was an alcoholic who was often mired in denial and spent little time parenting.

With Emma being one of the younger children in the family, it's also likely her behavior was influenced by her older siblings, who set for her an example of breaking societal conventions. At eighteen, her sister, Tillie, married German immigrant Otto Lorenz. Emma was two years old. When she was three, Tillie gave birth to a son, Frederick. Early in her marriage, Tillie divorced Otto, and Fred was raised primarily by his father and stepmother. Tillie married a Mr. Vinson, and then was either widowed or divorced, and married Frank Wiggins. Tillie gave birth to a daughter, Edith, in Houston in 1897, after which they moved to Nebraska where Frank worked as a watchman for the railroad. By 1901 they moved back to Houston, where Frank and sixteen-year-old stepson Frederick were imprisoned for counterfeiting dollar coins. Two years later, Tillie died at the young age of thirty-seven when her daughter Edith was six. Cause of death unknown.

Emma's second sister, Lottie, married Anton Readler, a carpenter and first-generation German-American. They had three children, and then Lottie died at an even younger age than Tillie—she was thirty and left behind three children under the age of nine. Cause of death unknown.

Little is known of Emma's third sister, Wilhelmina. She died before 1910, and it is unlikely she married or had children.

Emma's brother, John, died at two, five years before Emma was born. Her second brother, Paul, was born about the time John died. Paul lived the longest and died in 1969, at the age 92. He married once, a feisty girl named Mary Gray from Louisiana. They had their feuds, but Mary held the family together. When Paul came home drunk, breaking dishes and yelling, Mary threw dishes, too, and yelled right back at him.

Emma's younger brother, Henry "Hy," moved out of his parents' home at the age of sixteen with his younger sister, Eva, who was thirteen. Hy died a mysterious death at the age of nineteen. Through the years, Eva married five times.

Using today's vernacular, we would call the Butterfrases a highly dysfunctional family. What made them dysfunctional stemmed from abuse and alcoholism and perhaps Peter's background of social and economic problems caused by having an unwed, single mother in the 1830s.

Americans historically have shown a high tolerance for violent behavior. In Emma's day, men were seen as having the right to dominate and control their wives to assert their role as a husband. Aggressive action was normal for both mothers and fathers in certain settings, such as getting their children to behave "properly."

Through the years, social reformers increased public awareness of the darker side of families—the hurt and neglected and the domestic violence that took place behind doors. Their solutions were not adequate and their efforts short-lived. The laws did not have enough deterrents to keep men from beating their wives or to keep children out of the work force and in school. Child labor may have had less to do with abusive parents, and more to do with the family's poverty. The women activists who fought against family abuse were largely ignored.

A case in New York City achieved widespread publicity, shocking the nation and opening the eyes of those who would rather not see. A two-year-old girl, Mary Ellen McCormack, was placed with a woman who abused her for years. In 1874, when Mary Ellen was ten, neighbors contacted a charity worker after hearing the girl's screams. The charity worker visited Mary Ellen's home and found her malnourished, bruised, and scarred. The woman did not personally intervene, but instead contacted asylums in an attempt to get Mary Ellen removed from the home. Her attempts failed, and she contacted the American Society for the Prevention of Cruelty to Animals.

Posing as a census worker, an investigator for the ASPCA went to the home. Within 24 hours, Mary Ellen was removed from the household. She was later adopted. People finally became informed that it was easier to protect an abused animal than it was a human being. Because of this case, the New York Society for the Prevention of Cruelty to Children was founded. By 1900, there were nearly 500 such organizations.

With the abuse largely being blamed on mental disturbances or poverty, law enforcement had a hard time dealing with such matters, and the cases were eventually referred to social caseworkers, whose work wasn't always funded, and they often found their jobs embroiled in political machinations.

Despite the efforts of social reformers, many Americans didn't think that it was anyone's business what went on in their households. If there was abuse, a child often didn't have anyone to turn to for help and usually left the home as soon as they were able—often in their teenage years, like Tillie, Lottie, Emma, Henry, and Eva. As adults, they found themselves in destructive relationships.

CHAPTER NINE

Ora

On a cloudy Saturday in September, Emma's brothers— twenty-three-year-old Paul and fourteen-year-old Hy— left their home in Houston and caught the 9:45 a.m. Galveston, Houston, and Henderson train to Galveston Island. Through the passing of the following oral story, my family no longer knows why Paul and Hy went to Galveston that day. Since it was Saturday, they may have been going to the beach, but it's also possible they had extra work to do on the island. They worked as painters—a trade learned from their father. By the grace of God, Paul's wife, Mary, and their baby, Sanders, did not accompany the young men on the trip.

***

Paul ~ September 8, 1900

The wind sprinkled light rain against the train window where Paul rested his head. As the storm worsened, the landscape became a blur, forcing the train to slow. He let out a breath of frustration.

Hy slept in the chair next to him, oblivious to the fact that their day was probably ruined.

At 10:35 a.m., they should've already arrived at Union Depot in Galveston but instead had only reached Virginia Point—eight miles northwest. Paul stood and paced the narrow aisle, the muggy air making him perspire. Even with the bad weather, the train was full. People swiped at sweaty brows and loosened collars. Women fanned their faces.

A bad feeling gnawed at Paul. The weather had come out of nowhere.

A gust of wind jostled the car, and Paul settled back into his seat. He elbowed Hy, who snorted awake. Paul asked, "What time did ya get in last night?"

"You ain't my father." Hy grumbled then crossed his arms over his chest and slumped back to sleep.

Paul knew full well that their father didn't care when Hy had come in. It was Paul's job to worry about his brother. Always had been.

As they crossed the rickety railroad bridge, winds blew from the north. The car swayed violently. Even on a good day, the unsteady trestles could rattle Paul's nerves. Gathering at the windows, people gasped at the sea's white caps two feet below the train. Expressions of fear and surprise crossed many faces. Paul tightened his jaw, trying to remain calm.

As the train came off the bridge, it was supposed to hit land, but water flowed above the tracks, slowing them to a sluggish crawl. He wished they'd never left Houston. Would they even be able to get home today? How would he get word to Mary?

Some of the crew disembarked and sloshed ahead of the slow-moving engine, pushing drifting debris out of the way with poles. A strong gust of wind struck the train broadside, and Hy sprang upright, spurting forth a curse. Women furrowed their brows at him.

Paul patted his back. "I don't like the look of this weather."

"Looks like we won't be able to work. Let's go to the beach instead." Hy raised his brows in question to his suggestion.

Paul shook his head. The beach in the rain did not sound like a good plan.

By the time the train reached 75th Street, close to a hundred feet of track had been washed away, forcing the train to stop. They were stranded. The winds blew stronger, whistling through the car, shifting the train back and forth. Alarmed at the building intensity of the storm, Paul had an overwhelming urge to check on Emma in the city.

Some of the men around him discussed wading into town to get help. The rain was so loud on the roof that the men had to raise their voices to be heard. Before anyone left for help, a steward came by and announced someone at Union Depot had realized their predicament and was sending a switch engine with coaches.

They waited about an hour in the hot and muggy coach before the rescue train arrived. To board it, passengers had to cross a fifteen-foot flooded area between the two tracks. With the fast-moving water almost waist-high, they had a hard time keeping a foothold. Paul and Hy helped women and children wade the distance, encouraging them to hold hands in a human chain.

Rain fell in sheets. Hats blew off. Hand-held items, suitcases, and umbrellas joined the flowing wreckage. But everyone made it across.

Soaking wet and settled into the new coach, they slowly headed to Union Depot, again with a crew walking ahead, pushing track ties and other debris out of the way.

Just as Paul saw the city ahead and breathed a sigh of relief, he smelled smoke. He opened the window and stuck his head into the pelting rain. Flames shot from the engine, and the train stopped again.

He and Hy decided to leave the train and try to make it to Emma's. They jumped from the car into water higher than their waists. The water rose so quickly, it doused the fire on the train, but also made it harder for the locomotive to move toward the station. The train inched slowly away while Paul and Hy trudged toward the city.

Galveston's streets had been paved with wooden blocks— which now floated everywhere along with barrels, crates, and telephone poles. Paul and Hy shoved the debris away and struggled to move forward. The curbs, built over a foot high, two feet on some corners, were meant to direct high tides away from buildings but were uselessly under water.

Surprisingly, there were people on the street looking as if they were out for a curiosity walk. Others seemed more concerned, striving toward higher ground or what they assumed would be a strong building. The water was too deep for the street cars to run.

A horse-drawn wagon passed, weighed down with people. A stranger in the wagon called out, telling those on the road to seek shelter in one of the brick buildings downtown.

The howling wind pushed against Paul and Hy as they worked their way closer to Emma's bordello. They passed shops and saloons still conducting business.

Hy grinned and rolled his eyes, shouting to Paul, "Want to stop for a beer?"

Paul shook his head, wondering how people could be so crazy.

***

Emma ~ September 8, 1900

Emma wasn't worried after all the girls had gone to find what they thought would be a safer place than the bordello. Over the past years, streets had flooded on many occasions during tropical squalls. She was used to the storms and expected them considering the island was a sandbar and less than a dozen feet above sea level.

But when the water had risen to just below the kitchen tabletop, she questioned her decision. Putting George on the table, she climbed up after him before he crawled away. She stood, bringing him into her arms. Surely the water had reached its height and would soon start receding.

Someone pounded on the back kitchen door, jiggling the handle, but the water kept it from opening. She thought she heard her name. The pounding stopped, then Paul's and Hy's faces stared at her through the large kitchen window. They looked as if they'd just walked out of the ocean.

Emma couldn't believe her eyes. She frowned. "What is y'all doing here?" she called over the howl of the wind.

George startled from her screeching voice and wailed unhappily.

The brothers didn't reply and obviously couldn't hear her. Paul wedged his fingers into the bottom of the window and lifted it up, then proceeded to climb in with Hy close behind. Water blew in with him, puddling on the sideboard.

"What—?"

"We come to see if you needed help." Paul's blond hair was plastered flat to his head. His eyes didn't seem to know where to settle until he looked at her face. His confusion turned to what might be fear.

She'd rarely seen him afraid. Maybe not since Tillie had hit Papa with a chair, and Paul had come to help. He had that same look in his eyes now.

"I'm fine." She shook her head at his attempted *rescue*. "These storms happen all the time. The water will go down soon." She was sure of it.

Shouting above the shrieking wind and rattling shutters, Paul explained what they'd seen and argued with her, repeating information to emphasize the danger. "Leave with us. People is heading downtown to the stronger buildings."

"I'm not going anywhere." Although determined to stay put, she was touched that her brothers' concern brought them to help her. "Since when did I ever need anyone to take care of me?"

Paul slammed his fist on the table, then pulled George from her arms, handing the baby to Hy.

George howled his displeasure.

Paul grabbed Emma around her waist and tossed her over his shoulder.

She pounded his back and kicked her legs. "Put me down!"

He pushed her over the sideboard toward the open window. She climbed out, resigned to do his ridiculous bidding. When she jumped to the ground, water nearly came to her chest. She licked her lips and realized it was salty. Ocean water.

Debris flew about, and something splashed into water nearby. The storm had grown much worse than she'd realized. She hated that Paul might be right, that she did need saving. Well, she'd at least show him she was brave.

Hy handed a screaming and red-faced George out the window and climbed out, with Paul behind him.

"Let's head for the five-story Tremont Hotel." Paul pointed southeast. "It's got to be one of the tallest buildings in town."

A large chunk of slate landed between them, hitting the water with a splash.

Emma jumped back, trying to shield little George.

More shingles landed close by. After a city-wide fire years ago, the roofs had been covered in slate. Those tiles were now being shot like missiles along with tin shingles, broken glass, and other debris.

They began to walk. Emma's heavy, wet skirt wrapped around her legs, making it hard to push through the water. She handed George to Hy and pulled off her skirt, swimming to get out of it, leaving only a thin, cotton petticoat on.

Through the sounds of the storm, George's wails were not lost to Emma. He kept reaching out to her. She needed to get him to a safe place. She hollered to Hy, "Cover Georgy's head with your hand."

Hy acknowledged her with a nod, placing his large hand on George, pulling his head tight to his chest.

The wind shrieked past them. Paul batted at an uprooted shrub that had barreled his way. They ducked away from tree limbs, bricks, fence posts, and other wreckage flying around them like weapons.

A stable collapsed. People screamed. A man passed holding his head. Blood seeped through his fingers.

Emma clung onto Paul, more scared than she cared to admit to herself much less her brothers.

"Let's move closer to the buildings," Paul called. "Fewer flying objects."

A piece of timber floated by with toads on it.

Wrapped tightly in Hy's arms, George continued crying as they trudged through water bogged with sand. They pushed toward downtown and soon became caught in a flow of people heading to the Tremont. Someone carried a suitcase and another a Tiffany lamp. Emma wondered if she should have gathered food before leaving.

With the water a little lower here, at the waist, it still swept quickly past them. At the hotel entrance, rescuers stood on the raised sidewalks, pulling people from the gushing waters and into the building.

Entering wet and exhausted, Emma followed her brothers out of the shallow water flowing into the lobby from the street. They maneuvered past hundreds of drenched people crowded on stairwells and in corridors. The man in front of them stopped every once in a while, asking if anyone had seen his family, describing them to others.

Blacks and whites huddled together, race having no boundaries, a sight Emma had never seen.

Paul found an open area in a second-floor hallway, and they settled in to wait out the storm.

Looking at her wet petticoat, she could clearly see her legs trembling from exhaustion. A few other women were in a state of undress. There was nothing to be done about it.

George fussed forlornly, worn out from his bawling. She removed his wet nappy but had no dry one to replace it. She took off his gown and rung it as dry as possible, then put it back on, tucking the extra length between his legs. She nursed him. Strangers turned their faces away. She didn't care what they thought. Never had.

George suckled himself to sleep.

The winds howled, and debris banged against the walls. For the most part, Emma stayed calm sitting between her large brothers, thinking the storm would soon pass.

When George awoke, he crawled a few yards away and then back again, obviously not knowing what to make of all the people who wouldn't coo or grin at him like he was used to.

Hundreds in the hallways, the hotel refugees complained that they wouldn't go into the outer rooms for fear that flying glass and plaster could injure them. Stories of damage were being told and passed down. Emma was shocked at hearing of houses floating off their foundations and children missing.

The hotel lost electricity and further darkened sometime in the late afternoon.

Someone lit a lamp down the hall, giving the scene a more ominous appearance with shadows on the walls and faint light glistening on wet, anxious faces. The wet plaster smelled ammonia like—almost like urine.

When Emma heard projectiles striking the eastern walls, it was obvious the winds had made a change from north to east. The windstorm gained velocity. She rocked George, whispering as soothingly as she could muster, "We'll be fine. We'll be fine."

Newly arriving refugees told stories of a tornado traveling up 23rd Street. "The water rose four feet in a matter of minutes," a thin young woman said. "Bodies are floating in the streets." She covered her eyes as if to block out the images. She stumbled past, a sob escaping.

Surely, she'd exaggerated. A tornado in the middle of a squall? Dead people?

The winds again shifted direction, this time from east to south. Circling winds. This wasn't a squall but a hurricane! Emma's heart thumped hard in her chest. Would they live?

A sudden scream from upstairs made her jump.

Many ran down the stairs as a man called out, "The hotel has lost its roof!" More people crowded into the hallway. Objects hit the building like rockets.

George cried out in alarm, crawling back to the safety of Emma's arms.

Emma pulled him closer and buried her face between Paul's arm and the wall. She hated her weakness.

Paul patted her leg.

She trembled, expecting the hotel would give way at any moment, and that each breath would be her last. She held tightly to George, who miraculously quieted. Paul took them both in his arms, and Hy leaned against her. Poor Hy! He'd only just turned fourteen and was probably as scared as she. Emma reached back to touch him, letting him know she understood.

Winds moaned, and the walls of the hotel sounded on the verge of collapse.

She squeezed her eyes shut. The night would never end.

Not knowing if God existed, she called out to Him in silent prayer. *Don't let it end this way. If I must die, save my baby. Thank you, God, that Eva is far from here. Take care of her. Don't let her turn out like me.*

There must have been over a thousand people in the hotel, hundreds in the corridor with Emma. More arrived every few minutes. Some bleeding and barely walking, others being carried. So many people, wet and dank, made her claustrophobic. She wanted to push her way out but had nowhere to go.

Many of them knelt in vocal prayer. Blacks sang hymns, and some whites joined in. Emma didn't know the words.

Mercifully, around 10 p.m., the winds slowed. Emma finally slept in Paul's arms, not wanting to know the horrors she would awaken to.

In the morning, stepping around sleeping and blurry-eyed people as she and her brothers wound their way downstairs, she realized most of the people had been injured in one way or another, many with dried blood on their faces and hair. Thank God she could walk, and her brothers and George had all fared well.

She stepped out of the hotel and froze.

Hy bumped against her back.

Paul made a noise in his throat as if he'd be sick.

In front of her was a sight no better than hell. Her stomach roiled.

Hundreds of human and animal bodies were strewn in every direction, many bloated and still floating where water remained trapped and hadn't left with the tide. Most of the dead had been stripped of clothing by the fierce winds and water currents.

Bile came to Emma's throat. She quickly swallowed it down. Clutching her baby, she whispered, "Oh, Georgy, can this be so?"

She looked to where groups of people stood at street corners, frightened and in shock, calling out names. Many walked up and down the stinking silt-covered streets, crying and wailing, their muddy bare feet bleeding from stepping on glass and other debris. Still others had blank expressions. Corpses lay in every direction. A half-naked girl of perhaps five, crumpled where she stood, hoarsely screaming for her mother. A woman picked her way around debris to get to the girl.

Horses, cattle, dogs, and other animals strayed throughout the streets. Anxious for human comfort or food, they ran up to anyone. A cow with enlarged udders bawled to be milked, its eyes shifting unnaturally.

Paul turned to Emma, the strain in his expression immeasurable. "You stay here with Georgy. We'll go see if your place is still standing and if we have a place to go . . . maybe food to eat."

Emma agreed, and they left. She instantly felt their absence. Could she do this alone? So many things she'd had to do on her own. But this? She turned from the scene and rushed back up the stairs, angry people complaining as she pushed her way past.

In the distance, bells rang out from the Ursuline Convent calling people to worship. Emma stopped. For the first time, she was tempted to follow the sound. But she was not worthy to enter a church, even though she had spent the night in fervent prayer. She slowly continued her climb up the stairs.

As the day warmed, the smell of wet plaster walls, sewage, and who knew what else became horrific. Emma ripped off the bottom of her petticoat and tied the fabric around her face, covering her nose. She tried to do the same for George, but he wouldn't let her, swiping at her hands. She nursed him again.

When he had his fill, she again moved farther up the stairs, as far away from the stench as possible. She wanted nothing more than to get off the island that once represented freedom but had become her prison.

***

Ora

The oral family story does not include when the Butterfrases returned to Houston. It would not have been the day after the storm, or even the second day. Through historical accounts, it is known that during the night of the storm, a ship had been pulled from its anchor and blown into the bay, destroying all three wooden railway trestles joining Galveston to the mainland. The wagon bridge had also been destroyed by the storm. No telegraph or phone lines remained. Galveston was cut off from the world.

Black men were forced at bayonet point to assist in loading the dead onto wagons, piling them like cord wood. The men were given goblets of whiskey throughout the day to help them withstand the gruesome task of finding and, in many cases, unburying the dead from the wreckage. On Monday, 700 bodies were taken eighteen miles out to sea and dumped, but many drifted back onto the beaches by the next day. Consequently, city officials decided on Tuesday to burn the dead on pyres. Plenty of loose lumber was collected to help with the business. Piles of it had accumulated from the destroyed homes, which had been swept into the water currents during the storm, and then amassed into large, sometimes twenty-feet-high piles of wreckage.

The black workforce wasn't enough to complete the appalling task of gathering the dead, and soon every able-bodied man was expected to assist in the work of digging out and collecting bodies. I can only assume Paul and Hy helped with the ghastly task. Large fires burned throughout the city, day and night. The air was too foul to allow time for identifying bodies before cremating them. An estimated 6,000 people died during the storm—an overwhelming number of those were children.

There was little to eat if you were one of the unlucky ones left homeless. At the Tremont Hotel, free bread and coffee were distributed throughout the first couple days. A pint of mineral water could be bought for twenty-five cents.

In the ninety-degree days that followed the storm, the stench of dead bodies and sewage drove people to find any way possible off the island. They camped at the wharves trying to find passage, even if it was to New Orleans or farther destinations. By the third day, ferries sailed people across the two-and-a-half mile-wide bay toward Houston. Hundreds of bodies still floated in the water, bumping into the boats as they glided north. A large ship in the distance was stranded on the grasslands.

Once across, the Butterfrases would have walked through waist-high water strewn with debris and the swollen bodies of dead animals and people. I picture George strapped to Emma, and Paul and Hy on either side of her, a hand on each of her arms. Once on the firm ground of the prairie, they walked seven miles to the closest working train that took them into Houston.

It was a story Paul told even into his old age—a nightmare to never be forgotten.

CHAPTER TEN

Ora

Galveston started rebuilding immediately, but Emma didn't go back. There wouldn't have been many customers because of the destruction and people vacating the island. I have no record to tell me if she missed prostituting her body and the money she received for it, or if she was thrilled to be away from that lifestyle. Coming so close to death, perhaps she made deals with God to change her behavior? I am not comfortable with guessing at the answer. This can be the disappointment of family history research. I am left with a skeleton of the facts.

Emma now lived with her family on Main Street in downtown Houston. I can't imagine she liked the situation. The house was crowded with seven adults and two babies. Paul and his wife were the landlords, not Peter and Mary, who no longer earned a steady paycheck, but lived off their son's mercy. Money was tight and Emma needed to pull her weight. I don't know what she did for employment, but it was at this time that she met someone to love.

***

Emma ~ Spring 1901

The slow organ music of "On the Banks of the Wabash, Far Away," flowed out the open doors of the auditorium. Emma entered to a crush of people lining the walls, with hundreds more crowded onto the dance floor. Strings of lights draped overhead, meeting in the center of the room, attached to an enormous chandelier.

It took Emma ten minutes to find Jack. Seeing a woman held closely to his body startled her. Jealousy tightened her chest. She didn't want any man's life mixed up with hers, but here she was falling for him. She tried to brush it off.

She moved back behind the crowd, closely watching Jack dance with the woman near to his age of forty. He was clean shaven, as usual. She liked that. His once reddish-blond hair had thinned and darkened to a dirty-blond instead of gray, and an indented crease was in his hair where his hat often sat. Well dressed, but not elegant, he wore his suitcoat unbuttoned, with a plaid double-breasted vest underneath. His pants were crisply creased down the front. He was a good dancer, one of the best on the floor. It was obvious in his step that he loved the movement of dance. She loved it too but wasn't as good a dancer as he.

When the music ended, she stepped out of the crowd, hoping Jack would see her.

He did, walking quickly her way, grinning his reticent smile. "Why so late tonight?" he asked, "I've been waitin' for ya."

"I needed Eva to come home to watch the baby."

They moved away. Onstage a pianist took his seat and started playing "Louisiana Rag." Jack hesitated, looking back at the dancefloor. Emma knew he wanted to dance the lively two-step, but she hoped to visit with him first. They had hours yet to dance.

Jack politely took her arm and moved them through the crowd. He always treated her like a lady, even though she had told him of her past.

Finding a vacant table was impossible. They went outside on the veranda and found two empty chairs, which they placed in a shadowed corner. A waiter came and they ordered drinks. Jack handed her a cigarette then placed one in his own mouth. He lit hers and then his. Exhaled smoke hovered around them in the humid air.

"Thank you for getting Hy the brick mason apprenticeship. He's much happier not being under his brother's rule at work." Emma took another drag.

"I'm happy for the kid. The foreman says he's a great worker." Spoken more quietly, he added, "To be honest, I did it for you."

Emma wasn't used to having someone look out for her, but Jack kept doing her favors. She wondered if she could get used to it. She stared into Jack's blue eyes.

He looked shyly away. He had a small nose and a few light freckles. He appeared German, like her father. His fingers strummed on his leg to the music. He was often restless. He suddenly turned. "I picked up a new job at McLaughlin and Company for a singular reason."

Surprise widened her eyes. He liked his job hauling bricks.

Before she responded, he went on, "I'm basically doing the same thing I've done for years—delivering bricks, cement, and the like, but this job keeps me in town." He stared at her as if waiting for her approval. "Would you want me around more? Maybe even consider marriage?" His pale skin blushed with the question.

He changed his job for her? Was it possible a normal life with a husband was in her future? "That's kind of you, Jack. Sure, I want you around more. But I need to think on the marriage idea."

Jack looked away and took a long pull on his cigarette. "I know I'm no big shot, like ones you've known."

Was he referring to past customers? "I don't desire a big shot." The words sounded false to her ears. It was the money the bigshots usually had that she desired. Jack worked a steady job and might make life comfortable for her, but he was right, he'd never be a big shot.

Jack and she had good times together. He was a friend, more than a lover. To think of him as a husband appealed to her, if he didn't try to control her. He had been passive with her so far. Maybe it could work? "Georgy goes where I go."

"I have no dispute with that. I had kids once, but their mother took 'em away."

She sat up straighter and her mouth fell open. "Why haven't you mentioned this before?"

"No need, I guess."

That was no answer. She had told him her past. Why hadn't he told her his? Was he hiding something?

Jack kept looking toward the open door to the auditorium. She was sure he wanted to dance. His restlessness showed in his hands and feet, which kept beat to the music. He chewed on his lip and smoked his cigarette like it was his last.

Their drinks arrived.

"How many children do you have and where is they now?" It was hard to mask the hurt and anger in her voice.

He dragged his eyes back to hers. "My son, Joe, he's sixteen and living on his own. The two girls live with their ma's sister."

"Do you ever see them?"

"Not in a long while. I'm a rebellious maverick, like you. It's something I like 'bout you." Jack finished his drink. "Hey, let's dance."

CHAPTER ELEVEN

Ora

Although I never knew Andrew Jackson "Jack" Hydrick in person, I've always called him my great-grandfather. But it turns out, he's not. All I truly carry from him is the Hydrick name.

When Emma was eighteen, she married Jack Hydrick on July 2, 1901. They were married by a minister of the First German Methodist Church in Houston. Jack was thirty-nine, twenty-one-years Emma's senior. His marriage to Emma was not his first.

I started my search for Jack when I took a genealogy class in college. I received no help with the investigation from my grandfather George, who was as tight-lipped about who he called his father as he was about background information on his mother. Jack often worked away from home, so I assumed George wasn't keeping secrets, he probably didn't know any facts about Jack.

I spent twenty years researching the Hydrick family, trying to connect to a man I never knew but wanted to know. I traveled to South Carolina, Georgia, Alabama, and Pennsylvania in search of my assumed progenitors. I wrote to those I thought might be connected to the Hydrick family asking if they knew of a Jack Hydrick. I went to a Hydrick family reunion in Alabama, trying to find my place amongst strangers.

I created pedigree charts, family group sheets, and extensive notes on every Hydrick in America. I know the earliest Hydrick settlers (1732) better than I knew my own great-grandfather. I was never successful in joining him to them. Too many secrets buried the connecting links. It would take yDNA tests (path of male ancestors from my father, brother and uncle) many years later to understand who I really was.

I can trace Jack no further back than to when he was eighteen, in the 1880 Williamson County, Texas, United States Federal Census. He was documented as an orphan, born in Alabama, and his parents were born in Mississippi. I found two seven-year-old Andrew Hydrick's (no Jacks or Jacksons) in the 1870 Alabama Census, but none in Mississippi. I've researched those two families with whom the Andrews were living, but with no definitive results of any of them being Jack's family.

Jack was born in 1862 into a time when fathers were dying in the Civil War, leaving children abandoned, and courthouses holding records of marriages and births were burned by the Union Army. I traveled to Alabama to check what orphans' books still remained in county courthouses, but yielded no results. I also researched all Hydricks in Mississippi, with no conclusive connections to Jack.

In the 1880 census, Jack was enumerated with a divorced, thirty-year-old woman named Emily Ford and her three-year-old son, Daniel. Jack is recorded as the head of the household, and his occupation is listed as a "farm hand." Whether or not he worked on Emily's farm or someone else's, I'm uncertain. I suspect Emily to be the head of the household, and Jack her farm hand. Perhaps the census enumerator had antiquated views about women being heads of households and assumed the head to be a young man? The situation of an eighteen-year-old male living with a divorced thirty-year-old female may be suspect and a clue to Jack's nature. Emily being divorced and admitting to it to the census taker is surprising in itself. Jack and Emily were going against social convention of the time—outliers in an unusual relationship.

Five years later in Austin, Jack married seventeen-year-old Belle Flint—four months *after* Belle had given birth to his son, Joseph Henry Hydrick, in nearby Round Rock. On his marriage record, it is written in longhand by the county clerk: "I Andrew Hydrick do solemnly swear that the parents of Miss Belle Flint herein have given their consent for my marriage with her sworn to and subscribed before me Sept 19 1885," and is signed with an X (his mark). Which leads me to believe Jack was illiterate.

It is thought Belle and Jack had a daughter about 1887 and then a second daughter, Annie Hydrick in 1890 or 1891. I cannot find a divorce record for Jack and Belle, but the lack of a divorce record isn't surprising for early Texas. I assume Jack and Belle divorced because on April 6, 1895, John Teague and Bell [sic] Hydrick were married in Travis County, Texas.

Jack and Belle's daughter, Annie can be found living with her aunt and uncle on her mother's side in 1900. She records that she doesn't know where her father was born. Because of that small piece of information missing from her memory, I've often wondered what part Jack played in Annie's life. Was he an absent father after the divorce or maybe even before? When Belle remarried, Annie would have been no more than five. Why she is living with her aunt and uncle five years later, and not with Belle and her new husband, I'm uncertain.

Jack worked for Butlers Brickyard. In October 1894, *The Galveston Daily News* ran an article announcing, "The first load of brick for the super structure of the Binz Building was hauled this morning by Andrew Hydrick." The Binz Building was Houston's first "skyscraper," standing six stories high.

When he wasn't hauling bricks, Jack had an interest in dancing. Right before Christmas 1896, two newspaper articles announced an invitation to attend a "delightful masquerade ball" given by Professor Geisecke's pupils at the Union Men's Hall on Main Street in Houston. Jack is among the few committee members for the ball.

In the *1899 Houston City Directory*, Jack's employment is recorded as a teamster, which in those days meant he drove a wagon hauling bricks and other materials related to brickmaking. He boarded at 3317 Washington Avenue, close to downtown Houston, and three miles northwest from where Emma lived. Butler Brick Company's main location was in Bastrop County, Texas, near Elgin, within a few miles of the Williamson County border and over one hundred and fifty miles from Houston. They had opened another facility because of Houston's surge in growth in the 1890s. I suspect this is what brought Jack to Houston from the Butler area of Bastrop County.

My grandfather, George, claimed Jack was his father, yet Jack didn't marry Emma until a year and a half after George's birth.

And as I mentioned earlier, George's yDNA is clearly from an Osborne family line.

Between George's birth and his parents' marriage, Jack was married by the Justice of the Peace to Florence D. Patillo in Houston on June 14, 1900. I can find no divorce record for Florence and Jack, but Florence was alive in 1901 when Jack married Emma a year later. Was Jack a bigamist, or is it a case of another missing divorce record? The 1910 Census records Florence as being married five years—it should be ten years if it was to Jack—she's enumerated with her maiden name of Patillo and living with her mother. I would assume she married someone else in 1905. She is recorded as having no children.

The *1900 Houston City Directory* records Jack as a teamster employed by H.P. McLaughlin, a seller of brick, cement, lime, and sand. He boarded at 818 Lakin Street, a block from his last known Washington Avenue address. In this same year, Jack cannot be found in the United States Federal Census in Houston or anywhere else in America. As already mentioned, Emma is in the census enumerated with her parents and siblings, living three miles from Jack's Lakin Street address. It would be a year before Jack and Emma married on July 2, 1901. On their marriage license, Jack had not signed with an X as on his and Belle's certificate, but instead misspelled and signed his name in a childlike hand: "A Hydrik."

When they married, Emma was pregnant with her second child.

CHAPTER TWELVE

Ora

Ernest Albert Hydrick was born to Jack and Emma on March 20, 1902. The Hydricks rented rooms at a house in the 2600 block of Center Street in Houston, a block from the Washington Avenue entrance of Glenwood Cemetery and Gardens. Unbeknownst to Emma, in seventy-three years' time, Howard Hughes would be buried at Glenwood Cemetery, a stone's throw distance from her home.

Jack and Emma's rooms probably shared a hallway and phone with other tenants. Jack was a reliable employee bringing home a consistent paycheck but was away from home more than he was there. He had gone back to work for Butler Brickyard, hauling brick supplies by mule-pulled wagons 170 miles between Butler Switch and Houston.

Emma stayed home with her two little boys.

***

Emma ~ November 8, 1903

On Sunday afternoon, Jack moved restlessly between the two rooms of their apartment. "I'm going to the dancehall whether you come or not," he called to Emma from the bedroom. "Why can't Eva watch the boys?"

Emma came in carrying a pitcher of warm water and a towel draped over her arm. Ernest toddled behind her, crying out his frustration that he wanted to be held.

Jack took the towel and placed it on the washstand.

Emma poured the water into a basin. "I told you a couple weeks ago," she talked loudly over Ernest's fussing, "she and Hy moved out on their own to get away from Papa, who's even more belligerent than usual. They need to pay rent now and she's working long hours."

"Blazes! She's a few weeks past thirteen and living with her sixteen-year-old brother? Is she gonna take after you and work the streets?"

Emma ignored the jab. Pushing the crumpled counterpane to the side, she sat at the end of the unmade bed. Ernest followed, grasping her skirts, laying his head on her lap. She rubbed his back, and his fussing quieted a bit.

George played in a corner with a small metal toy horse attached to a firemen's wagon that his Uncle Paul had given him. Paul, now a ladderman for the fire station, was a hero in George's eyes. George softly made noises mimicking his horse clomping and winnowing as he pushed the wagon and horse across the wooden floor.

Jack slipped his suspenders from his shoulders and took off his shirt, throwing it on the floor in a pile of dirty laundry he'd dropped when he arrived home Friday night. He stood in trousers and an undershirt, briskly rubbing a soap bar in the basin water, creating lather, then rubbed the suds in each arm pit while humming the chorus of "Bill Bailey" and tapping his foot to the tune.

Although she was about two months pregnant, Emma hadn't yet told Jack. It was another reason she didn't want to go dancing. She was exhausted most of the time. She wondered if she told him now of the pregnancy if he'd feel more obliged to stay home with her. If she told him and he still left, it would cause a hurt she wasn't willing to feel, so she decided to leave the news for another time.

Jack pulled a leather strop out from where it hung by one end attached to the wall and started sharpening his straight edge razor. Although most men went to a barber for a shave, Jack preferred to shave at home in peace and not be bothered by a talkative barber, as he said they all were.

Emma pulled a tin of tobacco and white rolling papers from her apron pocket and began making a cigarette. She carefully rolled-up the crushed leaves, licked the edge of the paper to keep it lying flat, then put it in her mouth and lit the end. The drag calmed her and she closed her eyes.

Ernest fussed again.

"Why's that kid always crying?" Jack complained.

"He's cutting a molar."

"I don't miss that racket while I'm gone." Jack hummed louder while he lathered a shaving brush in a porcelain cup of soap, then spread the soap on his face. He had grown a mustache that year and worked the brush around it. Well lathered, he scraped the razor down his cheek.

His comment rankled Emma. She clenched her teeth. "Who do you think gets to hear *that racket* while you're gone all week? And now you're gonna leave on a Sunday besides?" She was asking for a fight, but her week had been especially hard with morning sickness and hardly stepping out of the house. She spent too much time remembering what it felt like to be independent, with no one to be responsible for. She wanted to wear beautiful gowns and have men want her again.

Jack stopped humming and stared into the mirror at her reflection behind him. "Well, I sure as hell ain't gonna be chained to the house with a nag."

Emma stood and took Ernest in her arms. "Then go! And good riddance!" She walked into the main room and sat at the table, sitting Ernest roughly on her lap. She shook with anger and took another drag from her cigarette, which did nothing for her nerves this time. She refused to let Jack see her weak. She squared her shoulders and willed herself to stop shaking.

Ernest chewed on his fingers, trying to get his whole fist in his mouth. George came out of the bedroom, glanced at her sullenly and moved toward the settee, where he drove his little firemen's wagon across its cushion.

Noises from the bedroom told Emma Jack had opened his tin of pomade. She pictured him applying it to his hair and the ends of his mustache. She smelled the lemony-clove and floral aroma when he applied his eau de cologne. He was no longer humming.

Dressed in a suit with a derby hat on his head, Jack came out of the bedroom. He looked handsome. Jealousy and anger tightened Emma's throat. Did he have someone in mind he would be dancing with? Was he sleeping around? Using a whore?

She looked away from him. "Bring me home a bottle, would ya?"

"Like father, like daughter." He closed the door behind him. It was still light outside.

***

When the sun had gone behind the tree line, the electric streetlight at the corner radiated a soft yellow light through its glass chamber. From where Emma stood at her second-story window, gazing at the dark shadows of the lushly landscaped cemetery, she saw the park's ornately formal iron fencing and brick gate posts. A little further south, rolling hills with ravines winded their way toward an ox-bow shaped curve of Buffalo Bayou. It was a beautiful area, like no other in Houston.

There had been a Yellow Fever scare that summer and people had stayed home. But now with the cooler weather and lack of mosquitos, they were out in droves. On Sunday afternoons, streetcars brought people from all over the city, who strolled through the park's grounds where they picnicked near the three-tiered fountain or the new conservatory. It was late, and streetcars had arrived once again to pick up the picnickers. Emma wished she'd felt well enough to have taken the kids for a walk earlier, while it was still light. Maybe then she would have avoided the fight with Jack.

If she wasn't dependent on Jack's money, she wouldn't be feeling so vulnerable. She was upset at herself for being caught-up in the situation. It reminded her that she couldn't count on anyone. Yet, if she were honest with herself, her ultimate desire had always been to be loved and cared for, something she'd never had in her life and still couldn't obtain. She suspected that what Jack felt for her wasn't love. Was he using her like her customers had? She was a fool to have allowed herself to become dependent. But how could she work now with the two boys and another on the way?

Emma considered her sister, Tillie, who died in July, perhaps from Yellow Fever, but Mama wouldn't say. Tillie was the last of Emma's three older sisters to die. She wondered what it would be like to die. It sounded so much easier than raising three children. When she realized where she had let her thoughts take her, she reprimanded herself. "I can do this," she said under her breath.

She rubbed her hand on her stomach where there was no bump yet. Perhaps this one would be a girl? She'd like that.

Startled by a knock on the door, Emma turned. Ernest stirred on the rug where he'd fallen asleep. George stopped his play to watch his mother answer.

Eva stood in the hall, pale and red-eyed. She stepped in.

Emma shut the door. "What is it?"

"Papa's dead." Eva stared into Emma's eyes. "I don't know why I'm crying. I should be happy, right?" Tears trailed her cheeks.

Emma didn't know what to say. The hollowness inside confounded her thoughts.

"I mean," Eva went on, "he was never like a father to me. Balls, Paul was more a father than Papa ever were."

Eva's statement helped Emma's mind start thinking again. "Yes, we're both lucky to have Paul. How's Mama?"

"Oh, I don't know…about like she was when Tillie died. Sometimes I think she's dead inside herself. If I were her, I'd feel relief—no longer having to clean up vomit or wet trousers and linens. Ya know, for the last year she's been helping him with breathing treatments 'cause his lungs couldn't keep up."

Emma suddenly needed to sit down and moved toward the settee.

Eva wiped her eyes and went to George, who sat surrounded by jacks. "Hi there, Georgy." She knelt and patted his head and then bounced his small rubber ball and quickly grabbed a jack and the ball. She gave a sad, false laugh and handed them to him.

"Aunty Eva?" George intently focused on her with a question in his eyes. "Crying?"

"Aunty Eva will be better in a minute." She came to sit by Emma. "What do you s'pose will happen with Mama? I can't imagine Paul and Mary will let her live there now that there's no need for someone to care for Papa. Mary and Mama will kill each other."

"I can't reckon. Mary's been a saint to put up with Mama and her Southern belle dramatics."

"Well, she can't come live with Hy and me. There's no room."

"No room here, either. Jack wouldn't have it, anyway."

Emma's chest felt as if it would burst. She wished Jack would come home with that bottle. If she ever needed to get drunk, it was now.

Butterfras Photographs

people thought to be - L to R: Mary, Eva's
husband, Eva, Hy in background

Paul Butterfras   Eva Butterfras

CHAPTER THIRTEEN

Ora

The infant child of Mr and Mrs A.J. Hydrick died at 11 o'clock last night. The funeral will probably be held tomorrow morning. *The Houston Chronicle,* June 28, 1904.

The newspaper did not mention the gender of Emma's third child, nor how long he or she lived. I was surprised to find the obituary notice because I have found no marriage announcement for Jack and Emma, nor birth announcements for George and Ernest in newspapers. Who placed the announcement in the newspaper? Perhaps city officials or hospital staff? But I don't believe Emma went to a hospital for the birth of any of her children. Ernest reported he was born at home. My father once told me George was born on a kitchen table.

The state of Texas began a statewide registration of births and deaths in 1903, but it was as late as the 1930s before births were consistently recorded. Delayed birth indexes exist, but these were not officially recorded at the time of the event, and instead done on a voluntary basis to record that the birth took place earlier (no proof required). All three of Emma's children are not recorded in any Texas birth record, other than George, later in his life, recording his birth in the Delayed Texas Birth Index.

***

Emma ~ August 1904

The tropical storm blew rain sideways, sounding like thousands of tiny pebbles sprayed against the windowpane. Emma dreamed the house rocked and swayed in hurricane strength winds, coming off its foundation and floating like a boat. She was standing on the kitchen table again, with the water rising around her. Frightened this time, she prayed to God for deliverance.

"You drink too much." Jack yanked the bed linens off Emma and threw them on the floor.

Emma awoke to rain drumming at her window. Her head pulsed in pain. She opened her dry, swollen eyelids, which felt as if they were weighted down. The bedside lamp light sent a sharp pain through her eyes and into her head. She quickly closed them again. "Leave me alone."

"You need to get up. Your son has spilled his oatmeal and Ernest stinks to high heaven. I've got to head to Butler *now*. This storm's gonna slow me down at least a day. I've packed my own clothes and food, no thanks to you." He stepped away. "In fact…" he said louder and threateningly.

She opened her eyes in time to see him pick up her ivory hairbrush and slam it against the bureau's edge where it cut a dent in the wood. The handle stayed in his hand, but the broken top-half flew over his shoulder and landed on the floor with a crack. It might as well have hit Emma's head the noise hurt it so badly. She moaned.

Jack's usual fair complexion bloomed beet red. "I've had enough," he yelled. "You won't be seeing me darken your doorway again."

Emma sat up quickly, feeling as if she might vomit. She swayed. Her mouth was extremely dry, but her heart raced fast enough to get her talking. "What do you mean?"

"I mean…I've had it. You've turned into a drunkard since the baby died. Hell, people lose babes all the time." He threw the brush handle at the wall and she cringed, worried the neighbors would hear the thud. "We're better off, if you ask me."

How could he say that about his child? He had no natural human compassion. She shouldn't be surprised, people to him were nuisances.

"Your soul is black," she said with disgust. "It were your child—a human being. Do you have no heart?" Tears came to her eyes and instead of willing them away as she usually did in front of Jack, she let them fall. It was a release of grief she hadn't experienced since the baby's death. She threw her hands over her face and let the quaking sobs overtake her.

"Oh please, and you're suddenly the saint of all mothers? How were you going to care for three when you can't keep the other two dressed in clean clothes and fed square meals?" He paced the floor.

Jack was right about her mothering. Even before the death of the baby she was often depressed and lonely during the week while Jack was gone, and she didn't give enough attention to the boys. Lately, she experienced the same disinterest on the weekends when Jack was there.

"Well, what do you have to say?"

She wiped her wet cheeks. "I can do better."

Jack laughed in derision. "It's too late. I've made up my mind. I can hardly stand to look at you anymore."

Emma pushed her hair back. She imagined how horrible she must appear. "How am I to feed the boys? Where is we to live?"

"You know how to make money. Clean yourself up and sell your charms again."

"You'd leave your child?"

"I'll come visit him like I do my children in Pflugerville."

She didn't know he had had contact with his other children. She suspected he was lying. Was he really going to leave her and the boys? Anger and fear pushed its way past her guilt. "You bastard!" She threw her feet to the floor and stood. She was tall enough to be eye level with him. "Go then. We don't need you. You're right, I do know how to make money. More money than you ever brought to this hovel."

"You whore!" Jack's spittle flew in her face.

She wiped it off. "And what is you? The man who married a whore—a bastard. Stupid me. I believed you loved me." Emma choked on the word love. "I should know better than to trust a man. You might as well be my father. He never gave a damn for his children, either. But at least he didn't leave us. You're the lowest kind of man there is."

Jack walked past her and out the bedroom doorway. She followed him. He picked up his valise sitting near an overturned bowl of oatmeal and slammed the door as he left.

The kitchen faucet dripped to the sound of the rain. If she looked outside would there be dead, swollen bodies everywhere? The smell of corpses rotting in the sun came back to her as if she was on Galveston Island. Life had become a horror again.

George and Ernest clung to each other where they'd pushed themselves into a corner behind the settee. Both stared at her in fear.

CHAPTER FOURTEEN

Ora

We've learned much about the consequences of children of an alcoholic parent in the last fifty years. But I doubt Emma was aware her environment as a child would impact her personality and decision making as an adult. Many children of alcoholics don't learn how to handle stress well—not when their parent's coping skills included alcohol and denial. Emma was a victim of psychological and emotional suffering and left her parent's household as soon as she was able, as did her siblings.

The abuse and neglect may have been worse for Eva and Hy as the youngest. Their father was in the latter stages of alcoholism—characterized by a need for alcohol so great that the drinker can be in excruciating agony if he doesn't quench his thirst. Peter would have lost his appetite for food but found a stronger appetite for booze. His physical and mental strength would have also deteriorated due to damage to his vital organs, including liver disease, gastrointestinal disorders, ulcers, and heart failure.

Children of alcoholics constantly guess at what normal is. As they grow into adulthood, they can lose sight of how to structure a healthy life and develop relationships. They typically repress their feelings as if situations don't bother them. Often unsure of how to deal with hardships, they follow their parent's example and use alcohol as a quick relief from emotional turmoil. This is not considering genetic propensities.

Emma fell into this pattern. As much as she hated what drinking did to her father and her family, she didn't suffer losses well and used alcohol as an escape or buffer. To both Emma's salvation and demise, she was headstrong and rebellious. She probably gave the impression of strong self-esteem but living with an alcoholic parent inhibited her ability to appreciate her self-worth.

The last four Butterfras children were blessed with sympathetic and close relationships amongst each other, which probably helped their situation. Knowing they had someone for whom they could care, and someone who cared for them and would help if need be, may have been their saving grace. Emma being the person responsible for nurturing and caring for her younger siblings would've given her a feeling of being needed and wanted.

When Jack left, he did not divorce Emma. He simply never returned. He no longer appeared in Houston's city directory as a resident and may have moved permanently to Butler Switch, working in the brickyard there.

Emma once again found the strength to pick herself up and rented a home at 2218 Carr Street, east of downtown Houston. Eva, Hy, and her widowed mother moved in with her and the boys. I've attempted to obtain documentation showing who owned the home on Carr Street, but after multiple record searches and phone calls, I have been told by the Harris County Archives that the deed and tax records for 1904 no longer exist. That doesn't sit well with me, and I picture the record sitting in a damp, dark basement that no employee gets paid enough to search.

Emma's employment wasn't recorded in the city directory, although employment was normally recorded that year. I suspect she started prostituting again, this time in Houston, and without a madam. It would've been around this time that she probably met Howard Hughes Sr., who was known as a philanderer and someone who often visited prostitutes.

I will take Uncle Buddy's letter at face value: "Aunt Eva and her young Sister Emma of a Sat. nite used to go dancing at the finest ballroom in downtown Houston...One dance night she met a very hansom young dude she only introduced to Aunt Eva as Howard."

A popular "finest ballroom" in Houston was in the Rice Hotel. There were others. If Emma were truly dancing at the finest ballrooms, she would have been associating with some of

Houston's elite. Although Howard Sr. was not considered wealthy in 1904, he did come from a prominent family, as did his wife Allene, and they mixed with high society.

If Emma was impregnated by Howard Sr. and considering Howard Jr.'s birthdate to be September 24, 1905—more about this later—then his date of conception would have probably been between December 29, 1904 - January 06, 1905. Howard Sr. had married Allene Gano a short time before, on May 24, 1904, and then spent a few months in Europe honeymooning. Upon their return in September, they first settled in Beaumont and soon arrived in Houston, residing at the Rice Hotel.

Howard Sr. and Emma were in the right places at the right time.

CHAPTER FIFTEEN

Ora

Four years past the Civil War, in a time when the nation struggled to rise above its great losses, Howard Robard Hughes Sr. was born on September 9, 1869, in Lancaster, Missouri to Felix Turner and Jean "Jennie" Summerlin Hughes. His mother's ancestors had been from the south, giving Jennie strong sympathies for its plight, which caused considerable disagreements with Howard's Yankee father who had fought for the Union Army.

Lancaster was a small town in northcentral Missouri near the Iowa border and the county seat of Schuyler. History was happening around the Hughes' modest town. Not far from Lancaster, and in the same year as Howard Sr.'s birth, Jesse James became famous for robbing the Gallatin Missouri, Daviess County Savings Association and killing a cashier.

Howard Sr. was the second of seven children, four of whom lived to adulthood. Raised in modest luxury with a live-in French maid, his mother lavished her attentions on her children and gave them a classical education, while his father supported them with a successful law practice.

Before Howard Sr. turned eleven, his family moved to Keokuk, Iowa, on the Mississippi River, where his father not only practiced law, but became a mayor and judge. To Jennie's delight, Keokuk offered better schools and tutors for her precocious children. She implanted in them artistic ideals and the drive to excel. Howard Sr.'s brother Rupert later wrote: "My mother instilled the ambitions, and my father found the funds."

Howard Sr. had a mechanical aptitude and enjoyed tinkering with engines and clocks. He grew to be tall, straight backed, and flamboyant with a flair for the dramatic. Not always the stalwart son, he was restless and repeatedly in trouble at home and school. He once staged a cockfight behind his house, often fought with his siblings, and earned an unsavory reputation for having an eye for the ladies.

In his teens, he attended an all-male boarding school in St. Charles, Missouri, which provided a traditional education with military training. Although his father would have liked him to follow in his footsteps, Howard Sr. soon learned he had no interest in law, although he did give it some effort. He attended the 1893 school year at Harvard College but dropped out in 1894. He enrolled at Iowa State University to study law but did not graduate. He took the Iowa bar examination and passed, then joined his father's law firm, but as with his other endeavors, he quit the practice.

Where Howard Sr.'s siblings found successful careers as adults, Howard floundered. His older sister, Greta, trained in opera in both New York and Paris. His brother, Rupert, became a popular novelist and later a famous movie director and screenwriter. And his youngest brother Felix Jr. studied music in Europe and became a teacher of light opera among other musical endeavors.

Howard Sr. wrote: "I soon found the law a too-exacting mistress for a man of my talent, and quit her between dark and dawn, and have never since been back. I decided to search for my fortune under the surface of the earth."

In 1895, Howard Sr. left his family in Keokuk and followed various mining activities in Colorado, Indian Territory, Oklahoma, and Missouri. After six years in mining camps, he hadn't found the success or riches he'd hoped for. "If I accomplished nothing more, I at least learned something of the art of drilling wells with cable tools."

In 1901, when he was mining for lead in Joplin, Missouri, he heard of an oil strike near Beaumont, Texas called Spindletop. Howard Sr. wasn't the only one drawn to the oil gusher. Thousands streamed into Texas to find their own liquid gold. Howard Sr. wrote: I heard the roar in Joplin and made for the seat of disturbance. Beaumont in those days was no place for a divinity student. The reek of oil was everywhere. It filled the air, it painted the houses, it choked the lungs and stained men's souls. Such another excitement will not be seen for a generation. It will take that length of time to get together an equal number of fools and "come-on's" at one spot. I turned greaser and sank into the thick of it. Rough neck, owner, disowner, promoter, capitalist and "mark"—with each I can claim kin, for I have stood in the steps of each."

Howard Sr. learned all he could of the new and booming oil industry. He applied what he knew of drilling ore to tap oil reservoirs, eventually entering the drilling and contracting business. His income was not steady and his fortunes fluctuated. His brother, Rupert, wrote that Howard Sr. survived because of his "uncanny gift for extracting money from my father for his wildest schemes."

At the age of thirty-four, having tried and failed at many things, he somehow attracted Allene Stone Gano to be his companion. Even though his future was uncertain, she married him at the Gano home in Dallas on May 24, 1904. Allene was well-educated, cultured, refined, and raised by Harvard Law School graduate and prominent Dallas judge William Beriah Gano. Howard Sr.'s own father being a judge may have had some bearing on his acceptance into the Gano family. He was classically educated, after all, and knew how to act like a gentleman no matter how dirty his fingernails may have gotten.

Allene's mother, Jeanette de Lafayette Grissim, also from the Dallas socialite circle and known for her interests and talents in music and literature, was much like Howard Sr.'s mother. Jeanette also raised four children, Allene being her oldest. Refined Allene was a graceful and soft-spoken young woman who had high cheek bones and dark brown hair and eyes. Some of her fears and phobias may have been evident from the start of her marriage, like swooning at the sight of a cat, but who scrutinizes personality flaws when in love? And how could Howard Sr. have known to what extent those flaws would reach?

CHAPTER SIXTEEN

Ora

Emma's and Howard Sr.'s faults were glaring. Emma was a prostitute with deeply buried insecurities and perhaps too rebellious, and Howard Sr. a philanderer who spent money unwisely. Yet they also had strengths. Emma was kind to her siblings and strong-willed enough to get through a hard life, and Howard Sr. was mechanically minded, a good salesman, and an entrepreneur.

I feel a different sense of responsibility in putting Howard Hughes Sr. into fictionalized scenes than I do with Emma and those close to her. I've enjoyed getting to better know my great-grandmother, Emma. She is my ancestor. Howard Hughes Sr. is not.

Hopefully what I get on the page is a resemblance of Emma and Howard's possible relationship. Howard was a classically educated man of ingenuity and vision. To better understand him, I have read about Texas oilmen at the turn-of-the-nineteenth century and what little I could find in his son's biographies, and also a biography about his brother, Rupert. In the following scenes, I have used this information and extrapolated upon it in an attempt to bring him to life.

Uncle Buddy's letter to Aunt Jeanette mentioned that Emma and her sister, Eva, used to go dancing at the finest ballroom in downtown Houston and that one night, Emma introduced Eva to a man named Howard.

***

Emma ~ Late Autumn 1904

The smell of perfume and tobacco met Emma in the foyer of the Rice Hotel. She entered the dining room looking for anyone she might know. Someone new stood near the wall with the other gentlemen. Smoking a cigar, he listened intently to them. She wouldn't call him handsome, but that never mattered anyway. It was his straight-backed stature, proud angular face, and breeding that interested her. He was a gentleman; she was sure of it. She'd watched men for seven years and gotten to know the meaning of their mannerisms and characteristics, and she knew the spurious from the genuine.

When he finally glanced her way, she didn't look down as she should've. Her move was brazen, but if she knew men like she thought she did, it was the sign he was waiting for.

He smiled subtly, his dark brown eyes warm and interested. Then he turned back to the gentlemen as if the interchange had never happened.

Emma's interest heightened. She moved into the ballroom to see if he'd follow. She was immediately asked to waltz by a young man with a thick German accent. The familiar guttural sound reminded her of Papa's roared demands.

It wasn't easy having Mama live with her now, but life had been more pleasant since Papa passed. It had been years since he'd held a place in Emma's heart, and she didn't feel his loss. What good would it do to dwell on her childhood? Everything about Papa had disappointed her, just like Jack.

The waltz went long, but she enjoyed the dance. A professional in her trade, she knew when to laugh at her partner's jokes, smile seductively, or when to apply a little more pressure where her hand rested on his shoulder, and whisper something flirtatious in his ear. She picked up on her client's eagerness and manipulated him to her own interests.

When the music ended, he took her by the elbow and led her off the dance floor.

As she turned to thank him, she found his face closer than she'd expected. She recognized the desire in his eyes.

He shifted uneasily. "Vood ya be interested in keeping company tonight?"

She might have said yes if she hadn't caught a glimpse of the gentleman she'd viewed earlier, pushing himself politely through the crowd in her direction. She wasn't sure he had her company in mind, but she wanted him to consider it. "I apologize, but not tonight," she said to her dance partner. Dismissing him with a faint smile and a nod, she turned fully toward the gentleman approaching her.

He didn't miss the invitation and moved closer. "I couldn't help but notice your lovely face in this sea of good society." His accent was Northern. As she suspected, he was of fine breeding. His frame was thin and he stood much taller than her, and she liked that.

His large, heavy-lidded brown eyes were expressive with open interest, but also held caution. Although his brown hair was thinning, it wasn't gray, and she guessed him to be in his mid-thirties. His lips were slim, but his teeth nice and grin friendly, with a strong and angular jaw. She imagined herself touching it.

"Would you care to dance?" he asked.

"That would be splendid." She tried to sound as sophisticated as possible.

He took her by the arm back onto the floor into a large crush of people dancing another waltz.

He danced with ease, back straight and chin high. "I'm somewhat new in Houston. Have you lived here long?"

"All my life. What brings y'all here?"

"Ha! Searching for my fortune with that oil that anoints the blessed."

"Do you own a well?"

"I've invested in some land out in Humble. Whether it will bring liquid gold is yet to be determined." He guided her gracefully along the dancefloor. "But let's talk about you. Do you come here often?"

How much she told at this juncture was always tricky. If he was looking for companionship, she wanted him to know he'd come to the right girl, but she also didn't want to come off as a trashy whore who was paid too little. "I come here for amusement . . . on occasion."

"Ah. And that is *exactly* what I'm looking for."

Emma shivered in excitement, thinking their relationship could be for his pleasure and her financial gain. If she played her cards right, he'd become a regular customer.

"What's your name?" he asked.

"Emma. What's yours?"

"Howard, but you can call me Bo."

"I look forward to our continued friendship, Bo."

***

Emma ~ Early December 1904

The ornately carved, wooden double-doors of the ballroom stood propped open and the spirited tune of "Give My Regards to Broadway" made Emma want to dance.

"Is you sure they'll let me in?" Eva asked. "This place looks rather grand." Her sky-blue eyes mirrored her nervousness.

"You're with me—they'll let you in. Besides, you're so tall and curvy no one will know you're fifteen." Emma arched an eyebrow and grinned at her sister. "Nor will they care."

Eva giggled like the young girl she was.

Emma gave her a look of disapproval and a little shake of the head as they moved toward the cloakroom.

A black woman, dressed in a stiffly starched navy uniform covered by a full white apron helped remove their winter coats. She handed them tickets, which Emma tucked into the small, beaded bag hanging from a chain at her waist.

For a mother of two small boys, Emma had a figure as slim as when *she* was fifteen. Now twenty-two, she'd already lived a lifetime of trouble, but that was about to change if she had her way. She smoothed her hands over her tightly fitted gown and pulled her shoulders back before entering the ballroom.

She knew how to work a room. As if there to entertain, she glided about, meeting acquaintances, laughing and joking, introducing Eva, and acting as if she had no cares.

Without appearing to observe the men too closely, Emma often glanced about the room, looking for her friend, Bo. If he wasn't there, her night would be most likely wasted. It had been weeks since they'd first met, but they'd spent many nights together. They became so close that Emma laid her heart open to him and released some of the pain recently forced upon her. She'd grown fond of him, even attracted to him.

Drawing in a breath, she tried to shake her feelings of desire. There could be no lasting relationship. There would not be any promises between them. Bo was safe because he was married.

Although she wanted nothing more than to settle down with a decent man, it was too late for that. No decent man would have her. Not that Bo was decent, but he was the closest she was going to get.

About one hundred people swayed and whirled on the dance floor. The band played "In the Good Old Summertime."

An awkward fellow with fidgety hands and dirty fingernails, wearing what was probably a borrowed suit, approached Eva. "Wanna dance?"

"I'd be delighted. My name's Eva, what's yours?"

Cringing, Emma realized she needed to teach Eva how to not be too friendly with men who had no money or manners.

Moments later, Emma danced with a rich man so intoxicated he fell against her, almost knocking them both to the floor. After his second fumble, she left him before the song finished and moved about the room.

Smoky air diffused the light from the newly installed electrified chandeliers. She wandered close to a table of men dressed in evening attire, smoking cigars. Eaves-dropping on their conversations while watching the room for Bo, she listened to them speak of cattle, cotton prices, oil strikes, and the usual.

"I was hoping I'd find you here," a familiar voice whispered near her ear.

Emma acted surprised and smiled sincerely. "Bo, how pleasant to see you."

"Come, I have a small table in the dining room."

Emma followed him, and so did many eyes. It was common knowledge he was a married man and a philanderer. She knew nothing of Mrs. Hughes and didn't care to know. It was easier that way.

In the dining room, Bo took her elbow and directed her to a back table softly lit by a single candle. He flipped the reserved sign face down and then sat, unbuttoning his suitcoat as he did so. "What have you had to eat today?" he asked as he waived over a waiter.

Emma simpered and looked into his kind eyes. This was a gentleman. "The same as usual," she said, not wanting to admit to having nothing more than bread and cheese.

The waiter arrived, and Bo ordered her lamb chops with chestnut dressing, creamed asparagus, a baked apple, and a glass of wine. He ordered himself a sherry.

"Who's watching the boys?" he asked Emma.

"I put 'em to bed, and Hy said he'd stay home tonight."

"Any sign of that husband of yours?"

She shook her head. "I don't expect to see him again."

"Dare I ask if he's sent you money?"

Emma dropped her eyes and noticed the diamond pin in Bo's ascot, then quickly focused on the fine linen tablecloth, not wanting him to notice what she'd observed. "No."

His concern for her welfare was evident. She didn't think he was acting when he studied her with worriment in his expressive eyes. "Have you paid the back rent with the money I gave you?"

"Yes."

"How are you set for next month?"

She wasn't sure if he was questioning her to make certain she wasn't receiving money from other customers, so she answered cautiously. "I have enough, but not for food."

She wouldn't give just anyone these answers. Her business usually remained just that—her business, but Bo was different. He wanted to care for her and he made her feel secure, unlike her deceased father or missing husband.

"Would you like to spend some time together tonight?" Bo asked.

"That would be splendid." She grinned seductively to give him something to look forward to.

"I'd like to establish a deal with you. I will take care of your financial needs if you'll not have any other customers than myself."

"That would suit me fine." She meant what she said and hoped Bo heard the earnestness in her voice.

He reached for her hand as Eva appeared at their table.

"Oh, there you is." She glanced at Bo and then back to Emma, beaming with youthful enjoyment. Her once perfectly swept up brown hair had released locks at her neck and temple.

"Bo, let me introduce you to my sister, Eva." She gestured to Eva. "Eva, this is Bo."

Bo stood and gave a little bow. "You are as alluring as your sister." His platinum watch chain glimmered in the table's single candlelight. He flagged over the waiter while asking Eva, "Would you care to join us for supper?"

Eva looked to Emma with a question in her eyes. Emma nodded once to assure her it would be all right. She wanted Eva to share in the good fortune of her new relationship with Bo. Emma had told Bo all about Eva and the others who lived with her. Even if Eva didn't know Bo would be her benefactor, she wanted Eva to like him, which she was sure she would.

***

Emma ~ January 1905

Over the months, the hotels they stayed in offered amenities Emma wasn't used to but very much enjoyed, like down-filled mattresses, soft linen sheets, and a private water closet with a claw foot tub. Bo spared no expense and ordered room service with hors-d'oeuvres, oysters on the shell, fish chowders, creamed vegetables, and sumptuous cuts of beef—foods she never had at home.

"Would ya like brandy?" Emma asked Bo when he arrived after working at the oil field.

He removed his coat and threw it on the bed. "That would bring comfort to a weary day." He sat in an overstuffed chair near a side table and a low-lit, fluted floor lamp.

Bo wasn't a normal customer. He often wanted to have long discussions before and after intercourse. Through their intimate chats, he'd became a friend. She felt no sense of love from him, only friendship, although she was terribly attracted to him as a result of the way he treated her as if she were someone special.

Emma offered the glass of golden liquor and sat on the chair arm next to him. She kissed his head and smelled the familiar musky pomade she'd grown to love. "What happened today that brought on weariness?"

Bo sighed. "There aren't enough men who understand the movement of the cable and what's going on thousands of feet underground."

"What does it take to learn the like?"

"An instinctive technician's mind like mine. I've been working with cables for ten years, but even before, I'd grasped the mechanics of such things."

"You're the smartest man I know."

"And don't you forget it." Bo laughed.

He had a rather large ego, but she didn't mind stroking it if it got him to talk more.

"Actually, I can't leave-off thinking about drilling," he said. "Even in my sleep, I dream of boreholes, bull wheels, and iron drill strings. For a man of my talent, my mind won't rest until I find a better way to drill through the earth." He threw back his head and drained his glass.

Emma noticed his other hand balled in a fist. Often at first, Bo had a hard time relaxing. She tried music once, but it got him more agitated. He told her it reminded him of his siblings, who were all musical. She learned he relaxed better if she asked him about his day and let him talk out his frustrations, for he was often impatient with an event, a person, or even himself. She listened, but rarely offered advice. She knew nothing of the oil business.

She did know how to ask leading questions. "And what'll y'all do if you can't find that help you need?" Emma refilled his glass, then placed the decanter at his side on the end table near a bowl of nuts and fruit.

Howard's agitation calmed some as he sipped at the brandy. "I'll do it myself, as usual." He looked at her. "Tell me about the boys. Are they feeling better?"

George and Ernest had both been terribly sick with influenza. So sick, she had taken them to a doctor, which she'd never done before. "The doc gave 'em belladonna, and it done nothin' for 'em. I paid him all I had left of the month's food cash. They're gettin' better on their own all the same."

"Well, don't worry about money. I'll give you more before you leave. As long as you stay with me, you'll never need to worry about money." He patted her leg. "And what have you eaten today?"

Emma liked that he was attentive to her needs. He gave her a sense of security she had always desired. "I had egg an' toast this morning. Nothing since."

"Dear Emma! Your body is a vessel to contain your soul, but also an engine you need to feed. An engine slows down when not fed coal, so too do you need sustenance." He picked up a red apple from the bowl at his side. "Have some sweet fruit, for it's God's candy."

He often spoke in metaphors, which gave poetry to his speech. She found herself mesmerized by his northern accent and wealth of knowledge. She bit the apple. It *was* sweet.

He watched her eat. "Are you keeping to our agreement and not entertaining any other gentlemen but myself? You know how possessive I am. I'll always pay you liberally if you're mine." He smiled at her.

"I'm seeing no one but you."

Bo pulled a small box out of his vest pocket and handed it to her. She set the half-eaten apple aside and pulled the end of a blue bow to release it.

He watched her with amusement.

Sapphire earrings set in a gold art nouveau swirling design nestled inside the box. Pearls dangling at the ends of each.

She gasped. "Oh, they're lovely!" She swallowed hard, feeling tears burn the backs of her eyes.

"I told you I'd take care of you." Laughing, he set down his empty glass and wrapped an arm around her waist, placing his hand on her thigh. He seemed to enjoy giving the gift as much as she did receiving it.

"These is the best gift I've ever gotten."

"*These are.* Your grammar is atrocious."

His words wounded her, crushing her joy under the heavy hand of embarrassment. She usually tried to use correct English when she was with the upper class. Her emotions had overruled her focus.

"I'm sorry, darling. Having conversations with you is delightful. I should have never corrected your cute southern charm." He stood and pulled her up to him, wrapping his arms around her and bringing her close. He kissed her neck and then her ear. "You smell intoxicating."

CHAPTER SEVENTEEN

Ora

The few documents I've found that displayed Howard Hughes Sr.'s dialogue show he spoke with a dramatic and romantic flare, often using metaphors. Growing up in a home filled with culture and artistic ideals no doubt attributed to his speech and way of thinking.

Emma, on the other hand, grew up in the South with little education. Although she died long before I was born, I've followed the patterns of language in my father's family. They commonly used the incorrect grammar of "is" in place of "are," and "was" instead of "were," and the wrong tense of "come" instead of "came." As high-class as Emma probably wanted to be, Ernest, George and some of his children spoke this way, so possibly she did too. To create the scenes in this book, I have mimicked the speech patterns of both Howard Sr. and Emma.

Besides being a forward thinker, Howard Sr. was known to be charming, well-dressed, egotistical, and a philanderer. Always moving among the rich, his finances fluctuated the years he lived in Texas, although he spent money as if he always had it. His brother, Rupert, commented, "One year he had fifty thousand in the bank. The next he owed the bank fifty thousand."

***

Emma ~ February 1905

The tiniest slivered moon hung in the night sky. Emma guessed it was the reason Bo allowed himself to walk hand-in-hand down the street with her. Earlier in the gambling club, they had stood apart but near enough to know what the other was doing. They'd left after midnight with the energy to walk for hours.

Bo directed her toward the bayou where it was as dark as the oil he worshipped.

He was hard of hearing, so she leaned near his ear as they walked. "As a kid, I used to come to these banks with my brother, Paul. It were an exciting time when the city were being built right before our eyes. The activity and sounds of manufacturing was lively. People was coming from all over the world. We'd sit and watch the ships come and go, and I'd dream of traveling to faraway lands—London, Rome, Paris even!" She laughed. "I'd imagine the beautiful gowns I'd wear and the dashing fellows I'd meet." She grinned at the childish memories.

"Were you lonely as a child?" Bo asked.

"I didn't have time. I had to do all the chores and take care of my younger brother and sister."

Emma's shoe heel caught in the train of her tailored satin skirt, and she stumbled.

Bo caught her and kept his hand at her waist as they continued walking.

She lived for his affection and their genuine connection that she hadn't had with any other man. In the past, she'd enjoyed controlling men with intimacy, but Bo was different. She'd stepped back and let him control her. She sensed it made him happy. "Seems most of my childhood were spent trying to stay away from my father."

"Man should be the protector of woman. But as you have seen in your short life, he has the power to destroy them also." Bo shook his head. "I grew in an impenetrable haven of refuge that kept violence away. Education was always first and foremost—before the handing out of love, even."

There was silence as they entered a trail near the bayou covered in crushed shells. Cats slinked in and out of darkness. Moored ships rocked against their docks. The breeze blew a bit chilly, but having Bo's body close to hers was all she wanted.

"There was always enough money to finance whatever endeavor we might desire." Bo's voice sounded indifferent, and Emma wondered why she didn't hear more joy. "With your father having eleven mouths to feed, I can't imagine there was anything left for lovely Emma's interests?"

Emma sputtered in derision. "I could've stayed in school, but it meant remaining under my parents' roof. I couldn't get away fast enough. I never left completely though. Hy and Eva needed me. I didn't want them to have my childhood."

"My darling, your heart is as wide as the cosmos. How lucky a man am I." He tightened his embrace around her waist. "Do I dare tell you I have an empty place in my heart that hungers for love?"

His words filled Emma's soul. She'd been trying to keep her strong feelings at bay. She knew too well where love got her. But she'd never met a man like Bo. "Do I come close to filling that place?"

Bo stopped walking and kissed her on the cheek. "Closer than anyone. It's like I've been shipwrecked and alone with no fresh water—clinging to life through the pleasures of wealth. Money helps soften the emptiness, but once it's in my hands, I find I still have a hole to fill in my heart. I'm always thirsty and can't get enough to drink. I make sure the pleasures of life distract me from my need."

"I can fill your need."

Bo chuckled. "You, darling Emma, are like a full glass of water, quenching my thirst. I can't get enough of you."

She wanted to ask him to stay with her. Leave his wife and make her his. But she worried that if she voiced such things he'd feel threatened. How could she expect a man like him to marry a woman like her?

"What are your thoughts on pleasure, Emma? Certainly, a courtesan has experience enough of a man's needs to be a master teacher."

"In some instances, fillin' the desires of men gives me a sense of power. Perhaps even boosts my confidence." Emma hesitated. Should she share her feelings when she'd never completely thought them through? She decided to be honest. She trusted Bo. "It has often fooled me into feelin' wanted." *And at first dirty and ashamed.*

"Why do you say fooled you?"

"It's a challenge to control someone with my body. At first, having that control made me feel like I had a say in my future.

But then I learned that I had no control over fate. I have two sons, and my husband has left me."

"We are but clay to the potter. Those who should have molded you into a strong woman instead created cracks in your shield that threatened to shatter if you didn't keep making repairs."

"I'm not exactly sure what y'all mean, but if it's empathy you give, it comforts me."

"In all honesty, I'm probably not the comforter. Have you heard the saying, 'A man will guard a woman against every other man but himself?' That's me, I fear. What you and I do would be considered an immoral act by some. You, dear Emma, bear the brunt of the immoral act. The man—me—goes about his day as all days."

"You is taking too much fault. I were ruined before you come to me. You have been nothing but joy in my life." Tired of his negative talk, she turned to face him, putting her arms around his neck. "Let's go to a hotel room." She wanted to have him to herself again, laughing and carefree.

"Oh, you beautiful and dangerous creature, I need some bee's wax to stop my ears. Your siren's song is irresistible and lures me to my doom. Somewhere on that ship—" he pointed to the dark silhouette of a ship docked nearby "—there must be a mast you can lash me to."

Emma laughed. "What is you talking about?"

"Something I learned from an old fellow named Homer, who I met in school."

***

Emma ~ Early March 1905

The French doors to the terrace of the hotel room hung open, and an afternoon breeze cooled the room. White gauzy curtains gently blew inward, and the balminess of the expensive perfume Bo had bought Emma lingered delicately in the air. That morning, he'd sent her a note requesting her presence "for lunch and pleasure." Now that both had been satisfied, she sat in her red organza robe near the doors, capturing the breeze, having a hard time listening to Bo's conversation. When would be the best time to tell him she was pregnant? Three months along, the small swell of her abdomen lay under her hand. Bo had not seemed to notice.

"That perfume smells lovely."

His comment barely registered. "Mmhm," she replied.

"You've been out of sorts today. Do you not know you're the excitement to my life . . . always something to look forward to?" Now fully dressed and about to leave, he placed a hand on her shoulder. "I fear I'm not the same for you, and I must endeavor to improve myself."

"There's something on my mind." She stared at the rippling curtains, her heartbeat sounding in her ears. Could she tell him now?

He stepped in front of her and grasped both hands, pulling her up. "You can share all life's woes with me." He kissed her on the tip of the nose. "You know that. Have I not helped you through thus far?"

It was true, his compassion was always evident, and he gave her all she asked for. He made her feel like he'd be there for her throughout life, but she dared to hope it was true. "Do ya care so much for me?" She wanted him to say he loved her like she loved him.

"When I'm not with you, all I do is think about you. Never has a woman driven me to such distraction." He pulled her into his arms.

The warmth of his solid chest gave her a sense of security and his tenderness broke her indecision. She pulled away and stared into his eyes. Drawing in a deep breath, she said in a rush, "I'm pregnant with your child."

Bo pushed her away.

Her feeble smile instantly fell, her lips trembled.

With his brows drawn together, she'd never seen so much anger on his face. "How do I know it's mine?" he said through clenched teeth.

Normally awed by his dynamic displays of power, fear and disappointment throbbed so great in her chest she had to push her hand there against the pressure. Backing away, she bumped into the chair. She walked around it, then faced him again. "How can you say such a thing?"

"How do I know it's mine?" He repeated louder.

The words punched her in the stomach. Without thinking she placed her hand where the child grew. Her world spun back to every other man she'd known. In the end, no one wanted her—or their own child. A deep pain grew where her heart was. "Of course, it's yours. I've been with no other man."

Bo rubbed his face with both hands. He turned his back and paced the floor near the foot of the bed.

Through the months, Bo had given her everything she needed or asked for, plus extravagant gifts. Had she misinterpreted his kindness as love? She'd feared to hope he'd publicly claim the baby as his, but she did believe he'd take care of them . . . somehow.

Bo stopped pacing and gawked at her. Annoyance and disbelief played across his features. "I cannot know this child is mine until I see its face. Then I will decide what to do."

"The child is yours."

"Forgive my disbelief, but you are far from innocent, Emma."

Though he was right, it still hurt. Her eyes burned and a lump formed in her throat. She'd usually been able to manipulate men, but she wasn't sure how to get him on her side this time. She had pictured him as a doting father, eager to have his own child. Even though he'd never met George and Ernest, he went out of his way to ask after them and buy them gifts. If he didn't believe this baby his, hope for their future was lost. Fear crept into her heart, and she let the tears fall, expecting he would respond to her sincere emotions. "Will ya have your child live on the streets, poor and uneducated?"

"He's not my child," Bo said, this time sounding more like he was trying to convince himself. He threw his hands in the air and looked toward the ceiling. "Why, Emma?" he cried out, then turned and stomped out of the hotel room, slamming the door behind him.

She ran to the door and opened it.

He moved fast down the hallway, almost running.

"Come back. You can't leave me," she yelled, but he'd already turned the corner. Her words echoed back. She quickly closed the door before any guests opened theirs. She waited for hours, but Bo never returned.

Over the next few weeks, she sent him messages, but none were answered. She had let her feelings grow too deep for him and she mourned his loss. She constantly watched for him on the streets and all the places he'd taken her. But once again, her dreams were not reality, and her child would be born to her alone.

CHAPTER EIGHTEEN

Emma ~ March 11, 1905

Emma rarely saw Paul anymore. He worked as a fireman fifteen days straight with one day off. On this particular day off, his wife Mary invited Emma, Eva, Hy, Mama, and the two boys to a birthday party for their eldest son, Sanders, who was turning five. In no mood for a party or a family gathering, Emma went at the insistence of Eva, who had noticed Emma's sour mood and convinced her she needed to get out.

No one knew she was pregnant, and she dreaded them finding out. It wouldn't be long before her body would make the news obvious. Knowing Paul, he'd feel the baby was one more person he'd be responsible for, even though they were all taking care of themselves and Mama at the moment. But that wasn't going to last much longer for Emma's household, not without Bo's money.

A few months older than Sanders, George had never celebrated his own birthday, much less been to a birthday party. His quiet curiosity kept him close to Sanders as if he didn't want to miss out on anything.

From the kitchen, Mary carried out a tall white birthday cake with five lit candles, singing a birthday song as she walked into the dining room where everyone had gathered. Mama and her four little grandsons sat up to the table, the others stood. No one knew the words to Mary's song and waited politely as she sang. Except for spirited Hy, who clapped the beat.

Thrilled with the glowing cake and his mother's melody, Sanders grinned wide. George's eyes grew as big as quarters. Ernest and Paul Jr. sat mesmerized. Sanders, dressed in his best little Sunday suit with large lapels, clapped his hands in delight as his mother placed the cake in front of him.

"Blow out the candles," she said.

He did just that.

Mary was "a Catholic girl," as Mama called her. She attended church at the old, daunting edifice on Crawford Street. Emma had gone to their babies' baptisms, but she'd always felt uncomfortable in the building, like she couldn't breathe the air of those who frequented its space.

"Lent starts next week." Mary cut into the cake. "And before I give up desserts and other luxuries, I wanted to give Sanders a celebration."

Hy guffawed. "If giving up luxuries is a form of penance, then I must be a very penitent person."

Emma chuckled, but Paul gave Hy a look of annoyance. Her two brothers were opposite in almost every way. Paul was tall and blond, like Papa, and Hy was shorter, smaller-boned and dark like Mama. Hy always looked for the joke in any situation, and Paul had to appear sober and strong. He asserted his older-brother status on Emma and her siblings, and she allowed it. It gave him a role to play in a family that sometimes lacked direction.

"What does penitent mean," Eva asked.

"You're better off not knowing, Eva," Hy said. "I would hate for you to feel like you had to apologize for sneaking me some of those cigarettes from the dancehall the other night."

Mama furrowed her brow but said nothing.

Mary honored her with the first slice of cake. "There you go, Mama."

An hour later darkness fell, and Mama went to lie down in one of the kid's rooms while the children went outside to play.

"Stay out of the street, now," Eva called to the children from the screen door. She was far and above better with children than Emma.

The rest of the adults sat in the parlor, drinking coffee and smoking cigarettes. Spring was on its way. A pleasant night to have the door open, the screen door keeping out the bugs.

Listening to the children's laughter outside gave Emma a feeling of peace until she remembered with a dull ache, she was pregnant. She hadn't yet decided what to do.

"Those boys need a father," Paul suddenly said with no preamble, looking toward the screen door.

"You should be tellin' Jack that," Emma shot back with a tinge of anger.

"I wrote the mongrel a letter and told him to get his sorry-self home."

Surprised Paul took that much notice of her, Emma warmed to the feeling of protection. But what would she do if Jack came home and found her pregnant? He'd been gone far too long for the baby to be his. "Did he answer?"

"No." Paul inhaled on his cigarette, then blew smoke into the room. "Did you do something to make him leave?"

"Paul!" Eva said loudly, surprise creasing her brow.

"Well, she's not exactly the Virgin Mary," Hy added.

Mary made a sound of disgust in her throat and stood. "I'm going to do the dishes." She walked out.

Emma felt ganged-up on. Paul and Hy knew of her employment in Galveston when she was younger, but they didn't know about Bo. She told her family she was a hostess and coat-checker at the Rice Hotel. "If being busy caring for his son is a reason for leavin', then yes, I guess I did."

"You need to make time for your husband, not just your children," Paul squinted his eyes in her direction.

Indignation tightened her throat. "I don't need to prove to y'all what kind of wife I was."

"Now, Paul." Hy came to Emma's rescue. "I worked with the man and know for a fact he spent far too much time with other women."

Her stomach hardened in anger. She didn't know that. She'd suspected, but never knew. Her brothers would think it her fault Jack cheated then abandoned her—that she couldn't keep him satisfied. With her experience, it was shameful to be left for another woman—or was it women? She clenched her fists and lifted her chin higher. "What women?" She stared hard at Hy.

Hy's face colored at his blunder. "I thought ya knew."

"I suspected, but he never fessed-up."

"Well, at least he didn't leave you with another child," Paul said. "Eva can't always care for your kids. You need a man, and the boys need a father."

She'd been a fool to think she could tell Paul of her careless and awful situation. She'd taken care of herself this long; she'd keep on doing that. Men could not be counted on.

CHAPTER NINETEEN

Emma ~ End of March 1905

Emma waited for Hy to go to work and Mama to lie down for a nap before she approached Eva. "I'm gonna live in Galveston again. Rent is paid here through June, and I think if you find a job, you and Hy both can start saving and earn enough to keep on here. And I'll come see you often"

"But why is you moving?" Eva's expression was both sad and worried.

"I miss the life I had in Galveston." It was a lie, but ashamed of being yet another failure in her family's opinion, Emma decided to not share her pregnancy. She didn't plan to come back until after she gave birth. Secretly, she still hoped Bo would eventually acknowledge his child and offer her financial support. After all, he'd said he needed to see the baby before he decided. She prayed the child would look like him. If it did, maybe he'd even take her back.

"Besides," Emma tried to smile. "I depend on you too much to care for Georgy and Ernest. Won't you be glad for your freedom?"

"Not really." Eva shrugged. "They're good little boys, and they love their aunty. Can't I come with you?"

"They do love their aunty, but you can't come with us. Hy will need your salary to help pay rent. Like I said, I'll come visit." Again, the lie. Could Eva see it on her face?

Later that day, Emma was greeted by the familiar smells of train smoke, fried foods, and salty ocean air. She disembarked from the train in Galveston with George and Ernest in tow. She waited on the platform while a steward brought her two bags. She gave her thanks and tipped him a penny, which she regretted instantly. She needed to hang onto all the money she could.

"Now Georgy, remember I told y'all to hold your brother's hand. I has to carry the suitcases."

Five-year-old George frowned and held out his hand for Ernest. George had become a quiet, but obedient child, even if he performed tasks with annoyance.

Emma picked up the two bags. "Stay close by my side."

Still rebuilding from the hurricane, and not yet warm enough to attract many visitors, Galveston was somewhat empty, although doors to bars and shops were open to welcome the few. She quickened her step past the Tremont Hotel, not wanting to think about what she last experienced there. The sights and smells of dead bodies still occasionally came unbidden.

As she passed numerous bars, her mouth watered for whiskey. If only the children weren't with her.

Galveston had changed. For protection against future hurricanes and flooding, the city built a seventeen-foot seawall. Miraculously, they were in the process of raising homes and buildings to a higher grade, made possible by dredging slurry from the bay's bottom and pumping it into the city, raising whole city blocks—a noisy and dirty process. Many new homes stood where old ones had been washed away, while others were perched on stilts awaiting fill sand to be piped below them. The boardwalks Emma and the boys walked along were also elevated. The neighborhoods had been depleted of mature trees, but some new growth had sprouted, a promise of the island beauty Emma remembered.

She headed for Lillian Sullivan's home, not far past Postoffice Street, south on 25th. The walk was slow, the suitcases heavy, and Ernest tended to dawdle. George, in his impatience, pulled hard on his hand, which made Ernest cry.

"If you're good boys, I'll give y'all a taffy when we're settled."

The promise sped Ernest's feet for a time, but he soon fussed to be held.

"Not yet, Ernest," she said.

At the Sullivan's, Emma hid the suitcases behind a large oleander bush, stepped to the door, and tapped the brass knocker.

The door opened to a black maid dressed in a dark blue, full skirt and white blouse with a crisp white apron covering all. She eyed the children. "May I he'p ya?"

"I'd like to see Mrs. Sullivan, please."

The maid nodded once, showed them into the parlor, and left.

The home smelled of furniture oil and something like wet carpet. Emma wondered why they hadn't opened any windows.

She whispered to the boys. "If y'all don't sit real still and quiet, I'll swat ya one."

They sat on an oak-framed, orange velvet chaise sofa with their worn shoes dangling above a silk Persian rug. She gave them a stern look as a reminder to mind their manners.

Lillian entered the room wearing a fashionable blue and green plaid dress with three layers of ruffles across the bottom that swished when she walked. An embroidered collar covered her long neck. At her breast she wore a watch.

Emma stood. "Mrs. Sullivan, I'm not sure you remember me, but I worked in Galveston until the hurricane. My name is Emma Hydrick now. These is my boys, George and Ernest."

Lillian barely glanced at the boys. Barren herself, she probably had little interest. "I remember you." Her voice was deep for a woman's. "You made some good money in your time." Her eyes were unfeeling. A condescending expression played upon her face, and she kept her head high.

Emma hadn't forgotten how hard she was—nothing but business and the bottom line.

"Why have you come to me?" Lillian asked.

Emma's heart pounded fast against her chest. She didn't want to appear as if she were desperate, but instead trying to make a business deal that would be lucrative for them both. "I'm here to work again. I've been told you have homes for women who can trade services for the payment of rent."

Without looking at the boys, Lillian inclined her head their way. "I don't see how that can work with children in the house."

Emma suspected she would say as much and had a quick answer. "They is good boys and will stay in another room. You know I was one of the highest earners when here before. Nothing has changed. I've been keeping company with the wealthy in

Houston and still earning a high commission." Emma didn't tell her she'd been working on her own, a kept woman for one man, without a madam. She wanted Lillian to believe she still needed an overseer to bring her customers. It was a way to put a roof over their heads immediately.

Lillian squinted her eyes, but her formidable stature changed little. "I happen to have a house available, and I suppose we can make a business deal for a trial period. I expect you to entertain daily, sometimes four or five a day, depending on the number of docked ships."

"I remember the island system." Emma clenched her fists and looked away. She needed to feed her boys, and she knew no other means to get by. Still hoping Bo would come back, she couldn't bring herself to sell the sapphire earrings and other gifts he'd given her.

She contemplated Lillian, then confidently said, "You'll be pleased with my work."

Once obvious to all that she was pregnant, she would probably be put out. Unless she could convince the woman she'd work through her pregnancy as she had with George.

***

Emma was surprised the house Lillian let to her hadn't been washed away in the hurricane. Propped against the wind near the wharf, and in a neighborhood not yet raised to a new grade, it was an old, one-story shack with an outhouse in the backyard. The salt air had stripped its exterior of paint, and the gray boards had slits between them big enough to push a coin through.

Finishing with a customer, Emma handed him his hat. "Be sure and come see me again, ya hear." She grinned and acted pleased to have his business.

"You can bet on it," he said as he placed the hat on his head.

She showed him to the door, happy to close it behind him. He was the third that day and she needed to get supper made for the boys. She stashed the almost empty whiskey bottle in the cupboard and went to unlock the kids' bedroom.

Ernest was asleep near the foot of the bed, so she untied George's wrist from the bedpost first. "You've been a good, quiet boy, Georgy, and I'll give you some rice and beans as I promised."

George pinched up his pale face, silent and angry as he always was after being bound to the bed. But it was for his own good. She couldn't have him coming in on her or making a lot of noise while she serviced her customers.

Emma untied Ernest but left him asleep while she prepared supper.

***

Ora

One of my more interesting finds while at the Rosenberg Library was a sociological study about prostitution in early Galveston. The study stated that madams paid taxes on the real estate they owned, and by doing so, appeared like upstanding citizens. It was these "real estate" owned houses, known in the bawdy business as "cribs," where the madams kept some of their prostitutes. I checked on known addresses for Emma once she moved back to Galveston in 1905 and found the residences were owned by Mrs. Tim Sullivan. In the *Galveston City Directory*, Mrs. Sullivan's employment was listed as "real estate." Madams most commonly called their business "real estate."

CHAPTER TWENTY

Ora

When I pieced together information about when Jack left Emma, it appeared he went to work at the Butler Brickyard in Bastrop County. The clay pits there were next to the Texas and New Orleans Railroad, an active site for brickmaking and exporting. Starting in 1871, a community had grown up around the brickyard with a company store and brick houses for employees, many of whom farmed on the side. This community became known first as Butler Switch and later just Butler.

The lack of searchable records for Jack is not the norm when doing family history research. I researched my mother's family in Virginia and North Carolina and found a hundred-fold of documents—court and land records, newspaper articles, photos, people still living who supplied information about her family— far more than I learned about my father's family in twenty years of investigation.

I've come up with a few possible explanations. I think my mother's ancestors were honest people, working their fields, participating in community events and services, and looking for what happiness life would afford them. They tended to live on the same plots of land for generations—in the East where records were kept better than the new and rowdy West. Even my fourth great-grandmother, who was raped near New Bern, North Carolina in 1811, had her story preserved through the court's Bastardy Bonds records. The unfortunate woman had to stand in front of a courtroom full of men and explain why she was unmarried and "with child" so the court could decide who should pay for the child's upbringing. It seems harsh, but it was for the wellbeing of the child who needed a guardian to pay for his education, food, and boarding.

So too, Emma had little means of financial support in 1905. If she'd been better educated with higher self-esteem, perhaps she could have worked as a clerk or a teacher. She was living in the west, a "frontier of America's future," where such things were possible, but even there it was widely felt that working women kept men from jobs. There would be no court-appointed guardian for Emma's new child, nor for Emma and her two sons. She had to find a means on her own by which her family and forthcoming child would have food on the table and a roof over their heads.

***

Emma ~ End of June 1905

Dressed in a burgundy satin robe that flared wide at the sleeves, Emma opened the front door of her house to a customer. "Welcome to my home of pleasure." She smiled enticingly but said no more when she realized the short man in a shabby suit observed her with disgust.

He eyed her abdomen. "If I wanted to fornicate a fat, pregnant woman, I woulda stayed home with my wife. Ya two look alike, and I'll have no part of it. Ya ain't the whore I desire." He turned and walked away.

"Wait! Maybe I can make you a deal?"

Without turning back, he waved his hand in farewell and kept walking.

Emma closed the door. Some men didn't realize no matter her condition, she could do whatever they wanted her to do—fulfill the dreams they couldn't find elsewhere. He was the second one that week who'd rejected her. Six months pregnant, she had grown larger than she had with her other pregnancies, and it wasn't because she was eating more. Judging from Bo's size, she guessed her baby must be bigger than the others had been. Maybe her age and it being her fourth pregnancy accounted for some of her girth?

When the first customer had rejected her, Emma had to reimburse him the money he paid Lillian to bribe him not to tell her madam of his displeasure. It was the only money Emma had saved in the last few months. All that she made went to food for the three of them and booze for her customers and herself. Lillian hadn't sent Emma the customers promised. Business was still paltry because of the noise and mess of rebuilding. Not only that, but it was also hurricane season again and people were afraid to visit the island. Emma finally resorted to hawking Bo's gifts, receiving a fraction of their worth.

When a man was not her companion at night, Emma didn't sleep well. Besides fretting over not earning enough money, she worried about Lillian finding out she was pregnant. If she were kicked out of the house, where would they go? She couldn't bring herself to let Eva and Hy see her condition. She had written to Jack asking for money, with no response. She also wrote Bo numerous times, sending letters to his business address to convince him that the child was his, but she never received a word in reply. She planned to write him every week until he accepted his child.

She opened the door to the tiny room that held no more than two small cots with a narrow path between, and the boys glanced at her briefly, then continued their play with wooden horses Bo had given them months before. Emma hadn't had to tie them to their beds in weeks. They were good on their promise to stay in their room and play quietly. Even without a customer there, they had little interest in being near their mother. "No business today, boys. I'll have no money to buy food. We'll need to eat beans again."

"No," Ernest pouted.

George kept his mouth clamped tight, as if he hadn't heard.

Emma left and poured herself a glass of whiskey. Sitting at the kitchen table, she wrote:

> *Dearest Bo,*
> *I hope you're getting my letters and reading them. I don't want no companionship, only for you to believe I carry your child. You must know that I'm living in dire conditions in Galveston. I once knew you to be a kind man. You wouldn't want your child hungry like my two boys. Please help me with our desperate situation. What do I tell the child of a father who didn't want him? I know you would make a good father and could*

financially take care of the baby better than I. Please
consider raising it with your wife as its mother.

Emma sat back in an old chair that creaked under her weight. Why had she written that last line? Did she really feel that way? Was she ready to give away her child? It was true the child would have a better life with Bo, and she wouldn't have to worry about feeding a third. But what kind of mother gave away her baby? Her throat tightened. She grabbed the letter to wad it up but was interrupted by a knock.

She quickly stood and shushed the boys while shutting their door again, glad she hadn't changed out of her robe. Maybe they would eat more than beans.

She opened the door to Lillian Sullivan on her porch, a motorcar idling in the street behind her. A black driver in white cap and gloves—the same man who brought Emma's salary each week—briefly glanced her way.

Emma squared her shoulders, inwardly wishing she could hide her protruding abdomen.

Lillian looked her over in the same way the customer had earlier. "So, it's true, you're with child. So large, in fact, I'd guess you were pregnant when you came to me for our business deal."

Dread flowed through Emma. She would be fighting for her survival sooner than she'd anticipated. "Please, Mrs. Sullivan, won't you come in, and we can come to an agreement? I'm sure I still satisfy my customers."

Lillian stood firmly on the porch, seemingly with no intention of stepping into the house she owned. "Not if they won't even enter this house. I had a visit from your last john. Seems he had no interest in a whore with a swollen belly."

"But I've kept all the others happy." Emma lied. "There's many who see my charms. I'm favored—"

"You're obviously no longer favored. I haven't had a customer request you in weeks. I should have guessed the situation."

"Please! I'll take more customers and show ya I can earn money."

Lillian pointed a finely manicured finger at Emma. "I want you out."

"But—"

"No," she yelled.

Startled, Emma stepped back.

Lillian wagged her finger. "There are plenty to take your place—whores with no children. I could put two working girls in this house." She glanced over Emma's shoulder.

"I can work harder." The desperation in Emma's voice agitated her. Unshed tears burned her eyes.

"No!" Lillian gritted out of her teeth. "You have three days to find another place."

"Three days? Who will have me? Where will we go?"

"That's not my concern. I'll be sending my husband here to make sure you're out."

Emma kept herself from falling to her knees and begging, although that's exactly what she wanted to do. "Please, give me another chance to prove myself. That were only one shortsighted customer."

"No!" Lillian contorted into a vile matron, far from her usual refined mask.

A young man on a bicycle stopped in front of the house. Lillian turned to view him and then stepped off the porch and into her waiting motorcar.

The young man got off the bicycle with a paper in his hand. "Telegram for Emma Hydrick."

"Yes," she said absently and took the message while staring at the retreating car.

When she looked back, the young man stared at her with his hand out, palm up.

"I have no money to give you."

His shoulders dropped, and he walked back to his bicycle.

Emma closed the door and sat again at the table, staring at her unfinished letter to Bo. What was she to do? She glanced at the telegram and realized it was from Eva.

'Got notice today. Jack dead. Congestion.'

***

Ora

Jack died June 25, 1905, at about 4 p.m. His death certificate is sparse. It records the place of death as "Butler Switch," with the immediate cause of death "congestion." The duration of the illness had been three days, which leads me to believe he died of pneumonia. Although there are spaces for Jack's age and residence in the document, these spaces have lines drawn through them, making me think whoever was the informant for the death record—or the doctor himself—didn't know any details. Jack was recorded as Andrew Hydrick, white male, American citizen. No place of burial stated. The physician was W.E. Wood of Elgin. It does not record it on the death certificate, but both the physician and Jack had pregnant wives. I don't think Jack knew about his.

***

Emma ~ June 1905

June weather in Galveston was hard to predict. Usually it was rainy or humid, but sometimes it could be breezy and dry. This afternoon, dark clouds hung heavy, but rain hadn't fallen. Emma sat on her porch sipping the last of her whiskey from a glass.

George and Ernest dragged sticks through the dirt, making roads for their toy horses to gallop.

Emma fanned herself as she watched the dock workers stream by on foot or bicycles. Charles Koenig, one of her consistent and kinder customers, a German immigrant and neighbor who lived alone a few doors down, waved as he passed.

In her desperation for money, she wouldn't have to share with a madam, she called out to him. If she got caught working a deal behind Lillian's back, she'd be in trouble, but what did she have to lose? It would be satisfying to get back at Lillian.

Emma unbuttoned a couple top buttons and pulled her blouse off one shoulder. "Charlie, come visit for a while?" She grinned a smile that didn't reach her heart, then downed the last of her whiskey, setting the glass on the porch.

Carrying a lard tin and in clothes that hadn't seen a washboard in weeks, Charlie came to Emma and stood at the edge of the porch. "How you this evening?" he said with a thick accent.

"Are ya looking for companionship tonight? Ya know I always please."

"Mighty tired. Perhaps on payday?" His eyes displayed sadness.

"Oh, I see." Emma sighed. Charlie probably wasn't much better off than she. Without warning, tears brimmed her eyes.

"I offer friendship." He smiled, and for the first-time Emma realized he was missing two of his bottom front teeth. Had he lost them in a fight?

Emma couldn't imagine gentle Charlie fighting anyone. His offer of friendship caused more tears to fall. She didn't know how to answer him.

Charlie stepped onto the porch and placed a hand on her clothed shoulder. "Vhat has happened?" he said in broken English.

Her face hot with embarrassment, she fanned faster. "I've gotta leave here tomorrow and have no place to go but to my family in Houston. I don't want to go there. My sister and brothers would be annoyed about my condition." She waved a hand over her protruding belly. "But I see no other way."

Charlie's kind expression deepened with concern.

"Would you happen to have change for us to ride the train? I'll do anything for your pleasure—you know I will," she said as sweetly as she could.

Charlie shook his head. "Come. Live vith me."

Shocked at the suggestion, Emma wondered if she may have misunderstood his words.

"My home one bedroom. Vee share." Pink actually rose to his cheeks.

She wanted to laugh at the ridiculousness of his blush. For the first time in months, hope crept back into her chest. "Do you mean it, Charlie?"

He nodded once. "Vee find cot for boys."

Emma placed her fan in her lap and laid her hand over Charlie's, where it still rested on her shoulder. "You is the kindest man I've ever had come into my life." Her words were as true as any she'd ever uttered.

Charlie glanced away sheepishly. "I lonely man." His face and neck bloomed redder.

"I can do your cooking..." she pulled at the dirty cuff of his sleeve, "...and wash your clothes. Ya won't regret this."

"I vihl not." He confirmed with a nod.

CHAPTER TWENTY-ONE

Ora

Charles A. C. Koenig immigrated to America from Germany in 1891 at the age of twenty, but I could not find him in the 1900 Census in Texas. If he had family in Texas, they are unknown to me. There was a large Koenig family in Fredericksburg, Texas, whose descendants have documented their family tree. Charles Koenig does not appear in that genealogy. He is recorded in the *Galveston City Directory* as a dock worker, not to be mistaken with the other Charles H. Koenig in Galveston who worked for the railroad and was married.

My family said little of Charlie, but my grandmother Lucille, George's wife, told my father that Charlie was a kind man who helped her in time of need in 1929, which tells me he stayed close to the family for at least twenty-five years. I wish I knew details of his past and personality, so I understood what made him such a caring soul.

***

Emma ~ September 9, 1905

Charlie's home was much like the one Emma had rented from Lillian. It had running water, but no water closet. The outhouse in the backyard was as antiquated as hers had been. Electricity had recently been brought to the home through a low-hanging wire that draped across the yard, entering the house at the eaves near a window, cutting through the view Emma had of the next-door shack five feet away.

She stood at the deeply stained and gouged porcelain basin doing dishes in what could be called the kitchen. Pushing aside a dingy, once-white fabric curtain, she reached beneath the sink for the old knife she used for scraping the bottom of pans.

When dishes were done, she put them into one of two peeling green cabinets next to a dark wood-paneled icebox and a coal burning stove with two hotplates. Each night they ate at a table with four mismatched wooden chairs. Their only means of comfortable seating were two cushioned chairs set against a yellowing floral wallpaper-covered wall.

Charlie sat in one of the chairs, reading a German newspaper by lamplight. Occasionally he'd try to interpret an interesting story for Emma, stumbling through the translation. It was unusual for him to talk much otherwise. She'd learned his quiet nature was not because his English was rudimentary, but discovered he said little to his German friends as well. She found the silence welcoming.

Charlie's needs were simple, and he appreciated anything she did for him, like prepare his dinner for work. She didn't know a man could be so kind without expecting something in return. Charlie came home from work each day, gave her an embrace and asked after her wellbeing. Never did he yell or get angry at her or the children. Always thoughtful of her condition, he placed no demands on her and accepted what she gave. So why wasn't she happy and content?

On a cot pushed against the wall near the bedroom doorway, the boys lay awake, dressed in their nightclothes. A knock sounded at the door. Tonight was a rare occasion. She'd secured a girl to watch the boys.

Emma dried her hands, then opened the door to the new young neighbor from across the street. "Good evening, Dora. Come in."

The boys sat up, eyeing the stranger who would be their caretaker.

Emma took Dora by the arm and brought her to the cot. "These is the two boys. They know they is to do nothing but sleep while you're here." She gave them the look they knew as a threat of a spanking if they disobeyed.

"Yes, Mrs. Koenig."

Emma didn't correct her. It was best if the child thought her married to Charlie.

"We is going dancing and may be home rather late."

"Yes, ma'am."

Charlie set aside his newspaper and retrieved his hat. "Find cold cider . . . icebox." He pointed to the icebox, grinned at Dora, then cocked his elbow toward Emma in invitation.

The evening was warm for September. In silence, they strolled arm in arm to Garten Verein, a German social club. As they neared, Emma was surprised to see only the tiered octagonal dancing pavilion had survived the hurricane. It appeared that someone was in the process of returning the garden to its former glory. Emma remembered once playing croquet on the wide expanse of lawn. The pavilion was illuminated with strings of hundreds of small lights and an orchestra played "Meet Me in St. Louis, Louis." The atmosphere and music lightened her mood. Over a hundred-people stood about, or danced, or lounged on benches along flower-bordered pathways.

"Lovely," Charlie said.

"Yes, isn't it! Let's dance." Her heart kicked up a notch.

"I know little dancing."

"Well, then I'll teach you." Emma giggled.

Charlie's eyes grew wide in surprise.

She laughed again and squeezed his arm.

His full smile showed his missing teeth.

They danced for hours. Emma found her large belly to be a nuisance, but Charlie said he didn't mind. She minded and couldn't wait to deliver her baby. She vowed to never be pregnant again.

After midnight, the pavilion lights dimmed. People began leaving.

"Let's go for a drink, Charlie."

"Well..." Charlie was obviously weary. He didn't drink other than an occasional beer.

Emma missed drinking so much she could almost taste it. If she had any money at all, she'd keep some liquor hidden in the house. "Please! Let's stay out a bit longer?"

He nodded, and they continued their walk to a saloon on The Strand.

They entered the saloon in a fog of cigarette smoke. The interior walls were covered in dark mahogany paneling except for the wall behind the bar where there hung an ornate mirror surrounded by bottles of all varieties of alcohol. A piano player's hands tripped slowly over the keys as if he'd been doing it for hours and was ready to lie down on his bench and sleep. The smell of perspiring bodies, stale beer, and smoke reminded Emma of her past.

A drunkard bumped against Charlie on his way out.

Charlie said nothing and pulled Emma over to a small, vacant table.

As they sat on two-bit chairs, someone called Emma's name.

An old friend, Val, stumbled over. "Emma, it's been a long time." Val, not terribly attractive, but large in the bosom, leaned toward Charlie, her low-cut gown gaping open. "Come, both of you, and sit in our booth. Do you remember Cary? She's here too."

"Of course, I remember Cozy Cary." Emma grinned.

Val laughed at the inside joke. "Is this your man?" She winked at Charlie.

He stood and removed his hat, giving her a bow. "How'do," he said like a German cowboy, which made Emma chortle.

"This is the nicest fellow you'll ever meet." Emma squeezed Charlie's arm.

Charlie was good natured enough to join the other girls at the booth.

Emma drank on Charlie's dime. She felt bad about it but couldn't help herself. She craved whiskey and sometimes vodka. She promised him only one but was on her third when he interrupted her conversation with Val and Cary an hour later. "Perhaps time to send Dora home?"

"Oh, Charlie. Just a bit longer? They'll all be asleep anyway."

He gave her a bitter smile. "A bit." He sighed and leaned his head back against the booth, closing his eyelids. If she was lucky, he'd fall asleep.

It had been a grand night dancing with Charlie, but when she saw Val and memories of her past life had washed over her, she wanted to forget what she had become and remember the time before she had children, when she was free to do as she wanted. She made good money then and had beautiful clothes. When she was with Bo that happiness returned. He helped her forget how hard it'd been to be alone with two children. She missed his praise and especially missed their conversations. But often she hated him for what he'd done and blamed him for how things stood now. She still wrote him letters weekly, hoping for his response. She'd not given up and would go to him when she had the baby to convince him it was his.

Emma emptied her fourth glass, waved the waiter over, then turned to the girls. "How'sss businesss goin'?" The girls tittered at the question, which made her believe the question must be funny. Her raucous laugh was loud enough for customers to turn and stare at her. "What'sss y'all lookin' at? We got us a sssister-hood here that y'all is jealous of, is all."

Val and Cary tittered again, themselves obviously too drunk to think clearly.

Charlie stood and pulled at Emma. "It time to go."

"Oh Charlieee, the fun'sss just beginnin'." She whacked him away.

He furrowed his brow, grasping Emma's arm.

She slapped him hard in the face.

Stunned, he stared at her for a moment and then turned and walked out of the saloon alone.

***

Emma ~ September 22, 1905

Emma lay in bed on her side, big with child and unable to sleep. She stared into the darkness, feeling lonely and troubled, her pillow wet with tears. The baby moved within. Her time was coming due. Her stomach often tightened with contractions, but they never lasted more than a minute or so. She laid her hand where the child pushed against her womb, wondering how aware it was to her presence. She pushed back. What felt like a tiny limb trailed along her insides. More tears fell.

Lately, she'd been consumed with the idea of giving the baby away. She wondered if she would have the nerve to do it when the time came. What if it was a girl like the one she'd lost? She once thought Jack a demon for not caring that his child had died. Had she become a demon too?

She shifted, pushing herself closer to Charlie's back. He seemed to be peacefully asleep, and she envied him that. He'd been so kind to her and the boys, but they couldn't burden him further. She didn't like living off of him.

She needed to make plans for after the baby was born. If Bo took the baby and not her, she'd go back to prostitution—that is, if Lillian hadn't put out a bad word on her. There were plenty of madams in Galveston. She swallowed hard with dread at the thought of going back to the business. She was tired of it. Bo had changed everything. If there were any man who should care for her and her coming child, it was him.

Dare she hope Bo would take her back once he saw his child? She missed him terribly. He had made her feel valued—something no other man had done.

If Bo took neither of them, well, she'd have to climb that hill when she came to it. She wiped the tears from her face and rolled onto her back, but the weight of the baby made her much too uncomfortable, so she rolled back to her side.

Charlie stirred, but soon breathed again in slumber.

Emma couldn't turn off her mind enough to find the bliss of sleep. She kept going through her few options. If she had the baby in Galveston, it would be weeks before she was strong enough to travel to Houston and find Bo. As she lay in the dark, thinking it over, she realized she needed to have the baby in Houston. She needed to go to Bo soon, before it was born, and let him know of her plans.

Somehow, she had to convince him to take his child.

***

Emma ~ September 23, 1905

"Boys, where is you?" Emma grumbled, walking down the street on swollen, sore feet. After ten minutes of indignant searching, she peered down the alley behind the neighbors' houses to find George and Ernest playing ball in the mud with other children. The thought of having to clean them before getting on the train made her even more weary. She pushed loose strands of hair behind her ear and yelled in the harsh voice she used too often with the boys. "George. Ernest. Come now!"

They came running.

As they neared, she placed her hands on what used to be her hips. "You naughty boys. I should whip y'all for leavin' without tellin' me."

They bowed their heads and scooted around her as she swung out but missed them. "Run to Charlie's. I want y'all cleaned up by the time I get there."

They took off running, and she wearily plodded behind. She'd never been so large with child. Walking hurt. Moving hurt. Standing and sitting hurt. When she arrived home, the boys stood at the sink, splashing water all over their shirts and onto the floor.

Emma grimaced and narrowed her eyes. "Take those clothes off and put on your best."

They stared at her in surprised glee. Wearing their best meant going into town or on a picnic with the adults.

"We is goin' on a train ride. Do ya want to see your aunty?" Emma asked.

"Yes!" George said with a smile, a question in his eyes.

Emma left Charlie a simple note she hoped he could read to say goodbye and thank him for all he'd done for them. She told him she'd come get their belongings when they got back in town and pay him the train fare she'd taken from his hiding place in his dress shoe.

On the train, she had second thoughts. By going to Eva, she'd give away her condition, something she'd hoped to avoid, but she could think of no other way to make this work. If she brought the boys with her to visit Bo, he would be more likely to reject her, thinking he had more to take on than his baby and Emma. She also didn't want the boys to witness her begging Bo to take the baby, if it came to that. It would be better for them to not know what happened to the child if Bo took it. Maybe she would tell them it died.

She was betting on Eva being home on a Saturday. She wasn't sure how Eva could watch the boys the whole time she was recuperating, but perhaps between Hy and Mama, they would work it out. She scrubbed her hands over her face. There was no other choice.

They arrived on Carr Street near the end of day. Emma didn't bother to knock but walked into the small cottage near the outskirts of town. Lights had not yet been turned on, and it took Emma's eyes a moment to adjust.

Mama and Hy were nowhere to be seen, but Eva sat on the sofa, mending in her hands. She stared at Emma's girth, her mouth open in surprise. She'd grown more beautiful since Emma saw her last. Tall and thin with striking blue eyes, her long brown hair was styled in the fashion of the day on top of her head, loosely fanning around her face. Emma envied her youth.

"Aunty!" George ran to Eva.

She stood and took him into an embrace. "Finally, you come visit your aunty, you naughty boy. Where have you been?" She squeezed him tight.

Ernest hung back, perhaps too young to remember his Aunt Eva.

"We been at Charlie's. Didn't ya know?" George's brows furrowed. He looked to his mother.

Eva considered Emma, cocking her head.

Emma shifted uncomfortably. "I'll explain everything. I know this is a surprise, but I can't stay." She rushed on, not wanting to lose her nerve to follow through with her plan and feeling shame and sadness at having to endure Eva's shock. "I come to ask if you'd care for the boys for a couple weeks while I go have the baby."

"Well . . . sure. But . . ."—Eva creased her brow—". . . did ya at least bring 'em a change of clothes? Anything? Is you leaving now? It's late. Where exactly is ya goin'? A hospital?"

Emma was afraid if she stayed any longer, she'd have to explain everything. The less she said, the easier it would be. With as much as Eva loved children, Emma was sure she'd try to convince her to keep the baby. "Yes, a hospital." Emma hoped it was true. She turned to leave.

"Wait. What's goin' on?" Eva moved closer with her arm outstretched.

Emma backed away. "I can't tell ya now. Please, Eva. I'm desperate. Please watch the boys for me. I'm so sorry. I don't know what else to do." She needed to get out of there fast before she cried. "And don't tell Mama or the brothers about my . . . situation." She looked down.

"All right." Eva again stepped toward Emma with an outstretched hand.

Emma hurried out the door, moving as fast as her cumbersome body would let her. She walked down the street until the house was out of sight. Eva didn't follow. Emma turned the corner and headed toward downtown. Her mind kept replaying Eva's expression. With all the things Emma had done in her life, she'd never felt such shame at her situation and dropping the boys on Eva like that. She didn't deserve Eva's love.

Streetlights came on. Cloud cover made the night darker. It smelled like rain. She slowed her pace and rubbed a sore area on her lower back. She worried it might be a contraction. Where was she going to find Bo? She would try his business address in case he was working late. But it was Saturday, and he could be anywhere.

CHAPTER TWENTY-TWO

Ora

When gas bubbles seeped to the surface of the San Jacinto River, it led to the discovery of oil in Humble, Texas. In November 1904, Humble became a boomtown overnight. The following January a large gusher erupted at a well-head, exploding the population of the small town from a few hundred to several thousand. Oil from gushers pooled around derricks and flowed everywhere, including into tents. The town reeked of the nauseating smell of gas. Forges opened, constantly clanging hammers onto anvils to smooth the drill bits into proper dimensions.

Homes couldn't be built quick enough. Tents and corrugated iron shanty towns sprung up across the prairie. Land once selling for $10 an acre, sold for $20,000 an acre. There was no shortage of saloons, gambling, or dysentery. Heavy drinking and fighting among oil-field workers were nightly occurrences.

It was common for the *Houston Post* to report on the depths of oil wells in Humble. The December 8, 1904 edition reported on four of Howard Hughes's wells, three of which were around 500 feet deep, and one "blowed the derrick down, has subsided and the derrick was rebuilt today. They will commence drilling again as soon as machinery can be replaced." To Howard Sr.'s consternation, the fishtail bits used by drillers often broke. In not too many years, he would come up with a solution to that problem.

I drove to Humble—pronounced with a silent "h"—in January of 2016, in hopes to understand the oil rigging history and living situation of the Hughes's in 1905. The city is situated in Harris County, north of Houston. At Lone Star College, I perused their genealogy and local collection and visited the Humble Museum where on display are stories, photos, and artifacts of the oil-boom years. I discovered Walter B. Sharp organized an oil business in Humble called Moonshine Oil Company with partners Howard Hughes Sr. and Ed Prather.

Sometime in 1905, Howard Sr. moved from Houston to Humble with his wife Allene, who hated living in the filthy town.

***

Emma ~ Evening, September 23, 1905

Just as rain sprinkled the walkway, Emma arrived at Bo's place of business, one of the largest buildings in downtown Houston. No one was about but a friendly-faced young man mopping the immense marble foyer. He eyed her timidly, as if he didn't want her to know he saw her.

"Can you tell me if Mr. Hughes has been in this evening?"

"No, Ma'am. I ain't seen no one since my shift started at five."

"Does he often work evenings?"

"Not often. He ain't here much since moving to Humble."

"Humble?" The surprise in her voice must have made the janitor think he'd said more than he ought.

"Yes, well . . . many of the wildcatters live there."

Emma paced. How was she to find him in Humble? She was obsessed with the idea of convincing him he needed to see the baby when it was born. She needed him to take her back, or at least give her money.

Turning again to the janitor she rocked in place, anxiously trying to calm her mind. "Do y'all have his address?" She clenched her hands to calm her trembling.

The janitor stared at her as if she'd lost her senses. In her agitation, her mind probably was deteriorating.

"I'm the janitor, lady."

"Yes, of course." She left the building.

Emma trudged slowly to the train station in the rain. Her abdomen felt as if it hardened with each step, and she often stopped to rest. She was now sure she was in the early stages of labor, which made her all the more convinced she needed to get to Bo. She was hungry, cold, wet, and more vulnerable than she'd ever felt in her life. Her time was running out. She briefly considered going back to Eva, but that look of shock in her eyes when she saw Emma's stomach made her burn with shame. She was sure she'd get the same reaction if she went to Paul. Having the baby on the train would be preferable to explaining her reckless situation to either of them.

Emma bought a ticket to Humble with the few coins she had stolen from Charlie.

On the train, a middle-aged woman approached her, introducing herself as Mrs. Graves. She sat by Emma and clasped her hand. "I couldn't help but notice your distress. It's a bad night to be traveling. Can I help you find comfort?"

Having felt so alone moments before, the woman's kind words helped Emma gather courage. She sat up straighter and tried to tame her soaked and frizzy hair. "You is so kind. I fear my time's almost due. I'm making my way to a brother in Humble. He'll know what to do."

"Oh! You have family *there*? Humble is such an indecent place to visit. The oil strike has brought rough men by the thousands." She leaned in closer. "And harlots have followed them," she whispered.

Emma squeezed the woman's hand and laid back against the seat. "Yes," she said, tears burning her eyes. "Harlots tend to follow the ones with money."

Mrs. Graves clicked her tongue. "Where's your husband, poor dear?"

"He ran off," Emma said, thinking of both Jack and Bo.

"Well, I'm glad you have a brother to do you right. Will he meet you at the train depot?"

Emma panicked. Was this woman going to keep prying? "He doesn't have a telephone. Doesn't know I'm comin'."

"Oh dear! How can I assist you?"

"I'll be fine. I'm sure with all the people flocking there, as ya mentioned, there will be hacks to hire."

"I suppose you're right." Mrs. Graves squinted her eyes and shook her head.

A strong contraction sent pain like fire around to Emma's back and she sucked in air.

"Oh dear!" Mrs. Graves said again. "Maybe you ought to travel to Magnolia with me? I have a fine doctor we can call on."

She couldn't respond through the pain but was tempted to take Mrs. Graves up on the offer. But if she had the baby in Magnolia, how would she get to Bo so he'd see it? It was the same problem she'd had in Galveston, so she decided she'd see Bo tonight, then go to a hospital in Humble. As the pain started to subside, Emma said through clenched teeth, "I wouldn't dare . . . put ya out . . . like that."

Mrs. Graves's face drew down in worry. Why couldn't Emma have been given a mother like this? She suddenly realized she was still squeezing Mrs. Grave's hand. "Oh!" She released her. "Forgive me if I hurt ya."

"No trouble, dear. I've had a few of my own. Is this your first?"

"Yes," Emma lied.

"Well, it's as they say, you'll think you've gone into the depths of hell but ten minutes after it's over, you'll have forgotten the pain."

Why did women say such things? "Yes, well, thank you. Don't let me impose on your night."

"I have no plans on leaving you. Lean back and relax if you can. The ride is not long."

Emma laid her head against the seatback, hoping to not draw out anymore conversation, but she couldn't relax. The frantic idea of getting to Bo in time kept her heart racing.

She remembered what it felt like to be in his arms.

He had to take her back!

She had one more contraction before arriving in Humble. At the station, she bade farewell to Mrs. Graves, her short-lived, kind friend.

The train pulled away and left the platform dark. The rain fell harder in Humble than it had in Houston. There were no hacks waiting, although several people had disembarked with her and entered the small depot. She entered the building feeling desperate. "Is any of ya from Humble?" She called loudly to the five people within. "And can all y'all help me find a resident?"

Two men stepped closer. One took off his hat, the other stared as if no intelligence resided within. The one who removed his hat asked, "How can I he'p ya, Ma'am?"

"I have a message to deliver to a Mr. Howard Hughes. Do ya know where he lives?"

"'Spect all knows where he lives, if he be the same who owns Moonshine Oil?"

Emma tilted her head. "That would be him."

"There ain't yet no street signs where he's livin', but I can take you to him, if ya like?"

"I'd appreciate that. Thank you."

He put his hat back on. "We're waitin' for my Pa to bring the wagon 'round."

"Do you think it'll be long?" A contraction tightened her lower belly.

"Not long."

She gingerly lowered herself onto a cold, hard chair. Someone behind her opened a thermos of soup. He slurped it. The smell of tomatoes, garlic, and beans made her mouth water. Even if she was offered some, she wouldn't be able to eat but a couple bites. Her pains would probably make her throw it up.

At last her ride arrived. The men helped her onto the springboard seat, even offering her an umbrella. Lights shown through windows of numerous saloons up and down the street, men moving slowly amongst them and also toward a tent city that stretched farther back than Emma could see.

During the short ride, Emma obsessively rehearsed in her mind what she'd say to Bo—the same words she'd rehearsed during her sleepless nights in Galveston. *"Bo, remember all the pleasurable times we had? I love you and want to always look after your needs. Even if you can't live with us, please give your child and me a place to live where you can visit."*

They stopped under a large magnolia tree in front of a newly built, still unpainted, narrow but long house. A huge pig slept in the mud beneath the tree.

The father came around the wagon and took hold of the umbrella. "Let me take ya to the door." Meaning he didn't want to leave his umbrella with her, nor did he expect her to get wet.

Although she'd rather be alone when Bo first saw her, Emma couldn't think fast enough of what to say and nodded.

There was no defined road or curb, only mud that oozed into Emma's shoes through eyelet holes as she neared the door. Her heart thumped against her chest. She followed the man as if she were about to visit friends but felt more like she was going to lay down her life.

They stepped to the door, and the stranger knocked.

Although excited to see Bo again, Emma had an awful fear that he'd shout at her, spit on her, accuse her of trespassing and tell the man to take her to the police, or worse, to an asylum.

Footsteps rapped along a floor on the other side of the door. Her heart raced. She held her breath.

The door opened. A young girl, probably no older than fifteen, dressed in a light gray maid's uniform stood before them.

Emma let her breath out in a whoosh. Light spilled onto the porch, exposing the mud they'd tracked there. She felt like white trash. Another contraction hit hard and she grasped the arm of the stranger.

He gawked at her in surprise.

Staring at them with wide eyes, the maid asked, "May I help you?"

The stranger was still scrutinizing Emma, and she realized he expected her to say something. "Oh, um . . . is Mr. Hughes in?"

"Yes. May I say who's calling?"

"Mrs. Hydrick. I have a message to deliver."

"Please come in."

As soon as Emma lifted a foot to step into the house, the stranger quickly left. The contraction forced her to bend forward and grasp her large belly.

The maid, clearly flustered, waited for Emma to move away from the open door so she could shut it. Rain drummed hard on the porch roof.

Emma's contraction burned across her belly. She took shallow breaths. "Here," she finally said, the contraction subsiding enough for her to talk. "Help me off with my muddy shoes." She didn't want Bo to see her looking so shabby.

She lowered herself into a chair next to a finely-carved mahogany wall tree.

The maid untied and took off Emma's shoes, making little squeals at the mud on her fingers. She opened the door and placed the shoes on the porch, then came back, wiping her hands on her now streaked apron.

Sore, but with the worst of the contraction gone, Emma slowly stood.

"Please be seated in the parlor." The maid pointed to a settee in the room adjoining and then left.

Still uncertain about how Bo would react when he saw her, she didn't sit, but instead paced about the room in wet and soiled stockings, leaving shiny footprints in her stead. She looked at the parlor's contents. That one room was the size of Charlie's house, but the interior walls were unpainted and no pictures hung on the new wood that fitted together tightly with no open seams. The furniture consisted of a few pieces one would expect to see in a mansion—a massive Victorian style sideboard and cushioned seats covered in silk damask. She didn't want to sit on them in her wet clothes. A few minutes later, she became aware someone was in the room with her and turned.

Bo gaped at her as if she were an apparition. "May I help you, young woman?" What came out of his mouth made no sense.

Emma cried, losing everything she'd planned to say. "Yes, you can help me. I need you. I didn't know it would turn out like this. I'm in labor." She wiped the tears from her face. "You need to see the baby, as you said."

Bo's face turned whiter. He glanced over his shoulder. A woman stood in the hallway, six feet behind him. Bo's wife! Emma hadn't expected her to come to Humble but imagined her staying comfortably at the luxurious Rice Hotel in Houston.

"Who is that woman, Bo?" Her voice was not as Emma had imagined. It was sensual and sweet—kindly making an inquiry of a husband she adored, probably disbelieving the words she must have heard Emma say. Mrs. Hughes wore an ivory robe draped in French lace. Her long brown hair cascaded over her shoulders. It struck Emma that they could be sisters, but his wife was more beautiful. Emma felt sick with jealousy.

"It's someone I haven't seen in a long time. Just business, Allene. Go back to bed."

Allene squinted. She turned to leave, then changed her mind. "I'll have Judy bring in some tea while the water's hot. Would you care for some, Mrs—?"

"Hydrick. Yes, thank you," Emma heard herself say, as if she were in a dream—a dream in which she stood nude in front of strangers.

Allene left and Bo turned back to Emma. He didn't move from where he stood. He wasn't wearing a tie. His collar flopped unbuttoned. His suspenders draped to his thighs.

She wanted to go to him—to be held and told everything would be okay. Her tears fell unchecked.

"I need to get you out of here." Bo's hardened face was much like the last time Emma saw him at the hotel.

A contraction grabbed her before she realized it was coming. She backed to the settee and gingerly lowered herself, focusing on breathing through the pain.

Bo stood his ground with a hard look of impatience.

As the pain subsided, she asked, "Where will I go?"

"Damned if I know . . . or care. You've placed me in a tight situation here."

His cruel words struck Emma, and she covered her face.

"Look, Em . . . Mrs. Hydrick." Bo looked over his shoulder. "I don't know why you're doing this to me. That baby could be any man's. I've got standards to uphold—a business to run—and a wife . . ."

Emma hated him in that instant. All those dreams of him wanting his child once he saw it dissolved. "I have no money. I can't keep your child. If you'll not have it, then it must go to an orphanage. Is that what you want?"

"No, he doesn't." Allene came down the hall with a silver tray, a china set upon it. Tears in her eyes, she passed Bo and set the tray on the sideboard. She contemplated him with so much hurt Emma felt shame.

Bo stepped toward Allene and grasped her shoulders. "I don't know this woman." His words sounded false to Emma, and by Allene's expression, she was sure to her, also.

"Shut up, Howard." She shook off his hands. "I sent Judy home. We can speak candidly." She looked with scorn into Bo's face. "I despise you." She trembled. "I knew your carousing would come to something like this. How many times have you promised me otherwise?"

Would Allene kick Bo out, and Emma would get him after all? Crying, Bo took her in his arms. "I'm sorry, darling. I would have never hurt you intentionally."

Emma watched the man she'd loved so deeply weep onto the shoulder of the woman he truly loved. Her stomach contracted until she had the urge to vomit. She hoped he felt as much pain as she had these last few months.

What was going to take her from this nightmare?

At last, Allene pulled away. "It's a good thing I just arrived here and no one knows me. We need a doctor who doesn't know either of us. Is there one in this God-forsaken, filthy town?"

"I'll ring up the operator." Bo walked stiffly down the hall, as if in shock.

Emma and Allene stared at one another. Emma's chest tightened with guilt and shame and jealousy all at the same time. Allene had everything Emma wanted—lovely clothes, jewelry, society's respect, and Bo—and she was innocent in the whole affair, which made Emma even more jealous. She needed to leave. "Why call a doctor? Can someone take me to a hospital?"

"There isn't one in Humble and getting you to Houston in time would be difficult with the mud and rain. Hospitals are too public, anyway. You need to have the baby here. Secretly." Allene's eyes held so much pain. "Come to my room and put on my sleeping gown. We are going to tell the doctor you are my husband's wife. I am your sister."

Shock momentarily stunned Emma. She rigidly stood and followed Allene into her bedroom—her's and Bo's bedroom—a sanctuary Emma defiled by being there. The covers were turned back on the bed where Allene had recently lay.

Allene gave her a gown and left the room. Emma stripped from her wet clothes and put on the soft garment. It smelled like the sun and flowers. Tears fell again. How could she have done this to an innocent woman? The word *innocent* ricocheted in her mind until a contraction pulled at her womb. She laid on Allene's and

Bo's bed and pictured Allene in Bo's arms. "Please God, take me in childbirth."

The door opened and both Allene and Bo entered. Bo appeared in as much pain as she. He was suddenly a stranger.

"The closest doctor is in Houston," he said. "The streets are flooding. The doctor doesn't know if he can make it."

Emma closed her eyes and willed herself to die. "Leave me. I'll call if I need help."

"Emma! You can't deliver your own baby." Bo's anger seemed ridiculous at the moment.

Without opening her eyes, she said, "We all wish it to not enter this world."

"Don't talk nonsense. I'll go get the doctor myself if I have to," Bo said.

Bo and Allene left. A table lamp with a Tiffany shade sent amber light around the room. Emma stared at its jewel tones and gritted her teeth through more labor pains. A sticky flow of blood wet her legs and burning pain stung her lower abdomen.

Muffled conversations behind the door, between Allene and Bo drifted her way—sometimes Allene's voice would become shrill. Bo never yelled, but constantly spoke in soothing tones.

Emma hated losing control of the situation.

She wasn't sure how long she laid in pain and delirium before the door opened to a bright light coming from the hallway.

A stranger walked in. "Hello, Mrs. Hughes. I'm Doctor Oscar Norsworthy." He came to the bed and took up her hand. "Can you tell me how far apart your contractions are?"

"Every couple minutes. I'm bleeding."

The doctor drew back the covers. "There is more blood here than I would like to see." Although he said it as calmly as if he were discussing a scraped knee, Emma knew from past labors that she shouldn't be bleeding. She pushed herself up on her elbows and gawked at the bed sheets covered in more blood than she'd ever seen before. Falling onto her back, the world went black.

She awoke sometime later, but the delivery was a blur. Her only thought was to die. She pushed the baby out and heard the doctor's announcement that it was a boy, then she slipped back into darkness.

In and out of consciousness, she was sometimes aware of the doctor trying to stem the hemorrhaging. She called out to Eva, Georgy, and Ernest, apologizing for leaving them.

The next time she awoke, disappointed she had not died, the sun filtered through lacy drawn curtains. Every part of her body hurt.

A woman stood by her, calling Allene's name. Who was this woman? Why didn't Allene answer?

A baby cried.

"Allene," she said again. "Mrs. Hughes, can you hear me?" Irish. The accent was Irish. Emma focused on the dark-haired, blue-eyed woman standing at her bedside. She wore a white uniform and white square cap on her head. "Your baby's hungry. Are you strong enough to breastfeed?" She was looking at Emma.

"If I can do it lying down," Emma feebly replied.

"I can help you with that." The nurse directed Emma to lie on her side. A bulky cloth pad between her legs impeded her movement. She looked down. The sheets were as white as new snow.

The nurse opened Emma's robe and placed the baby on the bed and helped him attach to her breast. The familiar tug felt good somehow. A reminder of life.

Her son's hair was as dark brown as hers. His little face looked like a baby, nothing more. He wasn't a little Bo, or a little Emma—but a baby with skin much pinker than her pale breast. She viewed her hand and arm and found them to be almost as white as her sheets.

"You lost a lot of blood." The nurse stroked her hair. "The doctor has instructed that you stay in bed a couple weeks. Your husband has hired me to care for your needs. Don't worry, we'll get you strong enough to play with this wee lad. He's as healthy as ever a babe was."

CHAPTER TWENTY-THREE

Tis fate that flings the dice,
And as she flings
Of kings makes peasants,
And of peasants kings
—John Dryden

Ora

Biographers and personal acquaintances of Howard Hughes Jr. can't agree on the place, nor date of his birth. What's particularly interesting is that between January 1904 through January 1905, Howard Sr.'s and Allene's names were in the Texas newspapers no less than twenty-four times announcing events such as their wedding, honeymoon activities, where they played cards, went fishing, who visited their house, automobile racing events, Howard Sr.'s oil well activity, or when they went out of town. Why was their son's birth announcement not in the newspapers? It seemed an event far greater than the society news.

The state of Texas began a statewide registration of births and deaths in 1903, and yet Howard's birth was not recorded with the state when he was born in 1905. Howard Sr. studied law, his father was a lawyer and judge, and his father-in-law was a judge. Howard Sr. certainly must have understood the importance of filing a birth certificate, yet one was not filed.

Thirty-six years later, in 1941, Howard Hughes Jr. needed a certified birth record to prove his age for his government work during the war in Europe before America entered World War II. To obtain the birth record, two adults who could verify his birthdate needed to sign a notarized document to authenticate the information. Allene's sister, Annette Gano Lummis, and Howard

Sr.'s business partner's wife, Estelle Sharp, signed a document stating the birthdate as December 24, 1905.

Thirty-six years after the 1941 notarized birth record, and after the death of Howard Hughes Jr., in a court deposition by Annette Gano Lummis, she stated that she first saw Howard Jr. during a Christmas Eve dinner at the Rice Hotel in Houston "when he was two or three months old." Did Annette lie about the December 24 birth date or merely forget about the Christmas party? If she lied, why?

Estelle Sharp and Allene were good friends and said to be constant companions. If Allene was never pregnant, Estelle would have probably known it.

Allene's sister, Annette, lived in Dallas, but visited Houston often, and also probably would have known Allene was never pregnant. In fact, Annette had visited in July 1905. Allene could have trusted the two to keep the secret because they both cared for her deeply enough to protect her reputation and happiness.

Estelle Sharp died in 1965 and could not be deposed when Annette was.

On September 6, 1906, *The Houston Post* announced on page 10 that "Mrs. Howard Hughes and Master Howard Jr., leave today for Keokuk, Iowa, for a visit to Mr. Hughes' relatives. The Misses Gano of Dallas, who have been the guests of their sister, Mrs. Howard Hughes, have returned home." A month following the printing of this article, in the church records of Saint John's Episcopal Church in Keokuk, a baptism is recorded for the year 1906 on page 120, "Date: Oct 7. Name: Howard Robard. Parents: Howard R. and Allene Hughes. Sponsor: Mrs. W. B. Sharp. *Birth: September 24, 1905.*"

In Annette Gano Lummis's deposition, she also said Dr. Oscar L. Norsworthy was the attending physician to the birth of Howard Hughes and that the birth was so difficult for Allene that he advised her to not have any more children. Dr. Norsworthy was a highly respected doctor. It is curious that he also did not complete and file a birth certificate for Howard Hughes Jr.

In one Howard Hughes biography, Dr. Oscar Laertins Norsworthy is credited with delivering Howard Hughes Jr. in the Baptist Hospital in Houston, but there doesn't seem to have been a facility by this name at that time. The closest thing to it was identified by a charter as the Baptist Sanatorium downtown but wasn't filed until 1907. Leading to the establishment of the Sanatorium, a Baptist minister had established a charitable institution in Houston in 1904. It was an eighteen-bed facility open to all individuals regardless of race, religion, or ability to pay. I assume this would have been what was available in downtown for medical care in 1905, especially in a poverty case such as Emma's. It seems questionable whether Howard Sr. and Allene would have used such a facility, given their social status.

Despite some biographers' reports that Howard was born in a hospital, at least two biographers claimed him to have been born in a home at 1404 Crawford Street in Houston. If Howard Sr. and Allene were living in this home at the time of his birth, the closest hospital—St. Joseph Hospital at 1910 Crawford Street—would have been a few blocks (.2 miles) away. It wasn't until the *1907 Houston City Directory*, however, that records the Hugheses actually living at the Crawford Street address. Before that, they boarded at the Rice Hotel and then lived for a time in Humble, where it was known Allene complained about the filth and would not live there for long. Some biographers believed Humble to have been Howard Jr.'s birthplace, a small town without a hospital in 1905.

As I researched these facts, I reflected on how my Uncle Buddy was told the story of the birth of Howard Hughes by Eva in 1937, when he was thirteen. I wondered how much he may have been told that he forgot by the time he put it on paper in 1996. There may have been some crucial details that are now lost to history. He stated in his letter to Aunt Jeanette that Howard Hughes was born before Christmas 1905. Was he told that by Eva, or did he come to that through biographer's claims and the date Howard Hughes himself eventually claimed after his Aunt Annette signed her name to the notarized birth record?

I don't have the definitive answer as to Howard Hughes's birth date and place, but I do believe it was September 24, 1905, because of his baptismal record and Annette Gano Lummis's memories of meeting him at Christmas time when he was two or three months old.

An interesting tidbit to all of this is that Howard Hughes often claimed himself to be an orphan acquired by his parents in the dark of night.

***

Emma ~ September 24, 1905

Later that day, the nurse stepped out, and Bo came to the bedside. So weak, Emma couldn't raise her head. Even keeping her eyes open was difficult. It was better to keep them closed anyway. Seeing Bo brought back too many emotions. She tried hard to hate him.

"I've promised Allene that if she raises the child as our own, I'll settle down and live a proper family life." He cleared his throat. "If you approve of us raising your child, once you leave this house, I cannot ever see you again." Although he didn't sound angry anymore, he did sound like he was negotiating a business deal.

A lump formed in Emma's throat. She already knew she needed to cut Bo out of her heart but making the final decision to give away her baby was almost more than she could think about.

"He's a robust, healthy child. I thank you for that." He cleared his throat. "I hope as he grows, I can believe he's truly my son."

"He's yours." Emma said hoarsely.

Bo turned to leave. "Time will tell."

"Why did you change your mind about taking him?" Emma asked before he stepped out of the room.

"Allene can't have children. She thinks this might be the answer to having a child she can convince others is ours."

As the days passed, Allene came into the room on occasion to play the part of a concerned sister. Always uptight, her lips pressed firmly together, jaw set firm, she'd ask after Emma's wellbeing, and Emma replied in simple sentences to keep up the pretense for the nurse. Allene would glance at the baby in the bassinet, but never pick him up. Even though Allene had helped Emma in her time of need, Emma resented her presence and was glad she didn't come often.

The days were long as Emma recovered. She had never been so weak. The nurse, Sally, had to help her sit up for meals, which she didn't have the energy to finish.

After the first week, Emma was better able to move about. Her first trip out of bed, Sally helped her to a rocking chair and brought her the baby to nurse, then went to the bed and began stripping it of linens.

Emma brought him to her breast. He was a strong fellow, eating every two hours and always eager for it. "Take it easy there, Sonny." She'd started calling him Sonny because Bo had not yet offered a name. She wanted Bo to feel some kind of connection to the baby by naming him.

"The lad's gonna suck what little strength ya have right out of ya." Sally laughed.

Emma smiled. As Sonny nursed, she ran her finger along his soft cheek. "Do you think he looks like his father, Sally?"

"Nah. He's your boy, that one is. But they do change by the hour when they're wee ones."

"Yes, I suppose," Emma said. She needed him to look like Bo.

Emma rocked and hummed a lullaby, then thought better of it. She didn't want to allow herself to develop a strong connection to him. Somehow doing what she did with George and Ernest might permit that to happen.

The baby stretched and his tiny foot moved out of his gown. Emma held it and counted his toes again, then opened the gown to see the other faultless foot. At least she was giving Bo a perfect gift.

She found relief in knowing the baby would be cared for in style. He'd have the best education and move amongst high society. He'd never have to worry about where his next meal was coming from. Most likely he'd have a home like Bo grew up in— with culture, where his interests would be cultivated. With all these things assured, why was Emma still feeling uncertainty tug at her heart?

Again, Emma thought about Allene having everything Emma wanted—Bo, his lifestyle, and now her baby. Jealousy tightened her chest. She found herself wishing she knew Allene better. What kind of person was she? Would she dote on the boy or push him away knowing he wasn't hers but the son of a whore?

Emma needed to know Allene would make a good mother and make sure Emma's son would be cared for properly. Maybe she didn't need to give the baby up completely, but somehow still be part of his life? Hope at the thought released the tightness in her chest.

In sleep, the baby released her breast. She stared at him and the love she tried desperately not to feel set free warmth in her bosom. She brought him closer and kissed the top of his head.

Finished with making the bed, Sally came over. "Let me lay the laddy in his bassinet before I go to dinner."

She took the baby from Emma's arms, and Emma instantly felt the loss, as if it was a warning of what was to come.

Sally helped Emma back into bed, fluffing her pillows so she could sit up, then left the room.

Emma let herself cry quietly and didn't hear the door when it opened.

"Allene has gone out to buy infant supplies," Bo said. "May I look at the child?"

Emma quickly wiped her face. "Of course, he *is yours.*"

Bo stood over the bassinet.

"Pick him up."

"I'm not sure I know how to hold a baby."

"Tenderness is enough." She knew Bo's tenderness well and wished she hadn't let the thought enter her mind.

Bo picked up Sonny and brought him to his chest. He stiffly walked to the rocker in front of a window in the warm light of the setting sun, then gingerly sat. "He's sleeping and doesn't seem to mind my holding him."

"He's a good baby. Only cries when he's hungry."

Bo rocked and stared.

Emma found relief in watching the two together.

"What will ya name him?" she asked, finally conceding in her heart that she would allow Bo and Allene to raise Sonny.

"Allene and I have decided to name him after me, Howard Robard Hughes."

"I'm glad for that. I've been callin' him Sonny. Maybe you can too, so others can distinguish between him and yourself?"

"Yes, I suppose we can."

The answer didn't sound promising, but Emma would take whatever he'd give.

"Bo?" She swallowed hard to keep stinging tears from falling again and gave herself a moment before she continued. "Is there a way I can see him occasionally? I mean, he doesn't need to know I'm his mother. I don't know if I can bear never seein' him again." This time she couldn't hold back the tears, and they rolled down her cheeks.

Bo contemplated her with sympathy, and she saw in him the old Bo she used to know. "I don't know, Emma. That sounds risky. I'm sure Allene wouldn't approve. I told her I'd never see you again. We've both dealt her wrong, and she deserves what she's asking for."

Emma hated Allene. She searched quick for an answer. In desperation, she said, "Maybe someone else can bring him to me?"

"That won't work. I can't trust that they wouldn't discover the truth."

"Then bring him yourself, Bo. Please! We're the only two who will know."

Bo raised an eyebrow, looking unsure. "I'll consider it and let you know."

***

Emma ~ October 9, 1905

After two weeks, Sally was sent away, and Emma felt strong enough to leave. She was anxious to not live with Bo and Allene but didn't want to leave the baby or the comforts she'd experienced. Logic told her it was for the best, but her heart couldn't agree.

Emma tightly wrapped her chest in a long length of muslin to help suppress her milk. Once dressed, she knelt at the bassinet where Sonny slept on his tummy. She rubbed his back. "I wouldn't be able to do this if I didn't believe I'd see y'all again." The hope of a reunion gave her strength, and she didn't cry. "You're in a better place, little one." She wasn't sure she completely believed that, but she needed to. Had to. Or she couldn't walk out the door to start a new life without her third son.

Allene and a stranger conversed by the front door. Allene turned. "This man will take you to your family's home in

Houston. He has been paid." She handed Emma a red-cloth coin purse. "This is to help you after that."

Emma pushed her embarrassment and sadness aside, but tears threatened all the same, so she said nothing, tilted her head in acknowledgement and stepped away with the stranger. She could feel Allene's unsympathetic eyes on her back.

When she entered the home on Carr Street, Eva and the boys rushed to her.

"Mama," George said with more devotion than usual. He and Ernest wrapped their arms around her legs. Finally, the tears came. She quickly wiped them, but not before Eva questioned with her eyes.

Reverently, Eva asked, "Did the baby"—she hesitated—"not make it?"

It was a reprieve to Emma's emotions to answer Eva. "I delivered a healthy baby boy." Emma feebly smiled.

"Then where is he?"

Emma shook her head and looked pointedly at her boys who were still at her skirts. "Have you enjoyed your time with aunty?"

"Yes, Mama," they both chimed.

"Why was you gone so long?" George asked with the same look of uncertainty he often held in his eyes.

"Mama wasn't feeling well, and I needed to recover." Emma pulled them to the sofa and held both until they squirmed under her embrace. "You is two fine boys," she said as she released them, feeling the gratitude she should have felt years before.

They grinned at her praise.

"Is Mama here?" Emma asked Eva.

"Yes, she's lying down. She's been ailing more than usual." Eva stepped closer to the boys. "Run and play outside while I visit with your Ma."

When they left, Eva sat by Emma and took her hand. "Mama doesn't abide the children well. I don't know what she does in that room all day, but most days I serve her meals in there."

Emma shook her head. "Who watched the boys when you went to work?"

"I quit my job to care for your children." Eva rolled her eyes at Emma's surprise. "I was glad for the excuse."

Guilt tugged at Emma's heart. "Can Hy make the rent?"

"October was paid for with my last check. I'll need to find another job. Unless"—she raised her brows hopefully—"You will come live with us again?"

Emma had considered it but decided to try Galveston again. If Charlie wouldn't mind putting up with them a bit longer, while she healed, she hoped she'd find work. "No, I have a friend in Galveston where I left our belongings."

"Charlie. I heard about him from the boys."

Emma nodded. "I think I can earn more there." She pulled the coin purse from her bag. "Here." She gave Eva enough money for November's rent. "This is for watching my boys."

"Thanks." Eva drew down a brow. "Will you be all right?"

"Don't worry 'bout me." Emma's voice wavered. "What is ya now, fifteen?"

Eva sat up straighter. "I had my sixteenth birthday a few days ago."

"Oh, Eva." Emma hugged her sister. "Happy birthday. Did you celebrate?"

"I made a cake, which Mama turned her nose at. The boys and I had a grand time, though."

Emma figured Eva attempted to make her feel all was fine, but Emma knew better. They stared at one another for a moment, trying to read what was in each other's eyes. Emma was surprised when Eva asked, "Can you tell me anymore about the baby?"

"The least I tell ya, the better. Be comforted to know he's with a good Houston family and will most likely want for nothin'."

Eva held questions in her eyes but only nodded.

"It's for the best, Eva. I can hardly care for the two I have."

Eva brought her arms around Emma and held her tight.

Emma's milk dropped down and her breasts ached. She drew in a painful breath and tears stung her eyes.

CHAPTER TWENTY-FOUR

Ora

After examining the typical life of a prostitute and putting it together with the alcoholism I've seen in my family, I believe Emma experienced the weakness of drowning her sorrows in a bottle. She lived through many traumas—the abuse and neglect she suffered at home, losing so many of her siblings at a young age, men walking out on her, no hope for a better future, and the loss of an infant. But the worst had to be giving away her child and being left with the void of a missing son and the guilt for not behaving as a mother should.

No one is immune to trauma. It affects us all differently, yet is, in a sense the great equalizer—the thing that helps us have empathy and understanding for one another. When faced with trauma, some people distance themselves from the experience so they encounter less emotional pain. They might disconnect from people they were once close to. Typically, this alienation plummets their quality of life.

When someone isolates, it narrows his or her range of existence and the outside world may feel threatening. Healing, on the other hand, occurs during the process of engaging with people. That doesn't mean there's not an importance to pain and struggle, because it is through these experiences where we often realize what's truly important. All experiences have value.

I once read an interesting article about what trauma does to our genes and whether or not that trauma can be passed down to the next generation. Researchers call it epigenetic inheritance—the idea that environmental factors such as diet, smoking, and stress can affect the genes of our children and possibly grandchildren.

A study was performed on two groups of people. Group one consisted of Holocaust survivors and their descendants. Group two consisted of Jewish families and their descendants who lived outside of Europe and did not experience the Holocaust. Epigenetic tags were found on the same part of the gene associated with the regulation of stress hormones in both the Holocaust survivors and their offspring. The same correlation was not found on the gene in any of the control group and their children. The children of the Holocaust survivors may have altered stress hormones that can hamper their ability to bounce back from trauma and may suffer from anxiety disorders.

Whether or not Emma's trauma affected her descendants, it did affect her. I don't want to minimize her trauma by writing scenes based off circumstantial evidence. Through writing this book, I have often wondered if I am dishonoring Emma in any way. I hope I'm not. I might not respect the path she chose but connecting with her has helped me feel compassion for her and others who might have made similar choices. It has also helped me better understand who I am.

***

Emma ~ Evening of October 9, 1905

When Emma and the boys entered Charlie's house, its smallness struck her. What hit her next was the smell of fried fish and soiled clothing.

Charlie jumped up from his favorite chair and came to them, beaming with relief and joy. "At last, you back." He embraced Emma, then ruffled the hair on both boys' heads. "Miss me?" he asked them.

"Yes," they said in unison.

They weren't talkative boys, and their answer seemed to please Charlie. "Come. Have you eaten?"

Emma had lost her appetite when she'd walked through the door, but the boys weren't so disturbed by the unpleasant odors.

"No," George said.

"I hun-gee." Ernest climbed onto the chair at the kitchen table.

Charlie stared at Emma with eyebrows raised, waiting for a response. What good would it do to tell him she'd spent two weeks being pampered and served delicious food on a silver tray that she didn't have to pay for or prepare? Reality hit hard, and she ached to feel that same security she had at Bo's. Her body sagged.

"Come sit. Rest from travels." Charlie beckoned her.

At least he knew better than to ask her about the baby in front of the boys.

Charlie prepared a meal of cold, greasy fish, pickled eggs, and bread that he toasted at the stove. As the kids ate, he told them about a ship he unloaded at the docks that was full of children's toys from his home country of Germany. They were fascinated with his descriptions of colorfully painted wind-up cars, planes, and boats. Occasionally, Charlie directed the conversation toward Emma, but she said nothing and turned her head.

Later that night, as they lay in bed, Charlie did something he'd never done before. He held her while she cried.

The next night in bed he coaxed her to talk. "The baby die?"

"No, Charlie. He's with his father."

"You tell more?"

"Not tonight." She rolled away from him.

A few days went by. Charlie always came home from work with prepared meals or food he'd cook himself. He was patient and gentle with Emma. She often caught him staring at her from across the room.

Breasts aching and still weak from all the blood she'd lost, she had a hard time doing much of anything. She mostly stayed in bed. Over the days, Charlie scrutinized her too closely. She wanted to move out on her own but had no employment or strength to search for work. She couldn't sell her body in the state it was in.

One day, she tried walking to The Strand to find a job, but she was so tired and light-headed by the time she got there, she didn't have the energy to present herself as a capable worker. She entered a saloon to rest and didn't come out until she'd spent all the money she had left from what Allene had given her. Sadly, the alcohol wasn't enough to erase the memories of Sonny and Bo. She hated herself for what she'd become.

One night in bed, Charlie surprised her with questions. "Vhere you have baby?"

It was too dark to see his face, so Emma rolled onto her back and stared into the cold night air. "At the home of his father."

"You see baby ever again?"

"I'm uncertain, but I believe so." She hoped he wouldn't ask the same question about Bo. Bo's coldness toward her was still so painful she didn't want to dwell on it.

Charlie sighed. "You still heal?"

"It were a difficult birth. I lost a lot of blood."

"I don't want you voork for men."

This surprised Emma and before she answered, he said, "I know Model Laundry need you."

She hadn't told him she'd been considering looking for another job. Doing laundry wouldn't have been her first choice, but she wasn't surprised it was Charlie's.

"And you marry me?" Charlie asked.

She gasped. She couldn't have been more bewildered. How could anyone want her? "Charlie—"

"Don't say now. Think on it." He felt for her hand under the covers and grasped it.

"All right."

"If you get job, I know house vee rent. Two rooms."

Emma didn't answer. A void seemed to lay where her heart should be. She didn't love Charlie. Against all logic, she still loved Bo. If she married Charlie, would it mean putting an end to ever having Bo in her life? She hoped not. If men cheated, so could she. She stopped her thoughts there, realizing she was still hoping and dreaming about Bo. When would she stop?

Charlie stroked her hand.

At the moment, she didn't feel she had the strength to either marry Charlie or move out on her own with the boys.

"I think a lot vhen you gone. I miss you all and feared not come back. Vee can be family. Good for boys."

She figured Charlie would probably never be more than a dock worker and doubted he'd give her the security she was looking for. But he might be all she'd ever have.

CHAPTER TWENTY-FIVE

Ora

Charlie and Emma were married at the Galveston Courthouse on October 22, 1905, by Justice of the Peace Sydney T. Fontaine.

In 2016, when I went to the courthouse to find information regarding their marriage, I was surprised to be given the original, lovely marriage license with scrolled and beautiful handwriting. As fancy as the certificate was, it didn't tell me anything about the couple's state of mind or love for one another. If Charlie were that interested in marrying Emma and willing to take on her two boys, why did he not suggest it before she gave away her son? Or maybe he did ask her to marry him when she was pregnant, but she hadn't yet decided what to do with the expected child. It may be possible that the father of the baby (Bo?) may have wanted his son all along.

Charlie and Emma moved across from the train yard into another house owned by Lillian Sullivan at 3727 Church Street (Avenue F). Their view of weeds and stationary railroad cars would have faced northeast. The wharf at Galveston Bay, which they wouldn't have been able to see, but possibly would have heard, sat directly behind the railroad tracks. Charlie's work at the docks would have been within walking distance as was Postoffice Street, where I assume Emma once again worked at a bordello, possibly for Lillian Sullivan since they were renting from her.

1906 was a year of change for Emma. Her boys were growing up—George turned six and Ernest four. When her sixteen-year-old sister, Eva, was five months pregnant, she married John Little and later gave birth to a daughter, Florence, or "Flossie" as she was called, on June 20th.

A week after Flossie's birth, Emma's nineteen-year-old brother, Hy, died mysteriously. A long article in *The Houston Chronicle,* June 28, 1906, described how Hy's body was "found up the railroad track nine miles south of Houston" the night before. In the city jail, a black man by the name of John Lacy, was the principal witness. Mr. Lacy declared, "that the two had laid down upon the track to sleep. The noise of the approaching train had not awakened the white man." Lacy maintained that he'd made an effort but had not been able to save his companion. "The negro avers that the two were walking to Galveston together."

Hy suffered from a broken arm and ribs and a wound on his head. "After striking the body the train was stopped, the remains recovered and brought to the city...While it is stated that the boy was struck by the train, the circumstances under which he happened to be on the track are in doubt. The negro is being held for further examination."

I tried following this story through newspaper articles, but there wasn't anything more about a trial or Mr. Lacy. I think if Mr. Lacy had been guilty of foul play, he would have run from the scene, but he did not. I can't help but wonder if maybe Hy was drunk and passed out on the tracks.

I have also considered that Hy may have suffered severe symptoms of post-traumatic stress because of his experiences on Galveston Island after the 1900 hurricane when he had recently turned fourteen. He would have been one of the "men" recruited (forced?) to dig the dead from the tangled mounds of wreckage, looking for valuables or something on their bodies to identify them, then piled the bodies by the hundreds to be burned. How did Hy react to death on a massive scale? It was two years later, when he was sixteen, that he moved away from his parents and brother, taking thirteen-year-old Eva with him. They rented their own apartment. A lot of responsibility for teenagers, but apparently to them better than living at "home."

By the middle of 1906, of Emma's eight siblings, two remained alive—Paul and Eva. Emma was twenty-four years old.

***

Emma ~ January 1907

The chill of the morning air on Emma's bare skin woke her. She was alone, the bordello quiet. Although it was mid-morning, the sun's light barely penetrated the thick velvet curtains. She arose and dressed in the fancy, low-cut gown she'd worn the night before, putting on her old heavy coat over its gaudiness. She crept down the stairs and out into the crisp air. Few were about on a street that came alive in the evenings.

She walked her usual route. Near home, George and a neighbor boy swung from a rope thrown over the crossbar of a lamp post. Ernest was nowhere to be seen. Emma ground her teeth. George knew he was to keep an eye on him when she and Charlie were at work.

"Where's your brother," she called to George.

"He's inside. Said his tooth ached."

Emma sighed. They had no money for a dentist. She hoped it was only a new tooth coming in. He was almost five, after all.

When she entered the house, Ernest called from his room. "Mama, that you?"

"Yeah, Ernest," she said, and then sarcastically added, "I'm here to enjoy the comforts of home."

"My tooth hurts."

"Rinse your mouth with salt water," she called back as she stooped to pick up yesterday's mail—a few white envelopes that had dropped from the mail slot. She threw them on the table and got herself a drink of vodka. Sitting at the table, she took a glance through the mail. Bo's familiar handwriting gave her heart an extra beat. She ripped open the envelope and pulled out a half-sheet of paper with a few short lines written across it.

Please be advised... she read. Why did he address her like she was one of his hirelings? She clenched her jaw.

...my family will be leaving town soon.

Emma gripped the paper tighter, crinkling its edges.

We will be staying at the Rice Hotel until Monday morning. Come Sunday afternoon if you can.

It wasn't the first time he'd sent her a letter to inform when they'd be in public with the baby. In the letters, he always warned her to keep her distance and out of Allene's sight. *If not, I'll never tell you again where you can see the child,* he had cautioned. At these meetings, Emma never was able to hold the baby or even get close enough to see his eyes. One time at the Azalea Festival, the Hugheses didn't show up as promised.

Bo never found an excuse to bring Sonny to her in Galveston. She'd given up on that ever happening, and now it sounded like they were leaving Houston. She rubbed her eyes, leaned back in her chair and took a sip of her drink.

Soon after leaving Sonny behind, she'd decided she didn't want him to know she was his mother. A mother who gave away her child would look bad in his eyes, and she didn't want that.

That night she told Charlie, "I need to go to Houston tomorrow and stay a night with Eva and her husband."

Charlie laid the newspaper in his lap. "Shall vee all go?"

"No. I'm hoping for an opportunity to see Sonny."

Charlie squinted his eyes. "Don't forget how that turned out last time."

His cynicism made Emma wonder if he was jealous of Bo or the better lifestyle he'd given her other son. She'd always been honest with Charlie about her trips into Houston, and she didn't care how he felt about them.

"Yes, well…" Emma balled her fists. "They is leaving town, and I need to hope for the best."

On Sunday, she wore her most modest dress, many years old, but still nice enough to be presentable and not put her at risk of being escorted out of the fine hotel. At least her jeweled hairpiece was new, even if the jewels were rhinestones. She fidgeted with a trinket hanging from her choker and went to the front desk. She dropped her hand and squared her shoulders in front of the clerk. "Please advise Mr. Howard Hughes that Mrs. Koenig is here. I will await him in the dining room."

Seated in the almost full room, she ordered tea. She waited over an hour, worried they'd ask her to leave if she didn't order something more. As she waited, she peered about. Good memories of meeting Bo at the hotel flooded her mind—dining with him in this room, dancing in the ballroom, slipping out into the dark together and going someplace more private. Did he ever think of her with the same fond memories? Her time with Bo had been the happiest of her life.

Suddenly he stood before her, holding a dark-haired, dark-eyed, fifteen-month-old child clothed in a white dress with white stockings and gray kid slippers. Sonny's wide collar vee'd at his chest where a blue ribbon tied in a bow.

"Oh," Emma breathed. This was the closest she'd been to him since she nursed him at her breast. She regarded Bo, instantly crushed by the sour look on his face.

"I don't dare take a seat," Bo brusquely said. "You understand. I'm down here on the pretense that I needed to stretch my legs and offered to give my wife a rest from the child's needs."

She pressed her lips together and looked away. Disappointment pushed at her chest "Of course." She tried to arrange her face in a happy look for her son.

Sonny stared at her for a moment then wrapped both arms around his father's neck, pressing his face into Bo's lapels, peeking back at her. He resembled her family.

Her chest warmed with the discovery. She wanted to say something smug to Bo about his looks, but she didn't. She still wasn't sure if he considered the boy his own flesh and blood.

"I wanted you to see him before we left the state," Bo said.

Emma's heart stilled in her chest. "Where is you going?"

"It's oil business and not important."

It *was* important, and Emma wanted to say as much, but her anger was making her lose the baby's interest. Staring at the brightly lit chandeliers and other curiosities, Sonny appeared to be an inquisitive boy. He finally inspected her with his deep-brown eyes.

Not having been with him all these months, she still felt the same love she always had and grinned at him warmly. "Hello, little Sonny." Emma reached toward him and started to stand.

Bo brought his brows together. "Please don't touch him."

He might as well have slapped her hand. She plopped back down. Bo had the advantage, and if she did something that didn't please him, she feared he'd never allow her to see Sonny again.

"I don't see that these meetings do you or the child any good." Bo shifted Sonny to his other side.

"That's because you isn't the one living without your son."

"Yes, well, decisions were made at his birth, and Allene was right. Let's make a clean break of it, shall we?" He stared intently at Emma, as if it was a demand, not a question, then turned and quickly left.

What could she do but stare at his retreating frame?

Sonny didn't even try to look back at her.

A pain constricted her lungs, making it hard to breathe, and time stopped.

CHAPTER TWENTY-SIX

Ora

In the Howard Hughes biographies I've read, Allene Gano Hughes is portrayed as a strange and phobic person. Although this portrayal may be accurate, as I found evidence for understanding her character, I saw a woman who worried about her son and protected him—maybe too oppressively, but she did what she knew best. I hope.

Bo was rarely in town, traveling out into fields to wildcat for oil and later taking long trips across America to promote his roller bit invention. Allene often found herself acting as a single mother. She probably let her worries get away with her and experienced anxiety she didn't know how to suppress—which came out as over-protective mothering.

Allene's sisters, Annette and Martha, sometimes stayed in her home. Their mother had died in 1905, when the sisters were fourteen and twelve. They helped raise Howard Jr., and Annette even tutored him academically in his youth. I haven't read anything that suggested Sonny had nannies or tutors other than Annette. In a will Howard Jr. wrote in 1925, he set up a lifelong pension of $20 a week for two "colored household servants." Considering Allene's upbringing, it would be more than probable that she had someone to help care for Sonny when he was a baby.

Howard Sr. was known to have cheated on his wife on a regular basis. What had Allene's choices been if she knew about his infidelity? I suppose she could've left him, but she didn't have a living mother to go back to. Perhaps she could have remarried. But for some reason, she did not feel this was an option. Maybe keeping up appearances was an important objective? She lived in a time when the divorce rate was at eight percent, and you couldn't obtain one without revealing to the court significant cause of abuse, adultery, or abandonment. Often these facts were published in a local newspaper or whispered about at parties.

One testament to Allene's feelings for Howard Sr. was found by Howard Jr. among his father's papers. It was the last letter penned by Allene, written the night before the surgery that took her life. She said she knew about Bo's recent affair—with the model and actress Eleanor Boardman—and conveyed her hurt, but that she forgave him. She also wrote in the letter that she had a premonition of her death and expressed her deep love to Howard Sr. for the last time.

In my fictionalized scenes, I don't want to misrepresent or take anything away from Allene. I'm drawing a picture of a "what if" for Emma being the mother of Howard. It's probable Emma was his true mother, otherwise I wouldn't be writing this book. I'm also hoping others may read the book and offer information to add to the story.

In early 1907, the Hugheses moved from Houston to Shreveport, Louisiana, following the oil strikes in hopes of making it rich. They lived at the Caddo Hotel, overlooking the aptly named Red River. Howard Sr. formed the Caddo Company, an oil exploration firm, creating affiliations with riggers. The oil wells proved dry, and the Hugheses moved after six months to the newest hotbed of oil reconnaissance—Oil City. It was a small and dusty outpost in Louisiana, near the Texas border. They lived in an antiquated home where they had to pump water and do their business in an outhouse. To make ends meet, Howard Sr. worked not only the oil fields, but also as a deputy sheriff and postmaster.

By 1908, Howard Sr. had some successes in Oil City, but eventually encountered a flint barrier in the ground that caused the fishtail drilling bit to break, not an uncommon occurrence. In the Oyster Pub, a saloon in Shreveport, Howard Sr. met a millwright who had an idea for a drill bit that had two cone-shaped cutters that engaged and rotated in opposite directions. For $150, Howard Sr. bought his mock-up of the cutters made from wooden sewing spools.

Howard Sr.'s partner, Walter Sharp, was knowledgeable about oil field technology and also interested in improving drilling methods. Sharp lived two blocks from the pub at the Phoenix

Hotel. Howard Sr. went to the hotel to show Sharp the crudely made mock-up. Sharp saw its potential and gave Howard Sr. $1,500 with his approval to come-up with a drill bit that would penetrate the thick rock formations.

Howard Sr. gave Allene $500 of the money and left her and Sonny in Oil City while he traveled by train to Keokuk, Iowa, where he worked on the drill bit and acquired more funding from his father. His brother, Rupert, wrote that Howard Sr. had fastened a paper to a breadboard from the kitchen and sketched his model drill bit upon it. The drawing had no less than 166 cutting edges. The edges meshed against each other on three sharp, ribbed cones.

His father hired a St. Louis patent lawyer to file the necessary papers with the patent office in Washington, D.C. on November 20, 1908. On the patent, Howard Sr. was listed as the sole inventor. He took his drawings to a machine shop and had a prototype fabricated.

Knowing he was on to something, Howard Sr. sent word to Allene in Oil City to pack their bags and head to Houston, where he'd meet her later. I can imagine Allene was more than grateful to leave the shabby house. She headed back to Houston at the beginning of February 1909, where she stayed with her best friend, Estelle Sharp. Sonny was almost three-and-a-half. Estelle had a son, Dudley, for Howard Jr. to play with, who was six months older. The Sharp's lived in a lovely old house in the country by a lake with tall oak trees and a fragrant and finely manicured rose garden.

In March, Howard Sr. met up with his wife and child. They arrived at the Rice Hotel in a Buick Model C roadster and took up residence. The proprietors were more than happy to allow the rare automobile to be parked in front of their hotel to attract customers.

Allene must have thought Houston to be utopia compared to the foul squalor of Oil City. They settled into the Rice Hotel until they could acquire a more capacious home. City life allowed for meals in the hotel dining room, teas with other socialites in one of the hotel's parlors, and walks along the boardwalk with Sonny in hand, dressed in the most fashionable knickers, striped jackets and boots that covered his shins. In mid-May, they moved into a home in Bayridge, southeast of Houston. Estelle Sharp entertained with a luncheon in Allene's honor.

In June of 1909, the new steel bit invention of Howard Sr.'s was brought to Goose Creek oil field in Baytown, Texas, and attached to a pipe stem rig. Sent down a well that had previously defied conventional drills, the roller bit cut through fourteen feet of solid rock and was dubbed the "rock eater." The patents in Washington had still not been approved, so a Washington lawyer was hired and successfully got the patents granted on August 10, 1909. Howard Sr. and Walter Sharp formed the Sharp-Hughes Tool Company and produced the drill bits commercially, renting them on a royalty basis rather than selling them.

The foundation for a fortune was laid.

***

Emma ~ November 25, 1909

Emma hadn't been to Houston in almost a year and now came with the boys to Eva's for Thanksgiving. Charlie had to stay behind to work, and Eva's husband John tinkered in the garage with an old steam-powered automobile he was attempting to get running.

Sounds of George, Ernest, and Flossie—Eva's three-year-old daughter—playing in the street hardly registered as Emma read aloud one of the many articles Eva had cut from the society section of *The Houston Post*. This one was dated September 26th: "Chilton Gano, who has been the guest of Mr. and Mrs. Hughes at Bay Ridge Park all summer, has returned to Cornell, where he will resume his studies." Emma assumed Chilton to be Allene's brother, but most importantly, the article disclosed where Sonny was living. Bayridge Park was a prominent neighborhood across the bay from Goose Creek where Emma had heard Bo owned an oil well. She imagined herself going to Bayridge to catch a peek at her son.

Emma picked up another clipping from the pile Eva had saved for her, this one dated August 29, 1909. It was an advertisement for a Studebaker EMF 30, costing $1,350. The black-and-white drawing of the white-rimmed-tire automobile was accompanied by the names of owners—Howard Hughes one of them. She smiled. The Hugheses must be doing well financially. Thrilled they were back in town, she needed to figure out how to get back into Bo's life. The hope of being his mistress again made her shiver with anticipation.

With shaking hands, she set down the clipping and turned to Eva. "When did they start showing up in the newspaper again?"

Eva stopped basting the golden-brown turkey and lit a cigarette. It dangled as she talked. "Last February, Mrs. Hughes come to visit her friend, Estelle Sharp. Here..." Eva stepped forward and shuffled through the pile, pulling out a small society page clipping. She removed her cigarette and read, "'Mrs. Howard Hughes is the guest of Mr. and Mrs. W. B. Sharp during the absence of Mr. Hughes in the East.'" Eva crushed her cigarette into an overfull ashtray. "And then later..." Eva picked through the clippings again and pulled out another. "This one's dated March 30th, 'Howard Hughes, the well-known oil man, has returned to Houston after an extended visit to New York.'" She set it down. "But the story is that he were also in Iowa working on his new invention."

Emma nodded, satisfied that the Hugheses were so well engrained into society that she could trace their movements in the newspapers, but unhappy that Eva hadn't alerted her to the fact sooner. "Why didn't you tell me any of this?"

Eva's eyes opened wide in surprise. "All ya told me were to cut out articles referrin' to the Hugheses." She creased her brow. "Why? What do any of this mean to ya?"

"Never mind." Emma shook her head and looked away. "That turkey smells wonderful." She deliberately changed the subject. "Can I help you get everything on the table?" She gathered the clippings into a pile and put them into her bag then went to the icebox and removed the gelatin salad, cranberries, and olives. "Y'all need to let me repay the favor and come to Galveston for Christmas. We can have a shrimp fry on the beach."

Eva jumped at the idea and started telling Emma about how she'd like to take a break from her job at the laundry. Emma stopped listening and started imagining how she'd get back into Bo's life and see Sonny again. Hardly a day went by that she didn't think first of Sonny, then of Bo, wondering where they were and how they were doing. Judging by the newspaper clippings, it sounded like Allene was busy with society functions. Emma wondered what kind of mother she was to Sonny. Was he being raised by a nanny?

Now that she knew the Hugheses were financially secure, she was sure Sonny would have the life she didn't. The thought made her smile. She had to see him.

***

Emma didn't know why she hadn't thought of it sooner. *She* had the upper hand, not Bo. She was so consumed with the dreams of getting Bo back that she hadn't considered her leverage for seeing Sonny.

Having found the Hughes' address in a directory, Emma asked directions of the driver before she disembarked the streetcar in Bayridge Park with a few socialite young women and men. They were amusing each other with conversations of their recent trips to Europe—how plain they found the food in England and how seductive in France. Their jokes continued as they compared the food to its people. Emma quietly chuckled.

Bayridge had been up and coming since the 1900 hurricane. Many of the stately homes were newly built after the old were destroyed by winds and flooding. Every home on the bayside had a pier. A lone yacht sailed south toward Galveston, perhaps out to sea. It was winter, but Emma imagined the summers here were probably filled with water activities such as crabbing, swimming, and beach parties at night where clams were steamed on smoky embers.

An elderly woman dressed in a long fur coat and full Victorian skirts, gloves, and hat passed Emma and acknowledged her with a greeting. Emma did the same and wondered at the life people lived in this small community. She imagined she'd gone back in time to a place where everybody knew everyone and neighbors gathered for picnics, boat rides, and fishing.

The crisp breeze off the bay chilled, and she tightened her coat around her. She arrived at the Hughes's large house, which had verandas all the way around. She didn't hesitate for a moment before opening the gate and walking past a perfectly manicured winter lawn to the front door. A maid answered and before inviting her into the parlor, advised her that Mr. Hughes was away but Mrs. Hughes could entertain her.

The parlor smelled of sandalwood, was carpeted in oriental rugs, and wallpapered in a green and purple floral print. Emma recognized some of the ornate wooden furniture pieces from when she'd visited in Humble. They must be heirlooms. Over the years, she'd investigated Allene and found she was from an old family who'd been in America for generations, distinguished in battles and politics.

When Allene entered and saw Emma, her face turned ashen. "May I help you?" she asked, acting like, and probably hoping, she was seeing a ghost.

"Is Sonny home today? I were hopin' for a visit."

Allene was as beautiful and regal as ever, but her emotions betrayed her. She licked her lips and swayed slightly. "We had an agreement."

"You and Bo had the agreement. I told him I wanted to be able to see the boy now and again."

"Why haven't you come forward earlier with this desire?"

"I did. Bo knew it and would send word when and where I could see Sonny at a distance." She hoped her statement shocked Allene and would cause a rift between her and Bo. "I've decided it's not enough for me. I want to see him more often, to talk to him and make sure he's a happy boy."

"But..." Allene looked like she was going to be sick and placed her hand on her stomach. ". . . he never said . . . I wouldn't have allowed...of course he's happy."

"I need to judge that for myself." Emma sat down as if she'd been invited.

Allene sat across from her, smoothing her black skirt with trembling hands. "I can't believe Bo would agree to that. He's not going to like you being here."

"I don't care what Bo likes or doesn't like. If ya don't allow me to see Sonny, I'll tell your rector our secret."

Allene gasped and clenched her hands. "You wouldn't."

Emma watched her face closely. "I would. I'll also write letters to those in your haughty circle and let them know you is raising the son of a whore."

Allene fell back against her chair and closed her eyes for a moment. "What kind of visits do you expect to have with Sonny?" she said slowly, as if in resignation.

"I expect they'll be different each time. It depends on when I can get away and how much time I have. I can imagine a picnic would be nice."

Allene turned whiter.

"Maybe go to the fair or watch him in a school play? Ya know, the kinds of things mothers like to do with their children." Having leverage over Allene gave Emma a feeling of power. Not only was she trying to see Sonny, but she hoped to make Bo and Allene squirm. They had her son after all. And their life seemingly sailed along without a care.

"I cannot let you take him anywhere without a chaperone." Allene hesitated. "In fact, the chaperone will have to be me because I can't risk questions from others. People won't understand the time he spends with you."

"I suppose you is right. How will *you* feel being around the likes of me?"

Allene straightened and stared hard at Emma. "If you have the feelings of a mother, you'll want the best for him and not tell anyone, including him, who you really are."

"On that we can agree. I don't want him to know I'm his mother." For the first-time Emma felt a little disconcerted, as if she were giving away part of her heart all over again. She kept her chin high, not wanting Allene to know. "It will be best if I'm known as Mommy's friend, don't ya think?"

Allene looked away from Emma in disgust.

Emma despised her. She said coolly, "I want to see him now. Is he home?"

Allene nodded once, stiffly stood and walked away, then stopped and turned. "I'm not feeling well. Can this first visit be here in the parlor?"

Triumphant and guilty at the same time, Emma hated herself, yet was excited to talk to Sonny. Her conflicting emotions found expression in her quavering voice. "No, I'd like to take a walk with him through your *lovely* neighborhood." She tried to sound snobbish.

"But it's a cold day. He'll know something's wrong if I let him go outside. He could catch a chill. Infantile paralysis is easily contracted. The violent germs can even be carried by a well person."

"My boys is outside in all-weather with their playmates and is as healthy as can be."

"Sonny is a fragile child. I worry over him daily."

Emma was taken aback by the comment. In all her imaginings of Sonny, she never figured on him being sickly. She wondered if Allene was lying in an attempt to get them to remain in the parlor and away from the prying eyes of neighbors. "Is he often sick?"

"If I didn't observe him closely, I fear he would be. I check his throat, feet, and stools, and he takes mineral oil nightly."

Emma had never done such things with her boys. She imagined Allene would think her the worst of mothers. Or was Allene in the wrong? Emma became uneasy. "Let me judge for myself."

Allene left and returned with Sonny holding her hand.

Emma stood.

Tall for four and handsome, Sonny's hair had lightened in the way that brunets turn blond in childhood, and was swept across his forehead. His dark brown eyes were as inquisitive as she'd remembered when he was a baby at the Rice Hotel.

"Master Howard, this is Mother's friend, Mrs. Koenig."

"How do you do?" Sonny bowed formally.

Emma was flabbergasted at his manners. She couldn't speak for a moment. If Sonny didn't look so much like her and Mama, she'd think him a total stranger. "It's a pleasure to finally meet you." She had never been so formal with an adult, much less a child.

Allene held Sonny at a distance, so Emma reached a hand out as if she wanted to shake his.

Sonny let go of his mother's hand and stepped forward.

Emma took his small hand in hers while Allene drew into herself.

"Shall we visit for a moment?" Emma moved toward the settee, Sonny in tow.

They both sat, and Emma asked, "What do ya like to play, Sonny?"

Allene moved into a chair near them.

"My aunt sent me a tricycle from Paris. I ride it in the atrium. When it gets warm, Mother says I can ride outside."

Emma looked him over. His cheeks were plump, his coloring good. He appeared as healthy as could be. She was suspicious Allene was the type who coddled. Sonny would probably turn out spoiled with expectations of everyone serving him, and Emma wondered if she could somehow counteract that from happening. "Do ya often travel, Sonny?"

"No, but Father does. He travels on a train. He said I could go with him next time." Sonny's speech was clear and succinct. He was obviously an intelligent child.

They visited for about twenty minutes more. Sonny never hesitated in expressing himself to Emma, an adult and total stranger. For being four, he was unusually precocious.

When he got up to leave, he bowed again to Emma and said, "Thank you for such a nice visit." He then left the room, once again holding his mother's hand.

Emma's heart went with him, but she now knew she could see him whenever she wanted.

CHAPTER TWENTY-SEVEN

Ora

Before oil was discovered in Texas in 1901, petroleum was chiefly used to make kerosene for stoves and lamps. Gasoline was a by-product that was thrown away, and natural gas was burned off. When gasoline-powered automobiles were invented, practices changed slowly. The cars often broke down and were noisy and smelly. There were no gas stations. Instead, one bought the gasoline in canisters at the grocery store or had it delivered. The automobile owners carried full canisters in their cars when making long trips. The convenience and speed of getting from one place to another overruled the difficulties and gasoline was soon in great demand. Howard Sr.'s drill bit revolutionized drilling for oil and gas, helping the oil industry become the fastest-growing industry in the country, with Texas at its center. Houston went through a period of dramatic change and economic growth.

Even before the Hugheses became rich from the drill bit, they were a part of Houston's elite. Image was paramount to them, and they joined Christ Church Cathedral where they rubbed shoulders with its upper-class congregation. At age five, Sonny went to school in the parish house of the church, known as Miss Eichler's University. One of the pupils, Ella Rice, would one day marry Sonny. The children of the Houston oil industry leaders, such as Sharp, Cullinan, Autry, and Donoghue, all grew up playing with Sonny.

Howard Sr. situated his family in a home in the fashionable south side of Houston, four blocks from the Sharp's home. The area was a mecca for the city's rich and powerful with colonnaded mansions set in amongst rolling hills. The Hugheses joined the Houston Country Club.

Howard Sr. was rarely home, traveling from coast to coast in two private rail cars, one just for his wardrobe. He entertained prospective drill bit customers with opulent meals and presents. He was known to rent an entire wing of a hotel to throw extravagant parties for prospective customers.

Contrastingly, in 1910, Charlie and Emma moved out of the Church Street house to another dwelling owned by Lillian Sullivan, an upstairs apartment over a beer parlor at 618 38th Street, a couple blocks from the train yard. I suspect a problem with their landlord's husband may have compelled the move. Timothy Sullivan, Lillian's husband, owned the two rental homes next to the Koenig's, and he was in trouble with the Galveston City Health Office for having open cesspools in the backyards of these homes. According to a newspaper article, one cesspool was within fourteen-feet of his rental and twenty-two-feet away from the dwelling of another family—which would have been the Koenig's house.

Mr. Sullivan legally challenged the city health department in matters of sanitation and refused to allow them to dictate what he should do on his own property. Dr. Trueheart, a city health officer, said in court, "the owners of the property had dug new cesspools and thrown the dirt into the old uncleaned ones, thereby creating an unsanitary and dangerous nuisance."

But the cesspools may not have been the only reason for the Koenig's move. In 1910, prostitution went through some changes on Galveston Island. Police raids became more frequent and less predictable, making some of the women feel they needed male protection. A trade once ruled by madams had them taking a backseat to pimps who took a hefty cut of the earnings. Emma finally left prostitution and went to work for Model Laundry and Dye Works as a machine operator.

Because of the move and new employment, things changed for the worse financially for Emma and Charlie. Charlie left the docks and got a job as an ice handler for a brewery. I assume it was the beer parlor below their home. George, now ten, was considered old enough to be a wage earner for the household and found a job as both a messenger boy and bellhop for the Hotel Galvez, over two miles from his home. He rode his bike to work and all over the island, even as far as Houston to visit his cousin Sanders, Paul's son.

In a recorded interview in 1980, George claimed to have gone to Alamo School, but I can find no record of his attendance in any elementary school in the Scholastic Census of Galveston County. In 1909, Ernest attended school for that year only. George and Ernest were not kept out of school by their parents because they were living in a rural area with their time and energy needed for farming or hunting, like so many other children of the time. They were frontier city boys, kept out of school to earn a living.

Child labor was sometimes an answer for families in poverty. Social reform to help get children back in school and away from the workplace was typically implemented by women volunteers of community organizations in big cities, not in Galveston. There was no government welfare or unemployment program to help families financially until 1935. In Galveston, church volunteers who were generally middle-to-upper-class women, helped families like Emma's, but it is unlikely that Emma would have accepted such help.

***

Emma ~ July 3, 1910

As Emma worked her tedious job at the laundry, she often thought about the Hugheses and wondered if they evaded her inquiries. According to the newspaper, the Hugheses moved again. They'd never told her this was their plan. Surely, they knew their lives were on exhibit in *The Houston Post* Society page. Ridiculous! She fed the hotel sheet, smelling of bleach, through the press and wiped the sweat from her temple, then shook her head in disgust. Was it worth having all that money if it meant being on display? She pictured herself wearing the newest styled gowns and opulent jewels and decided it would be worth it. They were lucky people. And she wanted what they had.

Emma worked ten-hour days. It'd been tough getting enough time off to spend a day, or even a few hours, with Sonny. He was in school now, which meant seeing him on a weekend or evening only. Allene supplied information whenever Emma sent correspondence, but she knew it was done begrudgingly. She clenched her jaw. That woman was one of the strangest Emma had come across—always fussing over Sonny. Emma hated that Allene was soft-spoken, regal, and gentle. It was obvious what Bo saw in her, and it bothered Emma that she was Allene's opposite. Her stomach hardened with jealousy.

Emma worked another sheet into the rollers, careful not to touch the long, hot, rotating canisters. Her hands were scarred from the burns they caused, the heat in the room from steam oppressive. Emma wiped her forehead again. Sometimes workers swooned from the temperatures. To the chagrin of the modest girls, Emma wore her thinnest dresses to work. It was those same foolish girls who were the ones fainting.

The laundry work was monotonously boring. Anyone without a brain could do it. But without skills to speak of, Emma couldn't find other work. She was right where Charlie wanted her to be, and it bothered her. After five years of marriage, she still didn't love him. They were comfortable together, she supposed, and he did give her boys some security. She knew too well how it felt to grow up without security. And it wasn't in Charlie to push his weight around and get violent with the boys, as her father had. She'd finally found a man she could trust but she didn't love him.

Emma fed another sheet through the rollers. The woman working by her side hated Emma, and they never conversed. So be it. She was used to being shunned by women who thought they were morally pure.

Usually Sunday was Emma's day off, but she'd changed shifts with another girl to have Monday off. She had plans to spend the Fourth of July with Sonny. During the times she'd spent with him, Bo was always out of town. Her hopes of Sonny having a father seemed to not be coming to fruition. In his absence, Allene smothered Sonny, which he didn't seem to mind. Emma did. Allene and Sonny's intimacy wasn't natural.

As time went on, Emma's desires for Bo waned. She still wasn't positive the love she thought they'd had had ever been real. And realistically, he seemed happy with his lifestyle on the road, and she didn't think he wanted to upset having his docile wife and child always there when he came home. Emma was more than sure he had whores wherever he went, probably favorites he visited in certain cities. He was that kind of man, with nothing more to offer than he'd already given her. Their time was over. Even with these sobering thoughts, it didn't stop her from sometimes dreaming of being his mistress again and having him shower her with gifts, and, most importantly, give her closer access to Sonny.

***

When Emma met Allene and Sonny at the agreed upon location near the San Jacinto Battleground Park, to her surprise, Bo made an appearance. But both he and Allene acted cold, hardly acknowledging Emma's arrival. Averting their eyes.

Sonny greeted her in a much kinder fashion. "Good afternoon, Mrs. Koenig. I hope you have been well."

She smiled at the handsome boy. "Yes, very well, thank you."

"I've rented a yacht at Burnet Bay." Bo didn't glance at Emma while he explained the plan for the day. "We shall have a day of fishing and later view the fireworks from the water."

Sonny clapped, thrilled with the plans. Emma wasn't surprised Bo had come up with a way to be near the party atmosphere, but far enough away from prying ears and eyes not to figure out who Emma was or why she was with them.

They rode in Bo's automobile to the pier where a yacht waited. Emma and Sonny sat in the backseat of the Studebaker with the top down. Sonny allowed Emma to drape her arm around him. Strange that she rarely thought to do the same with George and Ernest. Somehow, these times with Sonny were surreal. She stepped outside herself and became someone she wanted to be but wasn't.

Allene occasionally glanced back at them with a sour look not unseen through her motoring veil. "Is it too windy, Sonny? Father can put the top on."

"No Mother, it's wonderful!" Sonny said with a large grin on his face.

"Be sure and tell me if you get a chill."

Once on the boat, they cruised past other sailboats and yachts full of people celebrating in style, laughter and music floating across the water. The weather perfect, with clear blue skies as they sailed south through Burnet Bay towards Tabbs Bay. Bo helped Sonny bait a hook and then left him fishing while he maneuvered the boat through the crowded waters.

Allene felt the movement too keenly and excused herself to lie down in the cabin.

Emma went to the bow to recline. Removing her shift, she surveyed her new orange bathing suit with the low, square Dutch neckline, hoping her slender body appeared pleasing. The suit cost her $3.98, almost a week's wages. She opted to not wear the ugly black stockings that came with it.

She stretched out on a cushion and gloried in the sun and soft wind on her skin. The rocking of the boat soothed her cares. She closed her eyes and leaned back, all memories of the laundry work and Charlie and her boys buried in repulsion.

She must have dozed because when she opened her eyes, she found the motor quiet and Bo staring at her in a way she hadn't seen in years. She shifted into what she hoped to be a seductive recline and arched an eyebrow at him.

"How has life treated you, Emma?" His eyes smoldered warm, but he smiled like a snake.

She grinned at him as if there hadn't been so much history and heartache. "If you really want to know, it's been hell."

"I'm sorry to hear it. You've always had so much life in you, I'm surprised you haven't made a success of it."

Emma wondered where he was going with the conversation. "I'm no longer in the entertainment business."

Bo laughed. "That's a shame. You were one of the best *entertainers* I've ever known."

Was he mocking her? Should she feel hurt?

He anchored the boat and gaped at her with that old desire in his eyes as he approached the bow.

Emma caught her breath.

"Father," Sonny called from the stern, breaking their moment. "I've lost my bait again. Can you help me?"

Bo went to help his son.

Emma followed. "Do you have another fishing pole? I'd like to give it a try," Emma said, trying to shake off what just happened.

"Certainly." Bo went to retrieve one.

By the time he had her hook baited, Allene came back on deck and gave Emma's bare legs a look of disgust.

Allene stayed at Bo's side. There was never another opportunity to be alone with him, but Emma enjoyed her time fishing next to Sonny. He was inquisitive and asked many questions of all of them, acting as if he were an adult himself.

"How deep is the water, Father?" and "Should it not be salt water so close to the ocean?" and "Why do the fish not see the string attached to the bait?" When he caught a fish, he asked, "Why does the fishing rod bend and not break?"

Emma didn't know the answers and kept out of the interchanges until Bo and Allene drew close together, in a quiet conversation together.

"How's school going for you, Sonny?" Emma asked.

"I don't like school."

"Why not? You is such a smart boy."

"It's boring."

"Do you have nice playmates?"

"I suppose." He shrugged.

Was there a way she could observe him at school without being detected?

They anchored again near the mouth of Trinity Bay and ate out of a large picnic basket filled with watermelon, wine, cheese, caviar on crackers, and smoked salmon. As night came on, Emma's skin felt tight with too much sun. She slipped into her shift. She would have enjoyed a nap on the rocking boat, but suddenly fireworks burst from the sky over Morgan's Point.

Sonny exclaimed his awe with a gasp. "Look at the lovely colors."

The fireworks tumbled down toward the water, reflecting their glow. With a boom, more fireworks burst upward. Some showered so close Emma feared cinders would land on them. She laughed heartily.

Allene glared at her.

Sonny jumped up and down. "Did you see that, Mother? They are so close!"

"Yes," Emma answered automatically.

Allene squinted her eyes at her and turned to Bo. "Do you think we should move further away?" she asked him.

"Certainly not." Bo glanced at Emma, then grinned and winked.

She had been casting Bo out of her heart for years, and that one smile reeled him right back in.

CHAPTER TWENTY-EIGHT

Ora

The Sharp-Hughes Tool Company was so successful, they sponsored a Houston baseball team. In 1912, the Sharp-Hughes team played against the Coca Cola team. Walter Sharp became as rich and famous as Howard Hughes Sr. In fact, he was probably more loved by Houstonians, who believed him a man of character who invested in their city. Surprisingly, he died suddenly near the end of 1912, at the age of forty-two, probably of a ruptured appendix. He left his half interest in the tool company to his wife Estelle, Allene's best friend. The company retained its name of Sharp-Hughes, but in 1913, Estelle became alarmed over the way Howard Sr. spent money on frivolous parties and travel. She feared he'd bankrupt the company. Estelle made up the deficits, but eventually decided to sell her interest in the company to Ed Prather, an oil man and past business partner to both Sharp and Hughes. The sale made Estelle wealthy, and she became a philanthropist in Houston, spending her money on broadening the interests of young Houston women.

Sonny attended the Montrose School where he was often late and had little interest in learning. His three main playmates were Dudley Sharp, Mark Edwin Andrews, and Mary Cullinan. His best friend Dudley later said of him, "Howard was a strange boy. Very shy and very lonely."

***

Emma ~ November 1912

At dusk, Emma walked the mile between her house and Model Laundry. The days had gotten shorter and colder. Although it would have been a more direct route to pass through the bordello district, she avoided it. She'd tired of being the object of man's lust, and it depressed her to see the girls in their stylish clothing calling out seductively. Reminders of her past led to thoughts of Bo and the time he was friendly on the yacht. Once she got home and didn't hear from him, she came to her senses. Nothing had changed between them.

It had become too easy to blame men for her unhappiness.

Life was about getting through the monotonous job of passing laundry through the machines until she could finally go home to a bottle of whiskey. Charlie always stopped her at two glasses, but there were nights when she snuck more.

Uncharacteristically, this night George met her at the top of the stairs. The music from the beer parlor echoed up, and they both stepped inside their home and closed the door. The noise and music of the saloon vibrated the floor, but it was something they'd gotten used to and hardly acknowledged.

"I bell-hopped today for Mr. Rockefeller." George beamed. As he neared adolescence, his wiry, dish-water-blond hair had darkened, and his freckles were disappearing. Now that he was turning into a man, she tried to bring to memory who his father was—someone who probably resembled George, with gray eyes and a narrow face. As hard as she tried, she couldn't remember that face from the past.

"Mr. Rockefeller? John D.?" Emma asked, surprised.

"I reckon."

"He's the richest man in the world, son."

George nodded. "That's what they said at work. He just looked like an old man to me, but he must be rich because he tipped a dime when I took his bags to his room." George slid his hand in his pocket, probably fingering the coin. "Charlie told me to tell you he'd be out late playing cards, and that Aunt Eva sent another package. What's she always sending you those newspaper clippings for, anyway?"

"Where is it?"

"I think I left it on your chair."

Emma retrieved the package and opened it, pulling out a thick stack of papers. The last time Emma was with Eva, she told her the true reason behind wanting the clippings. Instead of judging Emma, as she thought Eva might, she was excited to know who her other nephew was and that he was part of a famous oil family in Houston. Eva laughed at herself for not figuring it out on her own. She continued her ritual of searching the newspapers for word of the Hugheses and often sent Emma thick envelopes full of society or business articles.

The largest clipping was actually two newspaper pages, folded over many times. Emma flattened them out on the table. The article was dated November 14, 1912. Written across the top of the front page, the headline read: "King's Ball was Scene of Gorgeous Splendor." The write-up was about an annual celebration called No-Tsu-Oh, which, as silly as it was, Houstonians took seriously. Emma quickly scanned the columns for information about the Hugheses. Bo's business partner Walter Sharp was featured in the center photo and had been crowned "Regent."

Emma flipped the page, and the next picture turned her stomach. Seven-year-old Sonny posed dressed as a royal page in a Louis IV costume, according to the caption. He wore a plumed hat, white satin breeches and blouse with gold lace. He was not smiling.

"What's all that about?" George stepped to the table.

Emma whiffed cigarette smoke, which confirmed her suspicions that he smoked behind her back. "The rich is crazy people. Look at how they play dress-up and act foolish while we is working hard for ten cents an hour."

"Yeah, well, I wouldn't mind being crazy for a while."

Emma shook her head. "You see this boy?" She pointed to the photo of Sonny and read the article aloud to George, who had little learning. "'*His outfit was lined with lavender satin and he wore satin slippers with jeweled buckles.*' Don't they have anything better to do with their time and money? What fools! They're turning him into a milksop, poor boy. I bet he hates it."

"Who is he, Ma?"

"Oh, the son of an old friend." Emma's heart ached a little with the partial lie. Guilt for not letting George know he had another brother caused her to shift about in her chair.

"He looks like a sissy."

"I do agree." Emma felt sad for Sonny and angry at Allene. The photo reminded her of how little influence she had in her son's life. She viewed George in his old, stained shirt and hand-me-down trousers that he cherished because they weren't knickers. Would George have more power to endure life's challenges than Sonny? Perhaps so, but probably not as many opportunities for success. "Success is measured by money in this world of ours," she said more to herself than George.

"Mr. Rockefeller said if I saved my tip, I'd be wealthy someday."

Emma's raw whiskey-throat sent out a bark. "You take his advice. I'll let you keep the dime if you save it." She knew it was soon to burn a hole in his pocket, and he'd spend it forthwith—probably on cigarettes.

CHAPTER TWENTY-NINE

Ora

In 1913, the Koenig's moved away from the upstairs dwelling over the beer parlor to a house at 4111 Avenue H, which no longer stands. I could not find tax information about its history. Charlie went back to working at the docks, while Emma continued at Model Laundry. At some point as a young child, Ernest worked as a messenger boy for Mackay Tel-Cable Company. I imagine this meant he bicycled around the island to deliver typed copies of telegraphed messages to the residents of Galveston. George continued his work as a bellhop at the Hotel Galvez.

When Emma's mother, Mary, moved in with them, the family dynamic changed. This is what could have initiated the move to Avenue H. The house probably had an extra bedroom for her. Since Peter's death in 1903, Mary had moved almost every year or two, living in the homes of Hy, Paul, Eva—now on her third marriage—and with the family of her deceased daughter, Lottie. Lottie's widower, Anton Readler, had remarried and was raising three of Mary's grandchildren.

If Hy had lived, he may have kept the responsibility of caring for his mother, as he was doing at the time of his death in 1906. In 1908, Mary filed suit in the district court against the Galveston, Houston and Henderson Railroad company to recover damages to the amount of $10,000 for the death of her son. As plaintiff, she alleged her son was her only support. In 1910, the Fifty-fifth District Court dismissed her suit for "want of prosecution."

1913 was the first time I found a record of Mary living with Emma in Galveston. Emma had reached her 31st birthday that year.

***

Emma ~ August 1913

Streetlights lit her way home in the dark by the time Emma got off work. She'd been working twelve-hour shifts to cover the two machine operators on leave after giving birth. Instead of the owner hiring more workers, he chose to work his employees longer hours until the new mothers returned.

Emma walked home slowly, her feet aching with each step. The night air warm, she wiped moisture from her neck and rubbed a sore spot on her lower back, groaning in discomfort.

She stepped into her house and the disappointment at not smelling supper added to her exhaustion. Mama sat in Emma's favorite chair, which rankled her further. She wanted nothing more than to sit and take her shoes off before eating supper, but it wasn't worth asking Mama to move or ask why she hadn't made the meal. Emma knew the answers.

"Where's Charlie?" Emma asked.

"Georgy didn't come home. Charlie went to the hotel to find out when he left and if anyone knows his whereabouts."

Emma sighed and sat in Charlie's chair. "He probably rode his bike to Paul's again." She wasn't worried. "George is fourteen, almost a man. He knows how to take care of hisself." He would balk if Emma interfered with his life.

She took her shoes off and massaged a foot. The pressure of her fingers on the sore spots sent sharp pains up her leg, yet the massaging somehow felt good.

Mama stared at her as if contemplating and finally said, "You wasn't much older when you left home. If you'd been around more, maybe you'd have learned to make better decisions and teach Georgy to get a decent job like Paul did."

Paul was Mama's favorite, Emma had heard it before, but this time it dug deeper than usual. Perhaps because she was tired or because she was weary of her mother never saying anything nice, always finding fault and certainly not appreciative of what Emma did to pay for Mama's keep.

Heat rose to Emma's face. "You sit here all day expecting to be cared for, taking what I give without so much as a thank you." Her anger caused her voice to rise. "I took you in because Eva had enough of you."

Mama stared, speechless. Her thin, messy hair, now completely white and piled on her head, hung loose around her hairline. Emma remembered the days when she helped Mama look nice. Now animosity was imprinted in the deep wrinkles of Mama's face, and no one cared what she looked like.

Ernest stepped out of his bedroom, his jaw clenched and his eyes worried. "What's going on?"

Emma ignored him and turned to Mama. "You're only one person. One person! Why can't you take care of yourself?" Raising her voice with each word, the bitterness burned through her body. Like the shooting pains in her foot, somehow it felt good to let the soreness out.

"You disrespectful brat. You is the most selfish woman I've ever known." Mama's nostrils flared and lips puckered.

"Selfish?" Emma could hardly put into words her thoughts. The unfairness scorched her chest in outrage. "That's the pot calling the kettle black. You've always complained that you felt so poorly and could never do a thing for anyone—especially your own children." Emma stood. "Selfish—"

Charlie stepped into the house and quickly shut the door. "I can hear yelling from a block avay, voman."

The way he said 'voman' brought Emma instantly to memories of her cruel father. She wanted to slap him.

Charlie stepped closer. "Let's show respect. Maybe you should appreciate having a mother?"

"You know nothing. Just because your mother were a saint, don't mean they all is. Certainly not this woman." She threw her arm out toward Mama. "I might as well have not had a mother. She's been another child to raise along with Eva and Hy."

Mama cried and sputtered indistinguishable words.

Emma spun around. "Oh, please. Your imagined frailty is disgraceful." She picked up her shoes and quickly walked past Charlie and Ernest out the door.

Down the street, she sat on a curb and slipped her shoes on. She knew one place to find relief and headed to her favorite saloon.

Her anger didn't subside as she walked. Over and over, she played out the argument in her head. The hurtful words her mother had said tightened Emma's throat until she couldn't swallow. As a child, she'd turned off her expectations of Mama ever caring for her. As of late, to protect herself from hurt, she'd had to distance herself from the memories of the past and not expect Mama to be appreciative of a place to live and food in her belly.

Emma herself wasn't the best mother, but she deliberately never indulged her boys. She wanted them independent, unlike her mother. She was teaching them to take care of themselves— to stand on their own two feet. Life was hard, and they needed to endure well. Now that she'd seen how the Hugheses lived, she realized what life must have been like for Mama as a child. Mama still thought she needed someone to serve her night and day. She would never understand the value of self-reliance.

Emma thought about Sonny. Was Allene teaching him to be strong and independent? Emma didn't think so. Yet she was impressed with Sonny. Did she love Sonny more than George and Ernest? She spent the next ten minutes weighing it out in her mind and concluded that if she were raising Sonny, he would be a stronger person. She loved more and was envious of Sonny's *lifestyle*.

She loved her boys all the same, she reckoned. Each was a reminder of his father. George, the quiet and mysterious one she could never figure out, like she couldn't figure out who his father was. Ernest, with his easy-going nature, reminded her of Jack when they first met and the reason she fell in love with him. Sonny, with his mind for mechanics, was like Bo. Although wealthy, his father was strong and independent and certainly an entrepreneur, and she hoped these qualities would be taught to Sonny. She worried that Bo needed to be in Sonny's life more.

She was almost to the saloon when Ernest jogged up. "Come back home, Ma. I'm sure Granny didn't mean it, and Charlie's worried 'bout ya."

Her thirst for drink was stronger than her need to appease Ernest—or anyone at home. She didn't believe they cared about how she felt anyway. "You'll see me at home after Granny goes to bed. Now get on with y'all. You have an early day's work tomorrow." She pushed past Ernest and entered the saloon.

CHAPTER THIRTY

Ora

In 1913, at the age of eight, Sonny entered the Prosso School, a small private institution of ten teachers and thirty students. With an emphasis on individuality, Prosso prepared Houston's young elite for prep school in the East. The school was held in a small house owned by a husband-and-wife team who had both earned doctorates. A fellow classmate of Howard Jr.'s called it "a cram school," pushing the children to memorize as much as possible. She also remembered the wonderful picnic dinner party given for Howard Jr. by his mother, saying, "Every child in the school was invited."

The school had a strict learning structure that challenged Sonny to break from his shyness with peers. Pushed by his teachers, he gave a one-on-one recitation in each of his subjects every day.

As for the social aspect, the director reported to Howard Sr. that Sonny was being taunted and called "sissy" by the other boys. He also believed that Sonny had been "brought up to feel his superiority," which concerned the director enough to suggest to Howard Sr. that Sonny "needs to feel he is a part of the world, instead of the larger or better parts."

When Sonny was ten, he was made King of the May at Christ Church Cathedral's annual May Day celebration. His photograph appeared in the newspaper again as he stood regally in his satin costume. Allene may have had a hand in getting him crowned king. She'd written to the Church, "Howard is both tall and polite, and would make an excellent King of the May Fete. I feel the enclosed check for $250 might be used to ensure a successful day."

At the end of the year, Sonny asked for a black horse for Christmas. He was so certain he'd get the horse that when he sat on Santa's lap, he asked for a saddle. He received both saddle and horse on Christmas.

His playmate, Mary Cullinan, said, "We used to play at Dudley's. Dudley and Howard were both inventors and they had a workshop. It had all kinds of chemical things, not toys but real things…Playing any game, he [Sonny] always had some theory. And he wanted to know the mathematics of everything."

***

Emma ~ Spring 1915

On the Hughes's wide porch, Emma and Allene sat in black painted rattan chairs, more ornate than Emma had realized wicker furniture could be. Accompanied by a servant, Sonny stepped out. He'd grown tall, his hair now dark brown.

"It's nice to see you again, Mrs. Koenig," Sonny said. "I hope your visit will be pleasant. How long will you be able to stay?"

Allene cringed ever-so-slightly. She said as little as possible when Emma visited.

Emma raised her chin. "Only until dark, Sonny, then I must catch the train to Galveston."

"I do love Galveston. Mother took my cousins and me there recently. We had a delightful time."

"You must tell me next time you come."

Allene's mouth turned down and eyes hardened.

"I can show you the high dive at Crystal Palace bath house and rides at Electric Park, and we could go fishing off Bettison's pier." Emma grinned at Sonny, whose face lit with excitement. "There is no mosquitoes out at that pier," she added for Allene's benefit.

"I would enjoy that immensely."

Children's laughter caught Sonny's attention. A little girl and boy ran up to the white gate surrounding the yard. The girl called out, "Sonny, can you play?"

Sonny turned to Allene. "May I, Mother?"

Allene crinkled her brow. "Are you healthy Mary and Dudley?" she called out.

"Yes, Mrs. Hughes," they said in unison, no surprise evident by her question.

Neither was Emma surprised. She'd come to detest Allene's fixation on keeping Sonny healthy.

"All right children, you may play here in the yard for fifteen minutes."

Dudley unlatched the gate and Sonny met his friends at a wide, wooden swing hanging from a giant oak.

Emma and Allene didn't talk as they watched the youngsters at play. The children took turns swinging high, taking bets on who could go the farthest when they jumped off the swing. Sonny wasn't interested in swinging. Instead, he took a stick and marked the spots where Mary and Dudley landed.

He was a curious boy who seemed to observe everything. He seldom played like a child. When other kids laughed and shouted, he stayed quiet.

"Don't jump yet," he called to Dudley, who pumped his legs as he tried to get the swing to go as high as possible. "I want to work out the curve of the swing and estimate where you'll land."

Unusual child. *Her* child.

Dudley pumped so high that as he fell back the ropes of the swing slackened.

Sonny positioned himself where it looked like he had the best view, then threw a small twig to where he probably guessed Dudley would land. "Okay, jump!"

Dudley flew off the swing, Sonny watching his trajectory, while Dudley landed on top of the twig laughing. "Teach me how you figured that." He ran to Sonny.

Pumping her legs, Mary swung as high as she could, and again Sonny watched the curve of her flight, throwing a twig to pinpoint her potential landing spot. Her skirts billowed like a parachute as she sailed through the sky and landed on the twig.

"Okay, now you do it Sonny, while I watch," Dudley said.

Sonny stared at the ground. "I'd rather you did it again," he said quietly.

Dudley shrugged his shoulders and ran back to the swing for another flight through the air.

Sonny talked so well to adults, but he didn't seem to know how to be with other children.

CHAPTER THIRTY-ONE

Ora

Galveston's Model Laundry, Emma's place of employment, had been rebuilt into an impressive two-story, large commercial building in 1913. A square-shaped structure built of reinforced concrete with brick and tile facing, it had a flat roof. Decorative corbeling surrounded that roofline and parapets defined the corners. Six sections of large glass windows covered each side of the building, both upper and lower floors, making the building appear to be more glass than concrete—a modern look for the time. In the *1913 Galveston City Directory*, the advertisement for Model Laundry claimed the building to be "Our New Fire-Proof Home." It was the only steam laundry in Galveston at the time.

In the summer of 1915, both George and Ernest went to work for Model Laundry. On the day of a hurricane barreling toward Galveston, they were there with Emma.

***

Emma ~ August 17, 1915

Like a woman's high-pitched scream, the wind pushed its way into every crack of the building. It rattled the windows of the second floor until they shook as if they'd blow in at any moment. The air smelled of salty rain.

Emma's stomach soured with the emotions that came with haunting memories of the 1900 hurricane. Her weakest point in life had been that night. She didn't think she could withstand another like it.

Ernest came trotting up to her, having left his post as did many others. She straightened her shoulders and tried to not show the distress building in her gut.

Tall for thirteen, he stood over six feet with dark brown hair, a handsome face, and a deep cleft in his chin. He was almost the age Hy had been in 1900. "Do you think it's a hurricane, Ma?" His blue eyes widened with concern.

Emma pushed out a tense breath. "It might be." She managed to keep her voice from wavering. "Let's find George." She let go of the linen tablecloth that was partially through the rollers.

She hoped the new seawall would keep the flooding back, but there was nothing to keep flying debris from coming through the windows. Grabbing Ernest's elbow, she pulled him toward the center of the building, away from the windows, joining many other workers.

People shouted and called to one another, some left to go home.

As they searched for George, the electric lights went out. Emma's heart dropped, expecting the ceiling above to cave in like it had at the Tremont Hotel.

The windows barely let through enough light for them to continue their search. They had to approach half-a-dozen boys before finding George crouched near the dye vats with a friend.

"Damn storm!" Angry, not obviously scared, George glowered at no one specifically, then looked at Emma with sharp eyes. "You'd think they could have given us the day off. This morning people all over town warned the storm was going to be a hurricane. Should we go home?"

She'd experienced a lot of tropical storms since living on the island—since 1900 even—and this could be just that. "I'm not sure if we is better off tryin' to get home or stayin' where we is. In nineteen-hundred, people went to the strongest built structures." Was this new building a strong structure? She glanced around to gauge what others were doing. Maybe twenty were within vision and talking amongst themselves. "This building is well built, but the windows worry me," Emma said.

An awning from downstairs tore off and flipped up into a window near them. The awning's metal frame broke the glass. The shattering explosion dropped Emma to the floor. "Get down," she yelled.

Wind howled through the room and more windows shattered as though missiles shot, launched from a cannon. Wind whipped at their hair and clothing. Debris landed close by. Rain pelted as if they were outside in the storm.

Emma licked her lips. Salt water. She felt faint. *Hold it together, Emma!*

Something large, maybe cement, hit Ernest on the arm, making him cry out.

Pushing her wet hair out of her eyes, Emma scrutinized his arm. It would bruise but hadn't broken skin or bone. "You'll be fine." She sounded unfeeling, but she didn't want her boys to panic or know her fear. For them she'd act as calm as possible, but she knew too well what could happen.

She bit her trembling lip as memories came unbidden of the stench and sight of bloated bodies, people wailing incoherently, massive piles of wood from destroyed homes strewn throughout the island. Burning pyres of bodies. She shuddered.

"Let's crawl between the machines," George yelled over the noise.

George's friend ran off with some other young men. Emma and the boys crawled under the dye vats as far away from the windows as possible. At fifteen, George was slender and somewhat small. But for Ernest, it was a tight squeeze.

The noise of metal, bricks, and laundry paraphernalia hitting against surfaces continued for hours. People from downstairs came up, yelling that the first floor was flooding. They crowded around Emma and the boys, giving them more protection from flying debris. Some cried out as they were injured, others bemoaned their fears or worries about loved ones not with them. Children screamed and wailed.

This time Emma couldn't pray. When did anyone—God or otherwise—help her with anything?

Shielded by the vats and people, the noise became somewhat dulled. Ernest lay on his stomach, his forehead on crossed arms. He sniffled.

Emma wanted to comfort him but was afraid if she reached out and placed a hand on his back, he'd sob uncontrollably. She didn't want that, so she turned away and tried to remember the last time she'd cried. Maybe it was when she'd left baby Sonny almost ten years ago.

After a while Ernest quieted and asked, "Do you think Charlie and Granny is all right?"

"I'm sure they's fine." Emma had been wondering about them also. If Charlie got to Mama, he would do all he could to protect her.

Late in the afternoon, it became quiet, without even the whistling of wind. With the sky still dark, Emma wondered if the eye of the storm was passing, or if it was over. If it was the eye, shouldn't the sky be clear?

People started moving away from where they hunkered under the vats. Some injured and bleeding. Fabric had been blown across machinery, onto people, and even hung from light fixtures. They used some of it to bandage cuts.

"You two stay here. I'm going to look out a window." *Please let there be no dead bodies in the streets.* She didn't want her boys to be left with that memory too.

She pushed herself out of their cramped space and stood on stiff, wobbly legs. As she moved with others toward the blown-out windows, her shoes crunched on broken glass. Every building in view sustained some kind of damage, one wooden structure leaned precariously. Water had risen at least four to five feet, flooding the streets. Some people cautiously ventured out of buildings, wading through water up to their thighs.

Not realizing she'd been holding her breath, she let it out slowly. There were no dead or bleeding bodies.

"Do you think it's over?" someone nervously yelled from a building below.

"Not likely," came a response.

A woman called, "There's injured people in here. What should we do?" She sounded near tears.

"Treat their injuries as well as possible," a much calmer voice replied. "Before moving them, wait for the storm to subside . . . if you can."

Emma moved back under the vats with the boys. "We need to wait a little longer." She didn't want to tell them that what they experienced may happen again with winds coming at them from the other direction.

George complained but stayed put.

Wet and exhausted, Ernest actually slept.

Many people left.

After another hour, George said, "I'm not waiting here no longer."

The winds hadn't returned, just the rain, and Emma could only hope they were safe. They scooted out.

"Let's stay near the vats in case we need the coverage again," she said.

"Why?" Ernest asked.

"I'm not staying." George's normally pale face turned red.

Before Emma replied, she smelled smoke. "Wait, George." She grabbed his sleeve.

He scowled, yanking his arm away, and moved to some boys near his age. But he didn't leave.

Others in the building gathered together, talking amongst themselves and wondering where the smoke came from and what they should do.

A woman by a window called out, "There's a building burning down the street. Nothing coming from below."

They waited. And waited. Evening fell, and it would be foolish to try and get home through flood waters in the dark. "We'll sleep here and go home in the morning," she said loud enough for George to hear.

"Ain't you worried about Granny and Charlie?" Ernest asked.

"There's nothing I can do for them now."

"Strike me blind! Why does that reply not surprise me?" George glowered at her as if he hated her.

"Let off, George." Ernest said.

"Shut up, Ern." George stalked over to Emma. "I bet you'd like some whiskey about now."

Ernest pushed him, and George raised a fist near Ernest's face. "Try that again and I'll knock you off your feet."

"Stop it!" Emma moved between them, wanting to smack George herself. "We've got enough problems without you two acting like fools."

They moved apart and settled in for the night. Emma slept fitfully. George stayed near his friends, Ernest near her. They arose at first light. The flood waters were gone and the sky blue.

On the way home, George walked in front, quiet about his thoughts as they passed homes missing siding, doors, and windows, some destroyed beyond repair. She watched him closely. Had the ravages of the storm sobered him?

The destruction was nowhere near as devastating as the storm in 1900. Talk on the street was that the seawall was partly damaged and resulted in the flooding. What frightened Emma the most was when she heard the causeway was damaged and no one would be leaving or coming to the island—relief would not reach them anytime soon. She hoped they had enough food and water.

They met Charlie on the street before they arrived home, his face visibly relieved. "I vahs on my vahy to laundry." He hugged each one of them. To Emma he said, "Granny and I vaited out storm upstairs and house held strong. Flood vahters ruined much furniture."

Inside the house, she found chairs, the table, a trunk, muddy bedding, and rugs all tangled together in a giant heap. According to Charlie, everything had floated up to the ceiling, and this was what they were left with when the swirling water receded.

Mama took one look at Emma and the boys and plopped onto the stairs, tears filling her eyes. She covered her face and sobbed in relief.

Touched, Emma didn't know how to respond. She pulled an upside-down chair off the top pile of furniture and unwound a muddy and ruined curtain intertwining its legs.

"It's all right, Granny," Ernest said, going to her and patting her on the shoulder.

"You so cold," Charlie whispered to Emma. He wasn't talking about the temperature of her skin.

She hated herself for how unfeeling she'd gotten toward people, but it was easier to not care. Certainly, less painful.

***

Ora

A tropical storm had tracked westward over the Atlantic Ocean in August 1915. As it barreled through the Caribbean Sea, it passed south of Puerto Rico, but made landfall in Jamaica where it caused heavy damage. The storm brushed the western tip of Cuba then became a hurricane. Winds rapidly intensified over the warm waters of the Gulf of Mexico. On August 17th, it hit Galveston at 135 mph, causing $50 million in damages and hundreds of injuries. There were eleven fatalities in downtown Galveston, forty-two more across the island, and one-hundred and two people were reported missing offshore and presumed dead.

Hydrick Photographs

George Neverson Hydrick

Ernest Albert Hydrick

CHAPTER THIRTY-TWO

Ora

From a taped oral interview administered by my father on July 6, 1980, my grandfather, George Hydrick, said, "My brother and I worked together at the Model Laundry in Galveston, Texas. We'd come home from work, get ready, and go to the beach to go swimming. After we come home swimming, we'd go dancing that night at the Crystal Palace. We'd have a good time! They had an Olympic size pool to jump into. I climbed a ninety-foot ladder to the tower. That was every Sunday—to show off, you know. Practically every Sunday. I was about seventeen—sixteen when I did that. They had a Crystal Palace park with all kinds of rides. It was an amusement park in those days. Those were the good old days!

"I was a marker in the laundry. Ernest was in charge of the laundry washing department."

***

Emma ~ End of 1915

Emma set her empty whiskey glass on the pile of unwashed dishes in the sink. She sighed heavily and then went to work peeling potatoes for supper.

The rumblings of an automobile in front of her house caused her to grumble. Gas-powered vehicles had become so commonplace on the island that Emma cursed the noise and stink. The automobile idled in front of her house. She threw the knife down with a clunk.

Wrapping a shawl around herself, she stepped out into the cold. She couldn't have been more surprised to find Paul tightening leather straps around a wicker basket at the back of the still-running auto, its exhaust puffing smoke into the air.

Her mood instantly changed. "What in heaven's name is you doing here?" she asked with a grin.

Paul glanced up. "Hey, sis." He wasn't smiling.

Same old serious Paul.

"Why don't you turn that noise off and come in?" she asked.

"Can't chance it with that crank. May never start again."

Emma rolled her eyes. The junker had a metal frame for a buggy cover, like a skeleton with no skin. Its black paint had faded to gray and chipped in places, as if it had been hit with a sledge hammer a few hundred times. It was small, with seating for two, and running boards that emerged like wings as they rose over the skinny, spoked wheels.

"Who pawned that pile of junk off on you?" Emma chuckled.

Even though she said it jokingly, Paul still didn't smile. He finished with the straps and came around the car, placing a hand on the cracking leather seat. "I have plans to fix her up."

Her? Emma rolled her eyes again. "Well, do we have to visit out here then?"

"I've come for Ma," Paul said. "Is she ready?"

Shocked, Emma's muscles tensed. "Does she know you is coming?"

"George sent me a cable that she's ready to come to my house. Said she wanted to leave Galveston."

Emma clenched her hands and her lungs constricted. "It's the first I've heard of it." Although it wouldn't bother her in the least if Mama left, she didn't appreciate decisions made behind her back. She pulled back her shoulders, alleviating some of the pain in her chest.

"Well?" Paul shifted from one foot to the other, avoiding eye contact. "Hell, Emma, what's that pile of garbage in front of your house?"

Emma didn't need to look to know he referred to the broken furniture and filthy rugs they had dragged out of the house after the storm. "Ruined by the hurricane."

"That one hit Houston hard, too, but it were three months ago." He looked at her in a way that made her feel small.

"Everyone's busy workin' all day. It'll get taken care of," she said.

"Well, tell the boys to burn it out back."

"Hey," George shouted and waved from down the street where he was walking with Ernest. Both boys ran toward them.

"Where you boys been? There's work here." Paul gave them as little a greeting as he had Emma and pointed to the pile of rubbish.

Ernest held up a chalkware monkey with painted black eyes and pointed ears. It had a slit in the back to insert coins. "Look what I won at Electric Park."

"*Everyone's* busy at work?" Paul said directly to Emma, mocking her.

Emma ignored him. "Your uncle's here to get Granny."

"Can I go, too?" George asked, hope evident on his face.

"I have room for one, and that's Granny," Paul said, pointing to his cracked leather seat.

"Awh!" George remarked. "I could stand on the running board."

"I could, too," Ernest added.

Emma was betrayed. She crossed her arms over her chest. "Bite the hand that feeds you, would ya?"

"I can't blame them," Paul remarked. "Look at yourself, Emma."

She hadn't washed or changed in two days. Threads hung at the hem of her old, dirty dress, torn across the bottom. Self-consciously, she pulled her hair back, realizing she'd forgotten to pin it up. Was she turning into her mother?

"And your breath is sour with drink."

Emma ran her tongue over her fuzzy teeth. "Who is you to judge me?"

"You used to care about what you looked like. What's happened to you?"

"Life," she snapped.

He took a step back.

"And these boys." She swung her arm out toward George and Ernest, as if accusing them of some terrible crime. "They make life hell. While they're out having a grand-old time, I'm making their meals and cleaning up after them."

"You old hag," George shouted.

Paul quickly turned and pushed George hard, knocking him on his butt.

"Hey!" George's face reddened.

"You don't talk to your mother that way." Paul's voice hardened with indignation.

George stood up, wiping off the seat of his pants. "You did."

"I stated the facts and didn't call her a name." Paul towered over George. He pointed a finger in his face. "You're a punk kid and need to show respect for your elders."

"Yes, sir." George jutted out his chin, still red in the face.

Emma wished she had such command over George's actions. Charlie was too soft on the boys. She had told him that a thousand times.

The door opened. Mama stepped out, dressed for travel with a duster over her dress, satchel in hand, obviously aware Paul had come for her. She had her good hat on and didn't look at Emma as she handed the bag to Paul. He took it and tied it into the wicker basket at the back of his vehicle.

Stepping closer to Paul, George said penitently, "Can I please come, too?"

Paul hesitated. "Ya need to earn your keep at my house, unlike how you do here."

"I can work," George said, looking hopeful.

Ernest kept opening and closing his mouth as if conflicted. He slid a gaze to Emma and then stood a little taller.

"I don't know." Paul looked to Emma.

The deep pain of betrayal tightened her chest. Again. Would she be relieved to have George and his back-talking attitude away from her? She stepped from the group, feeling abandoned. "You're nothing but trouble," she said to George. "I don't care where ya go."

George flinched. "Good riddance, then!"

Paul gave George a threatening look and then opened the door for Mama and helped her step up into the car.

"Thank you, Paul," Mama murmured, then sat and peeked at Emma from under the brim of her hat. "We'll be seeing you, then," she said, her face devoid of emotion.

Emma didn't know how to answer, so she nodded and went into the house.

She was finishing peeling potatoes when Charlie arrived home from the docks. He opened the door and cold air and the stink of his body wafted her way. His clothes were as filthy as hers. As she remembered the things Paul had said, her face warmed in embarrassment. She'd need to do laundry on her day off, although it was the last thing she wanted to do after doing it all week at work.

She stared toward the closed bedroom door where behind it Ernest probably lay on his bed, moping about being left behind.

Charlie had stopped acknowledging Emma's presence after a fight they'd had weeks before about her disinterest in his wellbeing and needs. She didn't tell him sex hurt because it would be admitting what that might mean, and she didn't want him hounding her about going to a doctor.

The power she once felt by fulfilling men's desires was gone. It appeared she no longer had a say in her destiny and Charlie had more power over her than she cared to think about.

She retrieved a new bottle of whiskey from the lower cupboard and a dirty glass from the top of the dishes in the sink. Rubbing her sore lower back, she poured herself some liquor.

Coming closer, Charlie said, "Vee hardly have no money to pay rent, yet you alvays have booze."

"I work damn hard for the money I spend. What makes ya think you can say such a thing to me?" He wasn't going to control her like her father controlled her mother.

Charlie squinted and stepped even closer, and she knew he wasn't going to let this conversation die. "Vee are family. My money our money. Boys' money our money. Yours not ours?"

"My money goes in the pot like all the rest. Don't try and make it sound like I don't care about my family."

He pointed a finger in her face, his eyes cold and hard. "If you love us, show it. You show no feelings."

Emma's pulse sped and she sputtered, "No feelings? Everything I do...*all* I do, is for this family."

"Drinking for family?"

"Oh, shut up, Charlie. Don't get high and mighty on me, ya bastard."

Charlie's nostrils flared. "When last time you touch me?"

He had her. She couldn't remember the last time she even wanted to be intimate. And to be honest, it had nothing to do with the physical pain. She looked away and started cutting the skin off an onion. "I no longer want to touch you." The minute she said it, she regretted it. Charlie had always been good to her. He didn't deserve her unkindness. But he shouldn't be trying to control her. He knew better than that.

He was quiet for a moment and then said, "Then vhy I here?"

"You can leave like all the rest." Her throat tightened.

"Vhat you mean?"

"Paul come and got Mama . . . and George." She swallowed hard. "Ernest wanted to go, too. God only knows why he didn't."

"Vhat you say? Granny gone?" He glanced around the room as if he just noticed it was empty. "George gone too?"

Emma nodded and chopped the onion; her knife so dull she had to saw. The bitter smell made her eyes water. She wiped at one with the back of her hand. If she didn't stay detached from Charlie's words, the tears would become real.

"Emma." Charlie's tone came careful and controlled. "You push everyone out of life. Vhy you do that?"

Why did she do that? She didn't think she did it deliberately. Maybe she wasn't like her mother after all, but more like her father. Hands trembling, she set down the knife, then leaned against the table. "Maybe it's time for you to go too."

His breath stopped short.

She couldn't look at him.

His footsteps faded away, then halted and without turning he said, "I agree. I don't vahnt to be near you anymore, but I love boys. I voen't go far—for Ernest—and maybe George come back."

***

Ora

Emma and Ernest moved into a house at 1620 Avenue L. This house still stands. It is a one story that sits on a street of two-story homes.

Considering what George said when he was interviewed by my father, he probably went to live with Paul multiple times. He said about his Uncle Paul, "He could have made a baseball team the way I understood it, counting Ernest and me." Paul had six sons and lived at 1813 Keene in Houston, near the fire station where he worked.

George said, "He partly raised me. I would move back and forth. Go to Galveston and then back to Houston. I show up, and he'd say 'What are you doing here?' I'd say 'I'd come up to see if I could ride my bicycle up here.' And I would go to see Uncle Paul. He was just like a father too."

George would never answer questions about his mother. When my father asked, "Do you remember anything more about your mother?"

George replied, "No, not a thing." (Taped oral interview administered by my father, July 6, 1980.)

How does someone not remember a thing about a person they lived with off and on—mostly on, I'm sure—for nineteen years?

CHAPTER THIRTY-THREE

Ora

In June of 1916, at the age of ten, Howard Jr. traveled by train to New York with his mother to meet with Howard Sr., who had been in the city for work. They then drove by chauffeured car to Camp Teedyuskung in the Poconos of Pennsylvania, where they left Howard Jr. on his own for the first time in his life.

While he participated in camp until August, Allene stayed in New York at the Vanderbilt Hotel. It appears it was hard for her to be away from Howard Jr., for she often sent letters to her husband regarding her worries and asked Howard Sr. to also send a letter and newspaper clippings about the dangers of "violent germs" to the camp director, Daniel Beard—one of the founders of the Boy Scouts of America—also known as "Chief."

In response, Howard Sr. received a letter from Chief: "Your boy seems to be holding his own here in camp. He is an interesting little chap, full of fun and well liked. Please tell his Mother that the last time I saw him he did not look a bit like he was going to cry. His mouth was open and he was yelling, but he was yelling to the rest of his stockade to hurry up, and get a move on. In fact, he has shown no signs of homesickness at all, and seems very happy."

Allene wasn't satisfied and begged her husband to go with her to retrieve the child. For Howard Jr.'s sake, his father was able to distract Allene by taking her to Newport, Rhode Island, where they mingled with New York and Philadelphia society.

Allene still worried even though Chief sent her a progress report: "Physical condition, bowels, feet, O.K. General appearance, better than when he first entered camp. Heart, much better now." The Instructor's report noted "He cannot stick to one thing very long, but he is doing fairly well in scoutcraft and never gives us any trouble. In birds his effort and deportment is good. In his other studies he is trying hard, but is easily discouraged. Needs someone to show him how and then make him do it."

Allene wrote Chief that she would be visiting her son so she could "see him for a few minutes" to determine his condition. She wrote: "His letters are so short and unsatisfactory that I feel I must talk to him if it is possible before I can decide about leaving him longer." Allene later took Sonny out of camp a few days earlier than planned because of a polio scare in the East.

America entered the Great War, April 6, 1917. Besides losing many young men to serve in the War, Galveston's economy suffered in other ways. The Secretary of War at the time, Newton D. Baker, cracked down on prostitution in an attempt to protect the soldiers from venereal disease. The War Department ordered all vice districts closed and enforced anti-prostitution laws. Between March and August, El Paso, Fort Worth, Galveston, Houston, San Antonio, and Waco officially stepped-up arrests of prostitutes. The Charmerlain–Kahn Act of 1918 provided the first federal funding specifically designated for controlling venereal disease.

Another hit to Galveston's commerce came when Houston finished its Ship Channel in 1917, which drastically reduced the commerce and number of ships using Galveston's port. It never regained its thriving economy.

Before America entered the War, Howard Sr. had been in negotiations to sell a combat device to the English and French. Using similar technology to his conical roller bit, he created a rotary drilling machine that drilled horizontally through the earth to bore mines under enemy trenches a thousand yards away and deposit explosives. Howard Sr. claimed it could do in two days what would normally take months. When the U.S. declared war, Howard Sr., along with his brother Rupert's help, offered the device to the American military. Although Hughes Tool Company made stokes mortars, molds for dummy bombs, and parts for a device used in training airplane machine gunners, red tape proved a hindrance for the rotary drilling device, and it was never used in the battlefield.

In the spring of 1917, Howard Sr. bought a sixty-foot yacht with six staterooms, mahogany floors, brass railings, gold fixtures and a crew of six. He christened it the *Rollerbit* and kept it docked in Galveston.

Sonny feared the excursions on the yacht might keep him from another summer at Camp Teedyuskung. He wrote Chief: "I don't think that I will be able to come up to camp this summer although I would like it very much. We just bought a boat and I think that we will stay here all summer except about one or two months. I hope that the camp is as nice this summer as it was last summer."

But Sonny fell sick in the spring, and his mother decided mountain air might help him after all. This time, Dudley Sharp attended camp with Sonny.

The day after the boys arrived, Allene sent a letter to Chief: "I hope the doctor will keep an eye on him, watching his feet and teeth, and see that he takes his Russian oil every night. I put a large bottle of it in his suitcase, but I am sure he was tempted to throw it out of the car window and he may have done it." She didn't want Howard or Dudley to take a long hike when they first got there, worrying it might tax their resistance. She also didn't want them to eat the camp's flapjacks. She wrote to the stockade leader: "...I am trying hard to overcome too much anxiety over my one chick but don't seem to make much headway...I am afraid you will find him pretty nervous this year. He was so much improved in that respect by last year's camp that I hoped he was outgrowing it and his supersensitiveness [sic] but it seems to have all come back this spring since he has not been so well. That is one reason I was particularly glad for you to have him in your stockade. I think you understand him well enough to help him over the many times he gets his feelings hurt...If you can help Howard to take the teasing without getting hurt and resentful we will surely be lastingly in your debt. Dudley makes friends so much more easily than Howard does and Howard feels that keenly too...If you can help him to forget himself, get along better with boys and perhaps teach him to keep his hut in order, I ask for nothing else."

Because of the War, many of the camp counselors from the previous summer were no longer there and Sonny found the changes not to his liking. It's also probable the other boys were bullying him. He wrote to his mother that he was "having bad dreams, not sleeping well, and feeling tired all the time."

Allene called and asked Chief to have a doctor examine Sonny and to excuse him from arithmetic classes since she was certain it was causing him headaches. Allene was reassured that Sonny was "doing splendidly...I have, so far, noticed no signs of nervousness from him and feel sure that he will be as much benefited in this respect as he was last summer. I am glad to say that I have noticed very few of his faults to which you have called my attention. However, I shall make every effort to rid him of his sensitiveness as much as possible."

It is believed that it was at this time when the Hugheses were in New York at the Vanderbilt Hotel, that Howard Sr. met Eleanor Boardman. To the chagrin of Eleanor's mother, Howard Sr. offered to arrange for the almost-nineteen-year-old to meet his brother, Rupert, who was writing stories for films, hoping he may help launch an acting career for Eleanor.

When Sonny returned from camp in August, Allene was so pleased with his appearance that she wrote to Chief, "He is in better condition, I think, than he has ever been...His cheeks are round and fat and rosy and he is full of 'pep.'"

***

Emma ~ Autumn 1917

When Emma saw the newspaper article about Bo's yacht, she'd asked to sail on it. The only day she could was a Sunday, and it took months before Bo finally agreed, explaining Sonny had been gone all summer.

Paying the extra money to have her hair styled, and wearing a new dress in a shorter style, Emma waited at the docks, which were quieter than usual because of the young men gone to war, and it being a Sunday in autumn. Chilly in the morning, she kept herself warm by pacing, waiting for the Hugheses to arrive. She worried they would stand her up. She walked along the dock, marveling at the sixty-foot yacht moored in its slip, in awe at its grandeur. The boat was painted white, with the mahogany pilot's house and cabin's top floor varnished a shiny, rich honey-orange. It was a beautiful cruiser, and she found herself anxious to sail.

Late morning, Sonny and Bo came walking her way. Sonny had grown tall and lanky, reminding her of Ernest. He wore long, navy trousers, and a suitcoat cut to his thin frame. He ambled as he walked, not like Bo who carried himself with confidence and purpose.

"You look well, Master Howard," she said, smiling warmly.

He appeared surprised to see her. "Thank you, Mrs. Koenig." He hopped onto the boat deck and held out a hand to assist her.

Bo came on slowly. It'd been a few year's since she'd seen him last, and he'd gained weight. As much as Sonny looked young and vigorous, Bo appeared old. Thinning hair and round spectacles made him look like a grandpa. She felt no attraction to him. Was she going to distance herself from all men?

Emma looked behind him. "Where's Allene?" she asked.

"She doesn't care for boating," Bo said. "It makes her sick."

Yes, Emma remembered that now. No wonder Sonny acted surprised to see her. Bo probably didn't tell either Allene or him that she would be joining them. If Allene had known Emma would be alone with her men, she would've braved the nausea. The day suddenly improved, making Emma grin.

Having no more interest in catching Bo's attentions, she hoped to spend the day visiting with Sonny.

Sonny quickly moved about the boat removing storage covers. A crew of six men arrived, and the yacht was soon out of its slip and sailing out to sea. The chilly air warmed after the coastal morning clouds burned away, but it was still cool enough for a coat.

The three fished off the aft. Sonny talkative, he told her about communicating with ships in the Gulf of Mexico and how he'd built himself a radio station in his bedroom. Other boys who shared his interest formed a radio club, also meeting in his bedroom.

"And what do you talk about on your radio?" Emma asked.

"Sometimes I don't talk at all, I send Morse Code messages."

"He stayed up all night teaching himself Morse Code," Bo said proudly.

"It sounds like you're spending a lot of time in your room."

"Oh, no. I have a workshop at Tool Co now and have all kinds of plans for things I can build."

"My son is a genius," Bo added.

Our son. "He is his father's son," she said, hoping Bo caught her meaning.

Bo beamed at Sonny. "He took a junked battery and an automobile starter motor to make a motorcycle."

Emma had seen a photo in the newspaper of Sonny standing in front of his motorized bicycle. She was as impressed as Bo seemed to be.

"He's an exceptional businessman to boot!" Bo chuckled. "He charges the neighbor kids a nickel to ride up and down Main Street on his bike."

They all laughed.

"He's liberated some spare parts from my old automobile steam engine. I have no doubt he'll come up with some other new invention."

"I'm proud of you," Emma said sincerely.

"Thank you, Mrs. Koenig." Sonny shyly glanced at her and then out to sea. He began telling her about Camp Teedyuskung in Pennsylvania.

Emma couldn't help but feel sad for her other boys who would never have the opportunities Sonny had. She'd made the right choice to have the Hugheses raise him.

When they turned and headed back to Galveston after supper, Emma found herself alone on deck. The days had been growing shorter and night was coming on. A sunset of reds and oranges lit the horizon. She pulled the collar of her coat around her ears to block the cold wind and marveled at nature's beauty. The day of sailing, fishing, visiting, and laughing brought regret. So many activities she was missing while working at the laundry, day in and day out. There was no escaping what her life had become.

She contemplated concerns about her future visits with Sonny and decided to have a word with Bo. She found him in a stateroom below deck reading *The Wall Street Journal*. As she entered, he set it down.

Being alone with him after so many years gave her pause. She found no allure to him whatsoever and wondered if her attraction had been to his lifestyle and money all along.

"Have you enjoyed your day at sea?" Bo put on a false smile.

She suspected he wanted her to be grateful to him. "Spending time with Sonny is always a pleasure."

"You have my hands tied on that one."

She averted her gaze. "Yes, I do. Thank you for not acting begrudgingly."

"It's much harder for Allene than for me." He smiled again, but this time waggled his eyebrows and patted the bench seat next to him. "Come sit," he said with an air of allurement.

Emma had no interest in his seductive maneuvers. She hadn't missed Charlie since he'd left, and she certainly hadn't missed the sex trade. She was done with men.

"No, thank you." She remained standing. "What's your plans for Sonny's schooling?"

Bo sighed. "I've been looking into prep schools in the East, hoping he'll eventually attend Harvard, my alma mater."

"It's been hard for me not seeing him for months at a time while he were gone this summer. I'd like to make some kind of plan for keepin' in touch with him when he's away to school."

"I'm not sure how to arrange that." Bo's face hardened.

"Maybe I can vacation with you when ya go to visit him at school?"

Bo choked on a laugh. "You've got to be joking."

Emma wasn't willing to give up so easily. "I'm not. How 'bout ya bring him home on holidays and invite me to see him?"

"Children grow up, Emma, and mothers need to let go of their boys and let them become men."

She hoped he'd said such things to Allene. She was the one who never seemed to be able to let Sonny go.

Flustered, she pushed forward. "Mothers have their say in how their son is raised. Mothers write their boys letters while they're away and receive letters back. Mothers receive correspondence from the school on how their son is progressing. I enjoy none of those things."

A noise in the hall stopped Bo from replying.

Emma stepped out of the room to see Sonny rushing up the steps to the topside. Her stomach dropped. How much had he heard?

Bo joined her in the hall, looking like he was going to be sick. "Do you think he heard?"

"I think he did."

Bo rubbed his face, aging before her eyes. "Let me take care of this. Say nothing."

When they dropped Emma off at the docks it was late. Sonny had made himself scarce after her conversation with Bo, and she wasn't able to tell him goodbye.

Through the weeks she worried about Sonny. What had Bo said to him? She should have spoken to Sonny herself. But would he have rejected her? Could she have survived that rejection? What must he now think of her? She could write him a letter but what if he hadn't heard her conversation with Bo, what would she say?

She wrote Bo at his office instead and waited impatiently for his response. When it came it was all she had feared. Sonny had heard their conversation. At Sonny's own request, Bo told Emma to stay out of his life. "For the boy's sake," he'd written. "Allene knows nothing of the blunder."

CHAPTER THIRTY-FOUR

Ora

In early 1918, the Hugheses made an end to leasing residences when they built a five-bedroom home on a corner lot at 3921 Yoakum Boulevard. It was an imposing two-story, brick house in the Montrose section of Houston, north of Rice Institute, one block from the three-story mansion of land developer and lawyer John Wiley Link. When establishing the planned suburb, Link had brought in seven train-carloads of palm trees to line the public walks in the neighborhood. A streetcar, the Montrose Line, ran through the suburb to give easy access to downtown.

By now, Howard Sr. was considered one of the city's leading businessmen. He still spent money lavishly and often sent his yacht by rail to California when he wanted to entertain West Coast oilmen. When his business partner, Ed Prather, couldn't cap Howard's spending, he found himself personally funding his excesses to keep the company out of the red. Eventually, as was the case with Estelle Sharp, Ed Prather sold out and Howard Sr. gained full control of Hughes Tool Company.

In the meantime, Emma and Ernest moved to yet another rental home at 3906 Ave J, also known as Broadway, the main thoroughfare in Galveston. Emma left Model Laundry and worked as an elevator operator, a much less labor-intensive job. She went back to using the last name of Hydrick and recorded herself as a "widow," even though Charlie still lived. I have found no divorce record. Maybe she discounted her life with Charlie altogether and considered herself widowed because of Jack's death?

For a short time, when George was nineteen, he moved back in with Emma and Ernest. He worked as a streetcar conductor for Galveston Electric Company. On September 12, 1918, he had registered for the United States War Draft, but was not called up before the Great War ended November 11, 1918.

During World War I, 53,402 Americans lost their lives in combat or became missing in action. Another 63,114 died from other causes, mostly the Spanish Influenza. Although 5,170 Texans died in the armed services, more than a third of those occurred inside the United States, many of them as a result of influenza. In the years 1918 and 1919, the Spanish Influenza Pandemic killed 675,000 Americans and possibly over twenty million worldwide.

I can't imagine how Allene reacted to the flu pandemic, for it didn't take a germaphobe to fear the virus.

***

Emma ~ July 10, 1919

Emma placed her feet into a white porcelain bowl filled with warm water and Epsom salts. "Ah," she sighed. Her feet and legs often swelled. Working the elevator had made life easier than the hard work at the laundry, but she still had to be on her feet much of the day and suffered from back pain and fatigue. She took a long swallow of whiskey.

George came out of his bedroom, surprising her.

"Oh, I thought you was at work?" She set her drink on an end table.

"They closed my car when someone dropped dead in it. Another flu victim." George walked over to the icebox and pulled out a beer. "They is washing the thing down and told me to do the same to my skin and clothes."

"Have you?"

"Yeah. Fewer people is getting sick, though. At least most of the cars is up and running everyday now."

"Did ya pay for that beer?" She pointed to the bottle in his hand.

It was obvious when George got mad. His normally pale complexion instantly turned red from his neck onto his cheeks.

"Why so many rules in this house?" He slammed the still unopened bottle on the drainboard. "I can take whatever I want out of Uncle Paul's icebox."

"Well, we isn't as rich as Paul. All the food in this house is available to you, but the alcohol we pay for separately. Ya know that."

"Uncle Paul ain't rich, and I don't wanna live by your damn rules."

If he wanted a fight, she wasn't going to give it to him. She'd been feeling weak all day and didn't care about anyone else's needs. She wiped the sweat from her temple and calmly said, "If you're going to live in this house, you're sure as hell going to live by my rules."

"Then I better leave. I don't need ya anymore, anyway."

"That's expected. It's a step toward independence to not need your ma." She refused to get riled by his attitude. She'd been hearing his same complaints for years now.

"You just isn't getting it," he said.

"Getting what?"

"Why is you not like other women?"

"What's that supposed to mean?"

"You never cry, for one thing. Do you have no feelings?"

Charlie had said something similar. She sighed. Not wanting to fight, she answered, "I don't feel great highs and lows."

"You can say that again. You's so unemotional."

"I can't help who I am."

"Oh, really? I've been watching, and you show no excitement—no affection." He ran his hand through his short hair and then swung out the other. "No interest in life."

Emma thought about that. It had been a long time since she experienced any kind of passion, but she'd always been against feminine drama and the way women sometimes acted weak. Maybe he was witnessing her sadness, for it did go deep. "I care."

"You care?" George's mouth hung open. "Exactly what does you care about?"

She cared about her three boys. Other than that, not much else, but it was hard to tell her boys she loved them. Vulnerable about displaying such feelings, instead of telling George right then that she loved him, she let anger tighten her chest. "I care 'bout keepin' ya fed and alive, like I've always done since you was born." If he knew what life was like—raising him at seventeen in a bordello. But she never told him those things. She couldn't. Better he didn't know his beginnings. He'd never brought up memories of being tied to the bed, either. Hopefully he knew that was for his own good. Or he'd forgotten.

"Well, I'm no baby anymore. And I don't need ya anymore either," he yelled.

He was right. She let the words cut her deeply, but kept her pain private. Charlie had said similar words when he told her he didn't want to be near her. But for George to say it was a different thing—a thing she hadn't figured out yet. And she had no idea how to remedy the reactions she was having to the feelings his rejection caused. "You's old enough to be on your own."

"Fine. I'm done with you. You was never the mother I wanted anyway." George went into his room and banged around for a while. After a time, he became quiet.

Emma finished her whiskey and had another.

Ernest came home from work and made sandwiches, but George wouldn't come out to eat.

Emma felt nauseated and weak the next morning. It wasn't the first time, and she pushed herself out of bed to prepare for work. Slowly walking to the kitchen, she passed George's room, finding his door ajar. She peered in. He was gone and so were all his belongings.

"George," she whispered, "come back again when you're ready."

Young men could be so unpredictable. She thought of Hy and how he'd died so young and tragically. She leaned against the door frame. "Please, George. Don't do anything stupid."

A foreboding tightened her chest.

She'd given everything she had to her boys, but somehow that wasn't enough. If she were to believe George, she'd have to conclude she was an unfeeling beast, void of emotion. A creature who didn't—or couldn't—show 'excitement, affection, or interest in life,' as he'd put it. George and Charlie had both thrown similar words at her. Those words must be the truth.

She'd lost Sonny, George, Bo, Jack, and Charlie. She'd try not to make the same mistake with Ernest.

CHAPTER THIRTY-FIVE

"She had not known the weight until she felt the freedom."
The Scarlet Letter by Nathaniel Hawthorne

Emma ~ August 3, 1919

"Ma, Ma, wake up!"

Emma swatted at Ernest to leave her be. Excruciating pain in her abdomen and legs overwhelmed her. Sleep was her single deliverance.

"Ma. What should I do?" Ernest wept above her.

Where was she? Bits of memory floated in and out. She had awakened in discomfort when it was still dark. That wasn't unusual. She had been doing that for months now and felt better once she got up and relieved her bladder. But last night was different.

She remembered now. She had been on her way to the bathroom when she slipped on something. Blood. She fell before the bathroom door. She must have passed out.

"Can ya get up?" Ernest shrieked with fear.

She rolled to her side and pushed the hair from her face before trying to sit up. She couldn't do it. "I need help." Her voice sounded foreign. Weak.

"There's blood all over your nightdress. You're bleeding, Ma." Ernest knelt next to her, trying to figure out where to grab hold to help her up. His eyes filled with fear and tears.

"I'm sick, son. I just need to recover. Can ya help me into bed?"

"Ya need to go to the hospital."

"We don't have money for that. The bleedin' will stop. It always has before."

"Before?" Ernest looked confused, then panicked. "I should run next door and get Tancy. She'll know what to do."

Emma drifted out, leaving her pain and decisions and Ernest's desperate eyes behind.

Next, she woke to the smell of antiseptic and something metallic. The room's heat suffocated her. "Open a window," she wanted to say, but was too lethargic to force the words past her lips. On her back again, this time she was on something softer than the floor. She opened her eyes to a high, white-plastered ceiling she'd never seen before. Her legs were bent with her knees perpendicular to her pelvis, her legs spread. Pain burned through her lower body.

Fingers probed. A hand, laid flat on her belly, pushed.

She screamed.

"She's awake," a male voice said. "Mrs. Hydrick, can you hear me?"

Emma was afraid of what might come out of her mouth if she opened it again. She groaned in agony and nodded.

A young, dark-haired, clean-shaven man leaned over her. "How long have you had this abnormal bleeding?" His voice was one of breeding. It reminded her of Bo.

"Off and on for months." Her hoarse words sounded like she had been drinking.

The man furrowed his thick brows. "Are you under the care of a doctor?"

"No money."

"Your life is at stake. Is that worth paying for?"

His superior attitude vexed her. "I can give ya my blood," she said.

"Well, no need for the added sacrifice. You don't have much of that left to give." He blew out his frustration and stepped away. "Clean her up and give her a shot of morphine. Send the tissue samples to pathology."

"Yes, doctor." A female voice answered.

Emma watched the doctor walk to a porcelain sink attached to a white wall. He wore a white coat. He washed his hands until they were no longer stained with crimson blood.

She was in a hospital. She'd never been in a hospital before.

"I can't stay here," she called to him. The extra exertion of talking made her head spin. She closed her eyes and swallowed hard. Nausea flooded her. She waited for it to subside before opening her eyes again. "Where am I?"

The young doctor walked back, drying his hands with a towel. "John Sealy Hospital, and I don't think you'll be getting up and leaving any time soon. You've lost too much blood." He threw the towel on a stainless-steel cart covered in bloody instruments, then walked around the head of her bed in the opposite direction of the sink.

Emma turned to watch him leave, the movement making her head swim again. This time she kept as still as possible. Her pain might be keeping her from thinking clearly. Apprehensive and vulnerable, she needed to get an idea of her surroundings. A white sheet hanging from thick wire kept her from seeing the room, but she could tell from the expanse of the ceiling that it was a spacious room. The doctor was close, speaking to someone on the other side of the sheet.

Most alarming of all, she could hear the rapid beats of her heart.

Suddenly a cold cloth wiped against her inner thigh.

She jumped, and more pain jolted through her abdomen. She clenched her fists and clasped her lips tightly closed before she screamed again. Instead the muffled wail sounded more like a thick whimper.

"Sorry, Mrs. Hydrick." The nurse stopped her cleansing and packed something cold between Emma's legs. "This should help the bleeding stop." She picked up a large, glass syringe. "I'll give you something for the pain."

The sting of the shot was minor compared to Emma's overall misery. She had experienced pain for so long she'd forgotten when it started. She was broken, and they were going to try and fix her, but it was too late.

A year or more ago, when intercourse started hurting, Emma knew. The girls at the brothel used to talk about such things. Her body was now rejecting the lifestyle she'd lived for well over a decade. Whiskey had deadened the pain at first, but not lately. At night she'd lay in the dark and feel it grow inside her—a foreign intruder that found fertile soil to blacken and corrode.

Trepidation jabbed at her chest, and she pushed it away. No, she would not let fear weaken her.

The nurse stepped to the stainless-steel cart where the doctor had thrown the towel. She was in her early twenties. Under her white cap, her hair was bobbed in a marcel wave.

Emma slid her eyes down to check the length of her skirt. It was mid-calf. This was a woman who would embrace emancipation. Emma suddenly felt old.

The nurse lifted Emma's legs out of the stirrups. "Can you lift up?" she asked, positioning Emma's feet flat and knees bent.

With great pain, Emma did as she was asked.

The nurse quickly slipped linens out from under her backside and slid an undergarment up to hold the large, cold pad in place. She positioned Emma's legs out straight.

They trembled uncontrollably. Emma willed them to stop, but they disobeyed.

The nurse draped a white blanket over Emma and tucked it tightly under her legs.

Emma was already so hot, she began to complain, but the tightness of the blanket felt reassuring somehow.

The nurse rubbed both legs with her hands. "They may tremble for a bit, but you'll soon feel better," she said kindly.

The touch of someone's hands, and the kindness of her words struck Emma as sincere. No stranger, especially a woman, ever talked to her like that before. Tears came into her eyes, but she couldn't let herself give in to them. She closed her eyes and swallowed hard.

The nurse laid a hand on her shoulder. "We'll try and make you comfortable."

Emma was afraid if she opened her eyes, her emotions would open up too.

"I need to make my rounds. Call if you need me. My name's Martha."

Emma tilted her chin toward her chest. When she heard Martha's steps fade, she opened her eyes and stared once again at the ceiling. Large lights with metal shades as big as bread-mixing bowls dropped six feet from the tall ceiling, but the brightest light came from down the expanse of the room where there must be a large window. The hanging sheet kept Emma from viewing the room, but from the sounds she assumed there were many patients.

A tear fell, and she quickly wiped it away. Her life was no longer in her control and the fear of that realization kept pushing its way forward, rolling over her like waves during a hurricane.

Sometime later, Martha returned. "How's your pain?"

"Less," Emma said, grateful for the morphine.

Martha helped her into a gown and pulled the hanging sheet away, revealing an immense room—as big or bigger than the ballrooms Emma used to dance in—and all done in white. White ceilings, walls, and floor. Even every bed was covered in white. The only things not white were the wrought-iron bed frames lining both sides of the long room. Emma had never seen anything like it. At the far end of the room, two narrow windows reached to the ceiling. Light spilled from them into every corner, brightening the white of the fabrics. It was a room cleansed of the world she'd lived in all her life.

Martha helped her slowly walk from the treatment bay to an empty bed, pushing aside the crisp linens that smelled like bleach. "Here you are."

As Emma laid down, the springs squeaked.

Martha pulled a curtained sheet completely around the bed, cocooning them in a small, safe space. "I need to insert a catheter to make sure your bladder can find relief."

Yes, it had been hard to urinate lately. Scared, she didn't want to show it. "Will it hurt?"

"Maybe a little. If you can stay relaxed, it will make it easier." Martha bent over. Again, fingers where they didn't belong.

Once the nurse was satisfied, she covered Emma and pulled the hanging sheet away, then left Emma feeling vulnerable again.

Hours later, the doctor came. He had the advantage, standing over her. "The lab results show carcinoma of the cervix. With this condition, we've been finding success with cutting away the tumors. I will operate immediately—"

"No, ya won't," Emma said, not surprised by the diagnosis, cutting off his decision, as if it were his decision anyway. "I'm dyin', and I'll not prolong it."

"But research has shown by removing cancerous tissues you can recover."

Doctors often withheld information from patients, especially women. He wasn't telling her everything; she could see it on his face. "I feel pain throughout my abdomen."

He looked away for a moment, shifting his weight to another foot. "I didn't want to upset you, but yes, that's expected. The cancer may have spread to other organs. When I do surgery, I'll look at those, too."

"When ya do surgery? I told ya, I won't have it."

"We have a benevolent fund that will pay for your care. You won't need to worry about the finances."

"I still won't have it."

He grunted. "Look, you have no medical training and the complete diagnosis will probably confuse you, but it's possible there are other issues causing your symptoms. I'm educated in this field and know what's best for you. Your feminine responses are making you act irrationally."

Emma rolled her eyes. "Who needs God when ya have a well-trained doctor?"

He stuck his chin out a little further.

She should be grateful her treatment would be free, but she honestly believed it would prolong the inevitable. "I just want relief from the pain. Since I won't have surgery," she stared hard into his eyes to make her point, "what can ya do for the pain?"

Hesitating, he clenched his jaw. His resolve melted away as his shoulders slumped. "We'll continue with morphine injections."

"Then that's all I ask."

Ernest came that evening. He stood next to the bed, his tall, lanky body shuffling from foot to foot. He crushed his flat cap in his hands, while glancing around the room.

Emma didn't want him there.

"Is you angry with me?" he asked.

She blew her breath out. "How'd ya get me here?"

He looked to the floor. "I thought you was dying so I ran and got Tancy. When we couldn't rouse ya, we woke Mr. Smith, and he brung ya here in his carriage."

Emma pictured the chaos she'd created and breathed a sigh of humiliation. She hated getting help from anyone. She clasped her hands together to stop them from trembling. "Did neighbors see?"

"Naw, I don't reckon." He wouldn't look her in the eyes.

She couldn't tell if he was lying. "I might be here a while, and I don't want ya comin' anymore."

His head jerked up. "But—"

Emma held up her hand to stop him. "I'm told there's whole rooms of patients with the flu. You stay away from here." She couldn't bear to lose gentle Ernest like she had George.

So much talking and worriment were making her tired. The warmth and weightlessness she'd felt with the morphine had worn off. She closed her eyes and continued slowly, "And don't tell Paul or Eva or . . . no one I'm here." She opened her eyes and grabbed his hand. "Ya hear me? No one!"

Sympathy from others would make her situation harder to bear. She wanted to deal with this alone. And what if they did catch the flu? She'd never forgive herself. She sighed and wished the nurse would come back with another shot of morphine.

Ernest appeared as if he'd cry. Seventeen-year-olds shouldn't cry. "Yes, ma'am."

Emma let go of him.

Clearing his throat, he wiped at his eyes. "How long ya gonna be here?"

In her heart she knew she wasn't going home, but she refused to tell him that. "I don't know, son." She pulled the covers to her chin. "I'm awfully tired. Ya go on now." Her emotions rose to her throat, closing it off. She couldn't tell him he'd soon be on his own. As hard as she'd tried to teach him to take care of himself, she hadn't taught him to not need love.

Soon after Ernest left, the nurse gave her a shot and turned off the overhead lights. Emma stared at the soft glow of a small desk lamp in the middle of the room. It drew her in and held her steady while patients slept and nurses crept about the room on rubber-soled shoes. She wanted to sleep, but her mind wouldn't shut down.

She thought about her conversation earlier with the doctor, wondering if she'd reacted more to his arrogance than to what he'd said. Was there a chance he could cure her? No, she was sure surgery wouldn't prolong her life for long—and if it did, it'd be a miserable existence. She didn't want Ernest having to care for her.

If there was a God, this was His retribution. He was punishing her as a father should.

She placed her hand on her abdomen. The swelling had gone down some since the nurse placed the catheter. Emma gently pushed, feeling for the knot she'd discovered weeks before. There it was, as hard as a stone and sensitive to the touch. She continued to probe with her fingers and found other lumps. Her body was rejecting life, becoming hard where it should be soft. She needed more than a doctor to fix her.

She would die, and she'd do it alone.

Death would free her of both physical misery and the pain of regret. The pain had been with her so long, it was hard to trace back to when it started. The same with the regret. Had the roots grown when she'd given her baby away? *Sonny. Oh, Sonny! What have I done to you?*

Or did the pain start earlier, when the men she'd wanted to love used and left her? Maybe even before that when she gave away her body as a child? Perhaps that's where the anguish started—at least where she'd become aware of the ache.

A sharp pain pierced her heart as she became lost in memories she'd pushed into a deep cavern. She'd lost herself as a child. Her father had robbed her of her best self and all the things that should have been. He stole from her, and Mama should have protected her.

That secret shame of what her father had done grew and twisted inside her like a tumorous cancer she wouldn't allow anyone to examine or cut out.

From that point forward she never dared to fully give anyone her love or her trust. She didn't know how to emotionally care for a man—quite a joke considering the hundreds she'd serviced. She was merchandise sold to whomever had coin. No one had to fight for her. She was easy, and they would probably say she did just fine. But what were those men looking for when she was chasing after love and security? Lust. Lust never fulfills the soul.

"God?" She closed her eyes and searched the air in the room and then searched her body for His presence. Something foreign and scarcely remembered from childhood was there with her. It filled her heart with longing. "Can I forgive the child that was me?" she whispered. With the words a gentle peace came into her soul and her worries were stilled. She finally cried, but there was no one to cry with her.

***

Ora

Emma died twelve days later in the John Sealy Hospital.

In the early twentieth century, it was noted that cervical cancer behaved like a sexually transmitted disease and was common in female sex workers, and rare in nuns. Women could also contract it from men who had multiple sex partners, even if they themselves did not.

In 1896, "X-ray" was discovered, and three years later researchers discovered radiation could cause cancer as well as cure it. In 1910, American surgeon Robert Abbe was the first to use radium in the treatment of cervical carcinoma. However, radiating the cancerous cells in the cervix did not become a common practice until the 1930s.

Women rarely have symptoms of cervical cancer in its early stages. Researchers now know cervical cancer is caused by a sexually transmitted virus called human papilloma virus (HPV). A few strains of the virus produce visible symptoms and cause an infection in the cervix which creates changes in the cells of women who have the added risk factors of smoking cigarettes, having sexual relations at a young age, and having multiple sex partners. Back then it was a common cause of death for prostitutes, whose average age at death was thirty-four. Emma was thirty-seven.

Excerpt of letter from George to my father, September 14, 1980:

> Now Rick, In reference to my past. I have told you I can not tell you a thing. As I grew up I never looked back.

As of now I am still looking forward. What you have found in research is fine. You will find more.

I left home telling no one. I went to Houston. Decided to join the U.S. Marines. Passed my mental and Physical exam. Was sworn in July 11, 1919 as a U.S. Marine and Proud of it. I never told no one after arriving at Parris Island, S.C.

While I was still in boot camp My mother died. I did not go home for her funeral.

Now pleas ask me no more let my past be. I will answer no more questions.

I have the opposite opinion as my grandfather. I've learned through researching the past and the life of Emma that no matter what happened, we will always stick together as a family. I belong to Emma, and she belongs to me.

CHAPTER THIRTY-SIX

Ora

Howard Jr. was thirteen when Emma died. He had spent the spring of that year at Mackinac Island, Michigan, recuperating from a mysterious illness which placed him in a wheelchair. A couple of months before, he suddenly couldn't walk. The doctors in Houston feared he had infantile paralysis. Howard Sr. called the leading pioneer in the study of polio research, Dr. Simon Flexner, who sent his assistant, Dr. H. T. Chickering to Houston. The doctor could not find the cause of Howard Jr.'s paralysis, but was sure it wasn't polio, and believed he would walk again. As mysteriously as it had come on, the problem with Howard Jr.'s legs resolved. That summer Howard Sr. wrote that he had begun to "pick up and become a perfectly normal boy."

Howard Jr. attended South End Junior High in Houston and did poor academically. By the fall of 1920, he was attending Fessenden School near Boston, Massachusetts, where he improved academically and, most especially, did well at the game of golf. During his year there, Howard Sr. dropped by for a visit and took him into New London, Connecticut, where Howard Jr. flew in his first airplane. It was the beginning of his lifelong love of flying.

Howard Jr. graduated from Fessenden in June of 1921. Afterward, he spent time at a branch of his father's tool company where he enrolled at Thacher School near Santa Barbara, California.

It was while he attended Thacher that his mother went in for minor "undisclosed" surgery at the Baptist Hospital in Houston. The death certificate records the surgery to be for "curettement," which would entail removing tissue or growths from a bodily cavity. Biographers have speculated the growth to be in the uterus, but the death certificate does not confirm that speculation. The death certificate records "death occurred during administration of gas anesthesia." She died March 29, 1922, under much secrecy to the cause of why she was in the hospital for surgery. If she too had contracted HPV (from her husband?), it would be an illness she'd try to keep from the public and maybe even from her family and friends. It might have been the reason for so much secrecy surrounding her death.

Howard Sr. sent a telegram to his sixteen-year-old son at Thacher, informing him his mother was ill and that he needed to return home immediately. Howard Sr. then asked his brother Rupert to meet Howard Jr. in Los Angeles and send him by train to Houston where he'd tell his son the full story. Rupert said he knew his brother's anguish and told Howard Jr. the news himself. Howard Jr. did not weep but instead shook his head and looked down in thoughtful silence.

Howard Jr. did not talk about his feelings over his mother's death. Those who knew him said he seemed to not grieve. A childhood friend came to visit Sonny the day after the funeral to pay his condolences. He said, "We were alone in this big house, and spent the entire time in Sonny's room, playing with his radio transmitter. I remember saying that I was sorry to hear about his mother, and he replied, 'By turning this knob, we can hear Cleveland.'"

Howard Sr. acted heartbroken over Allene's death, avoiding his home on Yoakum, saying it reminded him of her. He eventually stayed away from Houston altogether. He begged Allene's sister, Annette, to postpone her plans for marriage and help him care for Howard Jr. Annette had often lived with the Hugheses after her mother died young, and she had been living with them fulltime since 1919.

Annette agreed to care for Howard Jr. one year, after which she'd marry. They moved to California, but Howard Sr. stayed at the Ambassador Hotel in Los Angeles and Annette and Howard Jr., along with a cousin, stayed in a cottage surrounded by lush gardens at the Vista Del Arroyo Hotel in Pasadena.

Howard Sr. didn't stay in Los Angeles long, but instead chartered three railroad cars for a party of fourteen to attend the Kentucky Derby. He also went to New York and then sailed his yacht in the Caribbean and through the Panama Canal and back up to Los Angeles. He had no worries about his business in Houston, run by highly competent managers still bringing in record-breaking sales.

Now seventeen and standing 6'3", Howard Jr. returned to Thacher School in the fall, but early in 1923, Howard Sr. took him out of school, saying he thought he needed special tutoring. Sherman Thacher was against removing Howard Jr. from school and wrote a letter to Sr. about how Howard Jr. needed "more than most boys the contact with other fellows such as he gets in school; and I think your desire and tendency to indulge him in every way would probably be very hard for him to resist and probably not at all good for him." Sr. ignored his advice.

Even after taking Howard Jr. out of high school, his father still hoped to enroll him in college. He worked out an arrangement for Sonny to attend California Institute of Technology in Pasadena. Howard Sr. made an undisclosed donation to Cal Tech's scholarship fund. As Annette put it, "they were bribed to let him in."

Although still living at different hotels, the two Howards often got together on Sundays at Rupert Hughes's mansion in Los Angeles. Rupert's Sunday brunches were popular with famous actors and directors. Sonny was often chauffeured to the movie studio to roam freely on the set of *Souls for Sale*, a movie Rupert was filming. He dropped out of school and spent much of his time golfing while Howard Sr. partied at his hotel suites in Hollywood and New York.

Annette's year of caring for Howard Jr. ended the summer of 1923. She went to Houston and married her fiancé, Dr. Frederick Rice Lummis, but Howard Sr. soon talked the couple into living in his Yoakum Boulevard house and watching after Howard Jr., who was supposed to attend Rice Institute. Howard Sr. still would not live in the home. He seldom came to Houston, other than for a few meetings too important to miss.

Caring for Howard could not have been an easy responsibility. For instance, he would not carry a housekey and whenever he came home late, he broke a pane on a French door to be able to let himself in. Time after time a glazier needed to be called in to fix it.

Howard spent much of his time golfing and little time attending school. Dr. Lummis made comment of Howard, "He was impatient with learning things in the ordinary way. He wanted to know what he needed to know and didn't want to waste time. I think his genius lay in the ability to identify the people he needed to do what he wanted done."

Author Marguerite Johnston wrote, "If to be an introvert is to hold yourself to your own inner standards, then Howard Hughes was an introvert throughout his life. He did what he wished to do, what he expected of himself. Nonetheless, for years after, he considered the Lummises and the house on Yoakum as home."

On January 14, 1924, Howard Sr. was in a business meeting when he "suddenly rose to his feet, grasped at the desk before him convulsively, and fell to the floor." He died of a heart attack at fifty-four, leaving Sonny orphaned at eighteen, and was buried next to Allene at Glenwood Cemetery.

When Howard Sr. died, he left his son the heir to three-fourths of the Hughes Tool Company. The remaining one-quarter of the estate was left to Howard Sr.'s parents and his brother, Felix. Nothing was left to Rupert, who was already financially sound.

After Howard Jr. convinced a judge he was competent to run his father's company and should be declared a "legal adult," he persuaded his relatives to sell their portions of the tool company to him. Rupert believed Howard paid them much less than the shares were worth and his disappointment in his nephew's behavior is expressed in a lengthy, scathing letter written April 19, 1924, stating how Howard Jr. had good looks, magnetism, extraordinary intelligence, imagination, and ingenuity, but that his faults had become more splendid in moderation and dangerous in excess—those faults being selfishness and miserly thrift that gave him a tendency to give the least possible.

Speaking in the letter of Howard's absence of feeling toward his father's memory during a recent visit to Rupert's home, where

Howard's paternal grandparents also lived, Rupert wrote that he'd never heard Howard speak one word of love or praise for Howard Sr. or suggest memorializing him. Howard Jr. had spoken of his father in a joking and contemptuous manner, angering Rupert. When Howard's grandfather believed he was coming to Los Angeles for consolation over the death of Howard Sr., his grandfather was hurt to discover Howard Jr. had come to make the best possible settlement of his father's will and usurp from his family money that belonged to them. Rupert warned him that being so ungenerous would result in robbing his life of friendship, love, and passion—all those things that make life worthwhile.

But free from his parents' overpowering personalities, it was clear that Howard Jr. could think for himself, wanted independence, and wasn't going to let his relatives dictate what the rest of his life would encompass.

EPILOGUE

People often focus on Howard Jr.'s eccentric behavior and reclusive lifestyle. Because of that, we may lose sight of a large part of who he was. He had a brilliant mind and ambitious vision, striving relentlessly to attain his goals and build an empire that grossed millions. In his later years, he cared nothing about everyday luxuries even though he was sometimes surrounded by them. He treated his loyal employees well.

Among his achievements: Academy Award winning filmmaker, designed a series of airplanes, founded Hughes Aircraft Company, broke the speed record for flying a plane over land, set a record for transcontinental U.S. speed, set a new record for circumnavigating the globe—for which he was hailed as a hero and honored with a ticker-tape parade in New York City and celebrations around the country—worked on experimental military aircraft, designed the Hercules flying boat, participated in the Glomar Explorer, became one of Nevada's biggest employers and private landholders, donated money to many worthy causes, and most especially created Howard Hughes Medical Institute.

What would America, or this world for that matter, be like if Emma had raised Sonny?

I'm not even going to try and answer that question, but I can say that there were desperate lifelong struggles for George and Ernest that Sonny would have probably experienced too. In Sonny's case, money bought him opportunities. At his death in 1976, he was worth $2.5 billion (net worth equal to 11 billion in 2021).

In contrast, after Emma's death, Ernest lived at boarding houses within Galveston and Houston, and worked at Peerless Laundry and a branch of Model Laundry in Houston. He became a foreman and salesman for Model Laundry and worked there at least until 1942, but probably much longer. He married Thelma Derouen in 1924 and was widowed in 1969, then married Lily Newman in 1971. He had no children with either wife. He came into money at some point because my brother remembers he invested regularly in real estate and lived in an upper-middle class neighborhood. His home was surrounded by a manicured lawn with carefully tended flower beds and sat on a large lot covered with mature, beautifully aged oak trees full of Spanish moss. He developed an interest in aviation and flew small planes for pleasure. He died in 1989, at the age of eighty-seven.

My grandfather, George, met his wife, Lucille White, in Landover, Maryland in 1921, while still in the Marines and stationed in Washington, D.C.

Lucille said, "My mother didn't want me to marry a Marine. Neither did my sisters. None of them wanted me to marry a Marine. But I was going to marry a Marine anyhow because I was crazy about him. I loved him. I came home and I called my mother and my sisters up and I had told them where to come, and they never did come to be at my wedding. But I got married anyhow."

George left the Marine's after two and a half years. He received an honorable discharge because his wife was pregnant, and it was necessary for her to quit her job. He was the sole breadwinner.

He worked as a fireman, following in his uncle Paul's footsteps. Sadly, George had a serious drinking problem and treated Lucille abhorrently by having numerous affairs and often not coming home for days and weeks at a time, leaving his family with no food or money. He couldn't hold onto his fireman's career and wandered from job to job, state to state, taking Lucille and his many children with him.

On one of George's jaunts to another state, he took his family back to Houston, where he worked at a laundry company—not Model Laundry where Ernest worked. They lived with Eva and her fifth husband Bert at 117 Conoly Avenue. My father was born in Eva's home in 1928, and his mother named him Plymton from an old family surname, but Eva called him Sonny, which stuck, and that's what the family called him most of his life. He was

George's fourth child. When Plymton was still a baby, George came home one morning, "stone-blind drunk" leaning heavily against the milkman, with blood seeping from a broken nose. On his way home, he had driven his car off the road into an embankment and flipped it upside-down. The milkman found him passed out with the car motor still running.

Although I would love to know more of the story, I was told enough to know Charlie Koenig was still in George's life and tried to straighten him up. He failed, and in contrition gave Lucille enough money for her and her children to take the train back to her family in D.C.

George followed a few months later, begging Lucille to let him come back into her life. They lived with Lucille's widowed mother and handicapped sister in a small rowhome. George again worked as a marker at a laundry company. By now the country was in the Great Depression. George's ways hadn't changed, and he soon left Lucille again. She went to work at a dime store while her mother watched the kids. By 1935, George and Lucille were together once again, now with five children. They moved to Charleston, South Carolina, where George worked graveyard at a civil service electrical job on a naval base. A baby girl was born to Lucille and George but soon died. Lucille ran a café during the day. She brought her children to work, and my father remembered lying on a cot and watching her cook and do dishes.

In 1937, they went to Houston a second time and George again worked at the laundry. My father said during this time he had no food to eat for three days while his father was away somewhere. Lucille begged for food from the neighbors, and they gave her enough to get them through until George happened to show up. My father wrote, "When the bill collectors knocked on our door, we had to be very quiet until they went away thinking no one was home. Mom always kept the blinds closed." George and Lucille moved to Norfolk, Virginia that same year and had their seventh child, Jeanette.

In 1940, they moved to National City, California where Lucille said of George, "Most of the time he was out of work and messing around at the racetrack." My father said of this move that they lived in a "run-down shack of a house two blocks from the Pacific

Ocean. It had cracks between the boards of the house and you could look through them to outside." Two weeks after they moved into that house, the Imperial Valley Earthquake hit, and the building was condemned and pulled down.

In 1942, George worked at the North Island Naval Air Station, again in civil service of some capacity. Lucille divorced George. He dated numerous women and married his second wife, Alice Ferreira, in 1945 and had two sons by her. Alice had come to the marriage with another son. As so many other women in the situation of no male breadwinner home during the War, Lucille went to work as a riveter (picture the iconic poster of Rosie the Riveter) at Rohr Industries in Chula Vista in 1942 until WWII ended.

In 1946, four years after George started work for the civil service in San Diego, he "retired" from the job and changed the pattern of his on-again-off-again employment. He moved to Culver City, near Los Angeles, and took a position as an Aviation Electrical Inspector for North American Aviation, based in Downey, California. I'm unsure how he would have received the experience for the job, perhaps it was at the air station in San Diego. At this time, he was somehow doing so well financially, he bought a gas station and racehorses. He stayed at the North American Aviation job for almost twenty years. (Hughes Aircraft Company, under the control of the Hughes Tool Company, was based in Culver City. In the same year that George moved there, 1946, Howard Hughes was in a near-fatal crash while flying a XF-11 aircraft.)

By the time I knew my grandfather, he was in his sixties and had twenty grandchildren before me. I was of little interest to him, and my first memories of him are of feeling afraid. He was grumpy and impatient, easy to upset. We visited him when my family went to Disneyland because he lived near the theme park in the 1960s. To get there, I traveled in a camper with my parents and seven siblings. I can understand George wanting such a large group of restless children to play outside. Sometimes he gave us all a quarter, which we thought a great sum, and helped us realize perhaps he did have an interest in us—or he was paying us off to run along and go spend the money. On occasions where I could be close enough to overhear his conversations with my father, they usually spoke about George betting on racehorses or his recent bowling score.

George died in 1990 at the age of ninety.

George's ex-wife Lucille was a gentle and sweet woman who loved living in rural areas and had an affection for farm animals and rabbits. I respect her for raising my father in a way that helped him become successful and for the most part happy. Alcoholism continued with a few members in his family, but not with my father. He put himself through college, finally graduating with an Education degree while supporting seven children and a wife—I was the seventh child, and my parents did eventually have an eighth. He taught junior-high English, American history, and social studies in South Lake Tahoe, California, most of his career.

Researching this story, I've learned that decisions we make can impact generations, and this was evident with Mary, Paul's wife. She was a strong woman who made a difference in a troubled family. She raised six sons and stayed married to her husband. Her grandson said, "She was feisty, and Paul couldn't put anything over on her." I honor her for doing what others couldn't in the Butterfras family. Her descendants are better for it. Paul went back to painting buildings and furniture about 1918, before Emma died, and continued with the career most of his life. He died in 1969, at the age of ninety-two. Mary died seventeen years before him.

In 1935, Paul and Eva rented homes next door to each other at 1707 and 1709 Airline Drive in Houston. Flossie, Eva's daughter, married a barber named Elwin Fontenot and they rented the house on the other side of Eva, at 1711 Airline Drive. Eva and her fifth husband, Bert King, adopted Henry Taylor King, a son of Eva's fourth husband and a schoolteacher with whom he had an affair—a familiar scenario in the family.

Bert King was a cattleman and friendly to all who came to his home. He especially enjoyed teaching boys about cattle ranching and trading. One evening, when Eva and Bert were on a social outing hayride, Eva tried moving from the trailer to the tractor that Bert was driving and fell between the two, mangling her leg so badly that it had to be amputated.

Paul's grandson, Charlie Butterfras, told me he remembered Eva's kitchen window looked out at Paul's next door. Paul didn't own a phone, but Eva did. When a call came in for Paul on Eva's phone, she would pull a rope that ran between the two kitchen windows and ring a bell in Paul's house. Sometimes the rope was used to get their attention for other things, such as visiting. Charlie remembers the bell ringing and Mary calling to Eva, "What do you want," and Eva saying, "It's coffee time." Mary and Eva had a running joke between them. Eva called out at Mary from her window, "Hey Cat-licker," because she was a Catholic, and Mary would yell back at her, "Dog-licker." I guess they enjoyed the joke and knew what it meant.

Eva's grandsons remember her as a "hard" woman, although they have good memories of going to work with her at a carnival where she conducted sales at the ticket booth. They remember her as being slim, about five-feet-seven, with distinctive blue eyes and gray hair, and in constant pain with her false leg. The false leg gave her an extraordinary walk as she swung it out in front of her. She wore high-top boots to cover it. Eva died in 1957 at the age of sixty-seven.

"Mama" Mary Clark Butterfras, Emma's mother, died in 1922, outliving seven of her nine children. She was seventy-five. She was living with the widowed husband of her daughter, Lottie, at the time of her death.

As mentioned in the Introduction, Buddy wrote the letter about what Eva told him regarding Emma and Howard Hughes a few months before he died in 1996. I remember little of Uncle Buddy, my father's brother. Most people who knew him remember him as a sensitive man who had a drinking problem. His full name was Owen Elmer Hydrick. He was the second son of George and Lucille. He joined the armed forces right out of high school and served in WWII, then attended college on the GI Bill. He was the first in the family to graduate from college and was proud of it. He married around 1950 and had six children, one daughter and five sons.

***

Since I've been young, I've always wanted to understand where I came from. Winston Churchill once said, "The further you look back, the further you can look forward."

My brother recently made the comment, "I don't like it when you research Dad's family. You're always finding out things I don't want to know."

For me, it's the stories I'm looking for—no matter if they're admirable or dismal. I want to know how my ancestors' lives and decisions play into mine. I want to be able to say, "I understand."

Families can give us a sense of belonging and identity. We inherit personality traits, attributes, and physical characteristics. Does Emma reflect those onto me? William Shakespeare wrote, "Thou art thy mother's glass, and she in thee." The closest we can get to looking into eternity might be when we stand between two mirrors and see our image going into infinity. I see each image as a generation, linked together through blood. There are no missing generations.

Because of the lack of records connecting Jack Hydrick to his ancestors, I found some relief—after twenty years of researching his family—when I learned through yDNA that we were not Hydricks at all but Osbornes. Some of my brothers and other males in my family who carried the Hydrick name did not share my relief. They felt as if their world had been tilted a little sideways.

The danger of doing DNA is finding out who we are *not*. My family and I weren't the people we thought we were. We grew up with the name Hydrick, descending from Schwankfelder (a religious sect not unlike the Quakers) immigrants who came to America in the early 1700s, fleeing religious persecution. One of them went on to South Carolina where he bought land, had a large family, and developed a strong work ethic. We considered ourselves Germans who had been in America for centuries, helping form the country and adding to its greatness. But that family narrative was no longer correct.

Family identity. What does it mean? It's not like I found out my father wasn't my father or grandfather wasn't my grandfather. There was no shocking truth that pushed me so far off kilter that I struggled emotionally. It was my great-grandfather who had no connection to me. But somehow there was sorrow in letting the Hydricks go. Many members of my family who carry the name Hydrick have made comments that maybe they should change their name to Osborne. But that too feels foreign. As of now, no one has done it.

There is more to who we are. I had to ask myself, *what makes me who I am*? I had a new reality to deal with. The Osbornes have been in England since the 400s. My autosomal DNA test showed I'm 60% English and Northwestern Europe, and even though I descend from Peter Butterfass from Germany, my DNA sample claimed only 5% Germanic Europe ethnicity. Some of my siblings' DNA results show a much higher percentage. The luck of the draw? How important is ethnicity anyway?

And who was this English Osborne man that was a sperm donor to my genetic makeup? My heart wants to believe there was more of a relationship between Emma and him. Could they have cared for one another? Was Emma heartbroken when he didn't step forward to raise their son, George? In all probability, Mr. Osborne was long gone when Emma found out she was pregnant. It's possible Emma didn't even know her sperm donor's name. Had he been a sailor who shipped out soon after doing the deed?

So why so much fuss about who I am?

Osborne was a real man who lived on this earth and had experiences and feelings like the rest of us. If he could have seen the future of continuing his seed, his descendants numbering in the hundreds, the large family we've become, would he have wished things had been different? That he had had some communal connection to us?

And if family identity is something I cling to, should I not want my possible great-uncle, Howard Hughes, to be part of "us?" I do actually. And it's not a new feeling. The first book I read about Howard Hughes began with his death scene. I wept. I clenched my fists at the unfairness of his last years. I shouted in my head that if I had been there, I would've taken care of him. He wouldn't have felt alone.

If I could, I would heal my family. Throughout all the questions about what was or what could've been, my hope is that I came closer to making things right in some way. I want Emma to find peace and be absolved for what she did. Even if it wasn't Howard Hughes she gave away, she did give away a son. I want her to know she can be loved and accepted by her family.

I'm glad my father was looking for family history answers himself. I'm grateful there was something in him that wanted to know and understand his father's family. He helped tell Emma's story by corresponding with family members and interviewing my grandparents, leaving those treasures for me.

My dad died a week after I started writing this book. I was in Texas researching this story and flew to California for his funeral. Emma's story has helped me understand his upbringing, which in turn helps me forgive him for wrongs he caused me during my childhood. Maybe that is stated too simply, but Emma's story has aided my healing process.

Oftentimes family history is incomplete—a skeletal picture of a person and not the whole. My daughter did a puzzle recently and accidently pushed some pieces off the table onto the floor. The dog immediately scooped them up with his tongue and swallowed them down, because what usually falls off the table if not edibles? My daughter finished the puzzle, but of course it wasn't complete. It would never be complete. Which is probably the greatest frustration with family history research. There are always going to be missing pieces that, if there, would've made the puzzle more recognizable as a full life. I wrote Emma's scenes as historical fiction to try and fill in those missing pieces. I was, and am still, striving for the full story. My search has always been for the truth.

I never found that great piece of information proving beyond a doubt that Howard Hughes was my great-uncle. As far as I know, his DNA doesn't exist. I am disappointed to leave this book open-ended, but sometimes real life is that way.

I will continue the search.

POSTSCRIPT

The Psychological Makeup of Howard Hughes

Many have speculated over Howard Jr.'s mental health, both while he was living and after his death. The Houston law firm Andrews and Kurth, who represented Hughes' business interests, hired Dr. Raymond D. Fowler to conduct a psychological autopsy which would establish the mental status and level of functioning of Howard Jr. It took Dr. Fowler three years to create his report. He used correspondence written by Howard, interviews of his employees, friends, associates, and family members to get first-person accounts. Because of Howard's instructions to his employees that they file every written communication and summaries of all his calls, Howard's life was documented well concerning his business and some personal dealings. Also, because there was a world-wide search for his will after his death, there were many court testimonies and depositions from those who had known him, which Dr. Fowler also employed for his findings.

In May 1986, Dr. Fowler published a synopsis of his conclusions in the magazine *Psychology Today*. He established that Howard developed psychological problems from childhood, which were exacerbated by numerous head injuries and drug abuse.

He wrote, "Howard Hughes Jr. was the child of a hearty, extroverted but often absent father and a quiet, soft-spoken mother who focused her full attention on her only child." Allene worried about his feet, teeth, and bowels. She gave him nightly doses of mineral oil as a laxative.

According to his Aunt Annette, Howard was not separated from his mother until he went to summer camp at the age of ten.

As shown in a previous chapter, Allene worried incessantly about Howard and wrote her worries in letters sent to the camp director. Dr. Fowler stated in his report that Howard was shy and introverted, uncomfortable around children his age and more comfortable with adults. When Howard returned to Houston after his second year at camp, he complained of bad dreams, not sleeping well, and feeling tired all the time.

Dr. Fowler said that psychologists call this pattern of shy, anxious, socially uncomfortable behavior an "avoidant disorder." Children who suffer from it have difficulty making friends, avoid new social contacts and experiences, and fear looking foolish or being teased. Howard may have wanted friends, but his anxiety and lack of self-confidence made him awkward. It was hard for him to initiate social contact or to accept friendships when offered.

Howard's anxieties and social difficulties may well have been heightened by Allene's overprotectiveness and preoccupation with illness. He probably internalized her excessive fears for his health and used illness to escape social pressure. Terry Moore, a possible wife of Howard's said that the only time he received love and affection was when he was ill. Ava Gardner, a twenty-year on-again-off-again girlfriend, wrote that Howard had a remoteness about him. She suspected his partial deafness may have explained his dull conversations and shyness. She called him the Quiet Texan.

When he was twelve, he formed a shortwave radio club that met in his bedroom, but soon became ill and stayed out of school, which put an end to socializing with those boys. When he was thirteen, his symptoms worsened and he was suddenly unable to walk, but an absolute diagnosis was never made. The illness may have served as a way for Howard to avoid the social demands of his early teenage years, keeping him from attending school as he should have.

Howard developed a hearing problem which may have been hereditary because Howard Sr. was known to have been hard of hearing. During Howard Jr.'s enrollment in boarding school in California, the condition may have isolated him further because he complained of being lonely and unable to relate to other students. The avoidant behavior became a personality pattern as he spent much of his time at school alone, riding a horse.

Losing his mother when he was sixteen, and then his father at eighteen, caused Howard overconcern for his health, and he further withdrew socially. Dr. Fowler wrote, "The loss of the only two people with whom he had a close relationship deepened his fears of death and increased his vulnerability to later disorders."

If it is true that Emma was Howard's biological mother, dare I ask the question—how would he have acted if he knew he was the son of a prostitute? If he did know, at what age did he find out, and would that have made the difference in his behavior? It would be understandable for him to feel anger, hate and loathing toward the woman who gave him away or even shame and embarrassment because of her life choices. It would have also been confusing as to who his family actually was.

Children who are abandoned can suffer from feelings of rejection, identity development, and damaged self-esteem. They may have vulnerable and hurt feelings over the birthmother's choice to reject them yet keep her other children to raise. Their feelings of loss and grief may be triggered at any time in their life, not just when they discovered the truth.

Adolescence involves a search for self-identity, and if Howard had a gap in his search, he may have been confused as to who exactly he was and never have formulated a real sense of himself.

I find it fascinating that Howard didn't appear to grieve after the death of either of his parents, and that he seemed to have no true connection to his extended families. In a 1925 will, he left out bequests to his Hughes side of the family. Later in Howard's life, one of his staff members, James Whetton, said that one evening when he was manning the Operations desk at Romaine Street, he received a phone call from Rupert Hughes, who informed him he was Howard's uncle and wanted to talk to Howard. The following evening Howard called to pick up his messages. Whetton gave him the names of the various callers, his uncle being one of them. This was followed by several minutes of silence on Howard's end before he finally said, "Jim, I want everyone to understand that as far as I am concerned, I do not have a living relative on the face of the earth."

As stated earlier, and in Rupert's own words from his letter to Howard after the death of his father, "Since your father's death I have never heard you say one word in praise, make one suggestion of a memorial to him or show any desire to emphasize his greatness or the importance of his splendid achievements."

Howard let few people get close to him. He was famous for having loyal employees who dedicated themselves to his needs. This group was dubbed "The Mormon Mafia," since many of them belonged to The Church of Jesus Christ of Latter-day Saints. The highly specialized group of staff members Howard surrounded himself with for most of his adult life became his family, in a sense. He found people he could trust, who could show him they would be loyal no matter the circumstances. Is that not what family should do for us? According to many of his staff members, Howard was unfailingly loyal to them also.

When he was twenty, Howard proposed to Ella Rice, a socialite and a girl he grew up with. When Ella refused to marry him, his aunt Annette went to Ella's mother and convinced her that Howard shouldn't go to Hollywood alone "with all that money." Three weeks later, they were married. There's no evidence he loved Ella, but perhaps he did. If he did, he seemingly didn't know how to show it. Within the first years of their marriage, he ignored her and was unfaithful, which sounds amazingly similar to how his father treated his mother. After Howard divorced Ella and dated a succession of Hollywood starlets, his uncle Rupert made the comment, "He'd throw his mother down the stairs if it was to his advantage."

Dudley Sharp said of Howard's marriage, "Howard was just not the kind of person who would ever take care of a wife. He was always off doing something and he ran these peculiar hours. He didn't sleep much. He would have his business meetings in a car somewhere at 2:00 A.M. and he might disappear for a day or two without Ella's knowing where he was."

After the divorce he never returned to Houston for the rest of his life, other than one single 24-hour visit in 1938 when he was honored with a parade for the success of circling the world in a Lockheed monoplane with two rudders. Cheering people lined the route between the airport and Rice Hotel.

Dr. Fowler stated that Howard was more interested in social activities and relationships in his early twenties, displaying more creativity and drive. It was also a time where he exhibited the least psychopathology.

His unlimited funds attracted women. He had many girlfriends and asked numerous women to marry him, some of the women multiple times. Perhaps his father's example created emotional instability with female relationships? If his real mother was a prostitute, the fact could have added a whole other dimension to understanding his mental health in this regard.

Howard dated many famous movie actresses and Dr. Fowler stated he "seemed more interested in collecting them than in establishing serious relationships." Before he became a recluse, Howard was in contact with many people and active in the Hollywood social scene, becoming a friend to Cary Grant, with whom he spent personal time. But for the most part, his relationships were distant and cool. Fowler felt his detachment was heightened by his progressive hearing disorder, making conversations difficult, especially in crowded rooms and at parties.

Most of Howard's phobias, OCD tendencies, desires to live in seclusion, and pain-medication abuse are well known, and for my supposition are not necessary to discuss here, however, I do find it interesting that what is not talked a lot about is how Howard's head traumas may have played into some of these issues.

Howard crashed a small plane during the filming of *Hell's Angels*, crushing his cheekbone and requiring surgery. He crashed a seaplane near Long Island and another seaplane at Lake Mead where he severely gashed his head. He was deprived oxygen from a defective mask while in flight. In a car accident, he smashed his head into the windshield. His most serious accident happened in 1946 when he had a near-fatal crash in an experimental FX-11 fighter plane, slamming into homes in Beverly Hills. He broke numerous bones and suffered severe burns. His chest was crushed and a lung collapsed. His heart was displaced to one side of his chest. After this crash Howard became addicted to pain medication.

More recently the effects of concussions have been understood. To quote Dr. Fowler, "A single head injury, even if there is no apparent structural damage, can affect psychological functioning seriously and may exacerbate existing emotional problems. A series of traumas, such as Hughes had, greatly increases the probability of brain damage. The accidents, particularly those that occurred between 1939 and 1946, may have been both a cause and an effect of his increasing emotional disorder."

What Dr. Fowler didn't address in his article is how geniuses typically behave socially, even without the other factors of Howard's overly obsessive mother, absentee father, his hearing disability, plane crashes, and all the other problems discussed in this chapter.

Also, what would it have done to Howard's mental health to have known that Allene was not his biological mother? Would this have caused bitterness and anger toward both his parents? There are many factors to consider when trying to understand someone's mental makeup. As I stated in the beginning of this book, enlightenment is the added benefit of understanding human reasoning. And truth can bring empathy and healing.

DNA RESEARCH

It is believed Howard Hughes Sr. had no children other than Howard Hughes Jr. Two of Sr.'s siblings had no children. The third, his brother Rupert, had one daughter, Elspeth. But during Howard Jr.'s estate settlement proceedings in 1981, claims were made that Rupert was sterile from having mumps as a child and that Elspeth's father was someone with whom her mother had an affair. I don't know if Elspeth's descendants have been able to determine their Hughes relationships through DNA. But the Felix Hughes and Jean Summerlin (Sr.'s parents) family is possibly at the end of its biological lines. And it's probable that only DNA can prove the relationships between Howard Hughes and my family.

I hired Mckell Keeney, an experienced genetic genealogist. She researched the Hughes family and my family tree, analyzed my DNA matches, and encouraged me to ask my paternal aunt to take a DNA test, which Aunt Jeanette did. We used the results across numerous DNA testing sites.

If Emma was Howard Jr.'s mother, and if Howard had descendants in any of the commercial DNA company testing pools, then the match to my family would be between them and Jeanette's (Emma's) DNA. Any rogue children of Howard's would be half-first cousins to Jeanette, sharing an average of 440 centiMorgans of DNA. (A centiMorgan is a measure of genetic distance, indicating how closely one is related to another.) Any grandchildren of Howard's would be half-first cousins once removed to Jeanette, sharing an average of 224 centiMorgans of DNA. Any great-grandchildren of Howard's would be half-first cousins twice removed to my paternal aunt, sharing an average of 125 centiMorgans. It was determined Jeanette does not have any unaccounted-for DNA matches over 75 centiMorgans.

Jeanette does have numerous distant DNA matches (over 50) with the surname Hughes. But so far, they are not to the same ancestors of Howard Robard Hughes Sr. within a genealogically relevant time frame. We discovered that many people not in my family also had numerous DNA matches to people with the Hughes surname, and that this is not uncommon for many Americans of European ancestry.

My father's yDNA test years ago (with the defunct Sorenson Project) showed us his paternal ancestral line was likely to be Osborne, not Hydrick or Hughes. As outlined in this book, Emma did not marry Jack Hydrick until my grandfather George was about a year and a half old. George was then given the Hydrick name. Jeanette's autosomal DNA matches also show numerous Osborne/Orsborn matches.

Keeney advised me that since Howard Hughes Jr. had no known children, my family members who have DNA tested will not have any matches to help determine that my great-grandmother Emma Butterfras was indeed Howard Jr.'s mother. Due to the lack of known Hughes blood relatives to test, Howard's DNA is needed to determine a relationship between him and me. It is rumored DNA samples of him exist, perhaps held in his estate. The mysteries of his complex life are not yet solved.

~ ~ ~

I hope you enjoyed reading this story as much as I enjoyed researching and writing it. If you did, please consider leaving a rating and/or review on Amazon.

CHAPTER NOTES

Introduction

Page vi. **met him many times while living in Southern California**: At the time (approximately 1964), Buddy lived in North Hollywood, and I lived in Thousand Oaks. Buddy occasionally dropped off his two youngest boys to spend a week or more with my family.

Page vi. **his time on earth was coming to an end**: Buddy (given name Owen Elmer Hydrick) died July 28, 1996 *(California Death Index, 1940-1997)*. He wrote the letter to Jeanette three months before, April 13-17, 1996.

Page vii. **"1937 on a porch of a house on North Airline Dr, in Houston, Texas"**: Bert and Eva Butterfras King lived at 1709 Airline Drive, Houston, Texas; *Houston City Directory*, 1935 and 1936.

Page vii. **"Great Aunt Eva (the one legged lady)"**: Phone conversation with Larry King, grandson of Bert and Eva King, February 10, 2016; "Eva severely injured her leg on a social outing when trying to get from a hay trailer to the truck Bert was driving." Email letter from Larry King, grandson of Bert and Eva King, February 18, 2016; "Because of her injury, I remember she always used some sort of electrical device to, I believe, stimulate the remaining part of her leg. She seemed in constant pain with the leg."

Page vii. **"Uncle Bert cut his index finger off"**: I could not find documentation regarding how Bert lost a finger.

Page vii. **"He was the one who took the gas in France in World War I"**: 1.) *Applications for Headstones for U.S. Military Veterans, 1925-1941*. Microfilm publication M1916, 134 rolls. ARC ID: 596118. Records of the Office of the Quartermaster General, Record Group 92. National Archives at Washington, D.C.; Enlistment Date: April 27, 1918. Discharged: Feb 15, 1919 Service #2805847 from state of Texas. Grade: Private, Branch of Service: U.S. Army, Company H, 360th Infantry, 90th Division; *The 360 Infrantry: A History of the Activities and Operations of the 360th United States Infantry Regiment in the World War 1914-1918*, p. 61; Casualties among enlisted men in Company H covering the period from August 21, 1918 to November 11, 1918 records 127 men gassed (none mentioned by name). http://www.90thdivisionassoc.org/90thDivisionFolders/mervinbo oks/WWI360/WWI36001/WWI36001.htm.; 2.) *The Houston Post*, Saturday, April 20, 1918, p 11 – Call 145, the Draft of April 26 to May 1…Bert King.

Page viii. **"He was a horse trader"**: *1935 Houston City Directory*, p ; Bert King's employment "salesman." *1936 Houston City Directory*, p ; Bert King's employment "cattleman." *1930 United States Federal Census, Houston, Harris, Texas*; Roll: 2342; Page: 23A; Enumeration District: 0024; Image: 653.0; FHL microfilm: 2342076; Bert King "Occupation: Salesman, Industry: Live Stock."

Page viii. **"finest ballroom in downtown Houston"**: Other than private ballrooms in mansions, the finest ballrooms were typically found in hotels. The most famous hotel in downtown Houston in 1904-05 was the Rice Hotel. For history and photographs see Website *The Heritage Society at Sam Houston Park* at https://www.heritagesociety.org/rice-hotel .

Page viii. **"One dance night she met a very hansom young dude she only introduced to Aunt Eva as Howard"**: *1904 Houston City Directory* does not record Howard R. Hughes because he came to Houston late in that year, after the directory was enumerated. *1905-1906 Houston City Directory*, p. 153 "Hughes, Howard R., oil producer and dealer, boards at Rice Hotel."

Page viii. **"Just before Christmas 1905, Emma, who was living in Galveston, Tx"**: Emma is not recorded in the *1905 Galveston City Directory* because she came late in the year, after the directory was enumerated. In October 1905, she married Charles Koenig in Galveston. (see marriage information below)

Page viii. **"showed up at her place"**: *1905-1906 Houston City Directory* "Butterfass, Eva A Miss h 2218 Carr."

Page viii. **Hughes Tool and Die Co.**: In my research I could not find the company owned by Howard Hughes Sr. to go by this name. It was known as Hughes Tool Company. But Buddy's grandmother Emma and Uncle Ernest worked for Model Laundry and Dye Company. Maybe he mistakenly combined the two names?

Page viii. **In 1928 we lived in Houston when Plympton, P.G., or Rick was born**: Texas Birth Index, 1903-1997. Texas: Texas Department of State Health Services.

Page ix. **George was not there. He was on a cow ranch.**: George Hydrick Jr. interview with author over phone, March 28, 2016. - George Jr., the brother of Buddy, lived with Eva and her husband Bert as a young teen, about thirteen to fifteen years old he thinks. George worked for Bert rounding up horses and cattle. He said Bert was a quiet, good guy and didn't allow "booze or raising heck." He said Eva was a wonderful person. They would visit in the afternoon over tea and roll Bull Durham cigarettes.

Page ix. **Sometime in the early 2000s, Aunt Jeanette sent me a copy of the letter**: I no longer have the postdated envelope that Aunt Jeanette used to send me the letter. It was in the early 2000s to the best of my recollection.

Page ix. **old family photos**: Included with the letter was a photo album once belonging to my grandfather, George Hydrick. Most of the photos are from his military service in Cuba, although there were a few photos taken earlier and later in his life of his extended family and his children.

Page x. **fellow coworker, Chris**: Chris Luders and I worked for Steve's Custom Doors in Mesa, Arizona from 2004-2006.

Page xi. **online rumors that Howard Hughes's mother, Allene Gano Hughes, was never pregnant, and that the Hughes' neighbors said the child just showed up one day.**: In 2016 when I tried to track down these internet posts from approximately 2005, I could no longer find them. I am hoping with the publishing of this book, more information like this will come forward.

Page xi. **Allene traveled to Keokuk, Iowa many months later**: *The Houston Post*, Thursday, 6 Sep 1906, p 10 – "Mrs. Howard Hughes and Master Howard, Jr., leave today for Keokuk, Iowa, for a visit to Mr. Hughes' relatives."

Page xi. **Many months after Howard's birth, on October 7, 1906, Allene traveled to Keokuk, Iowa and had Howard Robard Hughes Jr. christened in St. John's Episcopal Church.**: Keokuk Iowa Saint John's Episcopal Church Baptismal Record, pp 120, 121. "Date: Oct 7. Name: Howard Robard. Parents: Howard R. and Allene Hughes. Sponsor: Mrs. W. B. Sharp. Birth: September 24, 1905."

Page xii. **Letter from Ernest Hydrick to his nephew Sonny Hydrick, Aug 25, 1980 in its entirety**: original in the possession of author, Ora Smith.

Page xii. **Letter from George to his son, Rick**: original in the possession of author, Ora Smith.

Chapter One

Page 2. **His paint-splattered overalls and hat**: 1882 through 1891 Houston Texas Directories - "Peter Butterfass occupation, painter and glazier for A. Bering and Bros."

Page 3. **photo hanging over the mantle**: Photo of Mary Clark Butterfass is in possession of Charlie Butterfras. It is approximately 2'x2-1/2' in size, in an ornate Victorian Era gold frame with original bowed glass. Mary appears to be in her late teens or early twenties, which would place the photo in the 1860s. (Also owned by Charlie Butterfras is a photo of Peter Butterfass in his elderly years, probably taken soon before he died in 1903.)

Page 4. **the move onto Hutchins Street**: *1892 Houston City Directory* - Location of residence 1714 Hutchins.

Page 5. **heading to Market Square, about a mile up Milam Street**: 1.) 1882 through 1891 Houston Texas Directories - Peter Butterfass' residence located at 298 Milam Street, corner of Leeland. The house no longer stands, but close by is Market Square Park (historic); 2.) Johnston, p 97.

Page 5. **some of the tallest three-to-four-story wood buildings in the city. Merchants, bakers, gunsmiths, and blacksmiths were all along the way**: Becker, p 60 (photograph of market on Milam Street).

Page 5. **sawmills, iron foundries, and brick kilns**: 1.) Johnston, p 82; 2.) Wilson, p 101-103

Chapter Two

Page 8. **Peter Butterfass...1835 with the label of bastard**: 1.) Deutschland Geburten und Taufen, 1558-1898, Name Petrus Butterfass, Event Date 1835, Gender Male, Birth Date 22 Mar 1835, Birth Year 1835, Christening Date 22 Mar 1835, Christening Place KATHOLISCH, LUDWIGSHOEHE, RHEINHESSEN, HESSE-DARMSTADT, Mother's Name Catharinae Butterfass, Maternal Grandfather's Name Philippi Butterfass. Citing this Record - Deutschland Geburten und Taufen, 1558-1898, database, FamilySearch (https://familysearch.org/ark:/61903/1:1:NZNK-S6T accessed 6

April 2016), FHL microfilm 49,084. Note: records mother's name only: Catharinae Butterfass and her father as Philippi Butterfass, which leads me to believe Catharinae was not married; 2.) Peter Butterfass Immigration Record (below) records birth year as 1835; 3.) 1870 and 1880 United States Federal Censuses record birth years as about 1834 (he probably hadn't yet had his birthday when census was taken); 4.) 1900 United States Federal Census records his birth month and day as "June 1837"; 5.) FindAGrave.com "Name Peter Butterfras, Birth June 1837 Hessen, Germany, Burial Houston, Harris County, Texas, United States of America, Death 8 November 1903 Houston, Harris County, Texas, United States of America." Note: Since the 1900 Census and FindAGrave are the only (late) records that don't match the 1835 birth date, I have concluded his birth year as 1835; 6.) Harris County Court Probate Minutes, Index Film #1009262, Vol F, Naturalizations, p 616 – "Butterfass, Peter, Country of Birth Germany, Date of Proceeding Nov 1869, Grant of Citizenship. Note: No birth date or age recorded.

Page 8. **Peter…a glazier and painter**: 1.) *1877 Houston City Directory* "Butterfass Peter, Painter for Pereira and Randolph."; 2.) 1882 through 1891 Houston Texas Directories - "Peter Butterfass occupation, painter and glazier for A. Bering and Bros."

Page 8. **thousands of artisans and household craftsmen sailing to America**: Website - *Ohio University*, "Hesse-Cassel" of the Encyclopedia of Revolutions of 1848 https://www.ohio.edu/chastain/dh/hessek.htm

Page 9. **had to show proof of at the French border**: Website *Genealogical Historical Services* - http://www.genhist.org/ghs_Havre_eng.htm "After the French government required in 1837 that Germans present a valid ticket at the French border, local offices began to be opened in Switzerland and the German states."

Page 9. **Le Havre was the thoroughfare of emigration from Germany**: Ibid.

Page 9. **no meals would be provided**: Ibid.

Page 10. **sailing on the SS Gallia**: New York Passenger Lists - Line: 28 Microfilm Serial: M237 Microfilm Roll: 97 List Number: 374 "Name: Peter Butterfass, Arrival Date: 21 Apr 1851, Estimated Birth Year: abt 1835 Age: 16 Gender: Male, Port of Departure: Le Havre, France, Destination: United States of

America. Place of Origin: Preußen, Ship Name: Gallia, Port of Arrival: New York"

Page 11. **sandstone walls of Castle Garden**: Note: Ellis Island did not open to immigrants until 1892.

Page 13. **the German Coast**: Website *Wikipedia*, "German Americans" https://en.wikipedia.org/wiki/German_Americans#Louisiana

Page 13. **Peter piloted a Louisiana Confederate gunboat during the Civil War**: This piece of information came from extrapolating a query my grandfather posted for his grandmother, Mary Butterfrass in the *Confederate Veteran* magazine May 1916 - "George Hydrick, care G.H.&H Railway Company, Galveston, Tex., would be glad to hear from any comrade of Peter Paul Butterfrass, who was pilot on the gunboat *Laura Hill*, which sailed from Burwick Bay to New Orleans and was destroyed in battle. Mr. Butterfrass then enlisted with the Sentilenia Rifles at Pattersonville, La. His widow is trying to secure a pension." https://archive.org/details/confederateveter24conf/page/n15/mode/2up The information given in that query does not correlate with historical evidence regarding Civil War history, but the clues led me to believe Peter piloted the *SS Diana* because it was after that battle when soldiers went to nearby Pattersonville and re-enlisted.

Page 13. *SS Diana*, **which was destroyed in April 1863**: Raphael, p 19, 39, 147-148. Note: Peter Butterfass was not mentioned in the book by name.

Page 14. **married the young and beautiful Mary Clark**: I could not find a marriage record for Peter Butterfass and Mary Clark in Louisiana, approximately early 1860s. I do however match DNA to Clark families in St. Martin Parish and Calcasieu Parish, Louisiana. Proof below of Mary Clark Butterfass being the mother of Emma Butterfras.

Page 14. **governmental distribution of food**: Website *64 Parishes* https://64parishes.org/entry/civil-war-louisiana – "For many Louisianans, starvation was a real threat, as armies either seized or destroyed food crops. Some planters, who possessed the means to move, fled to Texas, often with their slaves. Other Louisianans struggled to feed, clothe, and house themselves. The Confederate state government tried to help by allocating $5 million to soldiers' families and distributing food to those in need, but this amount did not prove sufficient to alleviate all of the state's suffering, especially in areas that saw repeated Union incursions."

Page 14. **German colonization in Texas had been encouraged since the early 1800s, resulting in one of the largest migrations from Europe**: Johnston, p 35.

Page 15. **In 1868, he relocated his small family**: Texas U.S. Voter Registration Lists 1867-1869 – "Name Peter Butterfass, Registry Date 18 Nov 1869, Residence Place Houston, County Harris, Line Number 3039, Archive Name Texas State Library and Archives, Archive Collection Title 1867 Voter Registration Lists, Archive Reel Number 6." Note: The year of Peter Butterfass moving his family to Texas is a guesstimate considering the birth years of his daughters, Tillie born 1865 in Louisianna, and Lottie born 1868 in Texas.

Chapter Three

Page 18. **At the time, New York was the only other city building an electric power plant.**: Johnston, p 92

Page 18. **Houston offered free public schools**: Ibid, p 90.

Page 18. **The city had two-hundred and thirty-four trains arriving and departing each day**: Ibid, p 92.

Page 18. **Mary is recorded as having given birth to nine children**: 1900 United States Federal Census, Census Place: Houston Ward 3, Harris, Texas; Page: 3; Enumeration District: 0078; FHL microfilm: 1241642 - Mary Butterfass is recorded as giving birth to 9 children, with 6 living. Lottie was dead by 1900 (see Chapter Eight notes), and John died in 1877 (see next). It stands to reason Wilhelmina was the third who died because I cannot find any marriage other records about her other than her christening in 1871 (see next).

Page 18. **deaths of both Wilhelmina and baby John**: 1.) Erst Deutsche Evangelische Lutherische Kirche, Houston, Harris, Texas for Wilhelmina Butterfass christened 3 Sep 1871. Death date unknown; 2.) *The Galveston Daily News*, 24 June 1877 - "The following people died this week...John Butterfass, 2 years, inflammation of kidneys."

Page 19. **"They was a close knit family. Emma and Eva—they stuck together."**: Taped Oral Interview of George Hydrick, given by Plymton Hydrick on July 6, 1980.

Page 19. **Lottie's daughter, Beulah**: Beulah Readler, U.S. Social Security Application Index 1936-2007, Ancestry.com – "Beulah Readler Biers, Birth Date: 23 Oct 1890, Birth Place: Houston Harr, Texas, Father: Antone Readler, Mother: Lottie Butterfras, Notes: Jul 1965: Name listed as BEULAH READLER BIERS

Page 19. **Her baby sister, Mabel**: Mabel Readler, U.S. Social Security Application Index 1936-2007, Ancestry.com – "Mable Ebelt, Birth Date: 25 Dec 1892, Issue year: 1973, Issue State: Texas, Last Residence: 77060, Houston, Harris, Texas, USA, Death Date: Mar 1980"

Page 20. **Lottie married and moved away when Emma was seven**: Texas U.S. Select County Marriage Index 1837-1965, FHL Film Number: 25225, Ancestry.com – "Name: Gertrude Butterfass, Gender: Female, Marriage Date: 16 Apr 1888 Marriage Place: Harris, Texas, United States, Spouse: Anthony Readler."

Page 20. **Tillie married when Emma was two**: 1.) The Galveston Daily News, Sunday, April 27, 1884, p. 2 "The following marriage licenses were issued from the county clerk's office for the week ending today: Otto Lorenz and Matilda Butterfass."; 2.) Texas Select County Marriage Records "Name Matilda Batterfass, Marriage Date 21 Apr 1884, Marriage Place Harris, Texas, USA, Spouse Otto Lorenz. Document Number 11583 Note: Family records show his full name as Charles Otto Lorenz.

Page 20. **Now divorced, Tillie lived in Galveston**: *The Galveston Daily News*, Tuesday, May 14, 1895, p. 3 "In the civil district clerk's office today the following suits were filed: John Lenz vs. Matilda Lenz, suit for divorce."

Page 20. **Tillie's son was eight**: Social Security Applications and Claims 1936-2007 Ancestry.com. [database on-line]. Provo, UT, USA, Name: Frederick Grover Lorenz, Gender: Male, Race: White, Birth Date: 26 Mar 1883, Birth Place: Houston Trav, Texas, Father: Charles O Lorenz, Mother: Mary M Butterfrass.

Page 21. **Garten Verein**: 1.) Gidley and Marines, pp 44-46; 2.) Bixel and Turner, p 6.

Page 24. **they reached Grand Central**: Later named Union Station in 1911.

Chapter Four

Page 26. **Panic of 1893**: 1.) Johnston, p 103; 2.) Website *Wikipedia*, "Panic of 1893" https://en.wikipedia.org/wiki/Panic_of_1893

Page 27. **his new job as an auditorium watchman**: *1899 Houston City Directory* "Butterfass Peter P, watchman, r. 1113 Taylor." Note: the year before *1898 Houston City Directory* "Butterfass, Peter, glazier, r. 1809 Hardy." I don't know why he changed occupations from a painter and window glazier, something he'd done for at least thirty-five years. I don't think it would be related to feebleness because a watchman was expected to guard a building to prevent crime, to watch out for fires, and to ensure that suspicious and unauthorized people did not prowl around under cover of darkness. Peter moved his family sometime between 1898-99. This would have been about the time Emma moved to Galveston. Paul married in May 1899, but the *1899 Houston City Directory* shows he is living with P.P., which I would expect was his father. He and his bride are enumerated with Peter Butterfass in the 1900 United States Federal Census and living at 2519 Main Street. That's three residences in three years. Perhaps the moves are related to Peter's drinking and/or lack of funds? In *1902 Houston City Directory* "Butterfass, Peter P. janitor Houston auditorium r. 2515 Main 3." Notice Peter is now a janitor and no longer a watchman. (It appears on GoogleMaps that the small, one-story home on Hardy still stands but the other sites have been commercialized.)

Chapter Five

Page 29. **newly found Butterfras cousin**: Charlie Butterfras interview with author at his home in Texas, Feb 6, 2016.

Page 29. **home on Main Street**: Peter Butterfass in 1900 United States Federal Census, Census Place: Houston Ward 3, Harris, Texas; Page: 3; Enumeration District: 0078; FHL microfilm: 1241642.

Page 29. **the other three weeks she lived and worked in Galveston**: Remmers, p 18. Note: It is thought that prostitutes took the week of their menstrual cycle off.

Page 29. **she traveled on a trolley one-and-a-half miles to Grand Central Depot**: Distance between her father's residence at 2515 Main Street to the depot (later named Union Station in 1911).

Page 29. **The daily Short Line to Galveston left late afternoon**: Train schedules in 1899 *The Houston Post* newspaper.

Page 31. **They slowly crossed above Galveston Bay, two miles wide. As the train swayed slightly along the flimsy wooden trestle**: Gidley and Marines, p 136.

Page 31. **Since the end of the Spanish-American War the year before, the wharf thrived as Galveston's lifeblood.**: Bixel and Turner, p 12.

Page 32. **shopped at the elegant stores.**: Remmers, p 10 – "The madams and their girls shopped at all the fine stores in Galveston."

Page 32. **Emma made a point of dressing more conservatively east of 25th Street, to not bring attention to herself.**: Ibid.

Page 32. **a man lighting gas streetlamps on one of the few streets that hadn't yet been electrified**: The first electric power plant in Texas was built at Galveston in the early 1880s but residents were slow getting power to their homes, depending on their economic status.

Page 32. **rows of white two-story houses had lattice-work porches shielding front doors from the view of passersby and green-shuttered windows closed for the night.**: Remmers, p 8.

Chapter Six

Page 35. **section of bordellos along Postoffice Street was famously known as "The Line."**: Remmers, p 5.

Page 35. **the day Emma's life changed forever**: Date of conception considering George Hydrick was born January 19, 1900 would have been approximately April 28, 1899. https://www.calculator.net/pregnancy-calculator.html

Page 35. **surpassing New Orleans to become the top cotton port in the nation**: Bixel and Turner, p 12 – "The 1900-1901 season was no exception…Galveston had surpassed New Orleans to become the top cotton port in the nation, and during 1899 had moved to second place (after New York) in wheat exports."

Page 35. **The city had a toleration-silence policy regarding prostitution.**: Price, p 72.

Page 35. **The bordellos in Galveston were segregated by race and economic standing**: Ibid, p 62, 63.

Page 37. **Not only her looks, but the overall décor of her bordello and the quality of amenities were reflected in the price she'd receive.**: Price, p 10.

Page 37. **Emma received sixty percent and the retired prostitute who managed the bordello forty percent**: Remmers, p 7.

Page 38. **pushed the sale of liquor and music and made sure that drinking guests didn't cause trouble for her girls**: Price, p 10, 12.

Page 38. **The gas-lighted doorway of the bordello was hidden behind lattice, concealing his identity from the gaze of others**: Remmers, p 6.

Page 38. **wall prints of delicate nude girls draped in sheer fabrics**: Ibid, p 10.

Page 39. **Some were tourists, others boisterous seaman, and sometimes a young boy or two from the nearby medical college.**: Price, p 21.

Page 40. **a pitcher of water and a towel**: Remmers, pp 6, 7.

Page 40. **glass transoms over the doors were left open**: Ibid, p 7.

Page 40. **prostitutes were required to take out a license for $2.50**: 1.) License for Prostitution https://frankamills.com/portfolio/oleander-hotel-galveston-texas 15 August 1881 for Madame Kitty, Galveston, Texas; 2.) In Remmers book p 10, she writes about girls needing to take out "health cards" and having to be examined biweekly by a doctor and tested for drugs. They displayed this certification in their bordello room. When Galveston was an "Open City," meaning prostitution was not outlawed, it was the city's major industry.

Page 41. **many girls with mental health problems**: Price, p 41.

Page 41. **birth control methods used in 1899**: Website *National Museum of Civil War Medicine*, "Mother's Friend: Birth Control in Nineteenth-Century America" February 5, 2017 - https://www.civilwarmed.org/birth-control/

Page 41. **he impregnated Emma and left behind his DNA to travel down three generations to myself**: In 2011,

Plymton Grover Hydrick had a yDNA (paternal) test performed with Sorensen Molecular Genealogy. When information was later uploaded onto Website *FamilyTreeDNA* and also Website *Ancestry*, it was determined he descended paternally from the Osborne family. In 2021, testing was performed with Plymton's sister's autosomal DNA and her closest matches to the Osborne's were through family lines that descended from Neverson Osborne/Orsborn. Making one wonder if Emma knew George's father well enough to give George the middle name of Neverson. With research, there were no records (including birth) found of a George Neverson Osborne.

Chapter Seven

Page 42. **article in the *New York Times* by Bruce Feiler**: "The Stories that Bind," March 15, 2013. https://www.nytimes.com/2013/03/17/fashion/the-family-stories-that-bind-us-this-life.html
Page 43. **There is no birth record for George**: At some point, a delayed birth record was filed by George under the name of George Neverson Hydrick. He was not required to show proof of claim. I did not find an address for Emma in January 1900. Six months later, in June 1900 she was enumerated in the United States Federal Census at her father's household. George is not enumerated there, nor could I find him enumerated anywhere in that year's census using the name of George Butterfras, George Hydrick, or George Osborne. According to Emma's brother Paul, three months after census Emma lived in Galveston when the hurricane hit.
Page 43. **Emma was enumerated in her father's home**: 4 June 1900, United States Federal Census, Year: 1900; Census Place: Houston Ward 3, Harris, Texas; Page: 3; Enumeration District: 0078; FHL microfilm: 1241642. Address: 2519 Main Street, Houston, Harris, Texas. (In 1900 Houston City Directory Jack Hydrick lives at 818 Lakin Street, Houston, three miles from Emma, but she did not marry him until July 1, 1901. It is not known when they met. Jack married Florence Patillo, June 14, 1900, 10 days after the census. He is not found in any United States Federal Census in 1900.)
Page 43. **autosomal DNA testing performed...George did carry the Butterfras genes**: Multiple DNA matches between me and other Butterfras family members on ancestry.com.

Page 45. **Mrs. E. W. Nichols, the matron of Bethesda Door of Hope**: Turner, 111.

Page 47. **rescue home...1311 27th Street**: Ibid., p 290

Page 47. **There's at least a thousand of us in this city**: Turner, p 290.

Chapter Eight

Page 48. **profession of prostitution**: Although I searched for years, I have no printed documentation that proves 100% that Emma was a prostitute. I believe she was because: 1. My Butterfras cousin believes it to be so; 2. The fact that Emma's landlord, Lillian Sullivan was in "real estate," which was common for madams; 3. Emma lived in Galveston away from her family by as early as 1899 (probably earlier) when she was sixteen; 4. Her first child born out of wedlock with no record of who the father was; 5. Emma died young of cervical cancer, a common demise for prostitutes; and 6. My grandfather's shame and refusal to talk about his mother and knowing nothing about his father.

Page 48. **Some estimate that 85% of prostitutes were sexually abused before they entered the profession**: Website *Rape   Is   at* https://www.rapeis.org/activism/prostitution/prostitutionfacts.htm l cited from Patricia Murphy, *Making the Connections: Women, Work, and Abuse*, Paul M. Deutsch Press, Orlando, Florida, 1993.

Page 48. **"not welcomed at home"**: Price, p

Page 49. **Tillie, married German immigrant Otto Lorenz**. 1.) *The Galveston Daily News*, Sunday, April 27, 1884, p. 2 "The following marriage licenses were issued from the county clerk's office for the week ending today: Otto Lorenz and Matilda Butterfass."; 2.) Texas Select County Marriage Records "Name Matilda Batterfass, Marriage Date 21 Apr 1884, Marriage Place Harris, Texas, USA, Spouse Otto Lorenz. Document Number 11583 Note: Family records show his full name as Charles Otto Lorenz.

Page 49. **Tillie gave birth to son Frederick**: Social Security Applications and Claims 1936-2007 Ancestry.com, Provo, UT, USA – "Name: Frederick Grover Lorenz, Gender: Male, Race: White, Birth Date: 26 Mar 1883, Birth Place: Houston Trav, Texas, Father: Charles O Lorenz, Mother: Mary M Butterfrass."

Page 49. **Tillie divorced Otto, Fred raised primarily by his father and stepmother**. 1.) *The Galveston Daily News*, Tuesday, May 14, 1895, p. 3 "In the civil district clerk's office today the following suits were filed: John Lenz vs. Matilda Lenz, suit for divorce." 2.) Texas, U.S., Death Certificates, 1903-1982 Ancestry.com. [database on-line]. Provo, UT, USA – "Fred Grover Lorenz Death Date: 31 Mar 1950, Death Place: Port Arthur, Jefferson, Texas, Father: C.O. Lorenz," mother's name and birth place recorded as "unknown," which makes me assume Tillie had not been in her son's life for a very long time.

Page 49. **Tillie married a Mr. Vinson**: family record.

Page 49. **Tillie…married Frank Wiggins**: *The Galveston Daily News*, Tuesday, 7 April 1895, p 3 – "Marriage Licenses … Frank Wiggins and Mrs. Matilda Vinson."

Page 49. **Tillie…gave birth to a daughter, Edith**: 1900 United States Federal Census, Washington, D.C. National Archives and Records Administration, Census Place: McCook, Red Willow, Nebraska; Page: 20; Enumeration District: 0162; FHL microfilm: 1240938 – "Frank Wiggins head of household, married 5 years, Tillie Wiggins wife, born Sep 1865 in Louisiana, father born in German, mother born in Louisiana, daughter Edith born Febry 1897 in Texas, 3 years old."

Page 49. **[Tillie and Frank Wiggins] moved to Nebraska**: see 1900 Census above.

Page 49. **Frank and sixteen-year-old stepson Frederick were imprisoned for counterfeiting dollar coins**: *Brenham Daily Banner* (Brenham, Tex.), Vol. 26, No. 49, Ed. 1 Tuesday, 26 Feb 1901 – "Frank Wiggins and his sixteen year old step-son have been arrested in Houston on a warrant issued by the United States Commissioner Tracy B. Dunn, charging them with having passed counterfeit money. The counterfeits alleged to have been passed by the accused are coins of the dollar denomination."

Page 49. **Tillie died at the young age of thirty-seven**: Magnolia Cemetery, Houston, Harris, Texas – "Barbara Matilda "Tillie" Butterfras Wiggins, Birth 3 Sep 1865 Louisiana, Death 13 Jul 1903 (aged 37)," Plot 41B, Findagrave Memorial ID 196526896.

Page 49. **Lottie married Anton Readler**: Texas U.S. Select County Marriage Index 1837-1965, FHL Film Number: 25225, Ancestry.com – "Name: Gertrude Butterfass, Gender:

Female, Marriage Date: 16 Apr 1888 Marriage Place: Harris, Texas, United States, Spouse: Anthony Readler."

Page 49. **...they had three children**: **1.** Beulah Readler, U.S. Social Security Application Index 1936-2007, Ancestry.com – "Beulah Readler Biers, Birth Date: 23 Oct 1890, Birth Place: Houston Harr, Texas, Father: Antone Readler, Mother: Lottie Butterfras, Notes: Jul 1965: Name listed as BEULAH READLER BIERS; **2.** Mabel Readler, U.S. Social Security Application Index 1936-2007, Ancestry.com – "Mable Ebelt, Birth Date: 25 Dec 1892, Issue year: 1973, Issue State: Texas, Last Residence: 77060, Houston, Harris, Texas, USA, Death Date: Mar 1980"; **3.** William Anton Readler, U.S. WWI Draft Registration Card – "William Anton Readler, Race: Caucasian (White), Marital Status: Single, Birth Date: 13 Dec 1895, Birth Place: Texas, USA, Residence Date: 1917-1918, Street Address: 2113 Washington, Houston, Harris, Texas."

Page 49. **Lottie died**: Magnolia Cemetery, Houston, Harris, Texas – "Charlotte Emilie Gertrude Readler, Birth Date: 24 Aug 1868, Birth Place: Houston, Harris County, Texas, Death Date: 13 Sep 1899, Death Place: Houston, Harris County, Texas, United States of America, Father: Peter Butterfras, Mother: Mary Butterfras, Spouse: Anthony Readler." Plot Lot 41B, Findagrave Memorial ID 196525710

Page 49. **Emma's brother, John, died at two**: *The Galveston Daily News*, 24 June 1877 - "The following people died this week...John Butterfass, 2 years, inflammation of kidneys."

Page 49. **Paul was born about the time John died**: U.S. WWI Draft Registration Card – "Paul Peter Butterfrass, Race: White, Birth Date: 19 May 1878, Residence Date: 1917-1918, Street Address: 1812 Chestnut St, Residence Place: Houston, Harris, Texas, Physical Build: Slender, Height Medium, Hair Color Brown, Eye Color Blue, Spouse: Mary Butterfras."

Page 49. **[Paul] died in 1969**: Texas U.S. Death Index 1903-2000 - "Name: Paul Butterfras, Death Date: 22 Jul 1969, Death County: Harris, Marital Status: Widowed."

Page 49. **[Paul married] Mary Gray from Louisiana**: Texas U.S. Select County Marriage Index, 1837-1965 FHL Film Number 1008072 – "Mary Gray, Marriage Date: 18 May 1899, Marriage Place: Brazoria, Texas, Spouse: Paul Butterfrass."

Page 50. **Hy moved out...at the age of sixteen with his younger sister, Eva, who was thirteen**: *1903 Houston City Directory* – "Butterfass Eva A. Miss, Opr Ineeda ldy, h 1712

Freeman," next line "Butterfass Henry, brickmason, h 1712 Freeman." The other Butterfras's listed are not at this address. Note: Eva's occupation abbreviations appear to mean 'Operator I need a lady' which makes one wonder if she was a prostitute also. But in her day there was a biscuit made by Nabisco called "Uneeda." Perhaps the name was misspelled, and Eva was an operator at the biscuit factory? But what would the ldy abbreviation mean?

Page 50. **Hy died**: 1.) *The Houston Chronicle*, June 28, 1906; 2.) *The Houston Post*, Thursday, June 28, 1906, p. 1; 3.) *The Houston Post*, Tuesday, July 17, 1906, p. 9.

Page 50. **Eva married five times**: 1. John Sellis Little; 2. Charles Jordan; 3. Barney F. Brown; 4. Richard Taylor; 5. Bert King.

Page 50. **[Peter's] single mother in the 1820s**: Deutschland Geburten und Taufen, 1558-1898, Name Petrus Butterfass (see Chapter Two notes).

Page 50. **[abuse] case in New York City...two-year-old girl, Mary Ellen McCormack**: Website *The New York Times,* article "Case Shined First Light on Abuse of Children" by Howard Markel, M.D., 14 Dec 2009. https://www.nytimes.com/2009/12/15/health/15abus.html

Page 51. **New York Society for the Prevention of Cruelty to Children was founded**: Ibid.

Chapter Nine

Page 52. **9:45 a.m. Galveston, Houston, and Henderson train to Galveston**: 1.) Weems, p 44; 2.) Bixel and Turner, p 20.

Page 53. **winds blew from the north**: Website – *Genealogy Trails* "Texas Genealogy Trails, Galveston 1900 Hurricane" http://genealogytrails.com/tex/state/galvestonhurr_exp.html Personal Experiences of Those Who Escaped.

Page 53. **sea's white caps two feet below the train**: Weems, p 44.

Page 53. **water flowed above the tracks**: Ibid, 53, 58.

Page 53. **crew disembarked...pushing drifting debris**: Bixel and Turner, p 20.

Page 54. **They waited about an hour in the hot and muggy coach before the rescue train arrived**: 1.) *Our Texas*

History - http://ourtexashistory.com/post_3.html "passengers were forced to transfer to a relief train on parallel tracks to complete their journey" 2.) Bixel and Turner, p 20.

Page 54. **slowly headed to Union Depot...crew walking ahead**: Larson, Erik, p 168.

Page 54. **water higher than their waists**: 1.) Bixel and Turner, p 20 – "arrived on the island around 1:00 P.M." 2.) Website – *Genealogy Trails* "Texas Genealogy Trails, Galveston 1900   Hurricane" http://genealogytrails.com/tex/state/galvestonhurr_exp.html Personal Experiences of Those Who Escaped. "At 1.15 we arrived at the Santa Fe union depot."

Page 54. **The water was too deep for the street cars to run.**: Bixel and Turner, p 23.

Page 55. **considering the island was a sandbar and less than a dozen feet above sea level.**: Bixel and Turner, p ix.

Page 55. **water had risen to just below the kitchen tabletop...argued with her for some time.**: Oral family story of Paul Butterfras in 1969 "When I got to Emma, water was up to the kitchen tabletop she stood on." Guesstimating this would have been approximately 2 P.M. since their train arrived about 1:15 P.M. Emma argued with Paul about leaving and felt the water would soon go down.

Page 56. **five-story Tremont Hotel**: 1.) Bixel and Turner, p 27: 2.) This ad ran two days before the storm - *The Houston Post*, Thursday, 6 Sep 1900, p 10 – "Tremont Hotel, Galveston, Texas. Now Refitted and Refurnished with Bathrooms, Furniture and Carpets. ELEGANT SUITES CAN BE SECURED. Rates are reasonable. Office Staff-W. A. Easton, J. Y. Bedell, H. A. Butler. G. E. Korst, proprietor."

Page 56. **After a city-wide fire years ago, the roofs had been covered in slate.**: Weems, p 84.

Page 58. **Blacks and whites huddled together, race having no boundaries.**: Bixel and Turner, p 30.

Page 58. **upstairs hallway...outer rooms...flying glass and plaster**: Website – *Genealogy Trails* "Texas Genealogy Trails,   Galveston   1900   Hurricane" http://genealogytrails.com/tex/state/galvestonhurr_exp.html Personal Experiences of Those Who Escaped.

Page 58. **The building lost electricity**: Greene and Kelly, p 24 – from the personal letter of Charles W. Law.

Page 59. **Circling winds**: 1.) Website *Genealogy Trails* "Texas Genealogy Trails, Galveston 1900 Hurricane" http://genealogytrails.com/tex/state/galvestonhurr_exp.html Personal Experiences of Those Who Escaped; 2.) Greene and Kelly, pp 53, 94.

Page 59. **"The hotel has lost its roof!"**: Website *Genealogy Trails* - "The roof was blown off and the skylights over the' rotunda fell in and fell through, crashing on the floor below."

Page 59. **There must have been over a thousand people in the hotel**: 1.) Bixel and Turner, p 27; 2.) Greene and Kelly, p 24 – from the personal letter of Charles W. Law.

Page 59. **vocal prayer...Blacks sang hymns**: Ibid., p 30.

Page 60. **Around 10 p.m., the winds slowed**.: Ibid., p 31.

Page 60. **Hundreds of human and animal bodies...floated and still floating**: 1.) United States Weather Bureau Office, Special Report of the Galveston Hurricane of September 8, 1900, by Isaac M. Cline, Local Forecast Official and Section Director, Galveston, Tex., September 23, 1900, found at https://vlab.noaa.gov/web/nws-heritage/-/galveston-storm-of-1900; 2.) Website *The 1900 Storm, Galveston Island, Texas* found at https://www.1900storm.com/nightofhorrors/

Page 60. **Many walked up and down the silt-covered streets, crying and wailing, their muddy bare feet bleeding from stepping on glass and other debris**.: Greene and Kelly, p 25.

Page 61. **bells rang out from the Ursuline Convent**: Bixel and Turner, p 43.

Page 61. **smell of decaying bodies**: Ibid., p 48. Temperatures for the few days after the hurricane hovered close to 90 degrees.

Page 61. **a ship had been pulled from its anchor and blown into the bay, destroying all three wooden railway trestles joining Galveston to the mainland**: Weems, p 103. The ship *Roma*, commanded by Captain Storm.

Page 61. **The wagon bridge had also been destroyed by the storm**.: Weems, p 44.

Page 61. **No telegraph or phone lines remained**.: Greene and Kelly, p 114.

Page 61. **Black men were forced at bayonet point**: Bixel and Turner, p 48.

Page 61. **700 bodies were taken eighteen miles out to sea...drifted back**: Ibid.

Page 61. **burn the dead on pyres**: Ibid.

Page 62. **An estimated 6,000 people died during the storm**: The number of deaths does not appear to be agreed upon, but the majority of estimates reach over 6,000 fatalities with thousands injured. The highest estimate was 12,000 fatalities. Greene and Kelly, p 70 – from the personal letter of Ida Smith Austin, "The loss of life will not fall short of six thousand. The property loss will reach the enormous sum of thirty millions. Over four thousand happy homes absolutely demolished and wreckage of these homes was piled from twenty to thirty feet high for miles along the gulf front, extending inland from three hundred to a thousand yards."

Page 62. **By the third day, ferries sailed people across**: Greene and Kelly, p 24.

Page 62. **destroying all three wooden railway trestles joining Galveston to the mainland**: Ibid, pp 47, 95, 124.

Page 62. **Hundreds of bodies still floated in the water**: Ibid, pp 26, 47.

Page 62. **walked seven miles to the closest working train that took them into Houston**.: Ibid, pp 47, 48 – from the personal letter of Walker W. Davis, "We found hundreds of corpses floating in the bay. When we got to the mainland we were happy. There was no railroad nearer than seven miles as everything had been washed away. We all started in and walked part of the time through water up to our waist, but still happy to be alive. After walking over the prairie over dead animals and human bodies we at last reached a relief train that had been sent down as far as they could get from Houston."

Chapter Ten

Page 63. **Emma now lived with her family on Main Street in downtown Houston**: It is assumed she moved into her parents' home after the hurricane since she was enumerated with them only a few months before in the United States Federal Census. No documents have been found for Emma's residence at this time. It is unlikely she returned to Galveston's devastation.

Page 63. **Paul and his wife were the landlords**: *1900 Houston City Directory* "Butterfass Paul, painter, r 1517 Shearn." I believe his father and mother are living with him at this address because Peter is listed right below Paul in the directory and residence (r) is listed as "same."

Page 64. **Jack [a dancer]...near to his age of forty**.: 1.) *The Galveston Daily News*, Vol. 55, No. 262, Ed. 1, Friday, December 11, 1896 – "Houston, TX Dec 19. The New Branch office of the Capitol Hotel is in receipt of an invitation to attend a mask ball, to be given by Prof. Geisecke's pupils at the Union Men's Hall 213-1/2 Main Street, Tuesday evening Dec 22. The invitation committee is composed of Walter Hueni Hamilton, Andrew Hydrick and Julian Jantzen. Reception Committee: Mrs. Maggie Draper, Miss Rachel Krantz, R.E. Harper, and W.L. Sandel. Floor Committee: O. Geisecke, Ben Blieden, and Andrew Hydrick. A number of invitations have been sent out."; 2.) *The Galveston Daily News*, Vol. 55, No. 274, Ed. 1, Wednesday, December 23, 1896 – "Houston, TX Dec 22 – Prof Geisecke's dance class gave a delightful masquerade ball at Union Men's Hall tonight, and a large number of persons enjoyed an exceedingly pleasant evening. The committees were as follows: Invitation...Andrew Hydrick. Floor...Andrew Hydrick."

Page 64. **Hy the brick mason apprenticeship**: *1903 Houston City Directory* – "Butterfass Henry, brickmason, h 1712 Freeman." I am not certain who obtained for Hy the apprenticeship but since Jack worked in the brick industry, I assume he may have.

Page 65. **new job at McLaughlin and Company**: *1900 Houston Directory* – "Jack Hydrick a teamster employed by H.P. McLaughlin. Boarding at 818 Lakin, Houston." Note: a "teamster" in 1900 meant he hauled a load of goods in a cart or wagon pulled by horses.

Page 66. **My son, Joe, he's sixteen and living on his own**.: 1.) Headstone located at Magnolia Cemetery in Magnolia, Montgomery County, Texas (Note: this is a different cemetery than the Magnolia Cemetery in Houston) – "Joseph H. Hydrick, Texas Sgt. B117 Supply Tn WWI, May 4, 1885 - Apr. 5, 1960." Note: I could not find Joe in the 1900 U.S. Census. I am not sure if he was living on his own in 1901, but he was not enumerated with his sister Annie at his aunt's home in 1910; 2.) *The Bastrop Advertiser*, Vol. 52, No. 41, Ed. 1, Saturday, December 24, 1904 – "Mr. Joe Hydrick of Greenville [NE of Dallas] was a guest of Mr. Ed Diviney with Miss Josie Flynt of Round Rock this last week, returning home December 18."; 3.) Joseph Hydrick worked for

I&GN Railroad and may have lived in numerous places. When he settled in Magnolia, Texas after 1920, he owned a dairy.

Page 66. **The two girls live with their ma's sister.**: I am not sure where Annie lived in 1901 but she lived with her mother's sister in 1910 (see Chapter Eleven notes). Her mother, Belle Flint Hydrick may have raised her. I can find no divorce record for Jack and Belle, but there is a marriage record 6 Apr 1895 for Bell Hydrick to John Teague in Travis County, Texas. Annie would have been about 4 years old. After 1895, I have found no other records for Belle Teague. Regarding her other daughter, there are no records found, only record of Ernest Hydrick writing to Ora Smith that there was a second sister who "married a Bohemian fellow." Joe, Annie, and the other sister would have been halfsiblings to Ernest, but he didn't know any of them in life, only heard about them and attended Joe's funeral at invitation.

Chapter Eleven

Page 67. **When Emma was eighteen, she married Jack Hydrick**: State of Texas County of Harris, County Clerk's Office #7431. "July 2, 1901 Andrew Hydrick with Miss Emma Butterfrass. Solemnized by W. A. Kinalke(?), Minister of the German Methodist Church, Houston, Texas." Emma records that she "is over 18 years of age." Signature of Jack is "A. Hydrik" and looks childlike in writing style. No signature required for the bride.

Page 67. **yDNA tests**: In 2011, Plymton Grover Hydrick, Rick Hannan Hydrick, and Paul Peter Hydrick had yDNA (paternal) tests performed with Sorensen Molecular Genealogy.

Page 68. **1880 Williamson County, Texas, United States Federal Census**: Census Place: Precinct 3, Williamson, Texas; Roll: 1332; Page: 478D; Enumeration District: 158. "Jackson Hydrum(?) head of household, white, male, 18 years old, orphan, single, farmhand, born in Alabama, parents born in Mississippi. He is enumerated with Emily Ford, white, female, 30 years old, divorced, born in Texas, and Emily's son Daniel, 3 years old.

Page 68. **Jack married seventeen-year-old Belle Flint**: The State of Texas, County of Travis Rites of Matrimony – "Andrew Hydrick and Miss Belle Flint, City of Austin 19 Sept 1885." Note on form "I Andrew Hydrick do solemnly swear that the parents of Miss Belle Flint herein have given their consent for my marriage with her. Sworn to and subscribed before me Sept 19, 1885. His mark X" (Andrew did not sign his name).

Page 68. **had a daughter about 1887**: there are no records found, only record of Ernest Hydrick writing there was a second sister who "married a Bohemian fellow."

Page 68. **second daughter, Annie Hydrick**: Record below and *1910 Austin City Directory* – "Hydrick, Annie Miss, clk, h. 204 Red River."

Page 69. **John Teague and Bell [sic] Hydrick were married**: John Teague and Bell Hydrick married 6 Apr 1895 in Travis County, Texas. Source film # 978167, Reference # 2:27W6M99.

Page 69. **Annie can be found living with her aunt and uncle**: 1910 United States Federal Census, enumerated with Philip and Mattie Fagan – "Annie Hydrick, Age 19, Birth Date: 1891, Birthplace: Texas, Home in 1910:   Austin   Ward   7, Travis, Texas, Street: Red River, Race: White, Relation to Head of House: Niece, Marital Status: Single, Mother's Birthplace: Illinois, Native Tongue: English, Occupation: Salesman, Industry: Retail Store."

Page 69. **October 1894, *The Galveston Daily News***: 1.) *The Galveston News*, Vol. 53, No. 217, Ed. 1 Friday, October 26, 1894, Local Notes (Galveston) – "The first load of brick for the super structure of the Binz Building was hauled this morning by Andrew Hydrick."; 2.) Becker, p 58 (photograph of Binz building).

Page 69. **1896, two newspaper articles**: 1.) *The Galveston Daily News*, Vol. 55, No. 262, Ed. 1 Friday, December 11, 1896 – "The New Branch office of the Capitol Hotel is in receipt of an invitation to attend a mask ball, to be given by Prof. Geisecke's pupils at the Union Men's Hall 213-1/2 Main Street, Tuesday evening Dec 22. The invitation committee is composed of Walter Hueni Hamilton, Andrew Hydrick and Julian Jantzen. Reception Committee: Mrs. Maggie Draper, Miss Rachel Krantz, R.E. Harper, and W.L. Sandel. Floor Committee: O. Geisecke, Ben Blieden, and Andrew Hydrick. A number of invitations have been sent out."; 2.) *The Galveston Daily News*, Vol. 55, No. 274, Ed. 1 Wednesday, December 23, 1896 – "Prof Geisecke's dance class gave a delightful masquerade ball at Union Men's Hall tonight, and a large number of persons enjoyed an exceedingly pleasant evening. The committees were as follows: Invitation...Andrew Hydrick. Floor...Andrew Hydrick."

Page 70. **married by the Justice of the Peace to Florence D. Patillo**: State of Texas County of Harris, County Clerk's Office, #6560, Holy Union of Matrimony "June 14, 1900, Solemnized by M.M. Donald, Justice of the Peace." Document not signed by Andrew Hydrick.

Page 70. **Jack and Emma married on July 2, 1901**: State of Texas County of Harris, County Clerk's Office #7431. "July 2, 1901 Andrew Hydrick with Miss Emma Butterfrass. Solemnized by W. A. Kinalke(?), Minister of the German Methodist Church, Houston, Texas." Emma records that she "is over 18 years of age." Signature of Jack is "A. Hydrik" and looks childlike in writing style. No signature required for the bride.

Chapter Twelve

Page 71. **Ernest Albert Hydrick was born**: 1.) Letter in author's possession from Ernest Hydrick dated August 25, 1980: "...another question is my records show I was born Sept. 5, 1903 Houston Tex 2600 Center St. My mother told me my birthday was on March 20, 1902 so I believed her."; 2.) Form for Family Record Scholastic Census records, 1909 "Hydrick, Ernest, birth 1901 Mar 20, age 8, residence 3727 Ave. F" Signed by Mrs. C. Koenig, 25 May 1909; 3.) I'm not sure where Ernest saw "records" that recorded birth as 1903. If he was born 1901, as school records indicate, I would suspect he is not the son of Jack Hydrick. It is my supposition that Emma claimed Ernest to be born in 1901 to get him into a different school grade. It appears Emma was pregnant or already had Ernest when she married Jack Hydrick, which would make Ernest's father suspect.

Page 71. **rented rooms at a house in the 2600 block of Center Street**: 1.) *1902 Houston City Directory* records Andrew J Hydrick living at 2209 Washington St., employed as teamster Butler Brick Yard; 2.) *1903 Houston City Directory* records Jack as bricklayer living at 2413 Center, Houston. His phone SW 2453.

Page 71. **she and Hy moved out on their own**: *1903 Houston City Directory* – "Butterfass Eva A. Miss, Opr Ineeda ldy, h 1712 Freeman," next line "Butterfass Henry, brickmason, h 1712 Freeman." The other Butterfras's listed are not at this address.

Page 72. **Paul, now a ladderman for the fire station**: *1902 Houston City Directory* "Butterfass, Paul, ladderman central fire station, r 2515 Main 3." (See Chapter Eighteen notes also.)

Page 74. **strolled through the park's grounds where they picnicked near the three-tiered fountain or the new conservatory**: History of Glenwood Cemetery found at 1.) Johnston, p 88; 2.) Becker, p 67 (photograph of old Glenwood Cemetery); 3.) Glenwood Cemetery pamphlet.

Page 74. **Tillie, who died in July**: Magnolia Cemetery, Houston, Harris, Texas – "Barbara Matilda "Tillie" Butterfras Wiggins, Birth 3 Sep 1865 Louisiana, Death 13 Jul 1903 (aged 37)," Plot 41B, Findagrave Memorial ID 196526896.

Page 75. **Papa's dead**: FindAGrave.com "Name Peter Butterfras, Birth June 1837 Hessen, Germany, Burial Houston, Harris County, Texas, United States of America, Death 8 November 1903 Houston, Harris County, Texas, United States of America." Note: Peter Butterfass bought Lot #41, Section B in Magnolia Cemetery, Houston on July 26, 1887. He is buried there with other family members.

Chapter Thirteen

Page 78. *The Houston Chronicle*, **June 28, 1904**. newspapers.com

Page 78. **All three of Emma's children are not recorded in any Texas birth record**: they are not found under the names of Butterfras, Butterfass, Osborne, Hydrick and variant spellings.

Page 78. **Delayed Texas Birth Index**: Beginning in 1903, births occurring in Texas should have been officially registered within the first year. If it didn't occur, or a person was born before 1903, they could apply for a "Delayed Certificate of Birth."

Chapter Fourteen

Page 83. **rented a home at 2218 Carr Street**: *1905-1906 Houston City Directory* – Hydrick, Emma (Mrs. Andrew J.), r. 2218 Carr."

Page 83 (and pp 86, 91, 96, 158). **Howard Hughes Sr ... known as a philanderer**: 1.) Hack 35, 36, 44; 2.) Dietrich, p 29, 32; 3.) Barlett and Steele, p 28; 4.) Brown and Broeske, p 10, 14, 22-23, 27, 30.

Page 84. **Howard Jr.'s birthdate to be September 24, 1905**: Keokuk Iowa Saint John's Episcopal Church Baptismal Record, pp 120, 121. "Date: Oct 7. Name: Howard Robard. Parents: Howard R. and Allene Hughes. Sponsor: Mrs. W. B. Sharp. Birth: September 24, 1905."

Page 84. **Howard Sr. had married Allene Gano... May 24, 1904**. 1.) *Austin American-Statesman* newspaper, 29 May 1904, p 9 – announcement of marriage (see Chapter Twenty-Three notes); 2.) Barlett and Steele, p 30; 3.)

Page 84. **spent a few months in Europe honeymooning.**: *The Houston Post*, Saturday, 17 Sep 1904, p. 7 – "Beaumont, Texas, September 16. Howard Hughes, the well-known oil man has returned to Beaumont after an absence of several months, during whch [sic] time he took unto himself a wife and enjoyed an extended bridal trip through Europe. Mrs. Hughes was formally Miss Alene [sic] Gano of Dallas. Mr. and Mrs. Hughes may make their permanent home in Beaumont."

Page 84. **Upon their return in September, they first settled in Beaumont**: *The Houston Post*, Saturday, 24 Sep 1904, p. 4 - "Mr. and Mrs. Howard Hughes were in Houston Thursday at the Rice hotel and have returned to their home in Beaumont. Mr. and Mrs. Hughes spent the summer abroad, and with a party of Dallas friends made an automobile tour of France. Mrs. Hughes was formally Miss Gano of Dallas."

Page 84. **and soon arrived in Houston, residing at the Rice Hotel.**: 1.) Barlett and Steele, p 30. 2.) "Records of the Class of 1897" Harvard College Fourth Report, p 218. 3.) *1905-1906 Houston City Directory*, p. 153 "Hughes, Howard R., oil producer and dealer, boards at Rice Hotel."

Chapter Fifteen

Page 85. **Howard Robard Hughes Sr. was born on September 9, 1869, in Lancaster, Missouri**: 1.) United States Passport Applications 1795-1925, FamilySearch.com, Certificate Number: 162691 "Name: Howard R. Hughes (and for wife Allene Hughes) Event Date: 16 Jan 1920 Event Place: Harris County, Texas, United States, Birth Date: 9 Sep 1869 Birthplace: Lancaster, Missouri, Father: Felix I(?) Hughes, born in Illinois, now residing in Keokuk, Iowa, Spouse's Name: Allene Hughes, born Georgetown, Kentucky on 14 July 1884, Occupation: Manufacturer, Intending to return to U.S. in 6 months, I intend to leave the United States from the port of New Orleans or Key West, Sailing on board the United Forces(?) Seawer(?) on receipt of passport.";   2.) https://www.findagrave.com/memorial/10675573/howard-robard-hughes

Page 85. **Howard's Yankee father who had fought for the Union Army in the Civil War.**: Barlett and Steele, p 26, 27.

Page 85. **family moved to Keokuk, Iowa**: Ibid.

Page 85. **Rupert later wrote: "My mother instilled the ambitions, and my father found the funds."**: Kemm, p 9.

Page 85. **Howard Sr. had a mechanical aptitude and enjoyed tinkering with engines and clocks.**: Barlett and Steele, p 27.

Page 86. **all-male boarding school in St. Charles, Missouri**: Kemm, p 11.

Page 86. **Harvard College but dropped out in 1894... He enrolled at Iowa State University to study law but did not graduate.**: Barlett and Steele, p 28.

Page 86. **Howard Sr. wrote: "I soon found the law a too-exacting mistress for a man of my talent, and quit her between dark and dawn, and have never since been back. I decided to search for my fortune under the surface of the earth."**: "Records of the Class of 1897" *Harvard College Fourth Report*, p 218.

Page 86. **"If I accomplished nothing more, I at least learned something of the art of drilling wells with cable tools."**: Ibid.

Page 86-87. **Howard Sr. wrote: I heard the roar in Joplin and made for the seat of disturbance. Beaumont in those days was no place for a divinity student. The reek of oil was everywhere. It filled the air, it painted the houses, it choked the lungs and stained men's souls. Such another excitement will not be seen for a generation. It will take that length of time to get together an equal number of fools and "come-on's" at one spot. I turned greaser and sank into the thick of it. Rough neck, owner, disowner, promoter, capitalist and "mark"—with each I can claim kin, for I have stood in the steps of each.**: Ibid.

Page 87. **Rupert wrote... "uncanny gift for extracting money from my father for his wildest schemes."**: Barlett and Steele, p 29.

Page 87. **she married him at the Gano home in Dallas on May 24, 1904.**: 1.) *Austin American-Statesman* newspaper, 29 May 1904, p 9 – announcement of marriage; 2.) Barlett and Steele, p 30.

Page 87. **Allene was well-educated, cultured, refined, and raised by Harvard Law School graduate and prominent Dallas judge William Beriah Gano.**: 1.) Barlett and Steele, p 29.; 2.) Death Certificate of Allene Gano Hughes, Texas Department of State Health Services Certificate #8529 (see Chapter Thirty-Six notes).

Page 87. **Allene's mother, Jeanette de Lafayette Grissim, also from the Dallas socialite circle**: Barlett and Steele, p 30.

Page 87. **like swooning at the sight of a cat**: Ibid.

Chapter Sixteen

Page 90. **having Mama live with her**: 1.) *1905-1906 Houston City Directory* – "Butterfass, Mary (wid Peter) h 2218 Carr"; 2.) *1905-1906 Houston City Directory* – Hydrick, Emma (Mrs. Andrew J.), r. 2218 Carr." Also in this home is Eva and Henry.

Page 91. **Howard, but you can call me Bo.**: *American Legends: The Life of Howard Hughes* by Charles River Editors, 2014, ebook location 98.

Chapter Seventeen

Page 97. **His brother, Rupert, commented, "One year he had fifty thousand in the bank. The next he owed the bank fifty thousand."**: Kemm, p 43.

Chapter Eighteen

Page 104. **worked as a fireman fifteen days straight with one day off.**: *The Houston Post*, Wednesday, September 17, 1902, p 3 – details an injury Paul Butterfras sustained while traveling down the street on the rear of the engine when it "...lost a wheel at the corner of Louisiana and Congress avenue. The machine was going at a rapid pace and when the wheel ws torn off, the three men were sent flying in different directions. Ollre and Butterfrass were badly shaken up and the latter is said to be injured internally. Wagner escaped with a few severe bruises and was able to be at work yesterday afternoon. Ollre and Butterfrass were sent home by order of Chief Arto."

Page 104. **eldest son, Sanders**: U.S. Social Security Death Index 1935-2014 -"Sanders A. Butterfras, Birth Date 11 Mar 1900, Issue year Before 1951, Issue State   Texas, Death Date 30 Apr 1990."

Page 104. **four little grandsons**: 1. Sanders 2. Paul 3. George 4. Ernest

Chapter Nineteen

Page 109. **built a seventeen-foot seawall**: 1.) Gidley and Marines, pp 15-23, pp 49-83.

Page 109. **raising homes and buildings to a higher grade**: Ibid.

Page 112. **sociological study about prostitution in early Galveston**: Granville Price, "A Social Study of a Segregated District," Master's thesis, University of Texas at Austin, 1930.

Page 112. **madams paid taxes on the real estate they owned, and by doing so, appeared like upstanding citizens**: Price, p 8.

Page 112. **Mrs. Sullivan's employment was listed as "real estate."**: *1932 Galveston City Directory* – "Mrs. Tim Sullivan, real estate."

Chapter Twenty

Page 113. **Butler Brickyard in Bastrop County**.: upon checking with the still operating Butler Brickyard, I was informed their employment records do not go back that far.

Page 113. **New Bern, North Carolina in 1811**: State vs John Taylor, Craven County North Carolina, 1812.

Page 118. **Jack died June 25, 1905, at about 4 p.m.**: State of Texas County of Travis Report of Death #1019 – "Andrew Hydrick, white, male, Caucasian, citizen, died on the 25th day of June 1905 at about 4 p.m., Place of Death Butler Switch. Residence (left blank), Immediate Cause Congestion, Contributory Cause Congestion. Duration 3 days. Signed W. E. Wood, address Elgin, Texas." I checked four nearby cemeteries and could not find a gravesite for Andrew Jackson Hydrick or any Hydrick.

Chapter Twenty-One

Page 120. **Charles A. Koenig immigrated to America from Germany in 1891**: 1910 United States Federal Census - Place: Galveston Ward 6, Galveston, Texas; Roll: T624_1554; Page: 6A; Enumeration District: 0118; FHL microfilm: 1375567.

Page 120. **He is recorded in the Galveston City Directory as a dock worker**: Galveston City Directories 1908 thru 1914.

Page 120. **helped her in time of need in 1929**: Taped Oral History of Lucille White Hydrick administered by Plymton Hydrick, her son, May 1980.

Page 122. **only the tiered octagonal dancing pavilion had survived**: Gidley and Marines, p 44.

Chapter Twenty-Two

Page 129. **In November 1904, Humble became a boomtown overnight**: Meaux, Introduction.

Page 129. **The following January a large gusher erupted**: Ibid.

Page 129. **Land once selling for $10 an acre, sold for $20,000 an acre.**: Ibid.

Page 130. **Walter B. Sharp organized an oil business in Humble called Moonshine Oil Company with partners Howard Hughes Sr. and Ed Prather**: 1.) Clark and Halbouty, p 154; 2.) Website *Social Networks and Archival Context* "Sharp, Walter B. (Walter Benona), 1870-1912" at https://snaccooperative.org/ark:/99166/w6pc4pb3 ; 3.) Johnston, p 123.

Page 130. **Sometime in 1905, Howard Sr. moved from Houston to Humble**: Hack, p 25.

Page 133. **a tent city**: Meaux, p 25.

Page 134. **There was no defined road or curb**: Ibid, p 16.

Page 137. **hospital…there isn't one in Humble**: 1.) The Falvey Hospital opened in 1918, Humble's first hospital (source: Humble Museum); 2.) Memories & Musings - "The Hospitals of Humble" by Julia Nation 16 Mar 2021.

Page 138. **Doctor Oscar Norsworthy**: Deposition of Annette Gano Lummis. August 2, 1977, p 8, Hughes Estate Texas.

Chapter Twenty-Three

Page 140. **between January 1904 through January 1905, Howard Sr.'s and Allene's names were in the Texas newspapers no less than twenty-four times announcing events such as their wedding, honeymoon activities, where they played cards, went fishing, who visited their house, automobile racing events, Howard Sr.'s oil well activity, or when they went out of town.**: newspaper samples of many 1.) *Austin American-Statesman*, Sunday, 29 May 1904, p 9 – "Cards have been received in the city announcing the marriage of Miss Allene Gano of Dallas to Mr. Edward [sic] Hughes of Beaumont on Tuesday, May 24. Miss Gano is an ex-University girl, and has many friends here whose best wishes follow her."; 2.) *The Houston Post*, Saturday, 17 Sep 1904, p 7 – "Returned from Europe. Beaumont, Texas, September 16. Howard Hughes, the well-known oil man, has returned to Beaumont after an absence of several months, during which time he took unto himself a wife and enjoyed an extended bridal trip through Europe. Mrs. Hughes was formerly Miss Alene [sic] Gano of Dallas. Mr. and Mrs. Hughes may make their permanent home in Beaumonth."; 3.) *The Houston Post*, Saturday, 24 Sep 1905, p 4 – "Mr. and Mrs. Howard Hughes were in Houston Thursday at the Rice hotel and have returned to their home in Beaumont. Mr. and Mrs. Hughes spent the summer abroad, and with a party of Dallas friends made an automobile tour of France. Mrs. Hughes was formerly Miss Gano of Dallas."; 4.) *The Galveston Daily News*, Sunday, 8 Jan 1905, p 18 – "Cards and Cotillion…among those present…Mrs. Howard Hughes"; 5.) *The Houston Post*, Wednesday, 5 Oct 1904, p 12 – "E.S. Charpiot to Howard R. Hughes, lots 3, 10, 39, 40, 57, 58, 87 and 88, Collier subdivision of the James Strange survey $650. J.P. Collier to Howard R. Hughes, lots 95 and 96, Collier subdivision of the James Strange survey $200."; 6.) *The Beaumont Enterprise*, Sunday, 9 Oct 1904, p 9 – "Mrs. Hughes joined Mr. Hughes in a visit to Dallas this week, where Mr. Hughes takes part in the automobile races."; 7.) *The Houston Post*, Sunday, 6 Nov 1904, p 16 – "Flower Parade Committee…Mrs. Howard Hughes."; 8.) *The*

Houston Post, Thursday, 24 Nov 1904, p 10 – "From a standing start Howard Hughes' red car Peerless pushed to the front..."; 9.) *The Galveston News*, Sunday, 18 Dec 1904, p 8 – "Howard Hughes of this city has gone to New Orleans on a business call."

Page 140. **Howard Sr. studied law, his father was lawyer and judge**: Kemm, p 32

Page 140. **and his father-in-law was a judge**.: Barlett and Steele, p 30.

Page 140. **certified birth record to prove his age for his government work**: Ibid, p 31.

Page 140. **notarized document to authenticate the information**.: Ibid.

Page 141. **in a court deposition by Annette Gano Lummis..."when he was two or three months old."**: Deposition of Annette Gano Lummis. August 2, 1977, p 8, Hughes Estate Texas.

Page 141. **Annette had visited in July 1905**.: *The Galveston Daily News*, Sunday, 2 July 1905, p 10 – "Miss Annette Gano of Dallas is visiting her sister, Mrs. Howard Hughes."

Page 141. **Estelle Sharp died in 1965 and could not be deposed when Annette was**.: Texas U.S. Death Certificates 1903-1982, Certificate #50969 – "Estelle Boughton Sharp Age: 92, Birth Date: 19 Jun 1873, Birth Place: Flint, Michigan, Residence: Houston, Harris, Texas, USA, Death Date: 30 Aug 1965, Death Place: Houston, Harris, Texas, USA, Father: Boughton." Ancestry.com

Page 141. **baptism is recorded for the year 1906**: 1.) Keokuk Iowa Saint John's Episcopal Church Baptismal Record, pp 120, 121. "Date: Oct 7. Name: Howard Robard. Parents: Howard R. and Allene Hughes. Sponsor: Mrs. W. B. Sharp. Birth: September 24, 1905."; 2) *The Houston Post*, Thursday, 6 Sep 1906, p 10 – "Mrs. Howard Hughes and Master Howard, Jr., leave today for Keokuk, Iowa, for a visit to Mr. Hughes' relatives."; 3.) *The Houston Post*, Sunday, 14 Oct 1906 – "Mr. and Mrs. Howard Hughes returned yesterday morning from Keokuk, Iowa, where Mrs. Hughes spent the past six weeks, the guest of relatives, Mr. and Mrs. Hughes stopped en route home at Chicago and St. Louis for the horse show."

Page 141. **Dr. Oscar L. Norsworthy was the attending physician to the birth of Howard Hughes**: Deposition of

Annette Gano Lummis. August 2, 1977, p 8, Hughes Estate Texas.

Page 141. **birth was so difficult for Allene that he advised her to not have any more children.**: Ibid. Note: I have wondered if this were true to Emma's story since she did not have any children after the 1905 delivery, even though she was only twenty-three and married Charles Koenig soon after.

Page 141. **In one Howard Hughes biography, Dr. Oscar Laertins Norsworthy is credited with delivering Howard Hughes Jr. in the Baptist Hospital in Houston**: Brown and Broeske, p 6.

Page 142. **Baptist Sanatorium downtown but wasn't filed until 1907.**: Website *The TMC Library* (Texas Archival Resources Online) at https://legacy.lib.utexas.edu/taro/hamtmc/00078/tmc-00078.html - "Founded on September 1, 1907 as the Baptist Sanitarium, Memorial Hospital began as a two-story, wood-framed building at the end of the trolley line on Lamar and Smith. It had 17 beds and eight trained nurses on staff."

Page 142. **Leading to the establishment of the Sanatorium, a Baptist minister had established a charitable institution in Houston in 1904.**: Website *Texas State Historical Association, Handbook of Texas* at https://www.tshaonline.org/handbook/entries/memorial-healthcare-system - "The system began in 1904 when a Baptist minister, Rev. Dennis R. Pevoto, established a charitable institution open to all individuals regardless of race, religion, or ability to pay."

Note of Interest: In 1908, Dr. Norsworthy built a four-story hospital on Rosalie Avenue in downtown Houston. In this thirty-five-bed hospital he'd begun to specialize in radiology. He offered the Rosalie Avenue hospital to the Texas Conference of the Methodist Episcopal Church in 1919. His hospital became the Methodist Hospital in the Texas Medical Center: 1.) Website *Rice History Corner* (Gleanings from the Rice University Archives) at https://ricehistorycorner.com/2017/09/25/would-have-graduated-with-the-class-of-1919/ ; 2.) Website *Houston Methodist* at https://www.houstonmethodist.org/newsroom/houston-methodist-celebrates-100-years-of-leading-medicine/ - "The Methodist Hospital started as a small hospital on Rosalie Street purchased to help the community through the Spanish flu epidemic." 3.) Johnston, p 221.

Page 142. **two biographers claimed him to have been born in a home at 1404 Crawford Street in Houston**.: 1.) Barlett and Steele, p 31.; 2.) Dietrich, p 30. Note: Both claim his birth date to have been Christmas Eve of 1905; 3.) Brown and Broeske, p 8, wrote that Howard Sr. returned to the Crawford home after Allene had her baby in the Baptist Hospital. Note: When Howard Hughes Jr. was fifteen, in *The Houston Post*, 23 Dec 1920, p 8 Headline - Mr. and Mrs. Hughes Dance for Howard Hughes Jr. and Dudley Sharp. "Mr. and Mrs. Howard Hughes' dance at the Country club Wednesday evening honoring Howard Hughes Jr. and Dudley Sharp was one of the very enjoyable affairs ushering in holiday week. The club was bright with Christmas decorations of holly and poinsettias. Punch was served during the evening and a refreshment course of ices, cakes, and confections was served from a prettily appointed Christmas table. About 150 guests participated in the pleasures of the evening." *Nothing was written about it being a birthday celebration for Howard Hughes. No explanation as to why Howard and Dudley were being honored, but Dudley's birthday*

Page 142. **the closest hospital—St. Joseph Hospital at 1910 Crawford Street—would have been a few blocks (.2 miles) away**: 1.) Johnston, p 96 - Saint Joseph Hospital opened in downtown Houston in 1887; 2.) https://ourtribune.com/life-2/memories-musings-by-julia-nation/24960-memories-musings-the-hospitals-of-humble.html "When care was needed, residents of Humble were treated at Saint Joseph" 20 miles away.

Page 142. **the Hugheses actually living at the Crawford Street address**: *1907 Houston City Directory,* p 151 – "Hughes, Howard R., oil operator, r. 1404 Crawford, 3. C. ph 315, Sw. ph 928."

Page 142. **boarded at the Rice Hotel**: *1905-1906 Houston City Directory*, p 153 – "Hughes, Howard R., oil producer and dealer, bds [boards] RICE HOTEL, 2. Sw. ph 3946."

Page 142. **lived for a time in Humble**: Hack, p 25.

Page 142. **Some biographers believed Humble to have been Howard Jr.'s birthplace.**: Ibid.

Page 142. **a small town without a hospital in 1905.**: 1.) The Falvey Hospital opened in 1918, Humble's first hospital (source: Humble Museum); 2.) *Memories & Musings* - "The Hospitals of Humble" by Julia Nation 16 Mar 2021.

Page 143. **claimed himself to be an orphan acquired by his parents in the dark of night**: *American Legends: The Life of Howard Hughes* by Charles River Editors, 2014, ebook location 90.

Page 145. **I've been calling him Sonny**: Hack, p 25.

Chapter Twenty-Four

Page 149. **Epigenetics...A study was performed on two groups of people**: Website *The Guardian*, article "Study of Holocaust Survivors Finds Trauma Passed on to Children's Genes" by Helen Thomson, 21 Aug 2015 at https://www.theguardian.com/science/2015/aug/21/study-of-holocaust-survivors-finds-trauma-passed-on-to-childrens-genes - Cited Website *Biological Psychiatry: A Journal of Psychiatric Neuroscience and Therapeutics* "Holocaust Exposure Induced Intergenerational Effects on FKBP5 Methylation" by Rachel Yehuda, Nikolaos P. Daskalakis, Linda M. Bierer, Torsten Klengel, Florian Holsboer, Elisabeth B. Binder, published 12 August 2015 at https://www.biologicalpsychiatryjournal.com/article/S0006-3223(15)00652-6/fulltext .

Chapter Twenty-Five

Page 153. **Charlie and Emma were married at the Galveston Courthouse on October 22, 1905**: 1.) Ancestry.com Reference ID v R p 466, GS Film Number 1009521, Digital Folder Number 004705727, Image Number 00249 "Name Charles A. Koenig, Event Type Marriage, Event Date 22 Oct 1905, Event Place Galveston, Texas, United States, Spouse's Name Emma Hydrick."; 2.) Original Marriage License #931 signed by Sydney T. Fontaine 23 October 1905. Note: Emma Hydrick/Koenig is not recorded in the *1905 Galveston City Directory*. She may have come to Galveston after the directory was enumerated.

Page 153. **another house owned by Lillian Sullivan at 3727 Church Street.**: 1.) Description and Estimate of the Present Cash Value Tax Records of Galveston (19 June 1906) found at Rosenberg Library 2016 - description of home built in 1906: first floor dwelling size 11'x24', 2 rooms, 2 porches, 0 baths. Owned by L.C. Sullivan. She also owned homes on Ave F (Church Street) at 3728, 3725, 3721, 3719. Homes at 3715 and

3717 may have possibly been jointly owned with husband, Tim Sullivan. She also owns dwellings on G Street at 3718 and 3728; 2.) *1908 Galveston City Directory* "Koenig, Chas C, wks S.P. whf, residence 3727 Church Street 4 [people in residence]"; 3.) Galveston City Directory 1908 "Koenig, Chas C, wks S.P. docks, residence 3727 Church Street 4 [people in residence]"; 4.) Form For Family Record Scholastic Census records, 1909 "Hydrick, Ernest, birth 1901 Mar 20, age 8, residence 3727 Ave. F" Signed by Mrs. C. Koenig, 25 May 1909. Note: No school record for George was found.

Page 153. **she married John Little**: *The Houston Post*, Sunday, 18 Feb 1906, p. 8 – "Marriage Licenses...John Sellis Little to Miss Eva Anna Butterfrass."

Page 153. **and later gave birth to a daughter, Florence**: U.S. Social Security Death Index 1935-2014 – "Flossie Fontenot, Birth Date 20 Jun 1906, Issue year Before 1951, Issue State Texas, Last Residence 77009, Houston, Harris, Texas, USA, Death Date Apr 1984."

Page 153. **Emma's nineteen-year-old brother, Hy died mysteriously**: 1.) *The Houston Chronicle*, June 28, 1906; 2.) *The Houston Post*, Thursday, June 28, 1906, p. 1; 3.) *The Houston Post*, Tuesday, July 17, 1906, p. 9.

Page 154. **John Lacy..."that the two had laid down upon the track to sleep. The noise of the approaching train had not awakened the white man." And "The negro avers that the two were walking to Galveston together."**: *The Houston Chronicle*, June 28, 1906.

Page 154. **men recruited (forced?) to dig the dead from wreckage, try to find valuables or something on their bodies to identify them, then pile them by the hundreds to be burned**.: Greene and Kelly, p 85 – from the personal memoir of Lloyd R. D. Fayling - "...by orders of the Mayor, brought to me by Father Kirwin, we marched to the foot of Tremont street, taking every able-bodied man, white or black, met with, and forced them at the bayonet point to assist in the awful work." And from the personal memoir of Mary Louise Bristol Hopkins, p 172 – "my two brothers...They were conscripted to help with the burying of the dead and getting people that were under the wreckage. They were told they must help and then they were told they had to dig. There was no identification and no prayers said or anything else, the bodies were just put in the ground. There were so many of them that they couldn't find anymore ground to bury them. They took them out to sea and then they washed back in again, so they had to be burned."

Page 155. **my family will be leaving town soon**: Barlett and Steele, p 31. The Hughes moved to Louisiana for oil exploration.

Chapter Twenty-Six

Page 159. **taking long trips across America to promote his roller bit invention**.: Hack, p 40.

Page 159. **Their mother had died in 1905**: FindAGrave.com "Name: Jeannette Gano, Birth Date: 27 Jul 1857, Birth Place: Fayette County, Kentucky, Death Date: 28 Feb 1905, Death Place: Dallas, Dallas County, Texas, Cemetery: Oakland Cemetery"

Page 159. **Annette even tutored him academically in his youth**.: Hack, p 41.

Page 159. **In a will Howard Jr. wrote in 1925**: Barlett and Steele, p 56-59

Page 160. **found by Howard Jr. among his father's papers**: Dietrich, p 32.

Page 160. **In early 1907, the Hugheses moved from Houston to Shreveport, Louisiana**: Hack, p 26.

Page 160. **oil reconnaissance—Oil City**.: Ibid.

Page 160. **Howard Sr....deputy sheriff and postmaster**: Ibid.

Page 160. **Howard Sr. met a millwright who had an idea for a drill bit**: Barlett and Steele, p 33.

Page 160. **For $150, Howard Sr. bought his mock-up**. Ibid.

Page 161. **Sharp lived...Phoenix Hotel**: Ibid, p 34.

Page 161. **fastened a paper to a breadboard from the kitchen and sketched his model drill bit upon it. The drawing had no less than 166 cutting edges**.: Kemm, p 43.

Page 161. **patent office in Washington, D.C. on November 20, 1908**: Barlett and Steele, p 34.

Page 161. **On the patent, Howard Sr. was listed as a sole inventor**.: Ibid.

Page 161. **February 1909, where she stayed with her best friend, Estelle Sharp**.: *The Houston Post*, Sunday, February 21, 1909, p 34 – "Mrs. Howard Hughes is the guest of

Mr. and Mrs. W. B. Sharp during the absence of Mr. Hughes in the East."

Page 161. **The Sharp's lived in a lovely old house in the country by a lake with tall oak trees and a fragrant and finely manicured rose garden**.: Ibid, p 129.

Page 161. **In March, Howard Sr. met up with his wife and child**.: *The Houston Post*, Tuesday, March 30, 1909, p 11 "Howard Hughes, the well-known oil man, has returned to Houston after an extended visit to New York."

Page 161. **Rice Hotel in a Buick Model C roadster**: Hack, p 27.

Page 162. **In mid-May, they moved into a home in Bayridge**: 1.) *The Houston Post*, Wednesday, 5 May 1909, p 10 – "Mr. and Mrs. Howard Hughes and son leave next week to spend the summer on the bay shore."; 2.) *The Houston Post*, Wednesday, 19 May 1909, p 10 – "Automobile Party. Mrs. B. F. Bonner will be the hostess of an outing Saturday in honor of Mrs. Frederick Hanford of New York to spend the day with Mrs. Howard Hughes at Bayridge. Mrs. Bonner will take Mrs. Hanford, Mrs. W. B. Sharp and other guests in her car for the day's trip."; 3.) *The Houston Post*, Wednesday, 26 May 1909, p 10 – "Society Personals. Mrs. Howard Hughes was in the city yesterday from Bay Ridge."; 4.) *The Houston Post*, Thursday 10 Jun 1909, p 10 – "Mrs. W. B. Sharp, who is visiting Mrs. Howard Hughes at Bay Ridge, spent yesterday in town, the guest of Mrs. E. F. Simms."; 5.) *The Houston Post*, Wednesday, 8 Sep 1909, p 9 – "Mrs. Howard Hughes and her sisters, the Misses Gano, came up from the bay to spend today in town."; 6.) *The Houston Post*, Sunday, 26 Sep 1909, p 3 – "News From the Bay Shore…Mrs. Ray Wiess was the guest of Mrs. Howard Hughes for several days at Bay Ridge last week." And "Chilton Gano, who has been the guest of Mr. and Mrs. Howard Hughes at Bay Ridge Park all summer, has returned to Cornell, where he will resume his studies."

Page 162. **June of 1909, the new steel bit invention**: Barlett and Steele, p 34.

Page 162. **patents granted on August 10, 1909**.: Ibid.

Page 162. **formed the Sharp-Hughes Tool Company**: Johnston, p 127.

Page 162. **Eva's husband John**: Texas U.S. Select County Marriage Index 1837-1965, FHL Film Number 000025230 – "Eva Annie Butterfrass, Marriage Date 17 Feb

1906, Marriage Place Harris, Texas, United States, Spouse John Sellis Little."

Page 163. **Mrs. Howard Hughes is the guest of Mr. and Mrs. W. B. Sharp**: *The Houston Post*, Sunday, February 21, 1909, p 34.

Page 163. **Howard Hughes, the well-known oil man, has returned to Houston**: *The Houston Post*, Tuesday, March 30, 1909, p 11.

Page 165. **she'd investigated Allene and found she was from an old family who'd been in America for generations, distinguished in battles and politics**.: Barlett and Steele, p 30.

Page 165. **your rector**: Ibid, p 35. Note: With many of Houston's prestigious citizens, the Hugheses were members of Christ Church Cathedral, an Episcopal church.

Page 166. **catch a chill…Infantile paralysis**: Barlett and Steele, p 39.

Page 167. **tricycle from Paris**: Hack, p 28.

Page 168. **He travels on a train**.: Barlett and Steele, p 38.

Chapter Twenty-Seven

Page 169. **one bought the gasoline in canisters at the grocery store or had it delivered**: Website *America Comes Alive* at https://americacomesalive.com/when-gasoline-powered-cars-were-first-used-where-did-they-get-gasoline/

Page 169. **drill bit revolutionized drilling for oil and gas, helping the oil industry become the fastest-growing industry in the country**: Barlett and Steele, p 36.

Page 169. **they joined Christ Church Cathedral**: The Episcopal Diocese of Texas (see above). Barlett and Steele, p 35.

Page 169. **Sonny went to school in the parish house of the church, known as Miss Eichler's University**.: Johnston, p 163, 326.

Page 169. **Ella Rice, would one day marry Sonny**: Kemm, p 165.

Page 169. **The children of the Houston oil industry leaders, such as Sharp, Cullinan, Autry, and Donoghue, all grew up playing with Sonny**.: Johnston, p 126.

Page 169. **home in the fashionable south side of Houston**: Barlett and Steele, p 44.

Page 169. **The Hugheses joined the Houston Country Club**.: Ibid, p 35.

Page 170. **two private rail cars, one just for his wardrobe**.: Hack, p 29.

Page 170. **an upstairs apartment over a beer parlor at 618 38th Street**: 1.) Description and Estimate of the Present Cash Value Tax Records of Galveston for 618 38th Street found at Rosenberg Library in 2016, description: 4 bd, 1 bath (L.C. Sullivan also owns dwellings on 38th Street at 610, 612, 614, 616); 2.) *1911 Galveston City Directory* – "Charles C. Koenig wks S.P. docks r. 618 38th st."

Page 170. **Timothy Sullivan...in trouble with the Galveston City Health Office**: *The Galveston Daily News*, Friday, July 28, 1911, p 12 regarding premises at 3715 and 3717 Avenue F – "...alleged nuisance said to exist on the property of Timothy Sullivan and David Fahey. This case is, it is said, to be contested legally...The condition described as existing in cesspools within 14' of dwellings of women and children and within 22' of another family were unsanitary in the extreme."

Page 170. **"the owners of the property had dug new cesspools and thrown the dirt into the old uncleaned ones, thereby creating an unsanitary and dangerous nuisance."**: *The Galveston Daily News*, Friday, July 28, 1911, p. 12.

Page 170. **pimps who took a hefty cut of the earnings**.: Remmers, p 10.

Page 170. **Emma...went to work for Model Laundry and Dye Works as a machine operator**.: Taped Oral Interview of George Hydrick, given by Plymton Hydrick on July 6, 1980.

Page 170. **Charlie left the docks and got a job as an ice handler for a brewery**.: 1910 United States Federal Census - Place: Galveston Ward 6, Galveston, Texas; Roll: T624_1554; Page: 6A; Enumeration District: 0118; FHL microfilm: 1375567. Charles Koenig recorded as "ice handler for Brewery." Immigration year 1891, born in Germany, age 39. Both George and Ernest are enumerated with "Koenig" surname.

Page 171. **In a recorded interview in 1980, George claimed to have gone to Alamo School**: No documentation found in public school records, but in 1910 United States Federal Census, George is recorded as attending school and can read and write. Evidenced by his letters to my father, his education appears to have been minimal.

Page 171. **1909, Ernest attended school for that year only**.: Form For Family Record Scholastic Census 1909 "Hydrick, Ernest, birth 1901 Mar 20, age 8, residence 3727 Ave. F" Signed by Mrs. C. Koenig, 25 May 1909."

Chapter Twenty-Eight

Page 177. **Walter Sharp...more loved by Houstonians...died suddenly near the end of 1912**: 1.) Website *Social Networks and Archival Context* "Sharp, Walter B. (Walter Benona), 1870-1912" at https://snaccooperative.org/ark:/99166/w6pc4pb3 ; 2.) Johnston, p 127.

Page 177. **Estelle became alarmed...frivolous parties and travel**.: Barlett and Steele, p 36.

Page 177. **Estelle...decided to sell her interest in the company to Ed Prather**: Ibid, p 38.

Page 177. **The sale made Estelle wealthy, and she became a philanthropist in Houston, spending her money on broadening the interests of young Houston women**.: Johnston, p 127.

Page 177. **Sonny attended the Montrose School**: Ibid, p 326.

Page 177. **His three main playmates were Dudley Sharp, Mark Edwin Andrews, and Mary Cullinan**.: Ibid, p 326.

Page 177. **"Howard was a strange boy. Very shy and very lonely."**: Brown and Broeske, p 12 - quote by Dudley Sharpe.

Page 178. **I bell-hopped today for Mr. Rockefeller**.: Paul Peter Hydrick interview with author in Arizona, March 2016 – "I remember Dad telling me he worked at the Galvez Hotel in Galveston as a bellhop...He said he had taken John D. Rockerfeller's bags and him to his hotel room. He said Mr. Rockefeller tipped him a dime and told him to save it and he would be wealthy someday. It burned a hole in his pocket, and he spent it forthwith."

Page 178. **King's Ball was Scene of Gorgeous Splendor**: *The Houston Post*, Thursday, November 14, 1912, p. 4 – includes photo of Howard Hughes Jr. dressed in costume.

Chapter Twenty-Nine

Page 181. **In 1913...house at 4111 Avenue H.**: *1913 Galveston Directory* – "Charles C. Koenig wks S.P. docks. r. 4111 H"

Page 181. **Ernest worked as a messenger boy for Mackay Tel-Cable Company**.: *1916 Galveston City Director* – "Hydrick, Ernest, messenger at Mackay Tel-Cable Co, rooms 1620 Ave L."

Page 181. **Emma's mother, Mary moved in with them**: *1914 Galveston Directory* – "Charles Koenig doc wkr, Emma A. Koenig, Mary Butterfrass (wid of Peter), 4111 Ave H."

Page 181. **Eva—now on her third marriage**: Husband – Barney F. Brown. 1910 United States Federal Census, Place: Houston Ward 1, Harris, Texas; Roll: T624_1559; Page: 13B; Enumeration District: 0049; FHL microfilm: 1375572. Also enumerated in household is Mary Butterfras (Eva's mother), Eva, and her daughter Flossie (mistakenly indexed as Mollie) Lyttle. Note: Eva may not have legally married Barney, but he boarded with Eva.

Page 181. **...Anton Readler, had remarried and was raising three of Mary's grandchildren**.: 1900 United States Federal Census, Place: Houston Ward 6, Harris, Texas; Page: 5; Enumeration District: 0067; FHL microfilm: 1241642. Enumerated with wife Ida Readler and Anton's three children by Lottie – Beulah, Mabel, Willie.

Page 181. **1908, Mary filed suit in the district court against Galveston, Houston and Henderson Railroad company to recover damages**: 1.) *The Houston Post*, Sunday, March 22, 1908, p. 13 with headline "Sues for Death of Her Son."; 2.) *The Houston Post*, Thursday, January 6, 1910, p 12 Fifty-fifth District Court – "Mary Butterfrass vs. Galveston, Houston and Henderson Railway Company, dismissed for want of prosecution.

Page 182. **He probably rode his bike to Paul's again**.: Taped Oral Interview of George Hydrick, given by Plymton Hydrick on July 6, 1980. Note: It was a common practice for George to ride his bike from Galveston to his Uncle Paul's home, a 47-mile trip.

Chapter Thirty

Page 185. **Sonny entered the Prosso School**: Barlett and Steele, p 35.

Page 185. **taunted and called "sissy"**: Brown and Broeske, p 12.

Page 185. **"Brought up to feel his superiority"**: Ibid.

Page 185. **King of the May at Christ Church Cathedral's annual May Day celebration**: Ibid.

Page 185. **"Howard is both tall and polite, and would make an excellent King of the May Fete. I feel the enclosed check for $250 might be used to ensure a successful day."**: Hack, p 30.

Page 186. **"We used to play at Dudley's. Dudley and Howard were both inventors and they had a workshop. It had all kinds of chemical things, not toys but real things...Playing any game, he [Sonny] always had some theory. And he wanted to know the mathematics of everything."**.: Jonhston, p 326 (see next).

Page 187. **taking bets on who could go the farthest when they jumped off the swing**.: Ibid. Full quote from Mary Cullinan Cravens – "Dudley and Howard were both inventors and they had a workshop. It had all kinds of chemical things, not toys but the real thing. They had a great big high swing, and we would swing high and make bets on who could go the farthest if they jumped out. The rest of us did it for fun. But Howard was trying to work out the curve of where you'd land—the trajectory. At that age! Ten or twelve! Playing any game, he always had some theory. And he wanted to know the mathematics of everything."

Chapter Thirty-One

Page 189. **Galveston's Model Laundry, Emma's place of employment**: *1914 Galveston City Directory* – "Koenig, Emma A Miss employed Model Laundry, residence 4111 Ave H 4."

Page 189. **Model Laundry...rebuilt into an impressive two-story, large commercial building in 1913**.: Website *Texas Historical Commission Atlas*; US Register of Historic Places; for photo see Model Laundry - Galveston, Texas at https://www.waymarking.com/waymarks/wm8CK1_Model_Laundry_Galveston_Texas

Page 189. **In the summer of 1915, both George and Ernest went to work for Model Laundry**.: Taped Oral Interview of George Hydrick, given by Plymton Hydrick on July 6, 1980. "But before that [leaving home in 1919] my brother and I worked together at the Model Laundry in Galveston, Texas...I was a marker in the laundry. Ernest was in charge of the laundry washing department."

Page 190. **She hoped the new seawall would keep the flooding back**: Gidley and Marines, pp 139-141.

Page 194. **Inside the house, she found chairs, the table, a trunk, muddy bedding, and rugs all tangled together in a giant heap**.: Taped Oral Interview of George Hydrick, given by Plymton Hydrick on July 6, 1980 – "And we couldn't get home because of the storm. The water was high. We went home the next day and not much was left. Everything had floated up to the roof. The chairs and table and trunk were on top of other things...the other furniture."

Page 195. **Tropical storm...became a hurricane...August 17th**: Website *Wikipedia* "1915 Galveston Hurricane."

Chapter Thirty-Two

Page 197. **Gas-powered vehicles had become so commonplace on the island**: Gidley and Marines, pp 136-137.

Page 199. **"Look what I won at Electric Park."**: Ibid., pp 28, 29.

Page 202. **Emma and Ernest moved into a house at 1620 Avenue L.**: 1.) Description and Estimate of the Present Cash Value Tax Records of Galveston found at Rosenberg Library 2016, description – cottage owned by Martin Ricke, value $750, possibly built in 1891; 2.) [postcard]

Page 203. **went to live with Paul multiple times**.: Taped Oral Interview of George Hydrick, given by Plymton Hydrick on July 6, 1980.

Page 203. **Paul had six sons and lived at 1813 Keene in Houston**: *1913 Houston City Directory*, p 205 – "Butterfrass, Paul P., driver Engine Co. #1 Central fire station, 1813 Keene, 7." Note: Paul lived at this address until 1918 when he moved to 1812 Chestnut Street, Houston. The only daughter Paul had was born and died in 1902. His sons were Sanders, Paul, Charlie, Frank, William and Johnnie, all of whom lived to adulthood. Sanders was three months younger than George Hydrick.

Chapter Thirty-Three

Page 204. **In June of 1916, at the age of ten, Howard Jr. traveled by train to New York with his mother to meet with Howard Sr**: Hack, p 31.

Page 204. **Camp Teedyuskung in the Poconos of Pennsylvania**: Barlett and Steele, pp 38-43 Note: Daniel Carter Beard papers, Manuscript Division, Library of Congress.

Page 204. **Daniel Beard—one of the founders of the Boy Scouts of America**: Ibid, p 38.

Page 205. **Newton D. Baker, cracked down on prostitution**: Website *Texas State Historical Association* "Prostitution"   at https://www.tshaonline.org/handbook/entries/prostitution

Page 205. **Howard Sr. had been in negotiations to sell a combat device to the English and French.**: 1.) Kemm, p 82, 83; 2.) Johnston, p 198.

Page 205. **Hughes Tool Company made stokes mortars, molds for dummy bombs**: Ibid.

Page 206. **In the spring of 1917, Howard Sr. bought a sixty-foot yacht**: Hack, p 33.

Page 206. **Dudley Sharp attended camp with Sonny.**: Barlett and Steele, p pp 42, 43.

Page 206. **Allene sent a letter to Chief**: Ibid, pp 39-43.

Page 208. **communicated with ships in the Gulf of Mexico and had built himself a radio station in his bedroom.**: Barlett and Steele, p 44.

Page 209. **He took a junked battery and an automobile starter motor to make a motorcycle**: Johnston, p 326

Page 209. **Emma had seen a photo in the newspaper of Sonny standing in front of his motorized bicycle.**: Ibid.

Page 209. **He charges the neighbor kids a nickel to ride up and down Main Street on his bike**: Ibid (Note: quoted by friend, Ed Andrews)

Page 210. **prep schools in the East, hoping he'll eventually attend Harvard, my alma mater.**: Barlett and Steele, p 46.

Chapter Thirty-Four

Page 212. **In early 1918, the Hugheses made an end to leasing residences...3921 Yoakum Boulevard**.: Barlett and Steele, p 44.

Page 212. **Link had brought in seven train-carloads of palm trees to line the public walks in the neighborhood. A streetcar, the Montrose Line, ran through the suburb to give easy access to downtown**.: Johnston, p 132.

Page 212. **sent his yacht by rail to California when he wanted to entertain West Coast oilmen**.: 1.) Barlett and Steele, p 36; 2.) Johnston, p 328 - "where he enjoyed entertaining movie stars."

Page 212. **Howard Sr. gained full control of Hughes Tool Company**: Barlett and Steele, p 38.

Page 212. **Emma and Ernest moved to yet another rental home at 3906 Ave J**: 1.) Galveston City Directory1919 – "Hydrick, Ernest A, employed Model Laundry and Dye Works, home 3906 Ave J"; 2.) U.S. Marine enlistment papers of George Neverson Hydrick record his mother's address as "3906 Broadway" [Ave J].

Page 212. **Emma...worked as an elevator operator**: Texas State Board of Healthy, Bureau of Vital Statistics, Standard Certificate of Death #24052, registered #424 – Galveston County, Galveston City, John Sealy Hospital - Occupation recorded as "elevator operator."

Page 212. **she went back to using the name Hydrick and recorded herself as a "widow"**: Ibid.

Page 212. **George...streetcar conductor for Galveston Electric Company**.: Note: there is a newspaper article in *The Houston Post*, Thursday, May 2, 1918, which lists George Hydrick as working for the Dickson Car Wheel Company. When my father asked George about this, he said that wasn't him. A WWI Draft Registration Card records there to be another George Hydrick living in Houston in 1916. He was born in 1877 in Hungary. Ancestry.com. U.S., World War I Draft Registration Cards, 1917-1918.

Page 213. **On September 12, 1918, he had registered for the United States War Draft**: WWI Draft Registration Card for "George Neverson Hydrick, address: 3906 J. Galveston, Galveston, Tex. Age in Years: 18. Date of Birth: Jan 19, 1900. Race: White. Citizen. Occupation: Street Car Conductor, Galveston Electric Co., 2028 I, Galveston, Galveston, Tex. Nearest Relative: mother, Mrs. Koenig and living at 2028 J(?)

Galveston, Galveston, Tex." Hard to read "description of applicant" but looks like color of eyes "grey" and color of hair "light." Ancestry.com. U.S., World War I Draft Registration Cards, 1917-1918 [database on-line]. Provo, UT, USA: Ancestry.com Operations Inc, 2005.

Page 213. **During World War I, 53,402 Americans lost their lives in combat or became missing in action. Another 63,114 died from other causes, mostly the Spanish Influenza**: Website *Military.com* "Memorial Day by the Numbers: Casualties of Every American War" at https://www.military.com/memorial-day/how-many-us-militay-members-died-each-american-war.html Note: "So a Great War-era soldier was almost as likely to perish due to trench foot or Spanish Flu as to a German bullet."

Page 213. **Although 5,170 Texans died in the armed services, more than a third of those occurred inside the United States, many of them as a result of influenza.**: Website *Texas State Historical Association* "World War I" at https://www.tshaonline.org/handbook/entries/world-war-i

Page 213. **In the years 1918 and 1919, the Spanish Influenza Pandemic killed 675,000 Americans and possibly over twenty million worldwide.**: Website *Stanford.edu* "The Influenza Pandemic of 1918" at https://virus.stanford.edu/uda/

Page 215. **He was gone and so were all his belongings.**: Taped Oral Interview of George Hydrick, given by Plymton Hydrick on July 6, 1980.

Chapter Thirty-Five

Page 220. **revealing an immense room—as big or bigger than the ballrooms...** and **...two narrow windows reached to the ceiling.**: Texas State Historical Association - https://tshaonline.org/handbook/online/articles/sbj01 photos and information regarding John Sealy Hospital.

Page 223. **She would die, and she'd do it alone.**: A typical death certificate has an informant to supply the needed vital information. There was not an informant recorded on Emma's death certificate, other than "Hospital Register." According to the death certificate, she was attended by J.H. Harris, M.D. from August 3 – 15, 1919.

Page 224. **Emma died twelve days later in the John Sealy Hospital.**: Texas State Board of Healthy, Bureau of Vital

Statistics, Standard Certificate of Death #24052, registered #424 – Galveston County, Galveston City, John Sealy Hospital…"Mrs Emma Hydrick, residence 3906 J. Length of residence in city or town where death occurred - 15 years. Female, White, Widow, born July 28, 1882, age 37…Cause of Death – Carcinoma of cervix; an operation precede death on 8/15/19 microscopic examination of tissues."

Page 224. **cervical cancer behaved like a sexually transmitted disease and was common in female sex workers, and rare in nuns.**: Website *National Library of Medicine* at https://pubmed.ncbi.nlm.nih.gov/14746027/

Page 224. **In 1896, "X-ray" was discovered**: Website *Wikipedia* "X-ray" at https://en.wikipedia.org/wiki/X-ray

Page 224. **Researchers now know cervical cancer is caused by a sexually transmitted virus called human papilloma virus (HPV).**: Website *National Library of Medicine* at https://pubmed.ncbi.nlm.nih.gov/14746027/

Page 224-225. **Excerpt of letter from George to my father, September 14, 1980**: George left home July 10, 1919, and enlisted with the U.S. Marines July 11, 1919 (see enlistment source below). Emma entered the hospital on August 3, 1919, dying 12 days later. Note: When interviewing George's children, George Jr., Lucille, Jeanette, and Paul, they all said their father never told them stories of his past other than one story he told Paul about Rockefeller visiting the Galvez Hotel. George Jr. mentioned that Sr. never talked about his mother. Jr. didn't know his grandmother's name was Emma until I told him.

Chapter Thirty-Six

Page 226. **Howard Jr…he had spent the spring of that year at Mackinac Island, Michigan**: Barlett and Steele, p 46.

Page 226. **infantile paralysis**: Ibid.

Page 226. **"pick up and become a perfectly normal boy."**: Ibid.

Page 226. **Howard Jr. attended South End Junior High in Houston and did poor academically.**: Ibid. (Note: Johnston, p 326 names the school South Central Junior High School.)

Page 226. **he was attending Fessenden School near Boston**: Dietrich, p 31.

Page 226. **graduated from Fessenden in June of 1921.**: https://www.fessenden.org/About/History "Graduates include statesmen, business leaders, and philanthropists such as Howard Hughes..."

Page 226. **he enrolled at Thacher School near Santa Barbara, California**: Kemm, p 121.

Page 227. **She died March 29, 1922.**: Death Certificate Texas, U.S., Death Certificates 1903-1982, Provo, UT, USA: Ancestry.com Original data: Texas Department of State Health Services Certificate #8529. "Name: Mrs. Allene Gano Hughes, Age: 38 Birth Date: 14 Jul 1883, Birth Place: Georgetown, Kentucky, Death Date: 29 Mar 1922, Death Place: Houston, Harris, Texas, USA, Father: Wm B Gano, Mother: Jeanette Grissim, Cause of death was as followed: Death occurred during administration of a gas anesthesia for curettement, Contributory (secondary): no cardiac pulmonary or nephritis disease was discovered at preotic(?) examination, Was there an autopsy: No, What test confirmed diagnosis: None. Signed: Gavin Hamilton, M.D., Informant: Miss Annette Gano of 3921 Yoakum Blvd."

Page 227. **shook his head and looked down in thoughtful silence**: Hack, p 45.

Page 227. **he seemed not to grieve.**: Ibid.

Page 227. **"We were alone in this big house, and spent the entire time in Sonny's room, playing with his radio transmitter. I remember saying that I was sorry to hear about his mother, and he replied, 'By turning this knob, we can hear Cleveland.'"**: Ibid. Note: Quote by friend Eliot Cage.

Page 227. **He begged Allene's sister, Annette, to postpone her plans for marriage and help him care for Howard Jr.**: Kemm, p 121.

Page 227. **Annette had often lived with the Hugheses after her mother died young**: Johnston, p 223.

Page 227. **had been living with them fulltime since 1919.**: 1.) Allene's death certificate confirms that Annette Gano (informant for certificate) considered the Yoakum address her home residence; 2.) Barlett and Steele, p 49.

Page 227. **They moved to California**: Kemm, p 121.

Page 227. **along with a cousin, stayed in a cottage surrounded by lush gardens at the Vista Del Arroyo Hotel in Pasadena.**: Brown and Broeske, p 26.

Page 228. **chartered three railroad cars for a party of fourteen to attend the Kentucky Derby**: Ibid, p 27.

Page 228. **He also went to New York and then sailed his yacht in the Caribbean and through the Panama Canal and back up to Los Angeles.**: Hack, p 47

Page 228. **He had no worries about his business in Houston, run by highly competent managers**: Barlett and Steele, p 52.

Page 228. **Howard Jr. returned to Thacher School in the fall**: Kemm, p 122.

Page 228. **Sherman Thacher…"more that most boys the contact with other fellows such as he gets in school; and I think your desire and tendency to indulge him in every way would probably be very hard for him to resist and probably not at all good for him."**: Barlett and Steele, p 50.

Page 228. **arrangement for Sonny to attend California Institute of Technology in Pasadena.**: Ibid, p 51.

Page 228. **"they were bribed to let him in."**: Barlett and Steele, p 51.

Page 228. **to roam freely on the set of *Souls for Sale***: Hack, p 47.

Page 228. **Annette…married fiancé, Dr. Frederick Rice Lummis**: Kemm, p 146

Page 228. **supposed to attend Rice Institute**: Ibid.

Page 229. **he would not carry a housekey and whenever he came home late, he broke a pain on a French door to be able to let himself in**: Johnston, p 328.

Page 229. **"He was impatient with learning things in the ordinary way. He wanted to know what he needed to know and didn't want to waste time. I think his genius lay in the ability to identify the people he needed to do what he wanted done."**: Ibid, p 329 - Quote by Dr. Frederick Rice Lummis.

Page 229. **"If to be an introvert is to hold yourself to your own inner standards, then Howard Hughes was an introvert throughout his life. He did what he wished to do, what he expected of himself. Nonetheless, for years after, he considered the Lummises and the house on Yoakum as home."**: Ibid - Quote by Marguerite Johnston.

Page 229. **On January 14, 1924, Howard Sr. was in a business meeting**: Texas U.S. Death Certificates 1903-1982, Certificate #371495 - "Name: Howard Robard Hughes, Age: 54, Birth Date: 9 Sep 1869, Birth Place: Keokuk, Iowa, Residence: 3921 St Yoakum, Death Date: 14 Jan 1924, Death Place:

Houston, Harris, Texas, USA, Father: Felix T Hughes, Informant: Jas. P. Houstonun, Cause of Death: Heart Failure – embolism of coronary artery, Duration: few minutes, Contributory: arteriosclerosis.

Page 229. **"suddenly rose to his feet, grasped at the desk before him convulsively, and fell to the floor.":** Barlett and Steele, p 52. Note: Quote from *Houston Chronical,* Jan 15, 1924. Death was also announced in *The Houston Post*, Tuesday, 15 Jan 1924, p 1.

Page 229. **was buried next to Allene at Glenwood Cemetery.**: https://www.findagrave.com/memorial/10675573/howard-robard-hughes Note: Howard Hughes Jr. is also buried there.

Page 229. **should be declared a "legal adult":** Dietrich, p 32.

Page 229. **he persuaded his relatives to sell their portions of the tool company to him**: Ibid.

Page 229. **expressed in a lengthy, scathing letter written April 19, 1924**: to read Rupert's letter in its entirety, see *Rupert Hughes: A Hollywood Legend*, p. 1-3.

Epilogue

Page 231. **At his death in 1976, he was worth $2.5 billion (net worth equal to 11 billion in 2021)**: https://www.celebritynetworth.com/richest-businessmen/richest-billionaires/howard-hughes-net-worth/

Page 231-232. **He became a foreman and salesman for Model Laundry and worked there at least until 1942**: 1.) Galveston City Directory 1921 – "Hydrick, Ernest, marker at Model Laundry and Dye Works, home 3202 Ave J."; 2.) Galveston City Directory 1923 – "Hydrick, Ernest, marker at Model Laundry and Dye Works, rooms at 2707 Ave J"; 3.) Ernest also shows up in Houston Directory for this year. I would assume he made the move to Houston in 1923-1924. Houston City Directory 1923-1924 – "Hydrick, Ernest marker at Peerless Laundry, rooms at Touraine Hotel." Note: 1925-1936 Houston City Directories show Ernest working for Model Laundry Co. as a foreman; 4.) 1940 United States Federal Census Houston, Harris, Texas; Roll: m-t0627-04190; Page: 7B; Enumeration District: 258-33 – "Occupation Salesman, Industry Laundry."; 5.) World War II Draft Card, National Archives at St. Louis; St. Louis,

Missouri; WWII Draft Registration Cards for Texas; Records of the Selective Service System 147; Box: 744, 16 Feb 1942 – "Residence 4031 Searle Dr, Houston; Employer Model Laundry 602 Prairie, Houston; Description 6' 180 lbs.; Physical Identification - paralyzed right leg and foot."

Page 232. **married Thelma Derouen in 1924**: Texas U.S. Select County Marriage Records 1837-1965, Ancestry - "Thelma M. De Ronen, Gender Female, Marriage Date 20 Sep 1924, Marriage Place Harris, Texas, USA, Spouse E. A. Hydrick, Document Number   64908."

Page 232. **widowed in 1969**: Texas Death Index, 1903-2000, Ancestry – "Thelma Hydrick, Death Date 16 Nov 1969, Death County Harris, Gender Female, Marital Status   Single.

Page 232. **married Lily Newman in 1971**.: Vital Records Harris County Texas Marriages 1971 #12348 Hydrick Ernest A., Age 68 to Newman, Lily, 52 04-Feb-1971.

Page 232. **He died in 1989, at the age of eighty-seven**.: Texas Death Index, 1964-1998 - Name Ernest Albert Hydrick, Gender Male, Event Date 08 Apr 1989, County Harris.

Page 232. **Geroge...while still in the Marines**: U.S. Marine Corp Service-Record Book of George Neverson Hydrick, Private U.S.M.C. July 11, 1919 – Jan 3, 1922 (Applied July 6, 1919). "Marine Barracks Parris Island, S.C., Date of birth January 19, 1899 [not 1900, as he claimed on other records], Houston, Texas. Occupation Clerk in Galveston, Texas. In case of emergency – Mother, Emma E. Hydrick at 3906 Broadway, Galveston, Tex." Special Duties – "Corral excellent, Radio Mechanic unsatisfactory, Orderly very good, Messman venereal disease." Expeditions - "Embarked on USS Kittery at Charleston, S.C. Sept 25, 1919. Sailed same date for foreign tropical shore service in CUBA...Embarked on board USS Henderson at Guantanamo Bay, Cuba March 1, 1921, sailed same date, arrived at Hampton Roads, Va. March 1921." Character "excellent" marks other than one comment "using profane and obscene language to N.C.O. 10/29/19."

Page 232. **"My mother didn't want me to marry a Marine..."**: Taped Oral History of Lucille White Hydrick administered by Plymton Hydrick, her son, May 1980 – "He started courting me, and then we got married, but my mother didn't want me to marry a Marine. Neither did my sisters. None of them wanted me to marry a Marine. But I was going to marry a Marine anyhow because I was crazy about him. I loved him.

So, one day from work we just got married. I had one of these girls that worked with me, and she was my best woman. And we went to the minister and got married. I come home and I called my mother and my sister up and I had told them where to come, and they never did come to be at my wedding. But I got married anyhow."

Page 232. **George left the Marine's after two years**.: U.S. Marine Corp Service-Record Book of George Neverson Hydrick, Private U.S.M.C. July 11, 1919 – Jan 3, 1922. Discharge 12/31/21 – "Own conv., Hon., Washington, D.C., character excellent." On Feb 24, 1931 George requested another copy of his discharge papers because he "misplaced or lost to civil service commission." Again, he records his birth as Jan 19, 1899, Houston, Texas. Another Discharge paper dated 1 March 1935 "This is to certify that the records of this office show that George Neverson HYDRICK, born January 19, 1899, at Houston, Texas, enlisted in the Marine Corps July 11, 1919, at Parris Island, S.C., and was honorably discharged, by special order of the Major General Commandant for his convenience, December 31, 1921, at Washington, D.C., a Private, with character "Excellent." Signed by L.D. Hermle, Major Asst. Adjutant and Inspector."

Page 232. **He worked as a fireman**: Taped Oral History of Lucille White Hydrick administered by Plymton Hydrick, her son, May 1980 – "They gave him an honorable discharge and he started as a fireman in Washington, DC. We was still living with my mother then."

Page 232. **worked at a laundry company**: Ibid. "Worked for awhile until he got on another rampage. He was working in the laundry. He was not working with his brother…some other laundry. I forgot the name of it."

Page 232. **They lived with Eva and her fifth husband Bert at 117 Conoly Avenue**.: Address supplied by Plymton Hydrick, but *1930 Houston City Directory* records Bert King living at 114 Conoly Avenue.

Page 232. **My father was born in Eva's home**: 1.) Family fact. Confirmed by a photo of my father standing in front of the house in 1969; 2.) Charlie Butterfras also confirmed it to be Eva's house in photo in interview with author at his home in Texas, Feb 6, 2016.

Page 232-233. **"stone-blind drunk" leaning heavily against the milkman**: Taped Oral History of Lucille White Hydrick administered by Plymton Hydrick, her son, May 1980 –

"He [George] was stone-blind drunk and he went off to sleep, I guess. And the milkman came along and found the motor running, and turned the motor off, and got him out of there and brought him home. We didn't take him to the hospital. Well, then I fixed him up and he went back to work. Worked for a while until he got on another rampage. He was working in the laundry. He was not working with his brother...some other laundry. I forgot the name of it. Doing clothes, or something. That's all he could get, I guess. This was during the Depression."

Page 233. **Charlie Koenig was still in George's life**: Ibid – "We was buying this house, so finally his step-father (not his father, his father was dead) come to me and he said he knew that your dad was running around having a good time and leaving us. Half the time we didn't have enough to eat. His stepfather was Charles Koenig. So, he told me, "Do you want to go back home to Washington, DC." I said, "Yes, I want to go back to Washington, DC." So, he said, "Well, I'll get your ticket." So, he got my ticket and sent me back to Washington, DC."

Page 234. **Lucille divorced George**.: Divorce record not found. Family believes it to have been about 1942 in California.

Page 235. **George died in 1990**: 1.) Washoe County District Health Department, Certificate of Death #011750 – "George Neverson Hydrick, date of death May 13, 1990...occupation Electrical Inspector, kind of business Aviation."; 2.) Obituary clipping (unknown newspaper) records George as "retired quality-control electrical inspector."

Page 235. **"She was feisty and Paul couldn't put anything over on her."**: Charlie Butterfras, interview with author at his home in Texas, Feb 6, 2016.

Page 235. **Paul...died in 1969**: Texas U.S. Death Index 1903-2000 - "Name: Paul Butterfras Death Date: 22 Jul 1969, Death County: Harris, Marital Status: Widowed."

Page 235. **1707 and 1709 Airline Drive in Houston**: 1.) Charlie Butterfras, interview with author at his home in Texas, Feb 6, 2016; 2.) Death Certificate of Eva King (below) 3.) Cemetery Record (below) of Eva Ann King.

Page 235. **married a barber named Elwin Fontenot...1711 Airline Drive**: 1.) 2.) When George Neverson Hydrick filled out his Social Security Application on April 9, 1937, he listed his address "1711 Airline Drive, Houston, Texas." I assume he lived with or was visiting the Fontenots at this time. On the same application he recorded his birth date as Jan 19,

1900. For his father, he recorded "Charles C. Hydrick (Deceased)," which leads me to believe he didn't know Jack Hydrick well enough to know his name. Perhaps it also means he considered Charles Koenig as a father? George may have been in Houston without his wife and five children because the month before his wife had lost her sixth child soon after birth in South Carolina.

Page 235. **Bert King was a cattleman and friendly to all who came to his home. He especially enjoyed teaching boys about cattle ranching and trading**.: Larry King phone conversation with author, Feb 8, 2016.

Page 236. **"Hey Cat-licker," because she was a Catholic, and Mary would yell back at her, "Dog-licker."**: Charlie Butterfras, interview with author at his home in Texas, Feb 6, 2016.

Page 236. **Eva's grandsons remember her as a "hard" woman, although they have good memories of going to work with her at a carnival where she conducted sales at the ticket booth**.: Larry King phone conversation with author, Feb 8, 2016.

Page 236. **Eva died in 1957**: 1.) Texas Department of Health, Bureau of Vital Statistics Certificate of Death #43869 Eva Anna King Date of Death 8/19/57, Date of Birth 10/5/89, Street Address 1707 Airline Dr., etc; 2.) Brookside Cemetery Record of Funeral #237, for "Mrs Eva Anna King, white, residence 1707 Airline, husband Bert, occupation Housewife, Date of Death August 19, 1957 10:35 am..."; 3) Obituary newspaper clipping from unknown newspaper.

Page 236. **Mary Clark Butterfras, Emma's mother, died in 1922**: Texas State Board of Health, Bureau of Vital Statistics, Standard Certificate of Death #34713 "Mrs Mary Butterfrass, residence 7002 Ave F (?) Magnolia, Female, White, Widow, date of birth Jan 10, 1833 [this is different from other documents recording a birth of April 1847], Informant: P. Butterfrass, Date of Death: Dec 19, 1922, St Joseph, Houston..."

Page 236. **living with widowed husband of her daughter, Lottie**: Mary Butterfrass is recorded twice in the 1920 United States Federal Census. Enumerated with Anton and Ida [2nd wife of Anton] Readler on 8 Jan 1920 (Houston, Harris County, Texas), and enumerated with John and J. [?Wilhelmina or another daughter?] Techa on 26 Apr 1920 (Magnolia Park City, Harris County, Texas). Recorded as "mother-in-law" to John Techa and "mother" to Ida Readler. Considering her residence was in Magnolia at death, I supposed she had been living with J. Techa.

Page 236. **Buddy...died in 1996**: U.S. Veterans' Gravesites ca.1775-2019, Ancestry - "Owen E Hydrick, Death Age 72, Birth Date 15 Feb 1924, Service Start Date 6 Feb 1943, Service End Date 15 Feb 1946, Death Date 28 Jul 1996, Interment Date 1 Aug 1996, Interment Place California, USA, Cemetery Address 22495 Van Buren Boulevard Riverside, CA 92518, Cemetery Riverside National Cemetery Plot Section 47 Site 3765, Notes Sn Us Navy World War II."

Postscript

Page 240. **Dr. Raymond D. Fowler...psychological autopsy**: Fowler, p 22-33

Page 240. **"Howard Hughes Jr. was the child of a hearty, extroverted but often absent father and a quiet, soft-spoken mother who focused her full attention on her only child."**: Ibid., p 24.

Page 241. **this pattern of shy, anxious, socially uncomfortable behavior an "avoidant disorder."**: Ibid., p 25.

Page 241. **Terry Moore, a possible wife of Howard's said that the only time he got love and affection was when he was ill.**: Moore, p 2.

Page 241. **Ava Gardner, a twenty-year on-again-off-again girlfriend, wrote that Howard had a remoteness about him. She suspected his partial deafness may have explained his dull conversations and shyness. She called him the Quiet Texan.**: Evans and Gardner, p 163.

Page 242. **"The loss of the only two people with whom he had a close relationship deepened his fears of death and increased his vulnerability to later disorders."**: Ibid., p 28.

Page 242. **In a 1925 will, he left out any bequests to his Hughes side of the family.**: Kemm, p 165.

Page 242. **James Whetton... "Jim, I want everyone to understand that as far as I am concerned, I do not have a living relative on the face of the earth."**: Whetton, Wadsworth, Thain, ebook location 34.

Page 243. **Rupert's own words... "Since your father's death I have never heard you say one word in praise, make one suggestion of a memorial to him or show any desire to** emphasize his greatness or the importance of his splendid achievements.": Kemm, p 3.

Page 243. **Rupert made the comment, "He'd throw his mother down the stairs if it was to his advantage.":** Ibid, p 205.

Page 243. **Annette... "with all that money.":** Fowler, p 28.

Page 243. **Three weeks later, they were married.**: Howard Hughes and Ella Rice married in the backyard garden of Ella's sister's home, Libbie Rice Farish on June 1, 1925. Johnston, p 329.

Page 243. **"Howard was just not the kind of person who would ever take care of a wife. He was always off doing something and he ran these peculiar hours. He didn't sleep much. He would have his business meetings in a car somewhere at 2:00 A.M. and he might disappear for a day or two without Ella's knowing where he was.":** Johnston, p 329.

Page 243. **After the divorce he never returned to Houston for the rest of his life, other than one single 24-hour visit.**: Real and Yenne, p 19.

Page 243. **in 1938 when he was honored with a parade for the success of circling the world:** Johnston, p 329, 330.

Page 244. **"seemed more interested in collecting them than in establishing serious relationships."** Fowler, p 28.

Page 244. **1946...Howard became addicted to pain medication:** Real and Yenne, pp 158, 159.

Page 245. **Dr. Fowler... "A single head injury, even if there is no apparent structural damage, can affect psychological functioning seriously and may exacerbate existing emotional problems. A series of traumas, such as Hughes had, greatly increases the probability of brain damage. The accidents, particularly those that occurred between 1939 and 1946, may have been both a cause and an effect of his increasing emotional disorder.".:** Fowler, p 29.

BIBLIOGRAPHY

Barlett, Donald L., and Steele, James B. *Howard Hughes: His Life and Madness*. New York, W.W. Norton & Company, 1979.

Barnstone, Howard. *The Galveston That Was*. New York, The Macmillan Company, 1966.

Becker, Ann Dunphy. *Images of America: Houston 1860-1900*. Charleston, South Carolina, Arcadia Publishing, 2010.

Bixel, Patricia Bellis, and Turner, Elizabeth Hayes. *Galveston and the 1900 Storm*. Austin, University of Texas, 2000.

Brown, Peter Harry, and Broeske, Pat H. *Howard Hughes: The Untold Story*. Cambridge, Massachusetts, First Da Capo Press, 2004.

Charles Rivers Editors. *American Legends: The Life of Howard Hughes*. Kindle ebook, 2014.

Clark, James A., and Halbouty, Michel T. *Spindletop: The True Story of the Oil Discovery That Changed the World*. New York, Random House, 1952.

Cline, Isaac Monroe. *Storms, Floods and Sunshine: An Autobiography*. Gretna, Pelican Publishing Co., 2000.

Dietrich, Noah. *Howard: The Amazing Mr. Hughes*. Greenwich, Connecticut, Fawcett Publications, 1972.

Evans, Peter, and Gardner, Ava. Ava Gardner: The Secret Conversations. New York, Simon & Schuster, reprint edition, 2014.

Fowler, Raymond. "Howard Hughes: A Psychological Autopsy" *Psychology Today*, May 1986, Vol. 20, Issue 5, pp 22-33.

Gidley, Jodi Wright, and Marines, Jennifer. *Galveston: A City on Stilts*. Charleston, South Carolina, Arcadia Publishing, 2008.

Greene, Casey Edward, and Kelly, Shelly Henley. *Through a Night of Horrors*. College Station, Texas A & M University Press, 2006.

-------- *Harvard College Fourth Report* "Records of the Class of 1897". Boston, Rockwell and Churchill Press, 1912.

Hack, Richard. *Hughes: The Private Diaries, Memos and Letters*. Beverly Hills, New Millenium Press, 2001.

Johnston, Marguerite. *Houston: The Unknown City 1836-1946*. College Station, Texas A&M University Press, 1991.

Kemm, James O. *Rupert Hughes: A Hollywood Legend*. Beverly Hills, Pomegranate Press, Ltd., 1997.

Larson, Erik. *Isaac's Storm: A Man, a Time, and the Deadliest Hurricane in History*. New York, Vintage Books, ebook 2000.

Meaux, Robert Dr., and Humble Museum. *Images of America: Humble*. Arcadia Publishing, 2013.

Price, Granville. "A Social Study of a Segregated District," Master's thesis, University of Texas at Austin, 1930. Rosenberg Library, GTHC-Reference Materials HQ 146 .A19 .G2 P8.

Raphael, Morris. *A Gunboat Named Diana: And Other Exciting Stories of Civil War Battles which Raged in the Bayou Country of Louisiana*. Detroit, Harlo, 1993.

Real, Jack G., with Bille Yenne. *The Asylum of Howard Hughes*. Xlibris Corporation, 2003.

Remmers, Mary W. *Going Down the Line: Galveston's Red-Light District Remembered*. M.W. Remmers, 1997.

Rundell, Walter Jr. *Early Texas Oil: A Photographic History, 1866-1936*. College Station, Texas A&M University Press, 1977.

Turner, Elizabeth Hayes. *Women, Culture, and Community: Religion and Reform in Galveston, 1880-1920*. Oxford University Press, 1997.

Weems, John Edward. *A Weekend in September*. New York, Henry Holt and Company, 1957.

Whetton, James J., and Wadsworth, James L., Thain, Wilbur S. *We Knew Howard Hughes: A Collection of Memoirs*. Book Wise Publishing, 2012.

Wilson, Ann Quin. *Native Houstonian: A Collective Portrait*. Virginia Beach, Virginia, The Donning Company/Publishers, 1982.

Other Books of Study

Bell, Jerry. *Howard Hughes: His Silence, Secrets and Success!*. Hawkes Publishing, 1976.

Burrough, Bryan. *The Big Rich: The Rise and Fall of the Greatest Texas Oil Fortunes*. Penguin Books, ebook 2009

Crane, Stephen. *Maggie: a Girl of the Streets*. Dancing Unicorn Books, ebook 2014.

Drosnin, Michael. *Citizen Hughes: In His Own Words, How Howard Hughes Tried to Buy America*. Broadway Books, Random House, 1985.

Dwiggins, Don. *Howard Hughes: The True Story*, "2-Hour Interview with the Man No One knows." Santa Monica, California, Werner Book Corporation, 1972.

Guthrie, Lee. *The Life and Loves of Cary Grant*. New York, Drake Publishers, 1977.

Hanna, David. *Ava: A Portrait of a Star*. New York, G.P. Putnam's Sons, 1960.

Hepburn, Katharine. *Me: Stories of My Life. New York*. The Random House, 1991.

Hill, Marilynn Wood. *Their Sisters' Keepers: Prostitution in New York City, 1830-1870*. Berkely, California, University of California Press, 1993.

Longworth, Karina. *Seduction: Sex, Lies, and Stardom in Howard Hughes's Hollywood*. Custom House, 2018. Kindle Edition.

McMurtry, Larry. *In a Narrow Grave: Essays on Texas*. Liveright, ebook 2018.

Moore, Terry. *The Beauty and the Billionaire*. New York, Pocket Books by Simon and Schuster, Inc., 1984.

Myers, Lois E. *Letters by Lamplight: A Woman's View of Everyday Life in South Texas, 1873-1883*. Waco, Baylor University Press, 1991.

Rutter, Michael. *Upstairs Girls: Prostitution in the American West*. Helena, Montana, Farcountry Press, 2005.

Rutter, Michael. *Boudoirs to Brothels: The intimate World of the Wild West Women*. Helena, Montana, Farcountry Press, 2014.

Sheridan, John Harris. *Howard Hughes: The Las Vegas Years - The Women, the Mormons, the Mafia*. AuthorHouse, ebook 2011.

Shulman, Irving. *Harlow: An Intimate Biography*. New York, Dell Publishing, 1964.

Website *Smithsonian National Air and Space Museum* - search for Howard Hughes for interesting videos, photographs, and articles.

Willett, Donald, and Curley, Stephen. *Invisible Texans: Women and Minorities in Texas History*. McGraw-Hill, 2004.

Acknowledgements

Thanks goes to my graduate studies mentor, Becky Bradway, who encouraged me to tell this story in a mixed genre because it was how I *saw* it. She often asked the pertinent questions to help delve further into a character's individual spirit and their motives and personality. Without Becky, I would not have believed I could tell Emma's story in a narrative fashion, yet also show the reader my own feelings and explorations, examining more closely my family identity.

Thank you to my family members, Carter, Christi, and Jill Hydrick, Don and June Carsten, Cindy Gibson, Heidi Smith, and Lisa Casillas for reading the first draft and believing in me. And thank you Rick and Don Hydrick for help with the final draft. Thank you also to my husband Hyrum and my five children, Hyrum, Taylor, Preston, Ian, and Makayla for being patient when Mom went back to school. I wrote this book in hopes that you would remember and care about your ancestors and that for you Emma's story connects your past to your future.

Thank you to my most helpful beta readers, who were Jo Ellen Guthrie, Rene Allen, Sandra Scott, Cindy Higginson, and Chris Luders, and critique group members Ann Lee Miller and Laura Zimmerman. Your advice was invaluable, and the friendships we forged an added gift I will treasure.

Thank you, Hernan and Ashley Arzac for letting me stay longer at your house than I should have while doing research in Houston and Galveston.

Thank you, Bruce, Charlie and Kay Butterfras for your hospitality, photographs, and information about the Butterfras family.

I appreciate the capable and friendly assistance received from the employees of Rosenberg Library in Galveston regarding genealogical resources available there. Finding Emma's residences and dwellings owned by Lillian Sullivan were a great find, as was the information available regarding early prostitution in Galveston.

Thank you to Wilkes University cohorts and faculty who always had my back and encouraged nothing but success and finding my voice. Most especially Bonnie Culver, Nancy McKinley, Kaylie Jones, Kevin Oderman, J. Michael Lennon, Taylor Polites, Bill Schneider, Joyce Anzalone, Deborah Cannon, Maura Nicholls Maros, Allison Richter, Donny Granza, Robert Peck, Donald Roe (RIP), Travis Schick, Melody Breyer Grell (RIP), Brian Thomas, Jeffrey Ford, Gabrielle Willis and Ronnie Stephens.

When deadlines loomed, I was able to turn to David M. Clare for additional research. His reports were professional and detailed with electronic photocopies of original records. I am most grateful to him for finding the newspaper clippings about Hy's death.

Manuscripts are never complete without a good editor's eye. Thank you, Karen Ball and Lori Freeland for making me appear to be an accomplished writer.

I enjoyed learning about genetic genealogy from Mckell Keeney. Her love for the subject was palpable. Because of that love, I'm sure she spent many more hours on my project than I paid her for. Thank you, Mckell, for all your help!

And lastly, thank you Aunt Jeanette Jackson for thinking of me as "the family historian" and knowing I would find interest in the letter written by Uncle Buddy. I hope I didn't let you down in trying to find the truth.

Also by Ora Smith

Children's Picture Book

A Christmas Story of Light

Heritage Fiction

The Pulse of His Soul: The Story of John Lothropp, a Forgotten Forefather

*The Cry of Her Heart (*A companion novella to *The Pulse of His Soul)*

White Oak River: A Story of Slavery's Secrets

*White Oak Plantation: Slavery's Deeper Roots (*a prequel novella to *White Oak River*)

Ora Smith, a genealogist who writes Heritage Fiction, creates fascinating stories about her ancestors based on true events. She loves nothing better than to be whisked off to past eras to meet those whose lives are worth sharing.

White Oak River: A Story of Slavery's Secrets

After giving birth to a son with dominant African traits, a white Southern enslaver must decide if she'll hold onto her bigotry at the cost of her heart.

When Caroline Gibson marries the Reverend John Mattocks, she leaves behind her privileged life, which she finds easier than leaving behind her prejudices. While she's content being served, John lives to serve others. Scorning his family's wealth and long-held practice of owning slaves, he chooses to follow his conscience, becoming an abolitionist preacher. But after Caroline gives birth to a son of African heritage, they both must face their vastly different beliefs. Their marriage mirrors the Civil War's failure to create a changed society, the turmoil not only leaving the nation in despair but their relationship as well. Can their love find deeper roots in forgiveness and acceptance?

This dramatic story of love, faith, family bonds, and discrimination is based on true events of the author's great-great-great-grandparents in coastal North Carolina.

White Oak Plantation: Slavery's Deeper Roots

An enslaved young woman craves a family. Her mistress desires status in society. Can an unlikely bond change their lives forever?

Most slaves long for freedom. Eighteen-year-old Spicey longs for a sister. As an orphaned house slave, she's desperate to belong to a family—even her mistress Caroline's family. But Caroline is more concerned with courting John, the local preacher, than noticing Spicey's devotion or caring for her needs. Caroline doesn't even think to look past Spicey's skin color to see their relationship for what it is. But when the decision to protect a runaway slave causes them both to risk everything, will the chains of slavery keep them bound to a world of lies and prejudices or be the catalyst that sets them free?

Rich in authentic details and unforgettable characters, Caroline, John, and Spicey's stories progress in White Oak River: A Story of

Slavery's Secrets. *Inspired by the author's own family events, the novel continues the struggles Caroline endured to overcome the scars of slavery.*

The Pulse of His Soul: The Story of John Lothropp, a Forgotten Forefather

Based on a true story of love and loss, family and faith.

At the height of Separatist suppression and enforced Anglican worship in England, Reverend John Lothropp meets and marries Hannah Howse. The witty, educated vicar's daughter immediately challenges his decision to put God before a wife. In a world spiraling into hypocrisy, tyranny, and betrayal, Hannah refuses to break from her Anglican roots. But when John comes face-to-face with his deep-seated convictions about religious freedom, he's forced to make a hard choice—renounce his orders with the Church of England to become an outlawed Separatist or conform and save his marriage, his family, and his life.

Considered one of the most important ministers to follow in the footsteps of the Plymouth Pilgrims, John Lothropp helped plant the seeds of religious freedom in America's soil and left a legacy of well-known individuals who influenced the nation's destiny.

The Cry of Her Heart

A companion novella to *The Pulse of His Soul*

Punished for her choice to leave the Church of England and meet illegally with the secret Separatist community, genteel Penninah Howse is thrown into Clink Prison with little chance of release. To survive prison under the evil of Bishop William Laud's tyranny, she must evade the advances of a malicious jailer, learn to live with a cruel cellmate, and battle the enemies of hunger, filth, vermin, and self-doubt. When Robert Linnell finally succeeds in buying visitation rights, her old and dear friend not only brings food, he brings hope. Is there a chance he'll find a way to secure her release? Or will this be her life forever?

About Ora Smith

Ora is an artist, genealogist, seamstress, lover of a good book, traveler, antiquer, upcycler, and history buff. She's one of those people who always has a project she's excited about. Although she's lived in Arizona since 1986, she spent her early life in Lake Tahoe, California, where her passion to write blossomed on a tranquil riverbank with a beautiful backdrop of the Sierra Nevada Mountains.

Get free novellas, sign up for Ora's newsletter, and get to know Ora at www.orasmith.com amazon.com/author/orasmith bookbub.com/authors/ora-smith facebook.com/AuthorOraSmith instagram.com/authororasmith twitter.com/AuthorOraSmith

I hope you enjoyed reading this story as much as I enjoyed researching and writing it. If you did, please consider leaving a rating and/or review on Amazon.

Made in the USA
Columbia, SC
04 March 2022

57204783R00200